Praise for *On Borrowed Wings*

"In Adele, Chandra Prasad has created an inspired and timeless heroine whose intelligence, imagination, and determination has you rooting for her from the very first page. Prasad's powerful prose matches the vital, urgent vigor of youth, particularly the bond of friendship. Her novel combines drama and a strong sense of place that provides both a lesson in history and a fine read."

—Sara Gruen, author of *Water for Elephants*

"*On Borrowed Wings* is an intriguing and moving debut novel about what happens when a young woman who is innocent and dreamy one moment, and insightful and bold the next, dares to cross gender barriers in order to attend the all-male Yale University of 1936. Prasad writes with the skill and confidence of an already seasoned author."

—Cristina Garcia, author of *Dreaming in Cuban*

"Full of high spirits and a rich sense of adventure, *On Borrowed Wings* takes the reader on Adele's intriguing journey as a young woman struggling to find herself in a man's world. Lovingly detailed and convincingly narrated, Chandra Prasad's novel offers a lush, deeply satisfying read."

—Diana Abu-Jaber, author of *Origin* and *Crescent*

"In Chandra Prasad's compelling debut novel, Adele Pietra, a poor yet ambitious girl from a Connecticut granite quarry town in the 1930s, assumes the identity of her deceased brother and attends Yale University. Throughout this page-turner, Adele faces the normal challenges of freshman year that any undergraduate would—meeting buddies, falling in love, keeping up with schoolwork—except she also carries the burden of keeping her true identity concealed. Prasad develops each character beautifully, and we soon begin to think of the intrepid heroine's friends as our own. This coming-of-age story is a great read, and I look forward to reading more of the writer's work in the future."

—Melissa Kagan, Lifetime Television

"Those who lament the death of the plot-driven literary novel will be delighted to discover Chandra Prasad's debut novel, *On Borrowed Wings*. Written in spare, elegant prose, this gem of a book is both rhetorically and dramatically compelling. It is, in short, a finely crafted page-turner."
—Jake Halpern, commentator on NPR's *All Things Considered* and author of *Fame Junkies*

"Prasad renders believable a girl who becomes herself in a most unlikely way."
—*Publishers Weekly*

"A splendid debut novel . . . Prasad explores the theme of identity in all its myriad forms—gender, race, class and identity—in a poignant tale about a young woman whose fate is forever changed when tragedy takes the lives of her father and brother."
—Connecticutcentral.com

"An exciting and thought-provoking journey through the political, social and sexual landscape of Yale in 1936."
—*Connecticut Post* online

"An impressive first effort."
—Fredricksburg.com

"Like its cross-dressing protagonist, Adele Pietra—who disguises herself as her dead brother, Charles, in order to matriculate at all-male Yale in 1936—this novel has two faces, both of them utterly charming: it's a compelling fish-out-of-water story and a sly commentary on gender and class. A big boola boola for Chandra Prasad and her witty and enjoyable debut."
—Natalie Danford, editor of the Best New American Voices series and author of *Inheritance*

"Prasad's characters—particularly her bold and subversive heroine—are complex human beings; they love, compete, survive, and imagine. In sumptuous prose, this novel both instructs and entertains. It crosses boundaries of culture, gender, and class, joyously wrestling with vital questions of life and literature: 'Who are we, and where do we come from?' At the heart of this brave book, the answer seems to be: We are ourselves, and can live by that alone."

—Neela Vaswani, author of *Where the Long Grass Bends*

"In a 1930s Yale bursting with secrets, one student harbors the greatest secret of all. Prasad creates a precisely true landscape of a long-ago world and makes us care deeply for Adele Pietra's struggle to find a place in it. Almost Shakespearean in its high-stakes gender-bending play, this beautifully wrought novel tenderly reveals the hidden places of town, gown, the body and the heart."

—Marc Wortman, author of *The Millionaires' Unit*

"*On Borrowed Wings* is a poised and unusual first novel, pivoting on the fascinating premise of a young woman posing as her dead brother at Yale. Prasad manages to give us a careful portrait of class, belonging, and prejudice, while keeping us wondering whether such a masquerade can really succeed."

—Marina Budhos, author of *Ask Me No Questions*

ON BORROWED
WINGS

A NOVEL

Chandra Prasad

W
WASHINGTON SQUARE PRESS
New York London Toronto Sydney

Washington Square Press
A Division of Simon & Schuster, Inc.
1230 Avenue of the Americas
New York, NY 10020

First Washington Square Books trade paperback edition November 2008

WASHINGTON SQUARE PRESS and colophon are registered trademarks of
Simon & Schuster, Inc.

For information about special discounts for bulk purchases,
please contact Simon & Schuster Special Sales at
1-800-456-6798 or business@simonandschuster.com.

Manufactured in the United States of America

1   3   5   7   9   10   8   6   4   2

The Library of Congress has cataloged the hardcover edition as follows:
Prasad, Chandra.
On borrowed wings : a novel / Chandra Prasad.
p. cm.
1. Women college students—Fiction. 2. False personation—Fiction.
3. Connecticut—Fiction. I. Title.
PS3616.R37O5 2007
813'.6—dc22   2006052623

ISBN-13: 978-0-7432-9782-0
ISBN-10:   0-7432-9782-2
ISBN-13: 978-0-7432-9783-7 (pbk)
ISBN-10:   0-7432-9783-0 (pbk)

To two great women in my life:
Angelina Jenkins, my grandmother,
and Bettina Perito, my aunt

ON BORROWED
WINGS

SUMMER

Chapter One

MOTHER ONCE SAID I'd marry a quarryman. She looked at me as we washed clothes in the giant steel washtub, two pairs of water-wrinkled hands scrubbing and soaking other people's laundry. We were elbow-deep in dirty suds and our fingers brushed under the foamy mounds.

"Some mistakes are bound to be repeated," she murmured.

We lived in Stony Creek, a granite town at a time when granite was going out of fashion. There were only three types of men here: Cottagers, rich, paunchy vacationers who swooped into our little Connecticut town in May and wiled away time on their sailboats through August; townsmen, small-time merchants and business owners who dreamed of becoming Cottagers; and quarrymen, men like my father, who worked with no thought to the future.

The quarrymen toiled twelve hours a day, six days a week. They didn't care that they smelled of granite dust and horses, grease and putty powder. They didn't care about cleaning the crescents of grime from underneath their fingernails. Even when they heard the foreman's emergency signal, three sharp shrieks of steam, they scarcely looked up from their work. In the face of a black powder explosion gone awry or the crushing finality of a wrongly cleaved stone, they remained undaunted.

I knew why they lived this way. They did it for the granite. Nowhere else on earth did such stone exist—mesmerizing collages of white quartz, pink and gray feldspar, black lodestone, winking glints of mica. Stony Creek granite was so striking, it graced the most majestic of architecture: the Battle Monument at West Point, the Newberry Library in Chicago, the Fulton Building in Pittsburgh, the foundations of the Statue of Liberty and the Brooklyn Bridge. The quarrymen of Stony Creek would wither and fall before the Cottagers, before the townsmen. But the fruits of their labor tethered them to a history that would stand forever.

"You'll marry one, Adele—I'm sure of it. His hands will be tough as buckskin, but you'll love him regardless," Mother told me, her breath warm in my ear as the steam of the wastewater rose around us.

I didn't say that she was wrong, that she couldn't know what would happen. I'd learned that from the quarry. Pa was a stonecutter and he cut the granite according to rift and grain, to what he could feel with his fingertips and see with his eyes. But there were cracks below the surface, cracks that betrayed the careful placement of a chisel and the pounding of a mallet. The most beautiful piece of stone could shatter into a pile of riprap. It all depended on where those cracks teased and wound, on where the stone would fracture when forced apart.

"Keep your eyes open, Adele. I don't know who it will be—a steam driller, boxer, derrickman, powderman? Maybe a stonecutter like your father?"

I turned away from her, feigning disinterest. "There's no predicting," I told her.

In May 1936 the sun, convinced of an early solstice, shone so warmly that the citizens of Stony Creek kept fresh handkerchiefs in every pocket to wipe off their perspiring faces. I kept three and used them all as I walked the mile from our boardinghouse to the quarry. I brought lunch to my brother, Charles, and to Pa. Despite the heat I basked in the freedom of my walks. Out of school until autumn, I was under the constant scrutiny of Mother, who always had a fresh pile of laundry that needed attention, and if not laundry, then some other chore. I welcomed any errand that took me out of her eyeshot.

Upon reaching the work site I would look for ways to dawdle. Sometimes I could convince one of the quarrymen to tell me a story. Most of the men didn't mind chatting as they worked. Still steeped in the lore of their ancestors, they spoke to understand where they'd come from and where they were now, how it had come to pass that they spent their days in a giant crevasse hacked out by their own hands. Maybe the granite itself kept them talking. The patterns in the stone were hypnotic, kaleidoscopic, powerfully inducive. Stare at them too long and you could start to see things, people and stories compressed between layers of sediment.

Old Man Richter, a stone loader, spun the best yarns. That day I passed him at the creek bank. Here, an estuary whooshed by fiercely before giving in to the sea. All around, the blades of the salt marsh bent under gentle winds. Old Man Richter was fishing for eel—a free lunch. He was up to his knees in the brackish water, stabbing the muddy bottom with a hand-fashioned spear: a pocketknife tied to a broom handle. His rolled-up sleeves and pants' legs revealed sinew and strength, the physique of a younger man. Yet he was the oldest worker in the quarry by at least a decade.

"Afternoon, Mr. Richter," I piped.

"Afternoon, Adele."

Though I knew I oughtn't—Mother wouldn't have liked it—I took off my shoes and waded into the creek. The water nibbled the hem of my skirt. The pebbles, slick with algae, felt smooth and cool under my feet. I sidled up to Mr. Richter carefully.

"Say, Adele, do you remember when the shanties were close to here? When they were only yards away? You could get out of bed and practically trip over the edge of the quarry."

"I think I'm too young to remember."

He squinted at me, his eyes settling on my long braids, on the smattering of freckles on the bridge of my nose.

"Oh, too young," he repeated. "Sixteen?"

Mr. Richter had always been a presence in my life. When I was a child he'd doted on me as if I were a favorite grandchild or niece.

He'd come to my Sunday tea parties, sitting outside on a make-believe chair between two of my make-believe friends. I'd pour sea-water from a chipped blue teapot Mother let me borrow and Mr. Richter would unearth linty sugar cubes from his pockets. He'd always remembered my birthdays, too. Once, he'd surprised me with a bicycle. It was a boy's bicycle and a little worse for wear, but how dazzled I'd felt when I'd laid eyes on it.

"Seventeen," I corrected.

His eyes widened merrily. "My! You'll have to pardon me."

"What was it like—living close to the quarry?" I asked him.

He jabbed the spear, stirring the already murky water. When the knife came up empty, he sighed. "Not so different, except for the black powder. There are accidents now, but not like then. No one knew what to expect from a blast, no matter how careful we planned it. My lord, we had to watch ourselves. Stone was always flying. My wife was sure I'd lose an eye. She was sure we'd all go blind eventually. She had big statues of all the saints lined up on the bureau. Every night she'd save a little of our dinner and offer it to them—a bribe to keep me safe." He smiled, the remainder of his teeth worn down and yellow-rotten. "A loon, that woman was."

Old Man Richter's spear emerged again. This time an inky, slippery-long fish dangled from the tip. Though the knife had plainly impaled it, still the eel squiggled.

"Want a bite?" he joked, waving the spear in the air.

He couldn't have expected girlish squeals or even blushing. Mr. Richter knew as well as anyone that I'd grown up around the quarry, that I was used to rough talk, and fish scales, and granite pebbles lodged in the soles of my shoes. One thing I would never be mistaken for was a Cottager's daughter.

"Cook it up and maybe I will," I told him, my words coming out so clipped and fearless they stopped him outright.

I pulled on my shoes and left Old Man Richter to skin and cook his lunch. After circling the work site several times I found Pa. He was sitting on an empty dynamite keg outside the cutting sheds. I was surprised to see him at rest—he seldom allowed himself a lunch break. I knew I had only a few minutes to give him his meal before he went back to work, his smile upon seeing me replaced by grim concentration.

Pa ate quickly, wheezing and coughing between bites. He'd tucked the dust mask Mother had sewn for him carelessly in a pocket. He'd promised to use it, but wore it only when representatives from the insurance company came for inspection—twice a year, like clock-work. It was obvious that he was resigned to his fate: silicosis, the stonecutter's black lung. He'd carved his tombstone five years back, at the age of thirty-four. All the stonecutters made this morbid gesture early. Everyone knew that their day was distressingly near, so much dust come back to haunt them.

"Delicious, Adele," he said. I smiled, though I knew he was lying. He ate the same lunch every day: cheese, homemade pickles, and salami tucked between slices of brown bread.

"You've been helping your mother?" he asked. I nodded. His eyes were kind, and I felt buoyed by them, like the channel markers that bobbed on the surface of Long Island Sound.

"But I hope you've saved some time for yourself," he continued, tilting back his head, lips parted as if to drink in the sun, the blue blaze of sky. "A day like this doesn't come around often." I, too, dipped back my head. Together, we watched the clouds drift past like elegant ladies in wispy white gowns.

"Francisco used to spend whole days like this—doing nothing," Pa said. "He never felt bad about it, either. No matter how much my mother yelled at him, or how much the teacher scolded him for skip-ping school, he didn't give a darn. He did things his own way, at his own pace, no matter what."

I loved to hear Pa talk about his brother and the adventures they'd shared as children. It didn't matter that I'd never met Francisco. In fact, my ignorance probably added to his allure. What I didn't know about Francisco, I had the privilege of imagining: the way his hair blew lazily in the wind, how his laugh lines made his face ruggedly handsome. Pa had disclosed some details over the years. I knew, for instance, that you couldn't pin Francisco down. He lived by neither calendar nor clock. A traveling musician, he possessed an aversion to routine and obligation. Pa said he preferred untrod continents, sun-blanched earth, pungent spices that came from across wide seas. Though he was younger than Pa, Francisco had already seen the greatest places in the world: the Taj Majal, the Great Wall of China, the pyramids. He sent Pa postcards of these distant wonders, but I'd never seen them. Pa kept them tucked away.

Sometimes, when I stared at the gray water in the laundry tub, I conjured Francisco's reflection, or rather, how I pictured it to be: something like Pa's, but livelier, a thrill about the lips, eyes brimming with intrigue. I'd feel my heart palpitating, and I'd worry Mother would notice that something was different, that I was acting strange. I knew if she asked me any questions, guilt would consume me and I'd blurt the whole thing: how I was infatuated with a relative I'd never met.

Staring at the clouds, Pa and I were quiet for a time. The silence was comforting—a lull rather than a void. I felt sustained by it, even nourished, the clutter and noise of the day secondary to the vista above. But the foreman's whistle sounded all too soon and Pa was back on his feet. His eyes shifted into focus. I was in the periphery now; his work, the splitting and drilling and polishing, at center. A pang of regret took me. I wished we'd had more time to daydream. My father seemed happiest when he slipped away from normal consciousness, forgetting for a precious clutch of seconds that he was at the mercy of his job, and Mother, and even, I suppose, of me.

"Hurry to Charles," he said, bending down to collect his tools. "He's in Tahiti." All the sheds were named after islands in the South Pacific. No one seemed to know why, exactly. But stonecutters are storymen, and I reckoned the blue of the tropics was more captivating than the muted shades of New England. "By now he'll be ravenous, I can bet you."

I found my brother surrounded by a cloud of dust that billowed from the cutting and carving machinery. A raggedy cap sat askew on his head, casting a shadow over his eyes. Engine grease marked his cheeks like war paint, contrasting starkly with his parchment-pale skin. His clothes and thick-soled shoes were coated with granite powder. Scrap rock sat in heaps and tumbling piles everywhere—the waste of splitting and cutting the dimension stone. The air inside the shed moved sluggishly—a hot, murky, amorphous mass quite unlike the clouds Pa and I had just admired.

"You're late again. I swear you do it on purpose," Charles said gruffly, eyeing the lunch pail. I removed a second sandwich and offered it to him. He snatched it like a street urchin stealing fruit from a stand. At the same time some of the men looked up, noting my arrival with interest. A long, low whistle escaped from the other side of the shed, followed by laughter. Girls were a rarity here. And even girls like me, perch-pole thin, sun-browned, and dressed in patched clothes, roused excitement.

"I can't keep waiting for you," he chastised.

"Sorry. I was just—I was talking with Pa."

I noticed that under his hat my brother's hair was damp. The blacksmiths must have dunked his head in the cooling barrel again, a common enough prank, but one usually reserved for tool boys and newcomers. Charles, a year older than I, had worked in the quarry every summer since he was eleven. By now he should have been one of the gang.

"Why do you let them do that?"

"It's not up to me," he charged, struggling to keep his voice low. "If it were—if I had any choice at all—I wouldn't be here. You know that."

"You shouldn't separate yourself."

Mid-chew, Charles glared at me. "And what would you know about that? You, who prance around like you're in some kind of fantasy land?"

I heard echoes of Mother in his talk. She, too, frowned upon the stonecutters, and all the quarrymen for that matter, even though she had married Pa, even though our lives were weighted with granite. "Their ribald talk, how it tires the ears!" she would say, always in front of Charles, who already eschewed the stonecutters' company, who already courted their ire. He acted like he was better than they were, but that would mean he was better than Pa, and surely he couldn't claim that.

"I should get going," I hastened. "Mother expects me back."

I wanted to say something else, something that would extinguish the flicker in his eyes, which threatened to spark, to explode into flame. But I couldn't say what I truly felt—that he could burn us all with his discontent.

"Isn't it nice to have that luxury? To leave when you want? To do what you want?"

"We all have duties."

"Duties? You have simple chores—things I could do blindfolded. You're so provincial, Adele. You don't even know how small this place is. When I think about all the things I'll do when I get out of here, all the people I'll meet and plans I'll make . . . I tell you it makes me want to throw in my tools this very instant."

His voice had risen and he was motioning broadly with his arms. But I didn't know what he was waving at—the dust clouds, the machinery noise, the resentment of his peers?

"We all have duties," I repeated, a little ashamed, knowing that I wasn't convincing anyone, least of all myself.

On my way home I walked slowly. By now Mother would be watching the clock, but the shoreline was simply too beautiful to rush past. Once again I took off my shoes, my toes sinking into the wet sand as I wandered the beach. The sharp salt air caught in my lungs and I felt heady, almost reckless, as I dug into the lunch pail and un-earthed the last sandwich. This I tore up and fed to the gulls that spun, zipped, and dove overhead, suspended as if on marionette strings between sky and sea.

I'd always had a fondness for seabirds. When I was very young I'd found a fledgling huddled on the beach, unable to fly. Its delicate, downy feathers had been soaked with sea spray. I'd cupped the bird in my hands gently, determined to make it my pet. Then I'd noticed its straw-thin legs, half-crippled, snarled in fishing line. For how long? I'd wondered. I'd spent hours untwisting and unknotting. Underneath the tangle, the bird's feathers had matted, the quills digging awkwardly, viciously, into its flesh. These I'd plucked with great reluctance, for by then the gull's pain had also been my own.

I didn't know if the animal would live, lame as it was. When at last I removed the line, it hobbled away, wanting nothing more to do with me. Wings beating frantically, it struggled to fly. I didn't think it could, but after tottering down a stretch of beach, yellow legs regaining purpose, it lifted. Aloft, it lurched, making desperate, lopsided bids to right itself. I thought it would careen into the water, but it found its way somehow, growing bolder, more confident, as if the fishing line I'd tucked into my apron were nothing more than a bad dream.

I'd smiled, joyous. But envious, too. I'd wished my life could be so suddenly changed. Despite what Charles thought, he and I weren't so different.

When I finally arrived home, I was intercepted on the front porch by Greta Prowl, our landlady. Miss Prowl owned and managed the house from her apartment on the first floor. My family lived in the apartment on the second. As I made my way up the porch steps, which were rickety and in need of a fresh whitewash, she stood up from her rocking chair. It was the perch on which she spent much of her day. She liked to peep over an open magazine or book, watching neighbors scurry past. I was sure she kept a running tally of their goings-on.

I passed and she leaned over to yank one of my braids, a hostile act disguised as playfulness. She had never liked me much, for reasons I didn't understand. Indeed, the older I became, the more her aversion manifested itself.

"It's about time you cut that hair, Adele Pietra. Don't know anyone else who wears it long and plaited like you do."

I shrugged, trying to get by, but she stood like a barricade.

"How is your father?" she asked. Her red lipstick had smeared clownishly. Despite the shade cast by the house's overhanging roof, she was perspiring heavily. Large wet spots soaked her underarms. A trail of sweat snailed past her ear.

"Fine."

"And your brother? He's fine, too, hey?"

"Sorry, Miss Prowl, but I need to get in the house. I'm late."

"Late for what? It seems to me you're following no one's schedule but your own." I wondered if she spied on me, not just here but down by the water, too. I gave her a hard look, hoping to break her momentum. Carmine laced the whites of her eyes. She smelled dankly of perfume and spirits.

"Your brother," she continued. "He's grown up handsome, he sure has. I can tell he'll go far. But you, you're taking a while to find your place."

"I don't know what you mean."

"Of course you do. You know that the options in this town are limited. Hell, they're downright measly."

I didn't reply, yet Miss Prowl seldom needed a second party to keep conversation flowing. She tugged fretfully at her blouse, which bunched at the waist, revealing her formidable girth. Her mouth pursed. At the same time, the lines on her forehead deepened, revealing her age, which she tried to conceal by way of carriage and dress.

"You're almost a woman now," she continued. "I remember Gertrude at your age—oh, all too well. Not that you two look much alike."

I knew she wasn't necessarily referring to my mother's appearance, but to her history—back in the days when she had been called Gertrude, Gertie, or, more commonly, Miss Mockleton. It was a subject gossips delighted in, which was why I suddenly saw no reason to mind my manners.

"Excuse me," I said coldly, reaching around her, making for the doorknob. "I have chores waiting." Miss Prowl's mouth opened in protest, but I slipped away before she could reply.

When I reached the second floor, Mother was already standing in the doorway, arms akimbo. "You're wasting your time, Adele. And mine, too."

"I'm sorry."

"Sorry, always sorry, but always late."

"Miss Prowl wanted to talk."

"Talking with Miss Prowl is no better than loitering around the workers. I've told you before what they think of girls who linger about the sheds." She sighed, smoothing her apron. "Have you had your lunch, at least?"

I nodded. "On the way home."

"I can't tell from the looks of you."

She clasped my wrist with her fingers, squeezing until she struck bone. The safe feeling I'd had since seeing Pa vanished completely.

"Well, have a little lemonade, at least," she continued. "I just made a pitcher."

I poured myself a glass and cut a few chips of ice from the melting block at the bottom of the icebox. Before I could take the first sip, though, Mother handed me the sewing basket. It was piled high with socks.

"I've been darning, but my eyes are tired," she admitted.

I thought she would retire to bed to rest. Instead, she followed me to the kitchen table and took a seat beside me as I threaded a needle. I was not as nimble as she, and my fingers felt clumsy under her stare. It was always this way.

For several minutes we sat in silence. Unlike Pa, Mother loathed moments of quiet reflection. Silence did not become her. She was a person of motion and purpose—all fluttering hands, fleet speech, and rapidly blinking eyes. She pretended to be idle only when she had news to share. I waited.

"Your father. By now you must realize his condition is getting worse," she said at last. She fingered the ruby brooch at her throat. But for my mother, no other quarryman's wife wore jewelry; no other quarryman's wife *owned* jewelry. The brooch was a remnant from her earlier life. Its sparkle caught the sheen of her eyes, an ardent glimmer that at once attracted people and kept them at bay.

"There is no easy way to say what I want to say, so I'm just going to come out with it: the security you've known—it is no longer guaranteed."

For many months, perhaps even a year, I'd heard Pa coughing through the walls at night. The noise pierced my dreams, keeping me awake and reeling with worry. Yet his coughing was so persistent, it seemed almost innocuous in its constancy.

"Your brother will move on," she continued. "It's in his nature to look forward. But you—I'm concerned that you have not yet thought about the future. You're so preoccupied, Adele. So dreamy. Most of the time I have no idea what you're thinking."

I watched her face rather than the needle until the sharp point struck my thumb. She swiftly grabbed my hand and wiped away the burgeoning bead of blood with a handkerchief. Her eyes strayed to the crimson blot, unnaturally bright on the starchy white cloth.

"He's been coughing a long time," I reasoned, watching the blood boil up again from the puncture. "His health is probably the same as it was."

"Your father's father died when he was thirty-four. He died in the quarry, his hands still clasping a cutting tool." Of course I knew this story already, and was upset that Mother would revisit it so casually. The crisp tone of her voice had turned my skin to gooseflesh.

"That was a different time, a harder time," I argued.

"Was it? Your grandfather died of dust in the lungs, and chances are your father will meet the same end. The only thing that's changed around here is the state of the industry. Before you were born, there were four companies mining the quarry. Now there's only Palanzas, and even they're shrinking. I don't know how much longer it will be before they start laying people off. Lord knows we all thought it would have happened already."

I cringed at her words, so brusque and incisive. Did the possibility of Pa's death stir nothing in her heart?

"What I am trying to say, Adele, is that you will need a man to take care of you."

"I have Pa," I cried indignantly.

"Aren't you listening, dearest? I'm talking about survival—yours and mine. I'll have no way to support you. We own nothing, not even this apartment. And Adele, listen to me, you're not a child anymore, much as you act like one."

"I know what you're getting at." And I did. She meant for me to marry; she'd hinted at it enough times. Mother had wed a quarryman, and more than once she'd called it a mistake—the worst she'd ever made. So why, then, did she expect me to hitch my life to a quarryman's too? I couldn't comprehend her logic. How could she assume that Charles would forge ahead and beyond, while she simultaneously believed I would retrace her steps, ensnaring myself in all the pits and traps she herself had already exposed?

Later, with the gift of hindsight, I would revisit Mother's motives with a clearer mind. I'd think that maybe she couldn't envision my life as different from hers because she was confined by her own example. Maybe, despite evidence to the contrary, she was a traditionalist at heart, believing that being a boy meant having special freedoms, while being a girl meant losing them. Her low expectations of me were not necessarily a sign of malevolence, I would try to convince myself. Maybe Mother's attitude toward me was simply a result of misguided thinking, favoritism, limited resources, or even unacknowledged jealousy. I didn't know at that moment, and even later, to be honest, I'd never be sure.

Mother didn't respond and I stood up. She rose, too. She was tall, taller than anyone else in the family, and as she faced me I found myself eye-level with the brooch.

"It will be yours someday," she said softly, following the trajectory of my gaze. I didn't tell her that I didn't like her jewelry: the brooch, or the matching necklace, bracelet, earrings, and ring she kept hidden under a loose floorboard. Such precious items sparked talk. They made enemies of the women who might have been our allies. Most of all, they reminded people that Mother was different, that she had once gripped privilege tight in her fist.

"I don't want it."

"Oh, Adele. You will, you will. You can't possibly be content with what you've got—this quarry, your secondhand books. You're my daughter, after all." But I knew I would never have her taste for finery and flash.

Her hand rested on my shoulder, long fingers digging into my flesh. Mother had beautiful hands despite hundreds of hours in the laundry washtub. Most nights she wrapped them in rags soaked in her special salve: cooking grease, honey, the comfrey root and lemon balm she grew in her little garden.

"Silvio Russo has been watching you for some time. He inquires about you whenever I see him. Adele, he is a reliable worker and by all accounts a good man. Even your father likes him."

Silvio was older than Pa—certainly too old for the likes of me. His face was a complicated map of wrinkles and planes, scars and pock-marks. It was a fascinating face, for it surely charted the course of his life, a life drawing toward a close. But mine was only just beginning.

"He's worked at the quarry for years. He's known this family for years," she continued.

If I weren't so shocked, I might have been outraged. Of all the men Mother might have suggested for me, she had picked one of the eldest and most beleaguered-looking quarrymen. Why, I wanted to demand, must I do as she had done and take another turn on this luckless wheel? Instead, I stayed quiet, frozen even, thinking about the pink rock of Stony Creek, how it would be Pa's undoing and maybe mine as well.

"Just consider it. That's all I ask," she continued, and I swear I caught a dash of resentment in her tone, just the tiniest shred. She searched my face, and I felt the familiar pressure of her eyes, how startlingly pretty they were, like her hands. "Remember that what you make of your future will affect me as well."

Her fingers slid from my shoulder then. My skin tingled where she had pressed. A moment later she left, leaving me to tend to the nick on my finger, which hadn't stopped bleeding.

That evening everything seemed a little different in our home. I noted the unmistakable pallor of Pa's face, how exhausted he seemed, slumped in his chair through dinner. I noted the friction between him and Mother, two ill-fitting granite blocks grinding each other down. I wondered if he knew of her plans for me. He said little during the meal, speaking only when addressed. Mother and Charles, on the other hand, talked endlessly of their favorite subject: the College Entrance Exam. Charles had been studying for it for a full year, and now it was nearly here—only two weeks away. If he did well, Mother swore the unheard-of would happen: a quarryman's son would go on to higher education.

Usually college was left to the Cottagers, but Mother had long shook her head at that notion. She said Charles made excellent marks in school. He had an insatiable hunger for learning—didn't his teachers always remark upon it? With the right recommendations and a full scholarship, of course a full scholarship, he would be poised for admission to the best universities. Perhaps even Yale. And that's when Charles's and Mother's eyes really glowed, for Yale to them would mean the ultimate escape: escape from this ramshackle house, from endless sacks of laundry, from this abyss of a town.

Yale was only twenty miles away, a short trip on the railway. Yet it had taken on the feel of a distant Canaan. I'd been to New Haven only once, but I'd been humbled by what I'd seen: young men dapper in their suits, all gloss, snap, and pomp, bustling with determination as I tried to look like I belonged, plunging my chafed hands into my pockets and wishing I'd styled my hair differently, not so much like a little girl's. The streets had been dazzling—York and Prospect and Whitney and Chapel—every one of them wide and grand, shaded by enormous elms, and I'd had no means of comparison, for the street on which we lived still turned to mud when it rained.

Mother and Charles had strolled through the city like they had every right to be there. They'd clutched each other's arms and pointed excitedly at sights that caught their fancy. What they saw was theirs and theirs alone. Pa and I, we walked two steps behind, staring at the sky like we always did when dreaming was preferable to real life.

When dinner ended I cleared the table. I scraped each plate clean, watching striper bones, snap peas, and bits of mashed potato fall into the waste bucket. Mother and Charles, meanwhile, prepared for the evening's studies. During the school year, Charles had plenty of time to pore over historical dates and mathematical theorems. But during the summer, with so many hours at the quarry, he confined his studying to the precious margins of his schedule—evenings and all day Sunday. Mother was always ready to lend a helping hand. She'd told me once that she herself had dreamed of higher education, long ago, before love and its many complications had intervened. She'd grown up in an educated household, after all, her father a celebrated scholar. I still remember the excitement in her voice when she'd talked about the number of books her parents had kept.

"Hundreds, Adele, simply *hundreds*."

I ran downstairs to fetch water from the pump, then returned to fill the sink, letting the dishes soak. From below, I could hear faint drifts of music. Bessie Smith crooned "A Good Man Is Hard to Find" while Miss Prowl sang along, her voice tipsy, quavering, rhythmless.

In the adjacent room, Mother repeated vocabulary words from a list. Charles struggled to define them. When he missed one, Mother would cluck disapprovingly. She'd recited the same list several weeks ago and I recalled all the words, even the ones that baffled my brother. I whispered the definitions to myself as I carried a blanket to Pa. He sat opposite Charles and Mother, in his favorite old chair, its springs long collapsed, giving it a tired, droopy look. His eyes were closed. He was seconds away from sleep, his breathing deep and somber. I draped the blanket over his chest, tucking the corners around his shoulders. His eyes opened briefly, brimming with thankfulness. In the past year he'd become so sensitive to changes in temperature. Even in the summer heat, a light breeze could make him shiver.

I sat on the floor at his feet. I was too old for such behavior, I knew. A proper young lady ought to sit on a chair, back straight, ankles crossed, hands folded in her lap, but somehow I felt better here, protecting Pa like a loyal dog might. Protecting him against what, or whom, I couldn't say, but it was enough simply to be near him. I listened to his breathing, the long exhalations nearly hypnotic, and soon I grew tired too. I forgot about the dishes in the sink, the darning I still hadn't finished. I slipped somewhere else, maybe in the sky with the gulls. Eyes closing, I ceased to hear Mother's questions, or Charles's nervous, stutter-ridden answers, until one word broke through the haze.

Ineluctable.

"That which is inescapable, irresistible," I answered, suddenly awake, but not knowing, not believing, I'd spoken.

"Adele!" Mother lashed.

I was alert now, alert enough to see the contours of her face, which were sharp, surely carved of ice. Charles had turned in his chair. His eyes met mine with such naked distaste I stood up to avoid further shame.

"I didn't realize," I whispered.

"If you know what's good for you, you'll finish those dishes," Mother said tartly.

I felt her gaze, prickly on my back as I hurried to the sink. My hands dove into the water, now scarcely warm, grease and food particles floating on the foamy surface. I washed, just as I helped wash the sacks of laundry. I washed mindlessly; better for girls to work this way.

Miss Prowl's music had stopped. I imagined that she'd fallen asleep awkwardly in her itchy-tight clothes, lipstick still smeared, whiskey bottle inches away. I imagined Mother and Charles leaning closer in the other room, their profiles mirroring each other: angular chins, high foreheads sloping into straight Grecian noses. They looked so alike, identically pleated yellow waves atop their heads, while Pa and I had been cursed with pettish curls, sooty as a grackle's breast. Sometimes I wondered if Mother was swayed by color alone. Maybe the battle lines had been drawn based on something as superficial as physical similarity.

I heard their whispers, scarcely audible over Pa's soft snores.

"You saw how she interferes. Isn't there something you can do?"

"Don't worry yourself over such trifles," Mother said, so resolutely I was sure he ought to believe her.

Chapter Two

WE HAD FEW photographs in our apartment—only two in fact. These hung beside the fireplace, which didn't work—squirrels had nested at the top of the chimney and Miss Prowl said it wasn't worth her while to hire a sweep. She'd like to have the job done, really she would, but she'd have to raise the rent to cover the expense.

The photographs were strikingly different. One was of Pa's mother, the grandmother from Italy whom I'd never met. She'd scarcely survived the journey here, Pa had said, and she'd died of a broken heart just two years after she'd arrived—too much to ask of her to have left her siblings, twelve in all, in a country across the sea.

She looked to be a sweetly plump woman, her proud face a perfect oval, and in that face I could see aspects of Pa. He'd inherited her wistful eyes, eyes that told the world that he'd never quite shown himself, but kept the best parts locked away. In the portrait, my grandmother's dark hair framed her face like a halo. It was only fitting: Pa called her his angel. And once, when I'd been very sick with pneumonia, he'd called me one, too.

"You and my mother—the only angels I've ever known," he'd said.

The other photograph showed Mother's parents, Alfred and Joanna Mockleton. I'd never met either of them, not because they had passed, but because they wanted nothing to do with our family. They'd disowned Mother the summer of 1917, the summer she'd met Pa. That's what Mother told me, and when she talked of this

time and of her youth in general, her voice would go low and con-
templative. She'd let slip intimate little dollops of her past, things she
would never ordinarily reveal.

She'd been a Cottager's daughter, a comely, coltish girl who carried herself like an aristocrat, who knew by instinct rather than by
lesson that she had something over the girls who lived in shanties,
over the town girls who stared enviously at her fashionable frocks, a
different wardrobe every season. She'd summered in a castle, or a
house that might have been a castle, a classic Victorian with spires
and a sixty-foot turret atop a hillside, a private road of crushed oyster shells winding to the entrance.

"It was our *cottage*," Mother said. "Isn't that a laugh?"

How her face would glisten when she described those careless,
incandescent years. She'd been free, no laundry, cleaning, or cooking—
such work was strictly for the servants. What were her duties, then? I
asked. Her duties, Mother explained, were to fill gloriously empty
hours with strawberry socials, trips to the beach, restaurants, moonlit
concerts, fish fries, dances at the various hotels. She spent her days
sleeping until noon, and then her evenings teetering on perilously high
heels, purchased in Milan, or was it Paris, and she'd been taller than the
boys, who gazed up at her like smitten pups. Sometimes she would join
her father on his sailboat, a red-and-white polka-dot scarf tied jauntily
around her hair, the ends rippling like flags. Sailing was her favorite
pastime, the wind in her face, briny water parting as the boat surged
ahead, and she at the prow, like a figurehead.

I asked her if she'd studied, if she'd gone to church.

Sure she'd studied—she'd loved to read and she'd had more tutors
than she could count. But she'd seldom gone to church in those days.
Her parents were Protestants, and though they loved God, they saw no
need for regular worship—so time-consuming, those church services.
Mother had never known that people could worship so passionately
until she'd met Pa. Those God-fearing Catholics were a different breed,
she explained, their hearts always bleeding, every conversation a dramatic exchange. They were a people she didn't care to consort with.

But Pa was a Catholic—hadn't she consorted with him?

That's when Mother always sighed, her girlish glow tossed off like a shawl. Yes, she'd consorted with him. That had been her first and greatest mistake. He'd been handsome, picture-show handsome, truly, with brooding eyes and that hair, hopelessly disheveled and exotically dark—hair that just begged for a woman's touch. She'd been coy at first: "Girls must *never* be forward, Adele. Then men know they have the upper hand."

Even under all that sweat and dirt, he'd caught her eye immediately. She was surprised she could see him at all, given the swarms of girls that were always buzzing around him. What must have driven those girls crazy was that he seemed oblivious to their attention. They'd follow him onto the dock, teasing and flirting, but he'd stand in a state of distraction, or was it torpidity, gazing at the sea rather than engaging in their daffy chatter. She'd never seen him so much as hold a girl's hand. Once or twice a girl, desperate for acknowledgment, had gone so far as to push him into the water, he gamely allowing himself to fall. How his admirers would coo when he emerged from the blue, that dazzling smile first, then the wet cling of his clothes against the hard contours of his body.

He was a challenge, all right, but Gertrude was game for a challenge. Like any determined competitor, she studied her target carefully: the juxtaposition between his deeply tanned skin and his white teeth (one tooth chipped, so dashingly roguish); his eyelashes, which were longer than her own; the way he could sit for an hour just staring at nothing. He was a thinker, she decided. Maybe an undiscovered genius. Being both beautiful and well-bred, she understood that fate often practiced favoritism when meting out its blessings.

When she'd felt sufficiently ready, she'd given a signal. Not a wink, no, that was too brazen. Just a lingering glance. He didn't respond, so she tried again, on another day. And again, on another day after that. On her fifth try he'd noticed her and approached, discreetly thank heavens. Lean yet muscled, his head tilted searchingly, his voice gentle, never insistent, this boy—Gianno was his name—was precisely the right boy to spawn the wrong sort of talk.

He'd asked her if she might like to get a sundae down at the Flying Point. He'd been shy, but not necessarily nervous. How refreshing a change from her usual sweaty-palmed suitors.

"Muffin-tin boys," she'd told me, for they were all the same: university-bound, overeager, haircuts approved by their mothers, blue-blood skin turned pink-pimpled under the sun. They pretended to listen to her, but their gazes moved centrifugally from her face, always toward her bosom. Her words disintegrated as the conversation shifted, always back to their lives. Something about plans to attend Princeton. Something about winning the Eastern Regional Debate Tournament. Something about an archeological expedition to Egypt, very dangerous.

She'd lost interest in those muffin-tin boys once and for all when she'd agreed to share a banana split with Pa. In between spoonfuls of whipped cream and hot fudge, she talked about her father, and what it was like being a Cottager, and feeling misunderstood, sometimes. Mostly she talked about being bored, though she had everything a girl could ask for. Still she felt there was more to life, more than simply being light-hearted, fun-loving, *ornamental*.

He didn't once interrupt. His silence meant painstaking attentiveness, surely. His dulcet eyes enveloped her. Except, sometimes his focus seemed to disperse, like sunlight spangling through a prism, and she'd wondered how she would possibly catch all of those wayward bits.

Mother had never told me the rest of the story. She didn't need to. I could decipher the rest for myself—how the dates matched, Charles born the spring of 1918, Mother and Pa married just before. I'd heard people whispering about the wedding: a simple, no-frills affair, no one from the bride's side in attendance, and the dress tailored just so, with an empire waist.

They whispered about it still—women like Miss Prowl. They gloated in Mother's shame, or the shame they thought she ought to have. But Mother refused to give them what they wanted. She carried herself high and straight, jewelry glistening at her throat, gazing above the brazen gapes. Her face was still lovely, but how did she do it? they gossiped spitefully. Must be through sheer force of will.

She was strong all right. But she'd never recovered from her greatest wound, the one inflicted by her parents when they'd refused to accept that she'd fallen in love with a penniless immigrant. A common work-hand. On top of everything, he was dark—almost *colored*—maybe a gypsy. They'd never trusted the Italians, a people who didn't seem to have the desire, the work ethic, or the brains to become productive Americans. Alfred used to say there were two types of Italian men: those with rings in their ears, and those with knives in their sleeves. Once Alfred had made the mistake of hiring an Italian as a gardener, and the fellow had come in drunk on his very first day, then passed out cold behind Alfred's prize-winning rosebush.

Clearly, their daughter's beau had been after only one thing. And now that he'd robbed her of that, he'd seek something else: the family fortune, carefully amassed and securely passed from generation to generation. Alfred would not let it change hands, never; he'd rather be struck dead. And so with angry fanfare they'd parted ways, parents and daughter, that summer. Not a word had been exchanged since Charles was born, not even a letter. Sometimes I overheard Pa suggest Mother make contact. He still mourned the passing of his own parents. What he'd give for one more day with his own sweet mother. But Mother always refused, saying she would bend her pride no more. She hadn't disgraced herself and she refused to act as if she had. She wasn't sorry and she wouldn't cry, not one tear, even on her worst day, when her hands were bleeding from the scrubbing, blistered from the iron. One day Alfred and Joanna would approach *her*, when she had proven them wrong, when she had redeemed herself through the very child they had shunned.

That's why it was so important for Charles to go to college. He would be the proof that she'd made the right decision after all. He would be her gateway *back*.

Sometimes I stared at the photograph of Alfred and Joanna, both so finely dressed, thin lips set in smug half smiles. I wondered if any harm could ever befall them, if it already had. Sometimes Mother would join me, both of us staring into that gilt frame.

"He was a literature professor," Mother once remarked, her voice steely. "Best in the country, his colleagues used to say. He hides in his books. That's why his heart doesn't pain."

The weeks that followed brought slow but discernible change, like droplets of freezing water giving way to the crystalline blade of an icicle. Charles claimed illness so that he could dedicate the last few days before the College Entrance Exam exclusively to studying. The foreman didn't believe Charles was ailing. He liked my brother even less than the other quarrymen did. Even so, he was fond of Pa, one of the better workers he had ever employed. It was for this reason, I surmised, that he accepted Charles's absence.

Charles took the exam on June 2. Though he'd gone into the test room nervous, he'd come out confident. He wouldn't find out his official scores until the end of July, however. The results, including those from the Scholastic Achievement Test, would be mailed to our home and to Yale, at which point the admissions board would determine the members of the incoming freshman class.

In the meantime, Charles and Mother took care to assemble the rest of his application: a complete record of his secondary school courses, an honorable dismissal for his final school year, and a statement of recommendation from his principal. For this last item, Mother decided nothing could be left to chance. Yale admitted roughly 850 students as freshmen. The vast majority would hail from private schools, posh private schools, where the boys had been groomed since infancy for world-class educations. A sizeable chunk of that majority would be admitted automatically. Mother knew this because Alfred had taught at Yale for part of his career. He'd spoken frequently of "the legacies": boys who were accepted into the university not on merit, but on lineage.

Charles had no such dispensation, which was why Mother decided to speak personally to Mr. Peck, principal of the Stony Creek Secondary School. Mr. Peck approved of my brother and of me. Both of us excelled in school. But Charles was clearly his favorite. The condescending lilt in his voice told me so, as if he were amused rather than impressed by my achievements—"Always top among your peers, Adele. But why work *so* hard?"

I didn't tell him that I scarcely worked at all. Most of the time the answers simply came to me. I remembered every word of every lesson that my teachers gave. I didn't try to remember; I just did. It was that way with reading, too. The sentences seemed to inscribe themselves on my brain. Whole pages lingered for years in my memory. Deep down, maybe I didn't want to study the way Charles did, hours at a time, teeth grinding in concentration.

Mother dressed well for her visit to Mr. Peck. She put on a fresh dress and a touch of rouge. She arranged her yellow locks busily with her fingers until they fell just the right way. She topped them off with a smart navy blue hat. I sat on her bed watching her spritz perfume onto the insides of her wrists. Moments later she knelt down, careful not to muss or rip her already mended stockings, pulled up the loose floorboard, and felt for the jewelry below.

"Aren't you going to put that on?" I asked. She'd slipped the ruby ring into her purse.

"Later," she said.

"Why do you need to go? Mr. Peck will write Charles a good recommendation. Why wouldn't he?"

She looked at me as if I were a half-wit. "It doesn't need to be good. It needs to be perfect. I'm seeing Mr. Peck to make sure he understands what perfect is."

Two hours later she returned with the same expression Charles had worn after the College Entrance Examination. Hesitant triumph was the only way to describe it. Her eyes were victorious, but her mouth indicated concern, for the proof of her win had yet to be furnished.

"I have a feeling, Adele," she said breathlessly. "After so much waiting, this may just work."

Seldom had I seen Mother in such high spirits. Once she had changed clothes, we started the daily washing and she didn't once complain about her chapped hands. At one point, she heard something jangle at the bottom of the washtub. She reached in and plucked out a silver dollar—a prize forgotten in a customer's pocket.

"Finders keepers." She laughed.

To my surprise, she gave the coin to me. It was the second time that day she'd parted with something of value. After dinner, when everyone was occupied, I crept into my parents' room. I lifted the floorboard to confirm that the ring hadn't found its way home.

If the change in our lives had been limited to missing jewelry or to Mother's mounting excitement, now feverish in pitch, I mightn't have worried so much. But there were other forces afoot, forces that entered our home, changing our patterns and behaviors. One was Silvio, who Mother continued to peddle. Indeed, she mentioned his name at almost every opportunity.

"I can invite Silvio to dinner this Sunday. We'll have lamb. I think you would enjoy his company, Adele."

"I'm not ready," I countered.

"You don't have to be *ready*. You just have to look nice and behave yourself."

Mother would retreat, but never for long. Home wasn't a safe haven any longer, but I soon realized that the quarry wasn't, either. Pa was there, and Old Man Richter. But it was Silvio who occupied my thoughts. Before, he'd been just another quarryman, mostly out of sight, running the derricks from the engine room. Now he'd become something else: an unlikely peril. Any glimpse of him made me cringe, turn in on myself. Mother said I must encourage him and perhaps I did, for whenever he entered my field of vision I stared, the same way I might have stared at a carnival freak. Lurid curiosity drove me. I wondered what it would be like to caress that face—the beaten leather skin, the chasmal creases. I imagined how it would be to kiss such a man.

Shuddering, I knew that it was my imagination that made Silvio grotesque. Yet my stomach still dropped when I heard his name. I wondered how much longer I could silently oblige Mother, pretending that I didn't mind marching in her footsteps. I looked at myself in the mirror that hung over my dresser. It was a wonder, I thought, that no one could see the shell that was beginning to form around me, pearly-hard and resistant.

If someone were to have asked me my favorite place in Stony Creek, I wouldn't have hesitated. It was a particular recess in the stone on the south side of the quarry. The cavity, roughly the size of a root cellar, seemed specially hewn for the human shape. It offered just the right slope to cradle my back and head. My feet on a rocky footrest, a book propped on my knees, I could read for hours without pause. The cavity dipped so low that there was only the pink granite that wreathed me, the sky overhead.

Pa knew of this place—he referred to it affectionately as my "cubby." When Mother, keen to bestow a new list of chores upon me, inquired where I was, Pa would tell her if I was walking the quarry path or digging for clams at the beach. But never did he divulge the existence of the cubby, and never did he give me away when I was holed up there. The hideout was one of our unspoken secrets, one of the reasons Pa was so dear to me.

The cavity happened to sit on the acme of one of the quarry's highest promontories. The winds that blew at that elevation were whistle-loud and trenchant. Pa would warn me, only half in jest, to stuff sand in my shoes so I wouldn't blow away. He wouldn't have been surprised to know that I'd sacrificed several handkerchiefs and a scarf to the fierce gales that rattled by. It would be easy, here, to lose one's footing; one push from the wind and the walls of the quarry would whiz by in a matter of moments. But the view from this level was worth the danger. I could see every rooftop and steeple in town, miles of Connecticut shoreline, sloops and barges navigating the white-capped Sound, and sometimes, on a clear day, the skyline of Long Island.

Within the cubby, I read anything and everything I could get my hands on: schoolbooks, maps, Miss Prowl's hand-me-downs, the castoffs of absentminded Cottagers, slim pickings from Stony Creek's town library, and the few novels Mother had held on to through the years. When the weather was warm and daylight extended into evening, sometimes Pa would venture to the cubby, too. Sitting beside me, he'd listen as I read aloud. He knew how to read and write, though not well, he was the first to admit. The fact that I could devour multiple books in a single sitting made him proud. He told me I had a knack for learning and must stay in school. A couple of times, when money was especially low or the laundry business especially busy, Mother had suggested keeping me home.

"Think how much more work we could get done," she'd tell my father.

But he always vetoed this proposition. He had two children, he reminded her, and boy or girl, they would remain in school for as long as he could keep them there. Given Mother's ambitious plans for my brother, that meant a long time indeed.

Late in July, on perhaps the hottest day of the whole summer, the postman delivered a letter addressed to my brother. It was a thin letter, unassuming. Because Charles seldom received mail, Mother's interest was piqued. It was too early to hear from Yale. Thus, the letter could be only one thing: the results of his College Entrance Examination. Charles was still at the quarry, but Mother would not be deterred. She ripped open the envelope with aplomb, her pupils dancing as they skimmed the contents of the certificate inside.

We were on the porch. Miss Prowl was not in her rocking chair and we'd taken this rare opportunity to relax without her meddlesome presence. Although it was an unspoken rule that no one else should sit in that rocker, Mother did so anyway. She didn't so much sit as collapse, a heap of raw nerves.

"Are you all right, Mother? Can I bring you a glass of water?"
She waved the certificate, fanning herself.

"His scores aren't as high as I'd hoped," she said. "But they're high enough. They should be high enough."

In that moment, I wanted to be happy, selflessly happy. My brother had competed with the rich boys, no doubt even with Cottagers' sons. He'd competed and he'd competed well. Yet I found myself more envious than glad. My lips broke into a flimsy smile. I mumbled something indistinct about his devotion to his studies, about Mother's fortitude and determination. Then I retreated into myself, into that shell, lest Mother notice my envy.

"Only one step left, Adele," she announced, her body trembling. "The formal letter from Yale should arrive soon. Then we'll know once and for all."

I thought back to that trip to New Haven, the Yale students so natty in their suits, mostly handsome faces, even the plainest ones alight with pride. I tried to picture Charles standing among them. He would be clutching books or a leather satchel and speaking of a football game or a difficult exam, maybe of a mixer that was coming up on the weekend, joking that he hoped the girls would be pretty. I tried to envision Charles beyond Stony Creek, beyond the granite juts, and I could—that was the rub! I could see him adapting well to a new environment, an environment that not long ago had seemed foreign, extreme. He'd come home on the odd weekend, during Christmas, certainly. He'd arrive with tales of his college adventures, and Mother would listen raptly, all her love concentrated, like sunlight focused through a magnifying glass.

"Let's splurge, Adele. A big gorgeous dinner—and a cake for dessert. Doesn't your brother deserve it?"

I forced wide my smile. "Of course."

"Is it someone's birthday?" came a question from below. And there was Miss Prowl, climbing the porch steps on her elephantine legs, veins woven through her thick calves like pieces of blue-green yarn.

"There's no birthday, Miss Prowl. Just a happy day," Mother replied, rising quickly from the rocker.

Miss Prowl looked around uncertainly. "And pray tell what makes it so happy?"

I began to shuffle my feet. Mother didn't like to tell Miss Prowl anything of importance. She said she might as well be broadcasting her personal affairs on the radio. By then, she had tucked the certificate back into the envelope, but not before Miss Prowl had stolen a glance.

"Nothing in particular," Mother replied, silencing me with a look.

"Have you received some news?" Miss Prowl angled.

"None. In fact, I was just telling Adele that we'd better start moving. We've been relaxing here as if we led lives of leisure."

Miss Prowl's stare snagged on Mother's brooch. The air seemed suddenly volatile. I wondered if Mother noticed, but she seemed too wrapped in her own thoughts.

For the rest of the afternoon she spoke scarcely a word, not even to mention Silvio. She remained in a giddy mood, capricious and not at all sensible, deciding that we could afford to ignore an overstuffed sack of laundry that had been delivered. The cake was her priority— a great big buttery lemon cake. Mother spent over an hour on its preparation, using the last of our eggs and molasses. When at last she tucked it tenderly into the oven, she indicated that I should wash the bowls and measuring cups.

"I'm going out for a while," she announced, digging through a jar of coins she kept in the cupboard. "I'm going to buy a frame. And I'm going to hang that certificate next to the photograph of my mother and father." She paused, her expression turning puckish. "Maybe *above* the photograph of my mother and father."

I willed myself to nod, pretending to share in her sly delight.

"Watch the cake," she remarked on her way out. "Be sure it doesn't burn."

But it didn't burn—it came out tempting and golden, smelling so delicious I had to resist stealing a bite before drizzling icing over the

top. I placed it on Mother's best dish, the one she used strictly for
guests. I set the table with similar care, buffing away smudges on the
plates with the bottom of my apron and polishing the utensils,
though they were only steel, not silver. On a whim, I ran outside to
pick a bouquet of larkspur, which grew freely along the border of
Miss Prowl's property. I laid one royal blue stem beside each plate—
the prettiest one beside Charles's.

Tonight would be a festive night, a joyous night, I told myself. I
repeated the sentiment when Charles and Pa returned home, Charles
a little gruff until he saw the certificate hung so conspicuously. He
was speechless, even when Pa clapped him on the back—"A job well
done, son"—and Mother's eyes swam with tears. He smiled at them.
Surely it was a magnanimous smile, a smile all of us could share in.
But his arms felt limp around my waist as I hugged him. The
embrace was a sham, and we both knew it.

We didn't eat heartily, even though Mother and I had prepared a
feast: bluefish with bread stuffing, baked corn chowder, raw cran-
berry salad, and Indian pudding. Pa didn't have much of an appetite.
I suspected his throat hurt, although he didn't complain. Nobody
commented on the setting of the table, nor on the flowers, but I told
myself it didn't matter. The family was together. And anyway, the
cake, so moist and spongy—a confectioner's prize—would surely
bring some cheer.

I cut it carefully, mindful not to break the edges, while Mother
poured cups of tea. But the first bite didn't taste right; the cake
had needed to bake longer. It doesn't matter, Mother assured me,
setting down her fork. We should count our blessings. You start,
Adele. And so I did, giving thanks for my family, for Charles's well-
deserved test score, for the food before us, which was bountiful,
even though these lean years had left so much of the country hungry and forlorn.

Pa's turn came, but he wasn't lucid enough to speak. Silently, I
chastised myself for not noticing before. He looked so faint. He
began to cough, softly at first, then in violent, convulsive spasms. He

covered his mouth with a napkin, and we half-expected the cloth to become speckled with blood. The doctor had told us to watch for it—this first telltale sign. But when Pa's coughing stopped, the napkin still looked clean.

"What he needs is a peaceful night's rest," Mother said, her voice scratchy.

No one could disagree. Better to let him sleep. Better not to worry in front of him. I led him to bed and pulled off his shoes, peeled off his socks. I asked him if he wanted me to stay, to watch over him, maybe to read something, but he shook his head, slumping on the mattress, already half-asleep.

Back at the table only three of us remained. Or were there two? I wondered. Without Pa around, Charles and Mother seemed like a single creature. They finished each other's sentences, then laughed in unison. I'd set candles on the table and the delicate, flickering light made their faces beautiful, achingly beautiful. My eyes hurt to stare. I thought Mother would protest when I began to clear the dishes— "No, Adele, sit with us. Share with us." But her eyes didn't stray from Charles's face, his hands, his hair. And though I'd willed it away, my envy crept back.

I retired early to my room, grateful to be alone, even as minutes earlier I had been grateful to be among others. I unbraided my hair and undressed, then lay in bed in a thin cotton shift, listening as Pa's coughing reverberated against the walls—a ghastly, consumptive sound. Although my eyelids drooped, I refused to sleep, not until Pa's coughing had subsided, not until he could rest too. I lit a lamp and lingered over one of Miss Prowl's secondhand donations: *Wuthering Heights*. I was reading it for the umpteenth time, struggling to slip out of my own reality and into the wild, windswept moors. For a while I managed to concentrate on Heathcliff's desperation rather than my own.

Time passed, how much I couldn't be sure. Eventually, I heard Charles and Mother rise, their chairs squeaking on the wood floor as they bade each other good night.

I waited for silence, for that coughing to break. But it didn't, never for more than a few minutes. In my mind's eye, I saw Pa's miserable lungs, blackened like the inside of a chimney, his every onerous breath passing through a brume of granite dust. I wondered if we should summon a doctor, even at this late hour. Surely Mother would know. Yet I didn't hear her voice through the wall like I sometimes did, the soft, patient coo she used when Pa was at his worst.

It mustn't be so bad, I told myself.

And yet I was filled with portent. The night was inky, without a hint of starlight, only my timid lamp to luminesce objects through the dim. And though I had opened my window, I swore the air wasn't seeping in. No wonder Pa was suffocating.

I had to get out; I needed room to breathe, so I rose, slipping my feet into unlaced shoes, wrapping myself in a pale shawl. I stole through the apartment, opening the door just wide enough to ease through. Then I tiptoed down the stairs, careful to avoid the fourth step down, the creaky step, lest I wake Miss Prowl, who was rumored to keep a billy club under her bed.

Once outside I breathed deep, gulping the air like I would water, hoping that by filling myself I might fill Pa, too. From under the porch came the shrill din of crickets. The bottom of my nightdress fluttered like the powdery wings of a moth. I tried, unsuccessfully, to keep it from blowing above my knees, vaguely aware of the eyes watching me in the darkness. They were green, flinty and alert, maybe even predatory, blinking briskly as they narrowed into slits.

"Mother, what are you doing out here?"

She laughed lightly. My first thought was that she was mocking my surprise. Then I felt ashamed for thinking such a thing, especially when she emerged from the shadows to wrap her long arms around my shoulders. The embrace was so tight I could hear her heart thumping, the whir of blood through her veins. Her body smelled faintly of the cake—yeasty and sweet. I wished, perhaps childishly, that we could always be this close.

"I'm so worried for Pa," I murmured.

She seemed not to hear me. Putting her hand on my head, she caressed my hair. She was gentle at first, but after a few moments her touch became rough, her fingernails scratching and catching painfully in the snarls. I almost told her to stop. But the desire to have her here beside me was greater than my discomfort, and so I held my tongue.

Chapter Three

THE QUARRY emergency signal: it was, more often than not, a false alarm. An explosion hadn't gone as planned, huge chunks of granite had dislodged haphazardly, causing a derrick to capsize. Or maybe there was a problem in the freight yard: a stone block had tumbled over the edge of a flatcar. Most of the time no one got hurt. But sometimes they did. There were minor accidents: burns from the boilers, a nasty gash from a poorly sharpened tool, a hammer coming down on a thumb, granite dust in the eyes, the cuff of a shirt caught in a polishing disk. And there were the accidents that the quarrymen remembered—the kind that time would not erase. Five years ago a worker had tried to fill the boiler with cold water instead of hot, instantly blowing up the boiler and the storage facility surrounding it. Two years before that, a man had climbed to the top of the tallest derrick to grease the pulley, but he'd looked down, panicked, suffered a dizzy spell. Some of the workers still remember him flailing in midair before hitting the ground.

The current foreman was unusually cautious, never hesitating to halt production when he heard a shout, an exclamation, even if it turned out to be a simple quarrel among the men. He was vigilant, maybe zealously vigilant, but he had to be. He lost at least a man a year to "unnatural causes." His employer, Palanza Brothers Granite, was the last in a memorable string of quarrying enterprises that dated back to 1858. Palanza had a reputation to uphold, one of quality, diligence, and reliability, but also of safety. The foreman knew that behind his back the men talked of unions and attorneys—one

accident called negligent and the lawsuits would pile up like hot-
cakes. If it came to that, the Palanzas might as well empty their pockets. In these troubled times jurors always sided with the poor man—
or the dead one.

Sometimes in a single month the emergency signal would blast
three times. I could hear it all the way from Miss Prowl's house. I
should have been used to the noise by now, but it never ceased to
make me shudder. Father said that he hadn't grown used to it either.
It still made him wince: not the thought of death, but of near-death.
Black powder blasts didn't always take lives. Sometimes they took
arms, legs, eyes, shards of sanity. And what would he be, Pa mused
aloud, if he spent the rest of his days in a bed or a wheelchair? What
would he be if he couldn't fend for himself or anyone else? He'd be
the opposite of his brother Francisco, that's what.

I was already on my way to the quarry, armed with lunch for Pa
and Charles. I was already on my way when I heard it—the three
sharp blasts of steam. I walked a little faster, then broke into a run, a
limber, startled run, my feet barely skimming the sandy path. So
long-legged and skinny, I was a natural sprinter, yet the path seemed
to go on forever, and when at last I arrived, my lungs stretched and
tight, I couldn't make sense of what was before me. The men were
scrambling in every direction, like ants whose hill had been toppled.
They were shouting, their voices blending together into one calami-
tous yelp. I called to one of them, Old Man Richter, but his face told
me he couldn't talk—or wouldn't. I tried to approach him, but got
swallowed in a swell of surging bodies. "Where's the foreman?"
someone yelled, and I wondered the same. No matter how chaotic
the circumstances, the foreman always made a point of being visible.

I moved on, pushing my way through the foundering clusters.
And I saw suddenly that their scrambling wasn't random after all.
The men were moving erratically in a single direction—to the site of
a derrick. It was the guy-wire derrick, the last of its kind. Heavy wires
anchored into the ground held up the central wood pole, which rose
to a height of a hundred feet. I saw immediately that the derrick

wasn't right. The boom had bent. The cable and skyhook were missing. At the bottom of the derrick sat a block of granite—an impossibly large block of granite, at least eight feet on all sides. The chain around it was loose and splayed. I didn't need the foreman to explain: anyone could see that those links had snapped. Jagged bits of metal had flown in all directions. The enormous stone had careened to the ground, leaving a deep welt in the earth. The skyhook could be anywhere—the explosive pop might have carried it to the edge of town.

There were rumblings of disbelief, of shock.

"Look at the size of that rock! The chain was too small by a mile."

"Did you hear? Six were taken. They're already with Doc Benson."

"How that metal traveled—like bullets."

"Six you say. Who were the men?"

But I didn't hear the answer. I was already running again, past Fiji, Tonga, Samoa, and the other work sheds, straight to the medical station. Doc Benson was always on-site—Palanza Brothers made sure of that. I told myself not to worry. Pa and Charles were stonecutters and stonecutters didn't die this way—swiftly, unexpectedly. They died always of silicosis, a disease that takes its time, so that family members can prepare.

And I wondered suddenly, legs pumping, head pounding, if I was prepared.

A pair of hands caught me just outside the door to the medical station. I fought against them. Arms flailing, I sent manic punches into the air.

"Hey, hold on, you can't go in there, Adele."

I couldn't have known, but for the hidden cracks in the granite. I looked at my captor and saw Silvio's careworn face. His arms coiled around me with stubborn concern. Up close, he didn't appear so menacing. His expression reminded me of sea glass, all the sharpness rubbed smooth.

"Let go."

"I can't," he said.

He didn't have to hold me much longer. The doctor himself emerged, his clothes stained with blood, dark clotted blood, the kind that pours straight from the heart.

"Who's this?" Doc Benson asked. His eyes lingered on my unraveling braids, the way my body was braced.

"The Pietra girl," Silvio breathed, loosening his hold. But I'd already wriggled free. I stood on my own two feet, supporting myself on a last feeble hope.

"Is my father in there?"

The doctor looked suddenly drained, nauseous, as if he, too, might need support. Carefully, finger by finger, he removed his sullied gloves.

"Miss Pietra, I'm sorry to inform you that your father and brother have passed. I tended to them myself, I can assure you of that. They felt no pain, no suffering. They died instantly."

Doc Benson's mouth seemed to move mechanically, as if the words were not his own. But they were—I'd heard them clearly, as clearly as I'd heard the emergency signal.

In the hours that followed, nothing else was as apprehensible. There were voices, so many, as Silvio half-led, half-dragged me away. I couldn't reconcile what was real from what I imagined: splinters of chain like shrapnel pummeling Pa's stomach and chest, Charles struck in the neck, clean through the jugular, by a single jagged link, two other men down and two more injured, blood spurting like fountains, some of the workers trying to stop the flow with their bare hands, with makeshift tourniquets torn from their own clothes, but still it came, in long scarlet rivulets, as they sobbed. The foreman had fled, unforgivably, like a general deserting his troops in their hour of need. He'd driven into town to make a frantic call to the Palanzas; then, someone said, he'd drunk an entire bottle of bourbon.

It was one of the worst accidents the quarry had ever seen—certainly the worst in recent memory. The next day two Palanza brothers came from Hartford to inspect the work site. Miss Prowl reported that they drove a Ford Model-A and wore handsome suits, straw skimmers, lapel pins, and fine gold pocket watches. One of them swung an ivory-handled cane as he walked. They fired the foreman within minutes ("Better pray for that poor soul. He's going to hell," Miss Prowl swore). Within hours they had brought lawyers and reporters—their own lawyers and reporters. Multiple versions of the accident started to circulate. The details got cloudy. Culpability was passed from person to person. The chain vanished—who had filched it? But no one could dispute the outcome: how four men were gone forever and how two others would be lucky to survive.

I asked Silvio if Pa and Charles had been outside the work sheds waiting for me. If I'd brought their lunches sooner, might they still be here?

He shook his head, mustering a sad smile. "I reckon not. When God makes a decision, there's no second-guessing it."

I thought about how Pa had carved his own tombstone years ago. He'd never considered carving one for Charles, too. I didn't blame him. Some preparations can never be made.

The skyhook had landed all the way in the Boy Scout camp, half a mile away. A scout had recognized it and brought it back to the quarry. But no one could look at it, let alone use it, so a couple of quarrymen rowed out into the Sound, said a few respectful words, and tossed it overboard.

In those long days following the accident, Mother and I moved automatically, unthinkingly, making funeral arrangements, opening letters of condolence, expecting any moment to wake up and discover that the terrible incident had never happened and that all was as it had been. But at six o'clock each evening neither Charles nor Pa walked though the door. Mother and I no longer added their clothes to the wash pile. We no longer beat the granite dust out of their shoes, nor did we set their places at the table. At noon, when I was supposed to bring lunch to the quarry, I lay in my bed and stared at the dusty blades of the long-broken ceiling fan.

The days themselves seemed different. Summer was at its peak, yet sudden winds trundled through the air, a portent of autumn.

We had visitors, but not many. In the years since Mother started living in Stony Creek—as opposed to merely summering here—she had managed to alienate a good portion of the population. She refused to engage in any neighborly chitchat, and acted with the utmost briskness and reserve when interacting with shopkeepers, neighbors, and acquaintances. Her demeanor, coupled with her jewelry and alpine height, lanced any chance of peaceable relations, and of course fueled the gossip surrounding our family. Mother didn't seek to win over the Cottagers, either, for they knew of her lot and turned up their noses as readily as she turned up hers.

Years ago, Mother had toyed with the idea of working in town, maybe taking a job as a clerk, teacher, or nurse—any position offering some challenge or stimulation. But she couldn't stomach the thought of working under people who weren't her equal ("people whose jealousy would have kept them from hiring me anyway," she claimed). In the end, out of the few options available, she'd preferred the lone toil of laundering. Other positions would have afforded more money and respectability, perhaps. But Mother's refuge—her ability to suffer discreetly—was priceless.

Of our handful of visitors, Miss Prowl was probably the most frequent. One afternoon she came for tea, announcing bounteously that she would overlook rent that month. Normally Mother would have resisted any gesture that smacked of pity, but this time she accepted Miss Prowl's offer with a faint nod. The stonecutters showed generosity too. They stopped by to give us Pa's and Charles's tools, newly cleaned, polished, and wrapped in oiled rags. It was a tradition among the men; they didn't know what else to give to a grieving family. Sometimes I went through Pa's tools at night, finding small solace in the soft clink of metal.

Though she didn't admit it, Mother concentrated exclusively on Charles's death. Her shrine was the certificate next to the fireplace. Several times a day I caught her standing before it, squinting as she read the words again and again, until their meaning disintegrated, until their weight collapsed what little sanctity we had left.

I left the house less often, making trips into town only when we were running low on necessities: flour, tooth powder, a new scrub brush to replace the one whose handle had broken. Acquaintances met my eyes with pity. They touched my shoulder lightly and told me to take care of Mother—she was my only family now. They told me that Charles and Pa were in a better place. But I resented their sentiment, which sounded cheap to me. I wondered where Charles and Pa had really gone. When granite dust is blown by the wind, it scatters harum-scarum; there's no way to trace it.

Mother stayed indoors almost all the time. I answered the door when the Cottagers' disimpassioned maids deposited sacks of laundry. Mine were the hands in the washtub's scalding water, the only ones to wrestle with stains, to twist hanks of fabric furiously, both to wring out excess water and to release my anguish. Mother was back in the house, maybe in bed, maybe lingering before the fireplace. She had stopped washing herself, the fresh scent of her skin replaced by an odor of decay that made my nostrils pinch. She who had so fastidiously bleached and scoured and scrubbed could no longer be bothered with cleanliness. Indeed, she had been living in the same musty mourning dress for days.

There were rumors that she'd gone mad. She ate only stale bread, people said. She gulped whole bottles of vinegar, mistaking it for wine. She scratched her head as if it were full of nits. She finally called herself by her rightful title: quarrywoman.

But the talebearers were wrong. Even inside our grim home, Mother still wore her jewelry. She was still fearsome in her lanky bearing. And she still spoke of the future.

"It is no longer a question of if, Adele, only of when. Before he passed, your father spoke with Silvio. He plans to ask for your hand. After all that's happened, I expect you to give him the answer he wants."

One Sunday afternoon I lay in my hidden cubby, my back conforming to the hard earthen contours. I realized I no longer cared about marriage, or even about life. I didn't care that my vision was tinged with death, or that my every thought was filmy and dull. I might as well have been that skyhook, now sunk fathoms down in sloshing gray water.

In the mornings I awoke with a salty crust of tears around my eyes—my grief struggling to surface when I was at my weakest, lost in sleep. But by day I would not allow myself to feel. My misery was muted; it had to be. If I faced it in earnest, I would truly drown.

Maybe it had started with the tangled seagull. Maybe it had been festering for years, feeding off desolation, isolation, and flagging hope. I can admit that it had surfaced in my consciousness, once or twice. I can admit that, like my brother, I wondered what it would be like to venture beyond Stony Creek. But at that moment the idea seemed spontaneous, born, almost, of its own volition.

Silvio was finally coming to dinner. There would be no coy formalities, no obligatory courting. Silvio was a decent man, that much I would admit. But my situation was indecent: a girl without a father was a girl for the taking.

Mother had told me to prepare.

"Put on your good dress, Adele—the blue calico with the lace collar. For the love of Pete, don't wear your hair in braids. Let it down. Brush it until it shines. Let him see you've left your girlhood behind."

I did as she instructed, to a point. I unraveled my hair until it streamed down my back. I hadn't cut it in ages, my stubbornness fed by snide comments like those from Miss Prowl. As I brushed them, the sable waves undulated. My dress was still draped across the bed. I stood only in my underclothes, my body an assemblage of straight, lean lines in the dresser mirror.

Through the closed door, I could hear Mother scurrying about. She'd set the table and lit tapers from the candle box. She'd scrubbed the apartment into immaculateness. Any residual odors of neglect and deterioration were hidden by the rich, savory smell of roasting lamb.

Since planning this dinner with Silvio, Mother had regained her purpose. At daybreak she'd taken a long bath, crushed calendula and lavender floating on the surface of the water. She had put away her mourning clothes. She had decided to forget that the postman had arrived this morning with a second letter for Charles. Yale had accepted him. Indeed, Yale had accepted them both.

On the floor of my room, a shiny pair of scissors glinted from atop the sewing basket. I reached for them, the smooth metal surprisingly cool to the touch. I pulled straight a lock of hair and clipped it close to my scalp. Seeing it there on the ground—long, wispy, and final, the first step made, no going back now—I was inspired. I snipped more, whole handfuls. Dark tendrils cascaded to the floor. My cheeks burned, yet my lips twined into a tear-away smile.

When I had finished, I inspected my image in the mirror. I'd done a crude job. Licks of hair sprouted about my head in wild whorls and barbed tufts. My appearance was no longer feminine, but rascally, skin stretched taut over flat cheekbones, eyes large and cagey, ears sticking out in larkish glee. I hung my head, but twin braids no longer flopped over my shoulders.

Opening the door with a steady hand, I walked with long strides, not the hesitant baby steps that were my habit in the house. I walked straight to the fireplace. I, too, had read Charles's certificate countless times. For me, its meaning had become distorted and rearranged, allowing for different interpretations.

I called to Mother, who came to me at once, concerned; never had she heard her daughter's voice like this: commanding, resolute. When she saw my shorn head, her shoulders slumped, her back caved. She tottered like an unmoored ship.

"How could you do this to me?" she asked.

"You'll see that it's for the best." I was surprised by my own tartness.

She grabbed the back of a chair—anything to keep herself upright. "Silvio won't look at you after this."

"He won't need to."

"What do you mean? Do you even know what you're saying?"

"We were only a year apart, Charles and I."

For several seconds Mother's eyes flickered between the certificate and the photograph of her parents. Her mouth opened in wordless wonder, seeing for the first time all that was possible.

"No," she said finally. "It's a foolish idea—foolish and disloyal."

"Mother, don't dismiss it so quickly. I've learned so much—on my own, reading. And I listened to the lessons you went over with Charles. I kept pace with him."

"You planned for this?"

"No, of course not. I just hoped that I'd have a chance too."

"A chance for what, Adele?"

For the kind of opportunities you threw away, I thought.

"Yale would have no way of knowing," I told her. "The accident scarcely made the local papers. They never printed any names. Palanza Brothers couldn't have kept it any quieter."

"It doesn't matter. Have you no sense of morality? Have you no respect?"

Suddenly stable, Mother released her grip on the chair and slinked toward me. I thought she would strike. Part of me would have welcomed a physical rebuke. I was ashamed of myself for crossing this boundary, for dancing across my brother's grave.

She reached out and I trembled, expecting my cheek to sting, but instead she touched my hair, or what was left of it.

"I've never seen this in you," she said.

She was so close I couldn't avert my eyes. Her face would have been a portraitist's delight: the contours both soft and precise, the colors—the subtle spray of rose across her cheeks, the swish of green in her eyes—unrivaled. Staring at her, I wanted to explain about the cracks in the granite, how she had no right to be surprised by death's haste, how no amount of planning could have ensured the future she'd favored. Instead, I instructed her to send Silvio away.

"Tell him I never want to see him again. Tell him anything you have to."

Surely she would refuse. Surely she would exorcise this stranger from my body with lashes and slaps. Yet she seemed wary of my sudden stoicism, eyeing me very carefully: the lopped-off hair, the rigid posture, the underclothes that hung loose on my frame.

Silvio arrived minutes later. I could hear his boots striking each step on the staircase. When he knocked, Mother opened the door only a crack. She whispered something gentle and apologetic—her daughter was ill, heartbroken, not at all herself. It was too soon after all. She asked him if he could find the patience to wait a bit longer.

There was a lull, a flash of time in which the future turned like a carousel, a churning of music and wild, brash color. I knew our turn had come when I heard Silvio's boots again, this time clopping down the stairs, two at a time—perhaps angrily, perhaps disappointedly. Mother closed the door and turned toward me steadily. Her eyes were unsparing.

"You're more my daughter than I thought," she said.

There was much work to be done—the kind of work that one would never consider if not for the bizarre circumstances Mother and I had chosen to embrace. The haircut had been my initiation, but it wasn't enough, even when Mother coaxed it into submission with hairdressing. There were my mannerisms, soft and intimate, too many self-conscious flicks of my hands to my face, a habit of cupping my palm around my mouth when I was about to laugh. And there was my gait, wider and sturdier than that of most girls, but a gait that had adjusted to skirts, not trousers.

Fortunately, my hands, rough and dark, passed muster. Mother told me to stop soothing them at night with her homemade balm. "They're right the way they are." Smiling, she added sheepishly, "I never thought I'd hear myself say that."

Some of the changes I enjoyed making. It was a relief, for instance, to toss aside the razor I used to shave my legs and underarms. I'd never been good at shaving, not since Mother had first showed me how, a cake of soap in one hand, a pitcher of warm water in the other—"never, *ever* go above the knees, Adele."

I was forever nicking myself with the blade, rills of blood oozing down my shins. The hair that I shaved was fine and downy, not like the coarse little wires that had dotted Charles's skin. Still, Mother insisted that it would look authentic enough if it grew out.

"You'll find out," she said with a smirk, "that there is considerable variation among men's bodies. And that men care more about some variations than others."

My voice was the last stronghold—light and gossamer as corn silk. Whole afternoons Mother and I worked on a deeper pitch. She gave me Charles's College Entrance Examination preparation materials, and these I read aloud with a voice that rose directly from my chest, the alto timbre of a different person.

"Remember your laugh, Adele. It will give you away. A laugh is spontaneous, free of guile. And *your* laugh is like a bell: high and sweet."

Each day, in between loads of laundry, we went through two lessons from Charles's books—a swift yet necessary pace, for Yale would welcome its incoming freshmen in a matter of weeks. Mother seemed surprised by my aptitude. So confident that no student could have been more exemplary than her firstborn, she was genuinely stunned to find one under her own roof. Yet if my ability caught her off guard, she was quick to cap her praise.

"I read as many books as I could get my hands on when I was your age, and where did it get me? History is full of accounts of curiosity ruining women. Just look at Eve."

Finally, there was my body itself—an entity that could not be tweaked or refashioned, only cloaked. Mother couldn't believe that after all these years of bemoaning my curveless shape, she at last had reason to celebrate it. In my room with the curtains drawn tight, she handed me one of Charles's shirts, one of his two pairs of pants, and his only jacket. I thought the mere giving of these items might trigger her melancholia. But by then we were too far gone for headlong emotion. We were charlatans now. We couldn't afford to wear our hearts on our sleeves when our sleeves were stuffed with tricks.

Mother had hemmed Charles's pants and adjusted the inseams. She'd shortened the jacket, taken in the shoulders, and put darts at the waist. I slipped into the guise of a boy, pretending that the clothes didn't still smell like my brother, that this elaborate ruse didn't touch me on some deeper, more disturbing level. For several minutes Mother fussed over me, tucking, pulling, buttoning, and straightening, pushing pins through ripples of extra fabric. She took a step back, but I could tell she wasn't satisfied.

"Take it off," she announced.

"Which part?"

"All of it."

Nearly naked, I stood, rueful, as she gathered the clothes and breezed from the room. I could hear her rummaging through drawers and cupboards. She started to sing softly—a little ditty she repeated over and over whenever she was sewing, something about a handsome young sailor braving a stormy sea.

I stayed in my room, staring intently at the mirror. I decided that in this short time I'd come a long way. My face was no longer so easily tipped by emotion. My eyes were mirrors rather than windows. I looked less like myself, more like the stranger who was emerging from within, an aloof and deceitful stranger who preferred closed shades and locked doors, but who nonetheless coveted freedom.

I'd learned my tricks from observing the men in the quarry all these years. Lately, too, I'd spent more time in town, standing wall-flower quiet, a scarf wound about my shorn head, watching the other sex talk, work, joke, and carouse. I'd decided that life was more thrilling for a man, much louder and crisper, each day a blustery free-for-all, no need for nuance or propriety. I'd always thought that the differences between a Cottager and a quarryman were considerable. But now I saw that all men were more similar than not. All spoke frankly, lived freely, and turned into lovesick fools at the sight of a pretty young Cottager.

I'd gained the most insight by standing outside the saloons in town in the evening, a habit that surely would have incensed Mother if ever she found out. She'd loosened her restrictions on me, perhaps exhausted by the extra hours we now spent together. The saloons were where I'd had the chance to see men at their most pared-down and truthful. When they lurched out the door, limbs loose from inebriation, eyes bleary, speech rougher than when they'd entered, I saw what fed them: lust. Lust for adventure, camaraderie, acknowledgment, money, women, security, a decent meal, peace of mind. It didn't necessarily matter what a man craved. All that mattered was that he craved something, and that this something dictated how he felt each night, once he bid adieu to his friends and stumbled back to his home, to his bed, where I imagined the white lull of sleep at last numbed his yearning.

I decided that if I were to be recognized as a man, I would have to yearn for something, too. Yet I wondered, was not wanting my present life the same thing as craving a new one?

Exactly twenty minutes after leaving my room, Mother returned. She carried a ribbon of cloth, several feet long, six inches wide, and elastic. I knew immediately what it was meant to do. I took it from her without speaking and wound it around my small breasts. When I had finished, Mother helped me to pin it in place. Then I donned the shirt again, the jacket and pants, too, and finally Charles's shoes, which were several sizes too big.

Mother took a step back and assessed me from head to toe. But still she wasn't satisfied. "One more thing," she said, taking a sock from her apron.

I was confused. Under Charles's shoes I was already wearing two thick woolen pairs. But Mother continued to dangle the sock, and soon enough I read her meaning. My hand flew to my mouth as giggles erupted. I tried to stop myself, but I couldn't, especially when Mother started to chuckle too. Soon we were clutching our bellies as long peals of laughter bounced off the walls, the echoes filling our

ears, making us howl even harder. How strange it was to let go like
this, as if we hadn't a care.

When at last we quieted, we collapsed on my bed and looked
guiltily at each other. I took the sock from her and swung it like a
pendulum.

"Do I really need this?"

She shrugged. "You never know. Boys are more physical than
girls. They like to play, to jostle. If during a tussle one happened to
brush . . . that part. Well, you understand."

She cupped my chin, but I didn't know if she did so out of fondness or because she was concerned for its softness.

"You're going to have to be quite an actress, Adele. We don't know
what kind of situations you'll encounter, but let's do our best to
anticipate."

We decided to write down every scenario we could imagine: the
troublesome and the advantageous, the exciting and the frightening.
Then we talked about the future. Mother had told me that I ought to
look at our ruse from both a short- and long-term perspective. The
short-term—my time at Yale—involved laying the groundwork: earn-
ing high marks, befriending people with influence, and motivating
them to help me. The long-term was about how I would make money
after graduation. This, of course, depended a great deal on the profession I chose. Mother, who came from old money, admitted she knew
little about the process of acquiring wealth. Alfred, being a professor,
hadn't contributed much to the family fortune. Mother called his
work "gentle" and dissuaded me from following his example.

"We must find you work with higher stakes and higher rewards.
Maybe law. If you are enterprising, you will establish a good reputation early on. You can start your own practice eventually."

What she didn't mention was just how long I'd have to pretend to
be male. Since Yale was the foundation of our future, it seemed that I
would have to keep Charles's identity indefinitely. I would need my
brother's name on my university diploma; I would need the cachet of

Yale to find a suitable job or to apply to graduate schools. To compete in a man's world, I would have to possess a man's privileges. Yet Mother and I had not resolved when and if I'd return to being myself, and I'd not harped on the matter, fearing what she would ultimately decide.

That night I slept in Charles's old trousers. I thought I would grow accustomed to them as I rolled about the bed, struggling to find a comfortable position. But when I awoke the next morning, all I felt was squeamish.

Since I'd cut my hair, I'd done my best to avoid Miss Prowl. Yet evasion was difficult, as nine times out of ten she was lolling about the porch, a bottle hidden in the folds of her skirt. I couldn't leave the house or enter it without seeing her gin-blossomed nose perched atop her day's reading.

I'd taken to using the back door. But one day she was there, about to enter as I was leaving, or so it appeared, for part of me knew that she had sniffed something amiss weeks ago and was now doing everything in her power to discover what it was. I reached self-consciously for my hair, but it was too late. I had no scarf or hat. She had already seen the change, and by now she certainly would have heard about it. I was the talk of the town. I'd ruined my already modest looks because of my grief, they said. Mother was on her way to the funny farm and now I wasn't far behind.

"What were you going for—a bob?" Miss Prowl snickered.

She'd shut the door, even though I'd made an effort to keep it open. Inside the narrow stairwell we were cloistered. To avoid touching her body, I pressed myself against the wall. The smell of her skin, winey and curdling, was thick. My eyes traveled to a fat mole on her neck. A single wiry hair sprung from it like an antenna.

"Really, Adele, don't you think you went a bit short? I almost didn't recognize you."

"You don't like it? I think it's very modern. It's exactly what I wanted."

She snickered again, more loudly, a bolder showing of her contempt. "If that's what you'd call modern, give me old-fashioned any day."

It would have been easy at that moment to pick on any of Miss Prowl's shortcomings: her fondness for alcohol, her rotund figure, her smeary face paint. But she'd shown Mother clemency by ignoring a month's rent, and no matter what my problems with her were, I knew I couldn't jeopardize our place in her house.

"How is your rheumatism, Miss Prowl? I hope it's improving; I understand it's a great torment to you."

She cradled one meaty hand with the other, showing me the fibrous, knotty joints in each finger. "Oh, it is. A real torment. Some days I just don't think I can make it out of bed—my knees feel as if they're covered in concrete."

In the drab, dark stairwell, I tentatively patted her hand.

We talked several more minutes about her aches and pains; or rather, she talked and I nodded sympathetically. I was grateful to have diverted her attention, yet just when I was preparing a good-bye, I heard Mother making her way down the stairs. Perhaps she had a load of laundry in her arms. Or perhaps she had somehow sensed my predicament.

There was no room to pass, and I hoped Miss Prowl would take the opportunity to part my company. Instead, she led the way outdoors, where all three of us assembled in the backyard.

It was high noon, startlingly bright, and we shaded our eyes with our hands. On the clothesline rows of shirts swayed, wooden pins keeping them from dancing away on the wind. Another batch of clothes soaked in the washtub. Years ago, when we had moved into the house, Miss Prowl had agreed that Mother could have the full run of the backyard for her laundry business. I could count on one hand the number of times I'd seen our landlady here, on this little barren plot, where not even the weeds dared to grow for fear of being poisoned with soap and bleach.

"It's something of a relief to visit, Gertrude," Miss Prowl said. "I've seen so little of you, and even less of your daughter."

"We've valued our privacy during this difficult time," Mother responded. Beside Miss Prowl, she seemed so tall and regal—a queen beside a crone.

"Of course you have. But too much privacy can be isolating. A young lady should be among people, wouldn't you agree?"

"Indeed I would. That's why I've decided that Adele will stay with my parents in Philadelphia. She will spend most of the year with them and come back only during the summer. They have the means to care for her properly. There is little for her now in Stony Creek, I'm afraid."

Both Miss Prowl and I responded to Mother's announcement with astonishment. Miss Prowl's was plain as day. Mine was kept in my sleeve along with the rest of my secrets.

"But you will need her now more than ever," our landlady protested. "And she will need you."

"Nonsense. This town has too many ghosts. I don't want my child haunted by despair, not when there's so much for her to see—and to do."

Mother's stopgap was so inspired I couldn't help but wonder if she'd come up with it on the spot or deliberated half the night. The lie worked on nearly every level. It allowed me to flee Stony Creek with minimal suspicion. It enabled me to return at any point. Most important, it was reasonable. Plenty of girls went to visit their grandparents for extended periods. But there was a flaw, an obvious one. Everyone knew that Mother and her parents were estranged. There was no way Miss Prowl would let this inconsistency slip by.

"So you've made peace with them at last?"

"I must insist upon my privacy. But if you must know, yes, we have reconciled. Adele is their grandchild, after all."

"And what about you, Gertrude? Will you also stay with them?"

"Me? My place is here with my husband and son. I could never uproot so suddenly."

Mercilessly, Miss Prowl tunneled deeper, certain that she would eventually uncover whatever it was we were concealing. "But what will you do without Adele to give you comfort? How will you manage?"

Mother took a deep breath. I waited, heart at a dead stop, for her to add flesh to the skeleton of this subterfuge.

"Manage? What a queer question, Miss Prowl. You must feel sorry for me, but I can't imagine why. We've lost a great deal, Adele and I, but we've never for a moment lost hope."

As the days flew by and the moment of my reckoning fast approached, Mother and I decided I needed to test my knowledge.

"Observing without doing isn't enough," she said. We both knew what she meant.

One Saturday we took the shoreline trolley to Branford, a town that was far enough from Stony Creek that we wouldn't be recognized, but not as far as New Haven, where I feared my courage would fail me. We sat in our regular clothes on the rattan seats, the rumble and hum of the motor in our ears. I ran my fingers nervously along the varnished wood, which had long ago been smoothed by the caress of travelers. Mother remained silent. We were terribly conscious of the old carpetbag at my feet, which was filled with the bits and pieces of my new wardrobe. Every once in a while, we were jolted out of our reverie by the strong metallic odor of an electric arc.

When we reached our stop, we exited the car grim-faced but resolute. Mother hunted for a place where I might change, but when she found none, we retreated to the outskirts of town. I undressed in a half-collapsed shed. Its only inhabitants were a couple of field mice. Mother kept guard, chiding me to move faster.

Mother had seen my costume many times, but perhaps here, away from home, the extent of our masquerade activated stronger emotions. Her cat eyes froze when I departed the shed. She stood rooted to the ground. Her immobility might have meant any number of things: shame, shock, disgust, reproach. Alarmed, I called to her softly. At first she seemed not to hear me, but then she shook off her doubts. She reached out, squeezing my hand as if to reassure us both.

We walked the distance back to town, talking of things we had so far avoided: how Mother had pawned off more jewelry to pay for a single room at Yale—"a roommate would be your undoing, Adele"; how I would need to visit a tailor in New Haven for finer clothing, things that my brother had never owned; how I must appropriate Charles's name and how I mustn't shudder at the sound of it. Finally, we talked of finances. Yale had awarded my brother a scholarship, but it would cover tuition alone. To pay for my board, books, and personal items, I would have to participate in a work-study program.

"You'll have your pick of them," Mother explained. "The admissions department told me that work-studies are tailored to a student's own interests. You can do just about anything: assist in a research project, aid a college master, work at the library or at the press. I've been assured that no matter what you do, you won't have to work more than eighteen hours a week."

"What's the pay?"

"Between two hundred and a thousand dollars, depending on the responsibilities involved."

"That's no pittance."

"No, it isn't," Mother replied.

The topic of the work-study troubled me. Until now, all I'd thought about was how I might conceal myself in order to conform. I was preoccupied with fitting in, blending in. I'd considered the opportunities that university life and scholarship would afford me, but only in the broadest sense. As for which goals and pursuits at Yale would be of a more personal nature, I hardly knew. That would have to change, I decided.

On that last stretch of road, my feet seemed lighter and I wandered along with head high and shoulders back. Inspired, I sized up the men who crossed my path before they had a chance to do the same to me. With a single luxurious swill I took in everything: children playing jacks along the dusty road, a spotted dog running past, two old men in a growly Ford Tudor. I walked as if I had a talisman, something sharp and lethal, stowed in my pocket. Surely the good citizens of Branford sensed it: my bright silver hook, capable of goring anyone and reeling him in. Eyes scampered across my person, for I radiated all that was rare and precious: self-confidence, salty disregard, the red-blooded vigor of youth. Beside me, Mother looked anxious. She clenched my arm in warning, but I didn't pay her much heed.

We entered the first shop we saw—Baldwin's store. It had a slightly disreputable look—the boards were warped, and some of the slate shingles on the steep-pitched roof were missing. But Mother nonetheless followed me inside. We glanced at the floor-to-ceiling shelves, at the chrome-handled oak refrigerators stocked with milk and meats and cheeses. A roll-top desk sat in a corner. A counter ran along one side of the store, so that no customer could access the more expensive cans, bottles, medicines, and remedies behind it. The girl minding the counter, a redhead with a round face, straightened at our approach. She had been idly pressing the buttons of a cash register, entertaining herself with the big metal clank of each button, the ding-ding spring of the cash drawer.

She eyed me as women had once eyed Charles.

"May I help you?"

"Yes," Mother said, stepping forward without hesitation. "I'd like a box of Higgins Aspirin."

The girl turned around and stood on her tiptoes, reaching for a high shelf. The back of her skirt clung to her peach-shaped bottom. She plucked the tin, then set it on the counter.

"And for you, sir?"

I stared at a huge striped lolly, one of a dozen that stood upright in a blue Ball jar, then decided it was something the old Adele would have chosen. The new Adele must be different, intrepid.

"I'll take a cigar," I announced. I maintained a throaty voice, facing the shopgirl head-on, deciding I had no choice but to overlook her coquettish smile. Beside me Mother shifted uncomfortably.

"Which kind?"

But here was a question I hadn't anticipated. I flipped through my memories of the men smoking outside the saloons. In vain, I tried to remember a brand, any brand. The girl seized upon my hesitation.

"These are popular," she said cheerfully, pointing to a box labeled Sun Ray. "So are these." She reached out for a yellow box with an Indian wearing a feather headdress on the lid.

"Which would you recommend?" I leaned into the counter. My belt buckle bumped against the wood. The sound seemed thunderously loud to my ears.

"Me?" she giggled, cheeks going the color of her hair. "I—I couldn't say. But my daddy smokes the Sun Rays."

I stared plainly into the girl's face, returning a bit of her bald-faced interest. "Well, I'll trust your daddy."

The girl's giddiness didn't abate as she stuffed our purchases into a brown paper sack. Mother nodded that I should pay and I did, using the wallet that had once belonged to my brother. I watched the girl as she counted out the change with one hand and twirled a curly lock with the other. As Mother and I left the store, I tipped my hat jauntily, mimicking a gesture I'd seen other men use. The girl waved to me blithely.

I thought Mother and I would spend the rest of the afternoon puttering around Branford, testing new waters. But after that first stop, she seemed hell-bent on returning home. I wondered if I'd flubbed my performance in the store or if her headache had worsened. She had already chewed one aspirin and was rustling about for a second. I trailed behind her as she stalked back to the derelict shed. Only after I'd changed my clothes did I dare ask for an explanation. But by then her mood had switched from gray to stormy.

"I don't understand—didn't I do all right?" I asked.

"A little too well, I'd say," she declared, taking my cigar and snapping it in two.

AUTUMN

Chapter Four

I REALIZED THAT if Mother and I were to be partners—something our circumstances demanded—then we would be unequal partners. As the date of my departure drew closer, she became increasingly recalcitrant, her headaches returning with alarming frequency and strength. Those last few days I studied the books on my own, I practiced on my own, and when I walked around the apartment in my trousers, Mother was nowhere to be seen.

Even so, it was clear that her mind was made. I would go to Yale, even if she couldn't always be there to say so.

"You'll pull me out of this granite wasteland, Adele," she'd muttered one evening after a wan dinner of fried eggs and mashed potatoes. And how similar those words were to the speeches she'd given Charles! "Maybe not immediately, but in time. You'll find a way to make enough money. Yale is a necessary stepping stone to better things."

Granite wasteland. Stepping stone. Such phrases did nothing but remind me of how I still loved Stony Creek, nostalgically, not altogether healthfully, the way a child might love a rag doll even as she grows too old for it. Although the thought of Yale left me breathless, a part of me suspected that I would find nothing as magnificent as those pink and gray blocks of stone, polished to a high sheen or left grainy and coarse. I wondered if any building at Yale or beyond would compare to the mountainous bluffs, the uncut headlands that harkened back to the earliest days, when there was nothing but rock, and sand, and sea.

On the day that I was to leave Stony Creek, I did two things. First, I visited Pa and Charles. I sat before each grave for upwards of an hour. I promised Pa that I would come back as soon as I could, and that I would try to make him proud of me in the meantime. To Charles, I had less to say. I knew that if he could have seen me dodging Miss Prowl's inquiries, collaborating with Mother, and dawdling outside saloons, he would have given me that old caustic look—or worse.

I plucked the dandelions that were growing around my brother's grave, digging them out by the roots until my fingernails were dirt-crusted and the edges of skin started to bleed. I think I did it as a sort of penance. I was sorry for his death, sorry that I had resented him so deeply. But I wasn't sorry about taking his place at Yale, and for that more intimate treachery, I could offer no atonement save the burden of guilt.

The second thing I did was to scoop up a handful of granite pebbles. I vowed to carry them with me in my pocket, every day if need be. I vowed not to forget where I'd come from, or who I was really, deep down, underneath not only my costume but also under this new skin, the one that had grown ever harder since the accident.

I was to take the ten o'clock morning train. Mother had decided not to see me off. She was in bed with the worst headache she could remember—a thunderous throbbing that refused to abate. Our farewell was shaky, somber, each of us half-expecting the other to put an end to the affair. Who would be the first, I wondered, to set eyes on that ratty carpetbag and decide that its contents weren't worth the price we might pay?

It wouldn't be Mother. She turned away as I was about to go. I imagined her biting her tongue, holding it with her teeth so it wouldn't lash out.

It was too dangerous to hug her; no kisses, either. I didn't even say good-bye as I closed the door to her room. Secretly, I was glad I would make this first step on my own. To break free of Mother's manacles—that was no small triumph.

All I carried with me on the train was the carpetbag and a woebegone suitcase. It surprised me that my world, swollen to the breaking point with fancies and fears, could be contained in these meager spaces. It surprised me that even before my anxiety had given way to full-fledged terror, I had already arrived to Union Station in New Haven. Somehow, I'd sat the whole ride in a state of rumination, staring at the sky and trees flying past, barely recalling the conductor coming by to claim my long green ticket. I'd shown no interest in anything or anyone, not to the chugging of the locomotive, nor to the deafening bites of steam from the engine room, nor to the roily clouds wafting up from the smokestack. I'd not even acknowledged the elder gentleman who sat beside me, methodically peeling a Macintosh with a paring knife.

I stepped onto the platform, one bag in each hand, and walked into the station. I thought back to the plan Mother and I had devised, a rickety plan that was built on unverified facts.

"Go straight to the ladies' washroom, Adele. Be sure no one else is inside—and that no one is watching you as you enter. Change as quickly as you can, but check that everything is done right—your hair, your shoes, the buttons on your vest. Make sure the latch is closed on the carpetbag once you put your frock and things inside. Then leave just as quickly as you entered. If someone happens to see you, shake your head and say something about a mistake—you thought you were in the men's washroom. Don't talk too long to anyone. And, for mercy's sake, no dawdling."

Mother hadn't known that the ladies' washroom would be flooded with weary travelers from Boston and beyond anxious to rinse their hands and powder the shine off their noses. I strolled in without incident, but leaving would be infinitely harder. I had to wait a full half-hour in a lavatory compartment, peering under the wood-slat door before the pumps and lace-ups and Mary Janes had all departed. The last shoes in the room finally fled from view and I was free to leave, which I did quickly and with fingers crossed. It would be all too easy for an overzealous policeman to put an end to my adventure even before it had begun.

Thankfully, my escape went unnoticed by the hurried travelers. I eased my way into the crowds, so different in my boy's clothes, more agile and deft and sure, and it was then that I fully immersed myself in the moment, weaving briskly through the helter-skelter, noticing that the people I passed were mostly boys, just my age, in newly shined shoes and suits a little rumpled from travel. They were likely my future classmates, for we all looked the same: an eager twinkle in our eyes, purpose to our steps.

In my hand I clutched the name and address of my dormitory: Durfee Hall. But I didn't need it. By now I had it memorized: 198 Elm Street, on the north side of campus. I waited outside the station for one of the taxicabs that swerved haphazardly in and out of the depot. The drivers must have looked forward to this day, one of the busiest of the year, when hundreds of students descended upon New Haven, each needing a lift to his new quarters. I waited in a long, tortuous line, the carpetbag feeling suddenly heavy in my hand.

Just when my apprehension felt intolerable and I thought I might as well get back on the train—any moment now someone would point to my perfectly hairless face and shout, "Look there, an impostor!"—a boy in line behind me tapped me on the back. I turned around wild-eyed, defensive. But surely this unassuming lad wouldn't be the one to see through my ruse. He was as slight as I, with a gaunt face monopolized by thick-rimmed spectacles. His fine dark hair stood upright on one side, as if he'd slept on the train with his head pressed against a window. He carried two bags, as I did, and his were just as tattered, especially in comparison to the fine leather suitcases and brass-ornamented trunks most of the other boys toted.

"The name's Harry. Harry Persky."

He stuck out a soft white hand, the tendons nearly visible through his skin. At the same time, he nodded toward the line. "Since we'll be standing here until the end of time, we might as well make each other's acquaintance. You're a Yale man, right? I could tell—never mind that nine out of ten fellows here are headed to the same place."

I shook his hand firmly, just as Mother and I had practiced.

"Charles Pietra."

"Italian, right? Took four years of Italian in school. I know Russian, Latin, and German, too. Why else you think they let me in?" But he continued before I could respond. "What dormitory did they assign you? I was late mailing back my room application. I'm stuck with a roommate way up on the third floor of Durfee. Who knows what this fellow will be like? Probably a hulking lug from Andover who likes to eat little guys for breakfast. That would be just my luck."

He paused for a moment before asking, "Say, you didn't go to Andover, did you?"

I smiled and shook my head, having taken a liking to this Harry Persky.

"I didn't suppose so. You don't look the prep-school type. No offense."

"None taken. Say, I'm in Durfee, too."

Harry's face brightened. "I thought so!" he exclaimed. "As soon as I saw you, I said to myself, 'I'm meant to know this fellow.' It wasn't silly Nostradamus prophesizing. But rather—I don't know—that you reminded me of myself."

And though Harry and I didn't bear a striking resemblance to each other in any way but build, we were similar. We didn't look as sure of ourselves as some of the other boys, whose sturdy, upright posture suggested immunity to nervous twitches and sidelong glances. Our demeanor was forced and shrill, a matter of avoiding eye contact, and thus shaky introductions; a matter of self-containment in the hopes of appearing mysterious, aloof, perhaps even suave; a matter of suppressing the disquieting knowledge that we were alone in a new place when other boys had already clustered boisterously in groups of twos, threes, and fours. And then, of course, there was the matter of our luggage: the travel pieces of the poor. These were our hallmark. We didn't need Nostradamus to enlighten us.

The line finally moved, and Harry and I shuffled forward.

"So where are you from?" he asked. "I'm from Manhattan."

"Stony Creek."

"Stony Peak?"

And here was where my heart just about stopped, for all the preparation in the world couldn't have readied me for the knowledge that my hometown, the place that encompassed everything I'd ever known, was entirely foreign to some—probably to most.

"Stony *Creek*. It's a little town in Connecticut, best known for . . ."

I halted, wondering if by some bizarre chance Harry Persky of Manhattan had heard of that awful day, when an accident in our little coastal town had ended the lives of four quarrymen. Perhaps the Palanza Brothers' hush money hadn't extended as far as I'd thought.

"For what?" he pressed.

"Best known for not being known at all."

Harry laughed, revealing a deep dimple in his pallid right cheek.

"Do you want to ride together—to Durfee?" I asked, to change the subject.

"Sure, except we have no way to get in."

"What?"

"We need to go to the Freshmen Registrar's Office. To pick up our room keys. Did you forget—have a few too many nips on the train, maybe?"

Adele would have been flustered by the insinuation, but Charles took it in stride. "I could use one right now, by golly."

Harry laughed again and I almost joined him, but caught myself.

An eternity passed before the boys in front of us hopped into a taxicab; we were next, our feet just behind a yellow marker painted on the cobblestones. It looked to me like a starting line, meant for a runner, and my feet itched to step, to sprint.

At last the doors of a taxicab closed around us. The stagnant air inside reeked of tobacco and cloves.

"Where you going—the Registrar?" the driver asked.

"Yes," Harry and I answered in unison.

"You boys freshmen?" The driver turned his head just far enough for us to see his profile: heavy, hooded eyes and a nose that had been broken but never reset.

"You bet, sir," I answered, and I could scarcely believe that that was the truth.

When I first stepped into my dormitory in Durfee Hall, I noted that it was almost identical in proportion to my room in Miss Prowl's boardinghouse. I was surprised by this. Mother constantly used words like "lavish" and "sumptuous" to describe Yale. Yet I wasn't disappointed. The modest size made me feel like I belonged.

The room was filled with basic amenities, as Mother had said it would be—a bedstead with a mattress, a feather pillow, a paint-chipped chiffonier, a bookcase and desk, two chairs, a floor lamp and desk lamp. A typed letter affixed to my door read that it was the occupant's responsibility to supply any other items he might need.

But this, too, Mother had already told me. I had a thick wad of bills in my wallet, more money than I'd ever carried, to buy whatever was necessary, which isn't to say I had a license to be frivolous.

"Buy what the other boys have—those items that you are noticeably lacking—but nothing more," Mother had warned. "As for your wardrobe, purchase only simple, well-made things. And be sure they're dark-colored. Anything light will show wear."

And this was something she had mentioned over and over—how I mustn't disclose our limited means, not only because we had to protect our privacy, but also because I'd be surrounded by the wealthy.

"The rich bask in the light of the rich," she'd said. "They hate poverty—it shadows them. I should know."

And this was true. I had only to remember how the Cottagers had stared distastefully at my patched, ragged clothes, how they'd walked wide arcs around me, as if hardship were catching.

Still, to act wealthy one needed the right props. How Mother had shuddered at the sight of that shabby carpetbag, but she'd realized a new travel trunk like the one she had had as a girl—teak-planked, lined with royal blue satin, covered with extravagant luggage labels:

Excelsior Hotel in Naples, Hotel La Plage in Marseille, Hotel Helvetia in Genova—was too much of a splurge. So many other expenses still awaited us.

"Sensibility is all that will matter anyway," she'd said, and it seemed she'd done the explaining as much to herself as to me. "Carpetbag or not, if you act as though you're entitled to things, people will assume you are. Many of the boys you'll meet have never been denied anything in their lives. It is second nature to them to expect the best."

Still, I wondered how I could imitate these boys when I didn't know a thing about having money. I would have to convince myself that a lifetime of watching Cottagers was enough to teach me what it was like to be one.

My thoughts were interrupted by Harry, who appeared like an apparition in my doorway, his skinny legs quivering even though he was at a standstill. It seemed to me that Harry was a person who would never be able to adapt. His awkwardness would be as impossible to change as his dimpled cheek or translucent skin.

"Not a bad room, Pietra. But it's smaller than mine. Of course, that's only fair. I've got to dig with that brute from Andover. He hasn't arrived yet. I've my fingers crossed that he's been rerouted to Harvard."

It turned out that Harry and I didn't live far apart—only across the hall. Durfee was an intimate place. It had four entryways, each facing the bustling Old Campus, a stately courtyard enclosed by Gothic buildings and gates and bisected with flagstone walkways. Each entryway in Durfee had its own stoop, on which rambunctious, chittering freshmen were already perched, and stairwell, which wound up four floors. The landings on each floor were flanked by suites, and each suite sported four or five rooms. Most were single rooms, meant for only one fellow, but a few—like Harry's—could house two.

The suites had their own common rooms: large spaces with fireplaces and huge bay windows. They had their own lavatories, too, and the lavatory in my suite had been the first place I'd inspected—

not out of bodily necessity, but to see what kind of privacy I'd have. Walking past several urinals and one toilet, I'd been disappointed to see no bathtub, but relieved that at least the shower stalls were separate. Before arriving to campus I'd fretted about all the obstacles before me. None seemed riskier than a daily bath.

Mother had said, "There are ways to wash yourself outside of a lavatory, Adele," and told me to get better acquainted with a bowl of water and a sponge. Granted, this was a logical solution—to wash in my room, a locked door between my body and curious eyes. But I would miss my daily soak terribly, so much so that I resolved, silently, to disregard Mother's advice and add bathing to the growing list of perils that I was willing to brave, even if it meant tiptoeing into the lavatory at three in the morning.

"Are you coming or not?" Harry asked me.

I'd been inspecting my mattress, which was thin and slightly soiled.

"Pietra, are you listening to me? I asked if you wanted to see my room. To compare."

"Oh? Sure, that would be swell," I answered, smoothing the bedsheets I'd laundered myself. I'd used too much starch and the cotton was stiff as paper.

On the way out, I introduced Harry to two of the fellows in my suite. I disliked how I sounded: apathetic and aloof. But my tone was necessary. These boys would see me at my most unguarded and vulnerable. They would sleep in rooms only a stone's throw from mine. For the sake of preservation, I'd need to distance myself, at least psychologically—even if it meant losing a chance at friendship.

I followed Harry to his room, which faced the hustle-bustle of Old Campus. Taking a seat, I watched him unpack. I was practically finished with my own room anyhow. There hadn't been much to put away. I'd dealt with my girls' clothes first, giving them temporary refuge in the bottom drawer of my desk, underneath a thin blanket. I was already thinking of how I'd need to stow them elsewhere eventually, somewhere safe, but I'd worry about that later.

"Want to look around campus when I'm through?" Harry asked. He was on his knees, a length of electrical wire in his hand, his eyeglasses askew, searching for the base plug, which he eventually located in the corner of his closet, along with a dust ball the size of my fist.

"Sure."

"We should go to Calhoun first."

I was about to ask why, then reminded myself of Yale's housing system, how all the freshmen lived together their first year but thereafter were assigned to Yale's eight residential colleges. Mother had made me memorize the names: Berkeley, Branford, Davenport, Jonathan Edwards, Pierson, Saybrook, Trumbull, and Calhoun. These names were mostly the monikers of men, powerful and well-connected men, some theologians, some inventors, some politicians, some visionaries, many a combination. But it seemed to me that the unifying element of all of them must have been immense wealth. In Stony Creek granite monuments were bought rather than earned. Perhaps, I surmised, immortality was the same.

Harry and I were both assigned to Calhoun, as were most of the freshmen who lived in Durfee. After freshman year Calhoun would be the center of our personal and academic lives. I knew this because I'd read the pamphlets Yale had mailed, and also because Charles had liked to talk about the college system. He'd wanted to be in Branford, the college with majestic Harkness tower and the most beautiful main court. He'd wanted to participate in its famous literary debates, wiling away whole nights arguing the finer points of modern political issues and timeless philosophical ones. I remembered how excited he'd been by the very idea of such conversation. It seemed that after all those wordless hours cutting stone, the only muscle he wished to exercise in the future was his tongue.

My college, Calhoun, was better known for athletics than for mental prowess. My brother had said that even though Yale's current residential system had been in place for only a few years, the individual colleges had already taken on distinct personalities. These personalities were encouraged by design. Each college was a community unto itself, gated and self-contained to foster camaraderie within rather than beyond. Each had its own dining hall, a master who presided over the student body like a patriarch, and a dean who acted as an advisor. The colleges vied against one another in football, hockey, squash, crew, golf, bowling—intercollege championships, Charles had said they were called. The rivalries were fierce. To win, each college had developed its own style, its own spirit, which further led to the feeling that while all students on campus were Yale men, they were first Davenport men, or Pierson men, or Trumbull men.

"Ready to go?" Harry asked.

He'd hung the last of his wrinkled shirts in the closet. As a matter of fact, I wasn't ready for a trip outside of Durfee, into the imbroglio of Old Campus. I would rather have hidden in my little room, those too-crisp sheets pulled over my head. But I didn't have to admit this to Harry, for just then his roommate arrived.

This newcomer wasn't the burly lad Harry had been dreading, but a weedy one, six feet and change. He had a mischievous look in his eyes like he'd just outwitted trouble, maybe outrun a police officer or seen a nun's habit lift in the breeze. His grin was crooked, cocksure. He was graceful, too, comfortable with the swoop of his shoulders, the long dangle of his arms.

"You must be my roommate," he said to me, setting down a box and extending a free hand. His eyes were unflinching, splashy as sunlight on snow. "Chadwick Foster. Wick for short. And you're Harry from New York."

Not sure what to do, I extended my hand. It all but disappeared within Wick's warm, spindly fingers.

I thought Harry would right the situation, but he didn't. It was left to me to explain. Wick seemed unfazed by the misunderstanding, however. He treated Harry and me with equal friendliness, opening the box he'd been carrying to show off a stack of records and a portable radio-phonograph.

"My contribution to the room," he announced bounteously.

Harry started to say how he'd left the better bed, the one farther from the door, as well as the bigger closet, when Wick's parents arrived. His mother wore a cheerful yellow suit with bright black buttons. Ill-dressed for a day of moving, she mostly paced what little space was left in the room, dabbing her eyes with a handkerchief. She was a tiny person, more like an oversized doll than a woman. Wick's father, by contrast, was towering and barrel-chested, with a sun-kissed face. He struck me as outdoorsy and athletic. Though he was smiling, a vein in his forehead bulged with worry.

Once all of Wick's luggage had been accounted for and Harry and I had mumbled bashfully through the introductions, Wick's father set himself down in a chair. Fingers laced in his lap, he began to speak about Wick's responsibilities these next four years, how he would need to learn to be a man, and to overcome his penchant for juvenile antics. During his lecture, his gaze occasionally drifted to Harry and me. I wavered uneasily between amusement and sadness. Though Wick's father sounded gruff at times, no one in the room could deny that he loved his son. Bidding farewell would be no easy task, I thought, as I listlessly fingered the stones in my pocket.

At last Wick's father stood up and shook his son's hand. His eyes were glistening. I hoped for everyone's sake he wouldn't cry, and he managed not to, even when Wick gave him a hard hug, those ropey arms perfect for the task.

Mr. and Mrs. Foster departed after a bittersweet and rather awkward round of kisses. When they closed the door behind them, Wick collapsed onto the floor, burying his face in his hands. Stunned, Harry and I stared at each other, believing we'd been left with a fledgling pushed too early from the nest. We stood shoulder-to-shoulder, gazing down at that gangly chap, who had knotted himself into a ball.

Eventually Harry knelt down and laid a hand on Wick's shoulder. I searched in vain for something to say, something appropriately reassuring. Just when we decided we ought to chase after the parents and beg them back, Wick looked up, his eyes perfectly dry. He revealed a smile so devilish, he might as well have picked the lock of heaven's gate.

"Freedom," he said, laughing. "Finally!"

Harry and I exchanged another incredulous look. We'd been duped all right, but there was no sense moping about it. Harry smiled and shook his head in disbelief. The anxiety in the room disappeared. It was replaced by music. Wick took out the radio-phonograph and played a tune I'd never heard before.

"Benny Goodman," he said, snapping his fingers. "You can't help but love him."

It was no wonder that I hadn't fallen in love with Benny Goodman earlier. The only music I was familiar with were Miss Prowl's scratchy tunes about wandering men and heartache. Sometimes, the Stony Creek Drum Corps played a free concert on the town green, but that kind of music was nothing like this—toe-tappingly jazzy and jubilantly new. Taking Wick's cue, Harry and I hunkered down on the floor, kicked off our shoes, and sprawled out with luxurious abandon.

Wick fished out a box of Camel cigarettes from the pocket of his sports coat and passed it to Harry and me. I refused at first, but Wick persisted—"Go on then, Charlie. Don't you smoke?"—and it seemed criminal to refuse him. Coming from his mouth, my name didn't sound so fraudulent. Or maybe it was that he called me "Charlie," a nickname Charles had always detested. He'd thought it too common and parochial. But I liked it—or rather, I liked the way it rolled off Wick's tongue.

Wick lit my cigarette, then Harry's, and finally his own, and I watched how he inhaled, so smoothly and naturally, like he'd done it a thousand times before, and probably he had. As for me, I struggled with that first inhalation. The smoke burned on the way down, leaving me singed. But Harry's initiation was worse: he drew the smoke straight into his stomach. He sputtered and hacked until Wick knocked him on the back. When poor Harry finally caught his breath, his cellophane skin sanguine, he told us the Camel brand was to blame.

"Really, I'm a Chesterfield man," he pleaded.

Harry and I were more cautious after that, ginger even, the cigarettes dangling more in our fingers than in our mouths. The three of us got to talking. Wick told us how he'd gone to Choate, a preparatory school in Wallingford, Connecticut. From the corner of my eye, I could see Harry's face soften as another false assumption was laid to rest. His roommate had gone to an elite school, but at least it wasn't the dreaded Andover.

"I wasn't what you'd call a model pupil," Wick said. "I never saw the beginning of the alphabet on my report card, if you understand my drift. I spent all my time with the dramatic club."

"What for?" I asked.

"The girls, of course! Choate ships in a new crop every season to play the female roles."

Harry leaned in conspiratorially. "Did you have any kissing scenes?"

"Kissing scenes?" Wick laughed. "A few, but rehearsing after hours was the best part."

"And I thought the chess club was a lark," Harry muttered ruefully.

Maybe it was the cigarettes, or the silver flask that Wick eventually pulled from another pocket in his coat, but quite soon I felt warmbellied, comfortable, and quite settled in. None of this seemed strange—the sound of my carefully modulated voice, the cold slate floor where I lounged without once adjusting my uncrossed legs, the flamboyant music, the company of these boys. I wasn't used to idling—dillydallying, Mother liked to call it. But how easy it was to chat about classes and clubs, the upcoming presidential election (did Alfie Landon stand a chance?), how the freshman football squad would most certainly crush Exeter, how life would be now that we were Yale men.

I didn't have much to say, not nearly as much as Wick. But still I could see why Charles had craved this kind of closeness. In Stony Creek, Mother had discouraged friendships. She'd said that the children of quarrymen were beneath my brother and me. She'd warned us not to waste our time on such coarse people. I'd argued that we, too, were a quarry family. But Mother had been outraged. The implication of inferior status always got her goat.

"Had circumstances been different, you and Charles would have been Cottagers," she'd flared.

And so I hadn't bothered to befriend girls my age. Nor had they bothered with me, what with Mother's puffed-up sense of importance. In time, all my attention had shifted to the sacks of laundry that landed on Miss Prowl's porch. I'd given myself over to the bristle of wet cloth and the heat of the iron. And when I'd needed a respite, I'd turned to Pa or to my books.

I took another slug from Wick's flask. The whiskey blistered, worse than the cigarettes.

"Do you fellows have steadies back home?" Wick asked us. He was smoothing his lacquered hair, his eyes twinkling and a little dreamy. I'd had my feet propped on one of his brand new–looking suitcases, but I felt suddenly like I was on my toes.

Harry shook his head. "I don't, but there's hope. The mixers are bound to bring a lot of girls. I hear the ratio is four to one."

"Girls to boys?" I asked.

"No, genius, blondes to brunettes. Of course girls to boys! Hey, Vassar supposedly has the prettiest skirts."

"What about you, Charlie?" Wick asked, turning in my direction.

I concentrated on my cigarette, watching the paper and tobacco disintegrate into smoke, a solid transformed into a vapor, hoping that I could pull off a similar trick with my own body.

"What—do I have a girl?" I asked.

"Yeah, back home."

My cheeks felt hot, but I told myself Wick and Harry probably didn't notice my discomfort. And even if they did, they'd never guess the source of it. I forced myself to bring the cigarette to my mouth, to inhale slowly, nonchalantly, as if this topic were like any other.

"I did," I said. "But I cut her loose. Told her if I were going away to school, I'd have to make a clean start."

Harry whistled. "Brave move, Pietra. I wouldn't have had the nerve."

"It wasn't as hard as you might think."

"Was she a looker?" Harry continued. "Did she cry when you told her? I can't stand it when dames make a fuss."

"I try not to think about her much. What's the use?"

A moment passed, then Wick sat up abruptly, dazzling us with his shiny-white, lopsided grin—a grin I was finding increasingly irresistible.

"I suppose we're all free men," he said. "Free to do whatever the hell we please. That calls for a toast."

So we passed the flask around once more, savoring those last fiery drops. I was glad we were sitting. My knees felt wobbly inside my secondhand trousers.

It must have been mid-afternoon by the time we emerged from Durfee, Wick, Harry, and I. Light-headed from the whiskey and cigarettes, we found Old Campus in a tumult. Freshmen continued to haul, roll, and push their baggage every which way. They arrived to Durfee and to freshman halls named Lawrance, Welch, and Van-Sheff. Many of the freshmen were still accompanied by their parents, mothers carrying tin boxes of homemade cookies and fathers offering admonishment and fat rolls of cash.

On the sun-dappled lawn of Old Campus, I felt nervous and exposed. It didn't matter that I'd covered every inch of my body except for my head and hands. I wasn't accustomed to meeting new people, and I was thankful I had Wick and Harry at my side. I believe Harry felt the same way, for he spent more time making asides to me than greeting his new classmates.

"That fellow there," he said, pointing. "He participated in the Olympic games. He's a swimmer. Took the bronze in the butterfly, I think. And that fellow yonder, over by the bench, his family's in oil. Guess he'll have a job when he graduates. The guy next to him—I hear his family owns half of Persia."

"How do you know all this?" I asked.

"I live in New York, don't I?"

Unlike Harry and me, Wick seemed perfectly content within this assortment of strangers. People congregated around him quickly and were loath to depart. Some were old classmates from Choate, clasping him on the shoulder and asking him how he'd spent his summer. But many were new faces. The Class of 1940 had only just met, but already some of the chaps stood out—and Wick was one of them. One might say it was his exceptional height or snappy smile, but I think it was his ease. While others pecked around nervously, Wick leaned casually against a gnarled elm. Though his eyes were welcoming, he made little effort to speak to others; that must have been why so many others made an effort to speak to him. One of these was Phineas Smith, a friend of Wick's from Choate.

Harry whispered, "If you ever wondered what the face of a legacy looks like, that's it. His father's the editor in chief of the *Chicago Tribune*. And his great-great-grandfather started the paper."

But the face of Phineas Smith—or Phin, as Wick called him—seemed ordinary enough to me. He was a handsome, if hard-looking, boy—stocky, sturdy, and well-built, eyes like ball bearings, chin rudely clefted. In the late-afternoon sun he was shadowed by Wick, and I suspected he had been in the same position at Choate. Yet there was no sign of rivalry between the two. In fact, Phin seemed attentive around Wick, hovering about him almost protectively.

When Wick made the introductions, his arm slung casually around my shoulders, Phin's stare turned steely. His handshake was a shade too firm. He struck me as the kind of person who established his allegiances quickly and fiercely.

"Good to meet you. Charlie, was it? As in charley horse?" Though I wasn't moved to smile, he laughed heartily.

"More like good-time Charlie."

"If you believe the stories," Wick added.

Phin stopped mid-chuckle, his lips taking an ornery shape. I couldn't account for this tension, which seemed to lack foundation.

"You fellows want to get something to eat?" Harry asked. I was glad for the interruption. We eyed Wick, our unofficial ringleader, who agreed it was the right time for dinner. According to our schedules, which we carried in our pockets—along with maps of the campus—the Freshman Rally began at 6:45, a mere hour away.

We made our way past the thinning crowds, across Elm Street, to another breathtaking quadrangle.

"Cross Campus," Harry said, and it seemed he knew more about Yale than the rest of us combined.

"Sterling Memorial Library is on your left," he continued, nodding to a building that resembled a heavily ornamented Gothic cathedral. "It opened six years ago. And there, of course, is good ol' Calhoun."

I nodded, as if I'd known all along.

We followed Harry to the University Dining Hall, home of Commons, where we were to take our meals. Vast and cavernous, Commons left me wide-eyed. Chandeliers dropped perilously from the four-story ceiling. College banners and portraits of eminent Yale alumni—many of whom Harry described in unsolicited detail—decorated the walls. The scent of rich, simmering foods wafted through the air, overpowering undercurrents of linseed oil and turpentine. Hundreds of boys swarmed about the round tables, which were bedecked with pressed white tablecloths, china, and sterling cutlery.

Here, I decided, was the Yale Mother and Charles had pined for.

We bobbed through the throngs and found four seats at an otherwise full table. Wick immediately struck up a conversation with the fellow seated next to him. From across the table I sensed Phin's shoulders tighten.

Mother had said I would eat well at Yale, and she was right. Maids in smart black uniforms with white lace collars served us bowls of soup from huge tureens. They filled our plates with boiled potatoes and hearty slabs of pink, pepper-crusted roast beef. They set down wedges of chocolate cake and lemon meringue pie. I hadn't eaten since morning and I was famished. Yet I was overwhelmed not only by the decadent food, but also by the experience of being served. I'd never eaten in a restaurant or a hotel, though both were numerous in the swankier sections of Stony Creek, and I wondered how the maids felt as they tended to us wordlessly. Their thoughts must have been similar to the ones I'd had while washing the Cottagers' clothes.

Phin, Wick, Harry, and I hurried through the meal so that we could be on the steps of Wright Hall, on Old Campus, in time for the start of the rally. I felt distracted as I walked with them. I found myself falling behind, staring dazedly at my surroundings. My eyes wandered to single elements: an ancient iron gate, ivy vines twisted about its rusty crooks and spokes; a resplendent panel of stained glass, its colors wistful in the waning light. As dusk descended, the buildings of the university were almost too wondrous to take in. I recognized limestone, trap rock, and brownstone, and I thought that Pa would have disapproved of the last. He'd told me once that brownstone wore down too quickly. It was the careless man's stone.

The raucous cheering at Wright Hall knocked me out of my reverie. I stood between Harry and Wick, watching the scene unfold. The university band, dressed in blue and white, played a series of off-key songs as the Yale cheerleaders chanted along. Then the band and cheerleaders formed a line, moving in torch-lit procession down a series of elm-lined streets. Harry, Wick, Phin, and I were swept along with the rest of the boys. We arrived at last, hearts swelling with excitement, to Memorial Hall, a circular building with a domed rotunda. Inside, white marble tablets engraved with the names of Yale men who had died serving their country seemed at odds with our mirthful group. But nothing could stop our momentum. We rushed through the grand doors of Woolsey, a concert hall that might as well have been a palace. The walls dripped with gold. Stately columns supported a gilded aquamarine ceiling. But the wonder of Woolsey was its organ. The enormous pipes rose ceremoniously from the base of the stage clear to the ceiling, and from those pipes came a series of notes so sublime, so near-holy, everybody scrambled to find seats.

From the stage, a man wearing a bow tie stepped forward. "Welcome, Class of 1940," he said, introducing himself as Dean Walden.

After taking several minutes to quiet us, Dean Walden went on to outline the pitfalls that awaited errant freshmen—moving pictures and bridge games, tipsiness and road trips that extended past the weekend. "Discipline is what will propel you toward excellence," he warned dourly, and we almost believed him.

Next, several seniors took the stage. Lawrence Kelley, the captain of the football team, promised that this year's players, as well as Handsome Dan, Yale's bulldog mascot, would prevail. Wick's ears perked up when R. L. Linkroum gave the Dramatic Association a boost. Other fellows talked about *The Yale News,* the *Yale Literary Magazine,* The Pundits, and the Corinthian Yacht Club.

By the time a representative from the Christian Association began to talk, we had grown restless. Dean Walden's speech about discipline seemed far away. We couldn't help but squirm and wriggle in Woolsey's unforgiving wood seats. A few boys in the back munched on bags of peanuts, shells flying into the air and crunching under idle feet. Whispers, snickers, and the odd cough accompanied the weakening strains of the Yale Glee Club. Wick was again sneaking sips from his flask—how and where he'd refilled it, I didn't know. He and Phin drank half of it before passing it to Harry and me. As I hid the offending object inside my jacket flap, I wondered what Mother would say if she could see me now.

Just as we surrendered ourselves to total impudence, the president of Yale stepped onto the stage. Something about James Rowland Angell set us straight. He looked nearly divine against those golden organ pipes, arms outstretched in welcome, his white suit radiant. Behind the spectacles clipped to the bridge of his nose, his eyes were serious. Though I sat twenty rows back, I could see he would tolerate no tomfoolery. Beside me, Harry gasped in reverence.

"You are at Yale, the finest university in this country and arguably in the world," he began, his voice filling the room as none before it had. "You are now part of a great tradition, an unparalleled heritage.

On you rest privileges only a lucky few can enjoy. And on you rest obligations to measure up to those privileges. We expect you to live up to your obligations and to seek to make your life significant for your friends, your college, your nation, and also for yourself."

These first words, above all, were the ones I revisited most frequently after that first day. President Angell went on to talk about vision, imagination, patriotism, moral courage, and intellectual liberty. He told us how the world was changing—faster than any of us could fathom, himself included—and that this change meant an early end to boyhood or an early start to manhood. It was up to us to decide which one it would be. Though I recorded his entire speech in my head, it was the idea of obligation that set me thinking. Here, in this vast hall, I was one of many. Yet I was also unutterably separate. Mr. Angell said there were exactly 848 of us. We hailed from forty states and six countries. But he didn't mention that there were two sexes. He didn't say that, until now, no girl had ever eaten in Commons with her classmates, or marched in the Yale Freshman Rally, or claimed a room in Durfee for her own. No girl had ever sat in this seat in Woolsey Hall during his speech, flanked by overwrought, breathless peers, her ribs aching from the thrill of it—and the fear.

President Angell's voice had risen to that vaulted ceiling, where cherubs strummed lyres against the heavens. We all have obligations, he'd said, and I knew he was right. But I'd be damned if mine were the same as the rest.

When we were at last released from the rally, we took our energy to the streets. New Haven was different by night. The grandeur of Yale appeared diluted and spectral. The moonlight reduced the university to a mere dream. Yet the city came alive. Window shades opened like eyelids, doors like hungry mouths. Music drifted from saloons and restaurants, raw and provocative, and the smoke of cigarettes created a seductive scrim through which to view the world. For the first time girls emerged, cheeks blooming, eyelashes elongated, lips stained fire-engine red. I wondered if they'd been locked up all day, captive in houses and offices and schools and nursing wards, their feet tucked into sensible shoes, their hair bolted down with bobby pins.

Wick, Harry, Phin, and I wandered the streets in a peppy state. We scooted by package stores selling Old Hickory straight rye, McCallum's Scotch, and Chilton gin, and picture shows advertising a smoldering Joan Crawford as *The Gorgeous Hussy*. We stood gaping in front of the elegant Shubert Theater, where *Boy Meets Girl* was playing. We passed the University Smoke Shop, opposite Bingham Hall, and read the signs in the windows: "Beer on draught and in bottles," "Pipes, Tobacco, and Smokers' articles of every description." We noted the names of scores of shops: haberdasheries, stores selling books, typewriters, used furniture, and hardware. We swerved by a lot of used cars and poked fun at Harry as he salivated over a lemon-yellow roadster.

Though I was overwhelmed by the events of the day and woozy from Wick's ever-flowing flask, the night restored my spirits. I felt energized, my apprehension quashed by the melded voices of hundreds of roving freshmen—"yearlings," one speaker had called us.

We meandered until our bellies forced us to a halt in front of a hole-in-the-wall diner, handwritten specials in the window advertising fifteen-cent cheeseburgers and five-cent Coca-Colas. The four of us shuffled inside and slumped into a corner booth. At a nearby table, two girls shared an egg cream from a pair of striped straws. They drew the attention of my companions casually and completely.

"Don't be such a goof, Persky," Phin said. "Quit staring." But Phin's own eyes, if not as rapacious, were at least as curious.

"I'd go over there right now if I thought they'd give me the time of day," Harry sighed.

"Oh, they'd give you more than that. These local skirts—they're a dime a dozen. Every one of them wants a Yale man on her arm—and a Yale man's money in her pocket."

"Will you look at the one on the right?" Harry continued. "That face, that figure. She could be a Botticelli. You know the painting I'm talking about? The one with the chesty girl in the seashell?"

"Venus," Wick offered.

"Yeah, that's it."

The eyes of the three boys drifted to the girl's snug cardigan sweater. The top two pearl buttons were undone, revealing a glimpse of her breasts, high and round and plush. I stared, too, uncomfortably, furtively. Under the elastic band Mother had made, my own meager breasts ached.

"I'll spring for your food if you ask her on a date," Phin told Harry.

"Sure, of course. And after she agrees, maybe I'll launch a bottle rocket to the moon."

Just then the counterman came by. I was relieved to gaze at the menu instead of that bursting sweater. But as soon as we ordered, conversation picked up where it had left off—with Phin advancing and Harry retreating. Wick was silent, but it wasn't until the girls had finished the last of their egg cream and were sliding out of their seats to leave that we found out why. A paper airplane crafted from a diner napkin sailed through the air, landing squarely on their table. The girls stopped mid-motion, staring at it before turning to us. Wick looked away, as if he had nothing to do with the matter.

The girls unfolded the napkin and giggled over what was inside—something Wick must have written. Bending their heads together, they seemed to agree on something. A minute later they walked over to us, dropping another napkin on our table. It was folded into a heart.

"Which one of you is Harry?" the Botticelli asked.

Up close her loveliness was less ethereal, though no less striking, her eyebrows plucked and lifted, her flawless skin ivory-smooth, shiny fawn-colored curls skimming her shoulders. And that jam-packed sweater—it was impossible not to stare. By contrast, the Botticelli's companion, a watchful, skittish girl whose hair fell like a curtain in front of her face, seemed to melt into the background.

Wick pointed at a petrified Harry.

"Well, Harry, I liked your poem. It was very romantic."

She was holding fast to the wrist of her nervous friend. Looping a lock of hair behind her ear, she smiled softly. Then she turned with a slow, intoxicating bending of the hips, following her companion out the door. Harry and Phin reached for the heart-shaped napkin at the same time, but Phin won. He unfolded it carelessly, tearing the edge. Harry cringed.

"'Dear Harry: We'll be here next Friday at eight,'" Phin read. "'Maybe we'll see you then.'"

"What did you do, Wick?" Harry begged, successfully grabbing the napkin from Phin. "How did you do it?"

Wick smiled. "I don't know what it is about poems, but girls love 'em."

"For Pete's sake—what did you write?"

"I don't remember the details. Suffice it to say, the word 'Venus' was used—twice."

"I can't believe it," Harry said. I couldn't tell whether he was wincing or beaming. "What the deuce do I do now?"

"You show up next Friday."

"I can't come alone. Someone's gotta be here with me."

"I don't think so. She's *your* goddess."

"Come on, Wick. Come with me. You have to! I'll make a fool of myself otherwise. It happens every time—I'm disastrous with girls. I fumble up compliments, trip over my own feet, make . . ."

"Listen, Harry," Wick interrupted. "Just remember you have four years. There's no need to tie yourself up your first week."

"Are you joking? I'd happily tie myself up with a girl like *that*."

At that pronouncement, our food arrived: four greasy cheeseburgers stacked with fried onions. Pouring ketchup from a little tin pitcher, Harry took a couple of bites. Then he began interrogating Wick on what he should wear, how he should act, what he should say. Phin kept to himself, taking neat, nimble bites. I kept to myself too, glad that no one had sought my opinion. I hadn't the least idea how to court a Botticelli, never having been one myself.

*   *   *

When we left the diner, I was determined to make my way to Durfee. So much had happened. I needed to sift through the events of the day, to make sense of them—indeed, to make sense of this new life. I knew I couldn't resolve anything here, conscious of my disguise, my deceit, and stepping in sync with these boys.

I tried to say good-bye, but Wick took my arm excitedly. "You can't head to bed, Charlie. This is our first night. Don't you understand? We can do anything, go anywhere. Why, we could steal that yellow roadster, if we had a mind to. We could take off for California, Africa, outer space. Come on, stay with us! You can sleep anytime."

His fingers sent electric impulses through my brother's old clothes. His eyes locked with mine and I could see little flecks of green floating in vernal pools. We were alone in that instant—or at least I thought we were, our gazes singular and charged, a crash of lightning suddenly and joltingly connecting two disparate points.

"Fine, fine. I'll stay," I said, turning away.

"Atta boy!"

We wandered about for another tireless hour, shouting across the streets to boys we'd met, hooting boldly at anyone who caught our fancy. When we grew bored, we walked back to Old Campus, entering through Phelps Hall, a resplendent archway that seemed like a portal back to university life. The night had turned cold for early autumn and I wished I'd wound a scarf around my neck as Wick had done. Its ends streamed as he ran ahead of the three of us, laughing mirthfully, making his way toward a life-size statue of a man in old-fashioned coattails.

"Nathan Hale," Harry announced, and by now there was no question that impromptu facts were his specialty and our burden to bear. "A graduate of Yale, of course. Also, the first American executed by the British for spying. This statue shows Hale right before he was hanged at the age of twenty-one. If you look carefully, you'll see his ankles and wrists are tied."

I stared in awe at that statue. Even in the face of death, the young man looked steadfast and undaunted, not a dash of fear in his eyes.

"He was a disaster as a spy," Harry said. "When he got caught he told the truth immediately. The poor chap signed his own life away."

By then Hale had a companion. Wick had climbed onto the pedestal and wrapped one arm around the lad's waist. Side by side, the two could have been twins: both tall, fair of face, and magnified—at least in my eyes—beyond human dimension.

Loopy-eyed and inspired, Wick began to sing, some silly ballad the Glee Club had warbled through during the Assembly. He remembered only the tune, not the words, and so he improvised his own patchy lyrics, most of them risqué. He swayed as he sang, his arm tethered to his bronze comrade, and he was quite a sight up there—a man with a boy's lust for life, a boy with a man's throaty bravado.

It might have been the alcohol—surely it was—for I suddenly felt hot inside that shivery night. I realized my fingers had curled into fists at the thought of Wick, at the thought of how he'd clutched my arm, ardently, or had I been mistaken? I started to wonder how it would feel to hold his hand, to touch him, anywhere, but especially some patch of skin that was taut and warm and secret. At the same time, I was scared, scared enough to retreat, to create some rash, middling excuse so that I could flee from the source of my craving.

"Hey, where are you going?" I heard in my wake. But I neither responded nor knew who had asked.

When I arrived home, well after midnight, my suitemates were already behind closed doors. Quietly, I filled a basin with water in the lavatory and washed my face with a cake of soap. In a mirror that hung over the sink, I peered into my own eyes and realized that they were different: damp, exuberant, animal-nervy—eyes that would have sent Mother into a tizzy.

When I was through, I went to my room and locked myself inside, hoping to lock my insecurities out. I was still thinking of Wick as I stripped off my clothes, then unbound my breasts. They were tender to the touch, my nipples pinched and swollen. Slipping into bed, I rubbed them gently, grateful to be laid bare at last.

Chapter Five

T HE NEXT TWO DAYS brought a flurry of activity. I met my freshman counselor, a haggard-faced professor who eagerly signed
my course schedule so that he could get back to his own work. I
joined Harry, Wick, and Phin for meals in Commons and tried not to
let my gaze stick to Wick for too long. I explored the streets beyond
the campus proper and drifted anonymously with the crowds into
Malley's, a class-act department store with shiny escalators, and the
Gamble Desmond Company, which was clean and large, but not as
gleaming-beautiful as Malley's. I loitered in front of the Taft Hotel
and watched ladies wrapped in chinchilla and mink slip coolly into
taxicabs. I planted myself on the top step of the post office and listened to people chat with one another about the weather and politics
and family visiting from out of town. I came to realize that New
Haven, though bigger than Stony Creek in every possible sense, still
had something of a small-town feel.

When I didn't want to be alone, I sought out Harry. One trip
found us in the Yale Co-op for textbooks. With the exception of some
science and language courses, all freshmen took the same core
courses—"guts," they were called—and book supplies for these were
already low. We were lucky to pick up what we could: *Chaucer's Complete Works, The Foundations of Biology, Romeo and Juliet,* a slim vol-
ume on the development of European civilization.

"What do you say we buy one copy of each and share?" Harry
asked. I agreed immediately, thinking back to our ragtag luggage.

For all the warnings Mother had issued, Yale had so far presented
no major obstacles. My confidence had risen in sync with the success

of our ruse. Perhaps it would have continued to rise had I not decided to get fitted for a suit.

There must have been ninety-nine tailors along York and Chapel streets. Thinking about Mother's advice on clothes, I popped into one that was small and nondescript and empty-looking, hoping I might be able to browse without detection. But I was soon intercepted by an aged clerk. He smelled of peppermints and castor oil. A measuring tape hung around his neck so casually, so fittingly, I suspected he never took it off.

"What can I do for you, young man?"

"I'm just looking around," I told him. But there was no use—he edged closer.

"You a freshman?"

"Yes, sir."

"And is the suit you're wearing the only one you've got?" I didn't answer. "Well, that won't do," he clucked.

I looked down at myself, wondering if I ought to be annoyed. Mother had altered Charles's suit so perfectly it fit me like a glove. I was contemplating a second only so that my shortage of clothes wouldn't be so apparent. Boys like Phin and Wick wore different outfits nearly every day.

The man sighed, sidling up even closer, so close I could see the mercury fillings in his teeth.

"Son, you seem like a sensible young man, so I'll be straight with you. Has anyone sat you down and told you about the apparel you'll need? This is Yale, you understand, and you don't want to be taken for a greenhorn. There are dinner parties and Master's teas, football games, nights at Mory's, dances with girls. Each of these occasions will call for different attire. Most boys come in needing a whole new wardrobe, from collar buttons to belts to saddle oxfords. Speaking of saddle oxfords, we got a line in just this week. Black and white—very fashionable right now. And on sale."

Despite sharing the cost of books with Harry, my wallet had slimmed. I knew I needed to watch my expenses.

"I don't know, sir. I'm on a budget."

"Aren't we all these days? I don't care what the president says; the economy's not getting any better. Fortunately, you won't find lower prices anywhere. And if you do, I'll beat any competitor by five percent—no, make that seven. I've got the biggest selection around: single- and double-breasted town suits in cheviots, worsteds, and flannels. English tweeds and Shetlands in plain-back and gusset. Arrow shirts, reversibles, polo coats, overcoats, evening clothes . . ."

"Sir, if you don't mind, I think one suit will do."

His voice dropped from insistent to intimate. "Son, look at your feet. You see them scuffed shoes? The worn soles? They don't send the right message. I been here, at this same location, for thirty-three years. I seen you Yale men come and go. And the one thing that always strikes me is how the better-dressed go further. Now, let's face it, you don't have size on your side. You're never gonna be the star of the football team. The least you can do is make the most of what you've got."

Ignoring my staggered expression, he rustled through a rack, pulling out a suit. On another rack he found a white shirt with the label "Carlton" and a tie with maroon stripes.

"Let's start with this," he declared. "The bare minimum."

Reluctantly, still wondering whether I ought to try to slip away, I followed him from one side of the store to another, to a partition covered by a navy curtain. The space was tiny: just enough room for a stool, a couple of hooks nailed to the wall, and one person. I drew the curtain tight and undressed as quickly as possible, conscious of the slope of my buttocks, the subtle curve of my hips, the sock tucked into my underwear, and of course the binding around my chest. I put on that shirt and suit as fast as I could, but not before my hands went clammy and my underarms damp.

When I was sure all my parts were concealed, I came out. The old man led me to an upside-down milk crate that served as a platform. In front of it was a large but cloudy cheval glass.

"Step up here," he indicated, pointing to the crate.

The clerk measured my waist, grunting in amusement at the size, and then the length of my pants from the waistband to the outside of my ankles. He made a motion to measure my inseam, his hand creeping up my leg, past the knee, higher and higher, matching my feverish temperature, but just then the door to the store jangled—a bell must have been tied to the inside knob—and I realized that though it was uncomfortable to be alone with the tailor, it would be worse to have company.

"What's wrong?" he asked when I stepped off the box.

"I don't know. I'm not feeling so well."

"Well, step on up and we'll get this done."

"No. I mean, I don't think so. I think I ought to go."

Leaving the clerk still crouched and puzzled, I rushed back to the partition. There, I collected Charles's clothes before heading toward the door, my head awhizz. I could feel perspiration streaming down the back of my neck, no doubt staining the collar of the shirt I probably couldn't afford.

"Hey, wait a minute, son. You gotta take off that suit. You haven't paid for anything." The clerk had stood up, the measuring tape trailing from his hand like a leash.

"I'll pay for it now and keep it on."

"The slacks are miles too long. You'll ruin them."

"I'll come back later and you can alter everything."

But already, I'd made up my mind to do it myself. Taking in a suit couldn't be so different from darning socks, could it?

"Really, boy, you're acting queer. What's wrong?"

I fumbled for my wallet.

"How much?" I demanded.

He thought for a moment, then walked over to me solemn-eyed, all business.

"For the hand-tailored Harris tweed suit? For the Carlton deluxe shirt in the popular wide-spread collar model? Thirty dollars even."

My eyebrows shot up.

He shrugged. "It's the lowest I can go."

But to escape I would have been willing to give him just about anything. I counted out the bills rapidly and thrust them into his hand. My wallet was now virtually empty.

"Come back when you're ready," he said, already eyeing his new customer. I nodded, opening the door. The cool of outside felt like freedom. I sucked it in, listening to the hems of my new pants slap against the sidewalk as I darted away.

I dashed back to Old Campus, to Durfee, all the way up to my room. Slamming shut the door, I changed back into Charles's suit. Shakily, I dug my hands into my pockets, reaching for those pebbles. Fingering them gently, I tried to catch my breath. I wasn't quite certain why I had panicked. Surely that old salesman wouldn't have touched me *there*. Surely he wouldn't have dared. But here in my room, safe but only temporarily, I knew that nothing was definite.

I sat on my bed, toying with the idea of cloistering myself here, coming out only to attend classes and to take my meals. I wondered if it was possible to keep entirely to myself for weeks, even for months, on end. Perhaps not, but it seemed like a good idea until Harry knocked on the door. I let him in hesitantly, like I was in the middle of something important, when all I was in the middle of was worry.

"Pietra, are you blind? Get out here. The Activities Rally's started."

Sure, I'd been aware of the colorful booths and the throngs of people on Old Campus as I'd run through, but I hadn't paid much notice. So much about Yale was new—I was in a state of perpetual surprise. A circus elephant could have tromped by and I doubted I would have batted an eye.

"What's the Activities Rally?"

Harry sighed at my ignorance. "Come, you must have heard about it. The officials of all the clubs gather here to advertise. They pitch and try to pick up new recruits. It's the best chance we'll have to chat with the upperclassmen. I've heard the secret societies scout for future members the second the freshmen walk onto campus."

Charles had talked a good deal about Yale's secret societies: Skull and Bones, Scroll and Key, Wolf's Head, Book and Snake, Berzelius. He'd wondered aloud about what they did, what kind of furtive rituals were held inside their huge, windowless meeting places scattered around campus, "tombs" they were called, and the very word had made Charles shiver. I'd remembered not caring much for the topic. I'd doubted that the truth about those societies could be half so tantalizing as what our imaginations conjured.

"So what, Harry?"

"It's true—they only take seniors. But we might get noticed early."

"*You* get noticed. I'm staying put."

"Pietra, you're missing out. You know you are. You're so darned stubborn."

He was right. I knew that becoming a hermit was not a realistic solution for my predicament, and so, after a little more bantering, I relented and accompanied him outside. Here, again, were the madding crowds and a cresting of energy so palpable it felt smothering. Boys bombarded the booths and tables. They jockeyed for position in line, boasting of what they'd done before and what they could do now. Though classes started only the next day, my classmates were already determined to make themselves known.

I walked with Harry nervously, following chalk arrows drawn on the flagstones to tables and display booths advertising sports teams, comedy groups, debating societies, political organizations, literary circles, singing groups like the Whiffenpoofs and the Spizzwinks, a juggling club called the Anti-Gravity Society. We listened to a dozen pitchmen before Harry lingered in front of a booth for the Yale Chess Club. After a few minutes I grew restless and continued on, my discontent and sense of isolation growing. The organizations here seemed so distant from all that I'd known, from anything I'd even remotely imagined, that I saw no way to breach the space between.

I crept on, hoping no one would notice how I hung meek and limp at the periphery, but someone did, a boy with conjoined eyebrows and an angry burst of forehead pimples. He tapped me on the shoulder, waiting for me to turn.

"Hello there! What's your name?" he asked.

I glanced at the banner above his booth: "The Fantastics—Yale's Newest Singing Group." He was wearing a silver pin on his chest with the same slogan.

"Charlie Pietra. Pleased to meet you," I said tentatively, extending my hand, simultaneously thinking how strange the ritual of the handshake was. Palm to palm—such an arbitrary way to greet someone—why not foot to foot or elbow to elbow? I'd never shaken hands with anyone before coming to New Haven, and here I'd done it with nearly every person I'd met.

"William Boyd!" he said ebulliently. "Ever sung before, Charlie?"

I wondered what he would say if I told him that the only time I ever sang was while mopping the floor, but that two times out of three Mother would hush me—"Adele, please, I could use some quiet." And I furthermore wondered what he would say if I told him I preferred humming, low and tuneless, a way for me to express myself without talking, to proclaim that I was there without opening my mouth.

"Not really."

"We could use another countertenor. That's what you are, right? Can you do falsetto? If you're not sure of joining, put your name on the sign-up sheet and come to the first meeting this Tuesday in Linsly-Chittenden. That building over yonder—you see it? Come at eight P.M. sharp. Then you can decide if you want to audition."

But already I knew I'd fit The Fantastics like a turkey fits a canary cage. I couldn't help but think, if I were to join an activity, it ought to be one that made sense. It ought to be one that gave me a chance to be myself—or whatever version of myself I'd become.

"Thanks," I said, retreating. "Maybe I'll come back." The same way I'd go back to the tailor, I thought.

Leaving William Boyd's smile a little strained, I scurried to find Harry. He was still hobnobbing with the chess club, too distracted to pay me any mind. He seemed to be fielding questions, his voice simultaneously apologetic and defensive.

"You're making a mistake about me. I just told you, didn't I? That's not my persuasion."

"What about your parents?" a fellow from the chess club pressed.

"Fine, yes, they are—but I'm not. Not that it matters."

Preoccupied, Harry nodded uncomfortably when I told him I was going. He didn't even ask where, not that I could have told him. I walked away hastily, as far from the crowds as I could, wandering indiscriminately for a good twenty minutes before I found myself in front of Sterling Library, the one building I'd so far avoided. I knew why. Sterling was so distinguished, all steeples and piers, carvings and august archways, that I pictured it as a place only Cottagers could go. I reached the steps and even then I hesitated, my eyes boring into the heavy oak doors, as foreboding as they were appealing.

I took a deep breath and looked down—the clerk was right, I really did need a new pair of shoes—and then I saw it: white quartz mingled with pink and gray feldspar, black lodestone, and hints of mica. Stony Creek granite, I'd bet my eyes on it. It ornamented every step leading to the library.

Delighted, I sank to my knees, rubbing the stone with my hands. I looked up toward the library, hunting for a date etched in a base block, or a plaque. Then I remembered Harry had said that Sterling, despite its bygone look, was finished only four years ago. It was possible, then, that Pa had touched this very stone. It was possible, even, that he'd cut it.

I don't know how long I lingered there—maybe minutes, maybe a whole hour. I let memories of Pa wash over me until I didn't feel so lonely, until that drenching, out-of-place feeling was a little more bearable. I remembered how Pa had been years ago, hair springy, blue-black, one tendril always drooping onto his forehead. How he'd

swept me onto his shoulders even when I was too old for it, Mother
shaking her head at the way my skirt flew up.

"You spoil her, Gianno. The more time she spends with you, the
more frivolous she gets."

"She's a child—she ought to be frivolous!" he'd responded.

He'd run around as I swung my legs, both of us gleeful and giddy.
"My best girl," he'd call me. Mother's face had dropped at the sound
of it.

I remembered the picnics, too. We'd had them up on the east end
of the quarry. It was still virgin land, slim-stalked birches marching
bravely all the way to the edge, where the granite juts left off suddenly. We'd spread a cloth on the stone—Mother's old picnic blanket, red-and-white gingham.

"I used to bring it on those long trips in Tuscany . . ." she'd remark,
but her words would leave off like the cliff, as perilous, too, for Pa
would cringe, knowing that the life his wife reminisced about was
nearly unfathomable now. And Mother knowing that the mere mention of her past shifted the mood.

We feasted on deviled eggs and ham sandwiches and fresh
peaches. We drank iced tea from jars, one jar with sugar—Charles
liked his sweet—but the sugar never quite dissolved, just sloshed like
silt at the bottom. When we'd filled our stomachs, my brother and I
would play hide-and-seek.

"But no running," Mother admonished. No, not so close to the
cliff.

She'd sink down, exhausted, laying her head on Pa's lap, staring
raptly into his face, trying to lock eyes with him, though he gazed
elsewhere.

When I was younger, it had always been like that: Mother aching
for Pa's attention, and Pa oblivious, his eyes—and no doubt his
thoughts—wandering. At first she'd act sweet: laughter and honeyed
talk. But her charms generally failed to entice. (Was it possible,
Mother wondered aloud, that Alfred had been right—that once the
thrill of the chase is over, a woman's worth diminishes?) Eventually,

exasperated, Mother would give up, lifting her lithesome body, shaking out her sleepy legs to draw attention to her dissatisfaction. Then she was off to scold us, the children, for nothing in particular, or perhaps for being there in the first place.

Rebounding from memory, I began to cry, right there on the steps of Sterling, in broad daylight, tears so heavy they fell rather than trickled. I was aghast that I'd let my guard down, that I'd lost control, but I couldn't stop. Burying my head in my arms, I sobbed so hard I grew thirsty, my eyes like broken spigots.

When my body at last stopped shaking and there were no tears left, I felt better, flushed out and clean. I realized I did have a place in New Haven, right here, even if no one knew it but me.

I reached into my pocket, took out all the pebbles but one, and lined them up in a row. There was no need to carry them around anymore. Pa had believed in signs, and he would have said that these steps were one—a piece of Stony Creek right here in New Haven. But Mother had always thought Pa too superstitious, "like all Italians—the whole batty lot of them." And it was true that Pa assigned value to simple, perhaps mundane things—black cats, broken mirrors, full moons, hats on beds. And it was also true that Mother sometimes spilled salt on purpose, just to pull his chain.

"Signs are for people who don't want to take control of their lives," she'd bite. "Signs are for people who don't make decisions, who want *an excuse.*"

I wondered what Mother would say if she were here with me, if she could see these steps for herself. I wondered if she could dismiss a sign written in stone.

I'd expected to receive a letter from Mother right away, that first week of classes. But one didn't arrive until the second week. I found it in my mailbox in Yale Station, a basement-level post office located in Wright Hall. I'd been given a brass key to my mailbox that first day, when Harry and I had gone to the Freshmen Registrar's Office.

My box was one of hundreds of tiny compartments, all of burnished oak with delicate crystal knobs. I thought how the post office might have been simple and plain, like the one in Stony Creek. But that wasn't the way of Yale.

I took the letter straight to my room. I wanted to look at it alone, no prying eyes peeping over my shoulder. I wanted to be able to hear Mother's voice in my head, to imagine her long fingers clutching a pen, her eyes lowered in concentration. We'd promised to write each other often—it was the safest way. Telephone conversations could be over-heard, and besides, we didn't even have a telephone in our Stony Creek apartment. The lines didn't extend to the outskirts of town.

And so here it was: the first letter—small, neat script on a single folded page. A faint rosewater scent still clung to the pores of the paper. I scanned the top and was surprised to see my name written boldly, precisely, no doubt intentionally.

My Adele,

I call you by your name because, try as I might, I cannot con-vince myself that you are anything but my daughter. I know it is a risk to address you frankly, to resist code and artifice. Yet compared to the risks you are taking each day, this one seems almost benign.

I think of you constantly since your departure. I wonder how you find your classes, your new surroundings, your schoolmates, even your dormitory. Are they all to your satisfaction? I wonder, too, if any unusual or inconvenient situations have arisen. In spite of our determination and lively imaginations, I realize we may have been ill-prepared for all that you will encounter. Perhaps you have already experienced strange and daunting things. Yet now that we have made the first steps, all we can do is stay the course. You are a pioneer, my daughter. And yours is an exploration into uncharted territory, a new world that may yet turn out to be flat. But, my dear, falling off the edge is not an option.

I hope you are heeding my advice and being frugal with your finances. With the rent and household expenses, I do not anticipate being able to save much in the coming months. Few customers have brought their bags since the onslaught of colder weather, and two hands work ever so much more slowly than four. But I trust my sacrifice will become a bounty so long as you remember our goal: freedom in the form of opportunity.

One last thing, my lamb. Remember that you are all I have in this world now, and I you. You must not trust your heart to any outsider, even if temptation rears its head. My hunch is that there is temptation aplenty in that new city of yours.

Faithfully,
Mother

In the silence of my room, I read the page once more before tearing it slowly, methodically, into tiny pieces. Mother and I had decided on this, too.

"Leave no evidence of our crime, Adele."

The word "crime" had surprised me. It was something I read only in newspapers and books. Surely Mother had meant to be softer in her phrasing. Surely she didn't see what we were doing as so lurid.

At my desk I picked up a pencil, ready to write an immediate reply. But I couldn't decide what to tell her—certainly not all of what floated around in my brain, certainly not even the half of it. She would disapprove of my friendships, of any fun or escapades. She would intuit my feelings for Wick, that sense of recklessness and excitement I felt whenever he was around. She would find out what she wanted to, anything at all. Mother had that power.

I set down my pencil. Before writing anything, I would need to weigh my words.

As I was sweeping the shredded bits of her letter into the waste bin, Harry appeared; I'd clean forgotten that we'd agreed to go together to Commons.

We had to be in the Payne Whitney Gymnasium for an athletic assessment by nine o'clock, Harry reminded me. So off we went for a quick breakfast: scrambled eggs, wheat toast coated in butter, a mysterious brown-pulpy pudding, and heaping bowls of applesauce. We finished faster than we needed to. We weren't running late, but Harry fretted that we were and urged, pushed, "Hurry up, Pietra," until mid-mouthful I followed him out.

"Aren't you worried about this test?" he asked. "I don't have any talent for sports, Pietra. Never have, never will."

I didn't say so, but I had no such reservations. I'd always been fast—and not just for a girl. From the time I could walk, I'd been able to outpace my brother on the path to the quarry. Doubled over, Charles would gasp, "Don't you know I let you win?"

Harry and I passed Phineas on the way into the gymnasium. He was on his way out, looking fit in his athletic clothes. He gave us the once-over, pausing at our broomstick legs and narrow shoulders, his smile wide by the time he thought to greet us.

"Good luck, boys," he guffed.

I laughed tensely. I was running out of patience with Phin. By now we ought to have been on friendly terms, what with all the time we'd spent together. But still he remained coiled and unpredictable, too much like a snake in the grass.

"Why would we need luck?" asked Harry, turning his back and marching on. I followed, shrugging at Phin, who now looked a little chagrined.

"*Sraka*," Harry muttered.

Inside the gymnasium we passed a huge desk. Behind it a heavyset, jowled man scrutinized us, then waved us through. We continued straight, bypassing the corridors on our right and left.

"Where are we going?" I asked Harry. "How many floors are there, anyway?"

"Nine."

"Incredible."

"You should see the swimming pools."

"The swimming pools?"

Harry cast me a sidelong look. "Don't you know about them? Heck, Pietra, sometimes I think you never knew anything about Yale before coming here."

"I know about the pools," I said coolly, choosing not to divulge that I'd never seen a swimming pool before. In Stony Creek, Cottagers didn't build swimming pools, preferring to swim in the Sound, which turned so dense and briny in the summer a trivet could float.

We paused in front of a flight of wide stone stairs leading up and peered at a directory on the wall, which told us, among other things, where the squash courts and fencing salon were located. I felt just as I had during the Activities Rally, like the great hand of fate had uprooted me from my humble station and flung me into a wonderland. Yale had to be the only place on earth where people swam in pools, ate with sterling cutlery, clashed swords for sport, and did it all with an air of breezy nonchalance. I realized at that moment that I couldn't wait to attend the athletic assessment. What a release it would be to run, to let my legs go loose and limber, to keep going until I outpaced my disbelief.

Harry said we needed to go to the fourth floor and I was off with a vengeance, taking the steps two at a time.

Behind me, Harry huffed, "Slow down! The assessment hasn't even started yet, Pietra."

I did slow at the top of the fourth staircase, where an iron heater hissed and rasped, its efforts drifting futilely out a half-open window. Before me, a hale-looking boy strolled past in only a swimsuit. His tanned skin glistened with water droplets, sun-freckles dotted his shoulders, and chlorine vapors haloed him. His tank-style swimsuit was made of heavy navy wool, clingy to the body, especially across the chest, where it dipped low enough to reveal the odd wiry black hair. His bare feet plip-plopped along the wood floor until he disappeared into a room marked "Lockers."

I watched as the door closed behind him and understood with jarring clarity the nakedness of this place, which smelled of damp bodies and heavy exertion. The odor of the work sheds without the granite dust. The scent of men.

Mother and I had anticipated how my coming to the gymnasium would be dangerous. I'd have to find a place to change my clothes, a forgotten corner, a poorly lighted nook. I'd have to do it quickly; I'd even practiced how fast I could doff one outfit and don another. Of course I'd considered what the consequences would be if I were to be discovered. Yet I hadn't realized I would discover things, too.

The thought of seeing a naked man made me wildly flustered. I was uneasy seeing even women's bodies, averting my eyes when Mother, hot from ironing in the kitchen, sometimes wriggled out of one old dress and into another. The only body I was comfortable with was my own, and maybe that was because it was board-flat, bland as oatmeal.

Out of breath, Harry made it up the last step.

"Better shoot me now," he said, his smile rueful.

Together we went into the locker room, where a short line had formed in front of a young man doling out athletic clothes from a voluminous wicker basket. Each boy in the line received a pair of gray athletic pants, a shirt with a "Y" across the chest, white cotton socks, and brand-new rubber-soled sneakers.

"What size?" the man asked me. I hesitated, as scared as I'd been in the tailor's shop. But the man was in a rush and thrust a pile of clothes into my arms when I didn't answer.

"Small," he said with finality. "Shoes?"

But here, too, I hadn't an idea. The man glanced down at my brother's too-large footwear, his brow knitted.

"Size eight, I suppose," he said, handing me a pair. "Next!"

"No, wait," I hastened. "I'm smaller."

"Fine," he retorted, switching the sneakers. "Take the seven then."

Joining Harry, I walked into an adjacent room, where a second fellow distributed scraps of paper. Each scrap contained a locker number and combination.

"Keep those papers," he told us, "until you memorize them."

I left Harry, muttering something about going to my locker, though I was really searching for a place to undress. Already, many of the boys were changing. I tried to walk with eyes averted, but still I caught snatches of skin: pink-white buttocks, pale thighs, muscular forearms, a ridged spine protruding from a bended back, shocks of hair billowing around the articles of manhood that women didn't talk about, except for Miss Prowl, and only when she was very drunk.

As I made my way, one boy turned, fully exposed before me. He seemed not to notice, or to care, that my eyes had widened at the dangle of his penis, heavily veined, slightly shriveled, a timid-looking thing. This wasn't how I expected a penis to be, the very thing that separated the sexes, that was compared in novels to guns and cannons, scepters and spears. Certainly I hadn't expected it to appear rosy and tacked-on, almost an anatomical afterthought.

And yet, I mused, how wonderful that men are nonchalant about their form! The group here in the locker room was behaving exactly the opposite of how a group of naked women might. Instead of cowering, hands and arms strategically covering forbidden parts, these boys reveled in their nakedness. They walked about briskly and boldly. They did not hurry to cover up. In fact, they even seemed to delay their changing by a minute or two, as if to bask.

I kept moving, barely realizing that I had cupped my hand to my mouth. A giggle threatened to erupt, a naughty, nervous, unmistakably girlish giggle. I was thinking how I was a pioneer, as Mother had written, even if this was not the uncharted territory she had meant.

Eventually, I found my changing place: a custodian's closet, unlocked and cluttered with brooms, mops, buckets, and cleansers. I slipped inside quickly, one glance back to make sure no one was watching. Still clutching my athletic clothes, I closed the door and found myself in perfect darkness. I undressed as quickly as I could, aware that the door might open at any time, and that one look could bring unspeakable consequences, worse even than dismissal. Mother had warned me.

Thrilled and keyed-up, I tugged on the clothes I'd been given, careful not to upset my bindings. When I was sure I looked as I should, I opened the door and exited, no one to see me, thank goodness, but this was only my first time in what would surely be a long year.

I found my locker and threw my regular clothes inside. Then I looked for Harry. When I couldn't find him, I followed a group of boys out the door, down a corridor. The line filtered through another door, into a large exercise room with brown brick walls and a hardwood floor that felt elastic under my feet. Or maybe that was my new sneakers, which were still too big.

Amid a sea of boys, a squat, fattish man blew a whistle. When he had our attention, he barked orders. We were to stand in rows, ten men to a row, until we were all in formation. As the throngs moved haphazardly into some semblance of order, I spotted Harry. He had positioned himself in the first row, right on the edge. He gave me a blithe little wave as if the impending assessment didn't alarm him. But in his eyes I detected a strange shrewdness, maybe even a knowingness, and I wondered briefly, the vinegar tang of fear in my mouth, if he had somehow guessed why I'd left him.

I found a place in the last row and obliged when the squat man, who I soon learned was named Coach Roota, told us to sit down. Having ceased his whistle-blowing, he was not as intimidating as he'd first appeared. He congratulated us on being at Yale, which he called just as fine a university for athletics as for academics. This earned a scoffing cough or two, which Coach Roota quickly quashed by waving a clipboard over his head. He proceeded to tell us that we were to perform a series of exercises: sit-ups, chin-ups, leg lifts, rowing sessions, and a one-mile run. We would be graded on these exercises, he explained. Then, from our scores we would be judged as either fit for sports or in need of corrective exercises.

"Being on the corrective exercises assignment list is nothing to be ashamed of," Coach Roota tried to assure us, although I gleaned from the panicked, dog-weary faces of my classmates that it most certainly was.

"Last year approximately sixty percent—the *majority*—of my freshmen were placed in case groups for corrective exercises. The most common deficiencies are in body posture and mechanics. The good news is that ninety percent of those men graduated from their groups within four months. They were able to join the sports of their choosing—without a handicap."

Sure that I had no handicap other than the obvious one, I felt confident. In fact, I felt ready for whatever Coach Roota asked of us. Rowing I was good at. Old Man Richter owned an ancient, weather-beaten dinghy, and he took me out fishing for snapper blues in the summer. I would row frantically as he cast and recast his line and hollered for me to move faster. As for the other exercises, they couldn't be too difficult. And anyway, it was the run that I longed for.

But I would have to wait for gratification. From a place unknown, or perhaps from the stale air of the gymnasium itself, another man emerged. He was the antithesis of Coach Roota: scrawny, angular, with eyes that bobbed in a jaundiced liquid. The man had a promi-nent bald patch, but the hair that remained was abundant and snow-white, protruding like plumes of raw cotton around the periphery of his head. So strange and foreboding was his presence that he reminded me of the scientist from Mary Shelley's book, another castoff Miss Prowl had given to me in one of her rare moments of charitableness.

Coach Roota introduced the man as Dr. Henrickson. He was here to perform the mandatory orthopedic tests.

" 'What exactly is the mandatory orthopedic test?,' many of you must wonder," Dr. Henrickson began, facing us and clasping his skeletal hands together. His voice was low, a bit caustic, and every bit as chilling as I'd imagined it might be.

"Well, soon I will invite each of you into my office. There, you will undress and I will examine you for any bodily aberrations or abnor-malities. I will also photograph you in bare form. These photographs and the results of my examination will help Coach Roota to deter-mine which of you are eligible for corrective exercises.

"Today, I will examine approximately twenty men. Those men whose names I do not call will be examined in subsequent visits to the gymnasium. All of you will be examined by the end of a one-month period. Any questions?"

But there were none. Intimidation had silenced us.

Though I thought it impossible, there was more bad news. Coach Roota again stepped forward and explained how all freshmen were required to pass a swim test—one hundred yards in under five minutes. He assured us that the test was easy: we could use any stroke we wished. But this was cold comfort when I considered what we'd have to wear: woolen swimsuits exactly like the one that gleaming swimmer had sported. There would be no way to hide in one. The bottom portion of the suit would hug an area I was obviously deficient in, while the top would showcase my meager endowments—meager, but endowments nonetheless. And then there was all that skin I'd show—smooth skin, fundamentally feminine skin.

Ignoring a round of groans and sighs, Coach Roota said that we could try to pass the swim test at any point during the year.

"You might even try it today, to get it over with. In any case, you *must* pass it before the end of your second semester or you will not be eligible to enter into your sophomore year."

Truth be told, swimming was another sport I excelled in. Mother couldn't understand how I could be so buoyant when I was "nothing but a bundle of bones." But I did float, as naturally as driftwood, and I could swim swiftly. The water was as familiar and comfortable a habitat to me as the path to the quarry. But it didn't matter that I could swim, only that I couldn't be seen swimming. I wasn't sure how to remedy the situation. I couldn't flee, as I'd fled from the tailor and the Activities Rally. Everyone would notice the lad who'd departed hastily and without permission. If no one else, Harry would catch me, then subject me to an interrogation.

With each passing second my stomach twisted tighter. But still I could envision no easy escape. The swim test I could put off. Coach Roota had said we had all year to pass it—all year to consider a way out. But the orthopedic exam could not be fought with procrastination.

In the midst of my distress, Dr. Henrickson called his first name—

a name that, mercifully, sounded nothing like Charles Pietra. Mean-while, Coach Roota bellowed his own set of names, mine included. We would be the first batch of fellows to undergo the exercise por-tion of the athletic assessment. Assistants emerged, among them the two men who had passed out our locker numbers and athletic clothes. These assistants, Coach Roota said, would help him to record our results.

We recruits were taken to a small room off the main exercise area, where a horizontal bar was suspended from the ceiling. Harry was not in my group, but I rolled my eyes at him on my way out, a gesture he returned.

Inside the adjoining room the boys and I formed a line. I was fifth from the front. By the time my turn came, dismay had made me impassioned and nervy. Lifted by the assistants to the bar, I clung with tenacious hands, pulling myself up until my chin was level with my clenched fingers and white knuckles. I elevated myself again and again, until I stopped counting in my head, until the rough, excited voices below went still with surprise. I refused to stop, even when my arms started shaking, the muscles so stressed they quivered. I descended only when the assistants decided that enough was enough, grabbing my legs and yanking me back down to earth.

"Twenty-nine," one said. He shook his head while jotting down the number.

I passed through the other exercises with similar pluck, including a rowing session not on a boat, but on a stationary machine with maneuverable oars and a sliding seat. I moved like I'd never moved before, the wraith of dread having possessed my body, giving it unreasonable ability. I performed as some quarry workers did during an accident. Sometimes the shock of a horrifying situation would give them a moment of staggering power, so that one would be able to lift single-handedly a five-hundred-pound stone from another's crushed leg.

It was the fear of Dr. Henrickson that gave me my strength—fear that my name would pass through his bloodless lips. I had no idea how he performed his examinations, but my mind conjured all sorts of sordid possibilities. I imagined the positions he asked the boys to assume as he took their photographs: bent, twisted, unnatural positions. I saw cold steel instruments in his pinched, wizened hands. He would use these instruments to probe the intimate folds and corridors of their bodies. And when he saw *my* body, why, those wasted lips would curl back in a combination of delight and disgust, his yellow teeth foggy with debris. His drippy eyes would travel to the door—better make sure it's locked, and the window shades drawn. This one's going to take a while.

By the time the run came, I was so panicked I thought I would retch. The exercise session was nearing an end. One of the assistants had already summoned most of the boys who were to be examined that day. Nevertheless, I was sure my luck would run out and I'd be among the final few.

My group was led up the stone steps of the Payne Whitney Gymnasium, up floors five through eight and the balcony levels in between, until at last we could climb no farther. Only we could: up all the way to the roof, where an outdoor track was the last thing to stand between brick and sky. The wind whistled in our ears and pricked our reddened faces. The cold crept through our clothes and slapped our sweaty, goose-pimpled skin.

That raw nip subsided when the assistant yelled "Go!" We were off, all of us, leaping from behind a chalky starting line into a full-fledged sprint, puffing and panting and wondering how many laps comprised a mile, for the track was of strange and ambiguous size. Before very long I stopped wondering and concentrated, instead, on the run itself. Though dashing on a track was nothing like tearing along the quarry path or a sandy shoreline, still I reveled in it.

Only my oversized sneakers kept me from total rapture. I made my way to the outer edge of the track and untied them, yanking them off, and my socks, too. I left everything orphaned and started again. The grainy track felt more natural under my bare feet, which were thick-soled, rather like my laundry-toughened hands. Seconds later I

caught up with the pack. Then I passed it, knowing not if I was in the
lead or laps behind, only that thoughts of Dr. Henrickson couldn't
catch me—not when I was going this fast.

Finally the assistant yelled "Stop!" and I slowed, my limbs jelly-
wobbly, my breathing labored. He announced that we were done for
the day. Some of the boys flung back their heads in thankfulness,
greedily gulping mouthfuls of air. One fell flat on the ground. Me—I
smiled until the cold made my teeth ache. I was so grateful to have
escaped Dr. Henrickson that I scarcely realized how exhausted I was.

Though the session was over, we weren't free to leave. Instead, we
were told to keep walking around the track, to cool our exerted legs.
We ambled in slow circles, like racehorses being breezed, until our
hearts stopped whizzing and our sweat felt like a clammy second
skin. Glad for the lack of company, I walked alone, until the assistant
came jogging up to me from behind. For a moment, I suspected the
worst: Dr. Henrickson had time for one more man after all. But the
assistant seemed too jovial to be the bearer of bad news. Toting my
shoes and socks, he gave me a smile.

"What's your secret?" he asked, handing over my things and slap-
ping me gaily on the back. He told me his name was Donald. Donald
Allen.

"What's my secret?" I asked, that queasy feeling returning.

"To all that stamina? If you don't mind my saying, it's a shame
you're such a small fellow. A few more inches and thirty more
pounds and you'd have been something."

I smiled weakly, unsure if this backhanded compliment was more
backhanded or compliment. But as I continued around the track,
which wound nowhere, just around itself, I decided that some questions weren't worth the trouble of speculation.

Back in the locker room I found Harry. Despite all the exercise, I
convinced him that we didn't need to shower—a dubious suggestion
that he was surprisingly quick to approve. Unlike the other boys,

Harry didn't feel comfortable with the intimacy of locker-room camaraderie. Maybe he even felt shy, saying, "You're right, Pietra. Who needs that kind of bother?"

We left Payne Whitney as we'd come in. On our way back to Durfee, I mentioned what the assistant had told me. Harry's eyes became so angry I thought his eyeglasses would steam. I hadn't seen him this way before and was amazed that he could be so dramatic.

"Those half-wits!" he exclaimed with a snort. "They're chumps, that's it, Coach Roota and his minions. They expect us to conform to the same dimensions, like eggs in a box. Well, can't they see we've got different makings, that we weren't all born of the same stock—sent to prep school at the age of thirteen with a crucifix in one hand and a football in the other?"

My first class started that afternoon and I'd have to eat lunch first, but when I arrived back to the dormitory all I wanted to do was bathe. Since being at Yale I'd often and surreptitiously carried a wet cloth from the lavatory to my room. But as the days passed I longed increasingly for a real soak, to scrub away the residue that the days had left behind. It was with relief, then, that I noticed only one of my suitemates was home, a quiet fellow named Marcus Patterson. He said hello as I walked by, but his tone made it clear that he was busy. Seeing that his concentration was wholly on the sketch pad and charcoals in his lap, I decided to chance the shower. I'd never used one before. We had a bathtub in Stony Creek, like everyone else.

The knobs and overhead nozzle of the shower gave me pause, but finally I doffed my clothes and stepped under the hard spray, which seemed to me inefficient and unruly. I wondered, how did people bathe like this, without *immersion*? Awkwardly I lathered up, the cake of soap slipping from my fingers once, then again, onto the wet tile floor. I struggled to rinse myself, the drizzle of water loud in my ears as I listened for the dreaded sound of the lavatory door opening—there was no lock. But thankfully, no one entered.

When I was through I wrapped an ankle-length bathrobe around my body, a purchase Mother had insisted on. I tucked my clothes under my arm and skittered past Marcus. Back in my room I remembered the confetti remains of the letter in my waste bin. I knew then what I had to write to Mother: not a careless blathering about the friends I'd made or the books I'd purchased, but a serious plea for help.

I wrote her plaintively about the swim test and the mandatory orthopedic exam, about how my next session in the gymnasium was only days away and how Dr. Henrickson might call my name then—or any day after. I told her I was taking enough chances; this was one I couldn't afford. I asked if she knew of a solution, and I was sure she did, or else that she would find one. Mother was industrious, a planner and a solver, that long neck of hers often craned as if she were peeking into the future.

I read the letter once. It was satisfactory—short and earnest. And when I sealed it shut, I felt better.

Yes, Mother would know what to do.

Phineas happened to be in my first class at Yale, The Foundations of Biology, and somehow it was appropriate to see him in that cold, sterile room, which stank of rancid-sweet formaldehyde, of curious things preserved. We sat next to each other cautiously, nodding like we were glad to see one another, when really we wished Wick were there too, to dissolve our discomfort. When someone came by to distribute pamphlets, we grabbed them with exaggerated eagerness, grateful for the distraction.

Behind a podium at the front of the room, the professor, Dr. Ernest Thatcher, introduced himself, saying we'd better get started right away. Everyone pick a laboratory partner, he instructed, the person you'll be working with throughout the semester. "Don't be shy," he said. "Make a new friend." Though Phin and I didn't immediately turn toward each other, we knew we would pair. Neither of us wanted the antagonism to surface.

To my surprise, Phin initiated the partnership, saying, "How about it, Good-time Charlie?"

"Sure," I agreed.

We dragged our chairs closer together as we leafed through our books. The illustrations were gruesome to behold—a frog split open from throat to belly, its skin peeled back, every organ labeled, the sight of those innards like the smell of the room: stomach-turning. Phin, his hand near his mouth, had more trouble coping than I, who had dodged dangling eels at the end of Old Man Richter's spear, who had gutted countless fish for Mother to fry, stinky, silvery scales under my fingernails even after I scrubbed them with a laundry brush.

Professor Thatcher spoke for the duration of the class, giving us an overview of what to expect in the coming months. Phin and the rest of my classmates scribbled notes on newly purchased paper, and I did, too—if only to seem like everyone else. But mostly I listened. My pencil became more and more ornamental. I absorbed the information, just as I had at school in Stony Creek. I relied on retention, knowing that I'd remember nearly everything the professor said if I only concentrated hard enough.

Eventually, my brain started to thrum, machine-like, shifts and gears turning as words and ideas filtered in, lingered, steeped, and settled comfortably, until the pencil finally dropped from my fingers with a clatter and rolled across the table, nearing the edge. Phineas caught it just before it fell.

"Looks like you'll want to borrow my notes after class," he said, raising one eyebrow comically, good-naturedly, so that I wondered if all this time I'd been judging him too harshly.

With classes well under way, my days took on a certain rhythm. Mother had said that establishing a schedule would prevent wasted time, wandering thoughts, the distractions that could derail our plan. She was right. Once I'd determined where I had to be at certain hours of the day, there was little of the freewheeling merriment that had characterized my first week at Yale. There were my classes, of course, and then labs and mandatory study groups. There were also several more trips to the Payne Whitney Gymnasium, where I continued to dodge Dr. Henrickson.

Wick, Harry, Phin, and I were frequently together in what spare time we had—we'd become a regular and near-famous foursome— and we met at least once each day, usually for some caper Wick had devised: playing an impromptu game of baseball on President Angell's manicured lawn, or sculpting the inedible mashed potatoes in Commons into zoo animals, or stealing the pickled human brain that sat on one of Professor Thatcher's shelves, leaving a farcical ransom note in its stead.

Harry frequently tracked me down, as he had on our first day at Yale. He would find me in my room, mention that he was on his way to Sterling Library, and ask if I wanted to come. Always I did. I welcomed the excuse to see those granite steps. Usually, Harry was in a rush to get inside and hit the books, but I'd try to linger. I'd ignore my friend's tapping foot and think of Pa.

Inside Sterling, Harry would settle quickly at one of the long tables, touching his finger to his tongue before turning the pages of a book he'd already combed through a dozen times before. I'd sit, too, idly eyeing my sparse notes. Sometimes I'd read for an hour or two, but never could I stay still for long. I'd have to excuse myself and Harry would look up, eyes brimming with impatience.

"Midterm exams are right around the corner," he'd remind me.

"Harry, classes just started."

"But you don't study. Not enough, anyway."

This sort of exchange went on until Harry and I were given a surprise test in Shakespeare: Histories and Tragedies—one of the classes we shared. The professor revealed that a single student had scored perfectly. He didn't say who.

Afterward, Harry asked me if I'd been the one.

"What makes you think that?"

"The way you study—or don't study—it's either one way or the other. You're either a genius or a misfit."

"I'm not a genius."

Harry searched for something in my eyes, some clue. "Even so, I know it's you."

"Look, I don't always score well," I hastened. "My Scholastic Achievement Test certainly wasn't perfect." This comment slipped off my tongue easily. More and more, I couldn't put a line between my brother and me.

Harry, who had no doubt scored well, seemed cheered by that.

But here, back in Sterling, I wasn't thinking of tests, only of the Stacks: the gargantuan portion of the library that contained fifteen stories of books. The mere prospect of those overflowing shelves thrilled me.

I knew I'd fall in love with the Stacks my very first time in its dusty bowels. I loved its half-darkness, the way the light filtered in so solemnly, as if fearing to enter. I loved the labyrinthian corridors, the toppling shelves climbing so high I felt closed in, lost yet also found.

That first time I'd looked for my old favorite: *Wuthering Heights.* To my astonishment I'd found eleven copies. They were perfect, not like the mildewed, yellow-papered specimen I'd inherited from Miss Prowl. Nor were they like the mysteries and adventure stories I occasionally found on the beach in Stony Creek, the forgotten debris of sunbathing Cottagers.

"We don't need their *leftovers,* Adele," Mother would tut whenever I brought them home. She was disgusted by the particles of sand caught in the chinks of the spines. Leeching off the Cottagers was beneath us, she said. Conversation would take a turn for the better, though, when Mother started to reminisce about the books she'd read as a child.

"Do you remember when I told you about the library my father kept in our house? How the bookshelves extended to the ceiling? You needed a ladder to reach the highest ones, so Father had one built. It moved on a groove all the way around the room, even around the corners. It was so clever."

Always I wanted to tell her how I'd heard the story many times. But instead I'd fall silent. When Mother was swept up in nostalgia, I hated to yank her back to reality.

Now that Mother and I were apart, sometimes I wished she could see the Stacks—a collection of books that trumped any other. Just being in those corridors soothed my spirit. I loved going in the evening, reading under a green-glass desk lamp, or sometimes under a thin beam of moonlight, believing maybe, just maybe, I was the only one in this dreamland of books. Upon each return I chose a different floor. I sought out dark crevices, long-forgotten nooks, the places where the shelves were dustiest and the books were just waiting for their pages to be rediscovered. I chose volumes arbitrarily. For one week I read nothing but novels with red covers, the next week biographies with blue. Sometimes I picked a number and counted the books from the beginning of a row until I reached that magic numeral. Other times I closed my eyes and ran my fingers along the spines, selecting my reading by touch.

The result of this slipshod process was variety. I would never have chosen to learn about Mayan hieroglyphics or President Rutherford Hayes of my own volition. Yet once I selected a book, I always read it cover to cover, forcing myself even to wade through the footnotes.

I came up for air only to check my brother's old pocket watch. Time was haphazard in the Stacks. Whole hours could slip past in the course of a minute, or so it seemed when the clanging of a bell indicated that the library was about to close. Sometimes I heard other sounds, too—the metallic clatter of the book-filled dumbwaiter as it climbed between floors, the whisper of turning pages, the scuffling of shoes. If I roamed for long enough, I'd inevitably spot someone hunkered down in a carrel or the adumbration of someone disappearing around a corner. And though I'd pretend otherwise, I'd know that there were other admirers, hushed and fleet as myself.

*   *   *

It was a surprise to spot them: stoneworkers, right here in New Haven. They were young, my age, give or take a few years, and they resembled the workers of Stony Creek: rough-and-tumble, skin surprisingly tender under dark smears of dust and grease. I smiled as I listened to them boast, quip, and tease. I drew closer, until I was at the periphery of where they worked. They were carving ornate flourishes above Memorial Gate outside Branford College. There were four of them, two standing on ladders, two on the ground sorting through the chisels, mallets, and hammers that sat in shallow, coverless toolboxes like the ones Pa and Charles had carried. Pa and Charles's boxes were now hidden in a closet in our apartment. Many times Mother had talked about burying them, or even pitching them into the sea, but sentimentality, it seemed, had won over recklessness.

The boys made crude jokes and brayed at any girls who passed. But their eyes seldom left the stone, and their hammers struck with a humbling precision. It was obvious that they took pride in their work, as Pa had.

Creeping closer, I wondered if they'd notice me and if they'd care; wondering, mostly, if they'd sense it—the kinship we shared—though I no longer shook granite dust from my clothes.

I didn't expect to be welcomed. The students of Yale and the artisans who worked for the university were notoriously combative. Harry said it was because Yale students considered stonecutters, bricklayers, and other laborers to be dimwitted. And the laborers—they thought Yale students hopelessly pompous. Once, Harry had shown me how the stone-carvers had wreaked a sort of permanent revenge. A frieze in Sterling Library depicted one student sleeping at his desk and a second lazing beneath a poster of a naked woman. Another carving portrayed a student studying a book, but the words inside read U. R. A. JOKE.

Despite this animosity, I was sure the workers here wouldn't lump me with the rest. Surely they would see it: the respect I felt for them, the affection. I set my sights on one. I would talk to him, I decided, say something pleasant about his work.

The boy wore navy coveralls and a sullied cap. A small, poorly etched tattoo—a star, a cross?—decorated the outside of his left hand. He stood low on a ladder, leaning down every so often to trade a tool with his comrade on the ground. There was something about his face I liked, although his complexion was coarse and pitted. It was only later that I realized he looked like a young version of Silvio.

Trying to swallow my nervousness, I strode over to him. The boy with the tattooed hand was limber-legged, a tool belt loose and jaunty about his hips. Like Wick, he seemed a magnet for attention. I hoped for a welcoming glance, maybe even a smile, something to set me at ease. But from above, his mouth crimped into a sneer.

"Yeah? What d'ya want?"

I backed up a step, instantly self-conscious. "Nothing. I just came over to tell you what a good job you're doing."

"You're joshing, right?"

"No. I really think you're doing fine work."

"You came all the way here to tell me that? Fellas, did you hear that? This little guy thinks we're doing fine work."

His hand opened and the chisel clattered noisily to the ground, only a few inches from my feet. Mockingly, he put that same hand over his heart.

"I've never felt so honored in all my life."

As the other boys peered at me, I backed up another step, angry with myself. I'd been naïve to think these fellows would sense our commonality. It was too many layers down, somewhere they couldn't even feel, never mind see.

The carver with the tattooed hand climbed down the rungs of the ladder, fast and aggressive, so that I wasn't sure whether he was coming to collect his tool or to launch a fist into my face. I picked up the chisel quickly, keeping it at my side so that he knew I had no intention of swinging it. He seemed cautious when I handed it back, looking around to see if I was on my own, if he could stomp me as easily as he thought he could.

"Who put you up to this, kid?"

"What do you mean?"

"You're here on a dare, right?"

I shook my head.

"Well, then, that makes you about the dumbest Yale man I've ever met."

"Maybe so."

"Why you so interested in what we're doing?"

"I don't know," I hedged, wondering if I could say what I wanted to. "My father and brother were stonecutters," I blurted.

"Oh yeah? And what does your mother do—fire the black powder?"

"I'm serious."

The boy eyed me guardedly. "So where you from?" he asked.

"Stony Creek."

"Yeah? We know some guys from there. Palanzas, right? Heck, I never heard of a stonecutter's kid going to Yale."

I sighed, not knowing what to say.

"So why aren't you a stonecutter like your father? Whatsa matter—hands too soft?"

A jovial sarcasm had replaced the grit in his voice. I was glad for the change. It reminded me of the way the men joked in the work sheds.

I got to thinking that maybe he should see my hands; they didn't look like they belonged to a dandy. I hadn't cut stone, but I'd scoured and scrubbed enough to gather a permanent collection of calluses and blisters. When Charles and I used to compare palms, mine were always rougher.

"Hey, Joe, whatcha doing down there? You on vacation?"

The fellow atop the other ladder flashed us a look of disdain. He looked older than the others. When his eyes found mine, I read their meaning. These workers might be in someone else's neighborhood, but their arms were anything but open.

"Who the dickens is that, anyway?" he continued.

That quickly, something changed. Whatever small headway the carver and I had made vanished. Joe squared his shoulders, belligerence returning to his face, even if it wasn't as authentic as before. He stalked back to the ladder, twirled the chisel, then slung it coolly into his work belt. We met each other's eyes once more but turned away briskly, bashfully, the both of us unsure how to end our conversation. The both of us wary of our own kind.

Exactly ten days after sending my letter to Mother, I found her response in my mailbox. How a surge of feelings overcame me: relief, hesitation, nervousness, even faintness of heart. I'd been waiting so anxiously for her note to arrive that I scarcely believed it was real—that powder-blue stationery a bit tarnished from travel, but still smelling faintly of roses.

I took it to my room, clenched and crumpled in my fist. Only when I'd locked my door and taken a deep breath did I read it.

Dearest Adele,

Your note elicited not the first jab of fear since your absence, but certainly the sharpest. I was not aware that athletics played such a prominent role in university life. Nor did I know that certain physical tests were compulsory. These were issues Charles and I never discussed. I suppose we hadn't needed to.

After much deliberation I have decided that a medical excuse is the most effective antidote to both the swim test and the orthopedic exam. I have already taken the liberty of mailing a letter written and signed by Doctor Benson to the proper party at Yale. It is not important that you know how I obtained this letter, only that you be familiar with its contents. The reason for your inability to participate in certain athletic proceedings, Adele, is a terrible accident. As a child, you suffered substantial burns from a fire in our home. The resulting scars, though not visible on your face and hands, are prominent elsewhere on your body. Throughout your life the dam-

age has caused you not only medical hardship, but also considerable social impairment.

Included in Doctor Benson's letter is a recent evaluation attesting to your general health and wellness, despite the accident. I have informed university officials that you do not need a second evaluation and that as your mother and benefactor, I will not allow you to endure the distress that would certainly accompany proceedings of such an intimate nature. Nevertheless, I assured Yale that you are fully capable of participating in those pursuits that require complete and standard dress. (With sports you were always one of the boys, Adele—running and jumping and lacking patience for more feminine pastimes.)

As you might expect, securing the letter from Doctor Benson cost me more than I wanted to give. Yet I had little choice in the matter. If you are to stay in New Haven, we will both have to learn to part with certain things.

Yours always,
Mother

I didn't sigh with relief after reading Mother's letter. Nor did I feel as if I'd been rescued. Rather, I had questions, even if I didn't necessarily want to know the answers. I wondered what exactly Mother had given up. I questioned what compensation she had offered Doc Benson. I puzzled over whether he was like most men, a little weak-kneed standing next to her. I wondered if she'd gone to him in a smart hat and lipstick, wearing the same dress she'd worn to see the principal of the Stony Creek Secondary School. Maybe she'd taken a piece of jewelry, or maybe she'd decided to save what was left for future use. If she'd gone empty-handed, she would have bartered with something else, maybe the clothing on her back, or maybe the long expanse of skin that lay underneath.

I shuddered at the image that emerged: Mother in her finery approaching Doc Benson's medical station, her neck rigid, her eyes aloof. She was a woman on a mission, determined to prevail even if she knew she wouldn't come out quite the same. I speculated about what she'd said to herself on the way there, maybe a phrase she'd often uttered to me: "All chores need to be done, even the unpleasant ones."

She would have left the station with hat askew, no more lipstick left on her mouth. But she'd have gained something, too: a letter. Signed and dated and stamped. A letter no one could refute, least of all Doc Benson.

Maybe Miss Prowl had been on the porch all that time. Maybe she'd seen Mother leave the house in her gloves and stockings, heading straight for the quarry path, and then observed her returning, noting that her legs were a little shaky and her demeanor not quite as proud. Miss Prowl would have a ball when she reached the same conclusion as I: how this impossibly supercilious woman had fallen, finally—fallen from grace and into a strange man's arms.

I felt sick, trembling with anger at Mother and at myself, too. I told myself I could be wrong. The sordid picture show in my head might be pure invention. Yet as I tore up the letter, little pieces falling from my fingers, I reminded myself that flesh had always been the basis of our deception. Flesh both hidden and exposed. I was convinced that Mother was doing her part as surely as I was doing mine.

Chapter Six

N EWS OF MY work-study came in the form of a letter, dropped by the postman into my box at Yale Station. On November 5, I was to report to the office of Joshua Cecil Spang, Ph.D., in Yale's Department of Social Demography and Intelligence. I was to bring with me this very same letter, which I would sign in Professor Spang's presence, thus officially commencing my yearlong service to him.

November 5 turned out to be a soggy, dreary day, the clouds hanging like wet wool in the sky, the streets puddled with gasoline rainbows. As I walked to Professor Spang's office, I thought not of our meeting, but of something more immediate—the walk itself. Already, in the short time I'd been at Yale, so much was familiar. I recognized the quirks of the campus: the perpetually stopped clock atop Harkness Hall, the skull-and-crossbones flag one student had brazenly hung out his window. I knew how many steps I'd have to take from Sterling Library to the gate of the Grove Street Cemetery. And I knew the spine-tingling inscription above that gate: "The Dead Shall Be Raised." I passed faces that I'd learned by heart—and not just the faces of my classmates. There was Amato the Shoeman, his cart permanently parked outside Woolsey Hall, his talent for delivering a knockout polish in two minutes flat indisputable. On Prospect Street, a vendor named Skinny Al sold five-cent hot dogs slathered in spicy Polish mustard and sauerkraut. Then there was the sad-looking old widow who wandered all the streets around campus. She was a hefty woman with a dirty face, asymmetrical eyes, and ratty-matted hair. She wore always an ancient coat of worsted wool. With its mother-of-pearl buttons and collar made of a whole mink, head and all, the coat still evoked the faint burnish of money.

Not surprisingly, Harry knew the widow's story, although I suspect he embellished it with his own flights of fancy. She'd lived in one of the grand old mansions on Whitney Avenue, he'd told me, one with white Corinthian columns and hedges trimmed into clever shapes. The widow had lost both her sons in the Great War. At first she'd done her best to put on a brave face, to convince herself that death could be justified by a noble cause. But one day courage had deserted her as she was leaving the house. Wrapping that very same coat tightly around her shoulders, she'd decided not to return to her old life, or what remained of it. She'd left a note for her husband telling him to remove the pot roast from the oven at 6 P.M. sharp. But he'd arrived late, and by then all that was left was a charred slab, its gamy smoke filling the house.

Whenever I crossed the widow's path, I could hear her talking to herself. Her speeches were strings of randomly arranged words—reasonable only to herself, perhaps. Except for the one time she had turned toward me as I'd passed, the only time I'd ever seen her show interest in something live and real. She'd pointed her finger and shouted, "You don't look at all like yourself, Josefina. Is that really you under there?"

After that, I crossed to the other side of the street when I saw her coming.

That day, the day of my meeting with Professor Spang, I didn't see the widow. In the mist and rain she could have been under any of dozens of bobbing black umbrellas. As I approached the building that housed the Department of Social Demography and Intelligence, the fact of the meeting finally hit me. I didn't know even one thing about the requirements of my work-study, or about the department itself, and my ignorance made me feel guilty and terribly uneasy. I cursed myself for not consulting with Harry.

After walking up two flights of stairs, I searched for Professor Spang's office, noting with a jolt how almost every door was closed, every room a secret haven. When I did find the professor's door, his name shiny on a brass plate, I knocked softly. I didn't want to interrupt him. I imagined he must be in the midst of something very impor- tant—a great thought, maybe. I wondered what sorts of things Ph.D.s pondered all day, certainly not the finer points of Skinny Al's hot dogs.

"Come in," a voice said. "And shut the door behind you."

I obeyed, my throat tight. I didn't raise my eyes to the owner of that resolute voice until the room was again sealed.

"Charles Pietra, I presume?"

"Professor Spang? Pleased to make your acquaintance." I won- dered if I ought to extend my hand. But when the professor didn't lean forward, I decided against it.

"And yours, son. You know why you're here, don't you?"

"Sir, my work-study, of course."

"Yes, that is the formal reason. But what is the personal one?"

"Sir?"

"I ask all my assistants the same question: What is your specific interest in this department?"

I had no ready answer. In the final days leading up to my depar- ture for Yale, when I'd been unable to choose from a list of possible work-studies, Mother had chosen for me. She'd picked this one almost arbitrarily, saying aloud with a little laugh that yes, by golly, she wanted the word "intelligence" associated with her child. I'd gone along willingly. Then, as now, I hadn't known what I wanted to do. That is, I hadn't known how to sort through the pile of opportunities that was building around me. By plucking even one from the heap, I worried I'd start an avalanche.

"Everyone knows about this department," I said finally. "It's the jewel of the university."

The professor smiled and picked a cashew out of a bowl on his desk. I wondered if he bought my answer. Even when he nodded complacently, I wasn't sure.

"The study we're about to conduct, Charles, is an especially important one. Now, there are studies I've done through the years that I've pursued because the money was available or because I wanted to beat my colleagues to the punch or even because I couldn't think of a reason why not. But this one's a little different. This study, if performed successfully, will serve as evidence in that infernal and never-ending debate: whether we are born as we are or molded by the society in which we live."

He paused. "Since you are a Yale man, I trust I know where you stand on the matter."

Having no idea which way I ought to stand, I sat, smack into one of the darkly upholstered chairs that flanked Professor Spang's desk. Once seated, I realized that the professor was either quite short or that his chair was set low. My gaze sloped downward as I peered at him.

"Sir, I'm sure we have the same stance."

"About the heritability of intelligence? Yes, I'm sure we do. Furthermore, I'm sure you come from a long line of impressive ancestors. I'm guessing your father was a Yale man?"

I didn't even hedge. "Of course."

"Of course," he repeated. "I like when I know where a man's parents have come from. Now, Charles—you go by 'Charles,' don't you?"

"Actually, sir, I prefer 'Charlie.' "

"Good. Well now, Charlie, we speak not only of intelligence, but also of virtue and vice, enterprise and sloth, even good and evil. This study couldn't be more timely, really, considering what's going on over there in Europe. Heck, we're seeing it in this country, too."

And here was where something changed in Professor Spang—not overtly, more of a subtle switch behind the eyes. He glanced jerkily at the closed door. He seemed to be making a decision. When he continued, finally, his voice was as quietly angry as it was earnest.

"Charlie, it used to be that we could keep them at bay. They would be corralled in their neighborhoods while we enjoyed ours. But they're encroaching. I see it every day on the streets—don't you? How they use our roads, our schools, our businesses. Some have even managed to steal our women. Pity all the mixed-blood brats they've borne. And look what they've done with our money—hoarded it in piles in their basements and attics. Sewn it into their mattresses. Spent it on drink and gambling and spurious entertainment. How else can you explain what's happening to this once-fine nation? I don't buy FDR's bull crap."

Huffing slightly, Professor Spang pushed back his chair and stood up. He began to pace. His shoes were stacked with the thickest heels I'd ever seen on a man, yet they scarcely boosted him past five feet. Through the thin light of the room—and it *was* thin, with the thick burgundy curtains drawn against the gloomy sky—I saw that Professor Spang's skin was waxy, his hair sandy-sparse. His eyes were jumpy and alert, the eyes of someone expecting important news. Bad news.

"You know what I'm talking about, don't you, son?" he continued, looking at the door once more before returning to his chair. "Just between you and me, that's really what this study will address—the meek and diseased, the criminal class, the paupers and prostitutes. Not only the predators, but even more important, the *scavengers*. They're immigrants mostly, though not all. They've come here because they know they won't have to do anything for themselves. They're leeches. And this ridiculous administration gives them hand-out after handout, draining the national treasure, draining what is rightfully ours, Charlie. Yours and mine.

"Men of our ilk, we must stay together if we're to keep the little that remains. That is where the study comes in. We must do our part to support the truth."

Professor Spang was beginning to look moist. His eyes shone salamander-wet. His cheeks and forehead glistened. Moreover, he was beginning to smell moist. I breathed shallowly as the mossy odor of his ardor filled the office.

"If you don't mind my asking, sir—what is my part in the study?"

"Well, you can see I'm a busy man. I don't leave this office much. I can't. There's too much to be done: statistics to compile, charts to design, analyses to correlate. Sometimes I even sleep here. I have a roll-away in the closet." At this, he motioned to a small door built unassumingly into the dark wood paneling.

"Right now I'm knee-deep in a piece for an academic journal about earth's carrying capacity and maintenance of the human population. It will take me another month to finish. For the study, I'll need someone to work the field. Someone to go to the homes of the subjects and collect data. Mainly, you'll be asking them questions to determine their levels of intellectual proficiency. You'll administer simple tests and take note of their oral and physical responses. It won't be easy work, I can tell you. It will be distasteful. You'll see plenty of screaming children, women who would never be mistaken for ladies, drunkards, and half-wits."

"Why would such people want to help us?" I said, trying to pronounce "such people" with the proper amount of repugnance.

"Because we'll speak a language they'll understand. We'll give each family five dollars to participate. Believe you me, son, that five dollars will sell itself. Especially when these people reproduce in such numbers—like rabbits, like mice!"

I remembered suddenly the silver dollar that Mother had found at the bottom of our washtub. I'd been so grateful to have it. All that day I'd felt for it in my pocket, its smooth, hard weightiness the very essence of good fortune.

"Let me make sure I understand," I said. "I'll go into the homes of the subjects. And the results of the tests I administer will help you to determine if certain people are naturally deficient? That biology, not circumstance, is responsible for their lack?"

"Their intellectual lack, yes. And in most cases their moral and physical lack, too."

"Yes, of course," I replied, a little hotly.

Professor Spang popped another cashew into his mouth. Silently, I imagined him choking on it.

"Charles—Charlie," he said, swallowing. "You'll have to exercise caution. I'm sure you're not accustomed to this breed of people.

Some of them do their laundering, cooking, sleeping, and shitting all in the same quarters. It's quite revolting, really."

I smiled thinly. "I appreciate your concern, Professor Spang. But I'm the man for the job—I'm from a place with the same type of divide."

"Oh yes? Where's that?"

I hesitated. "Stony Creek, sir. It's near here."

"Stony Creek," he repeated with obvious pleasure. "I spent a few summers there as a youth. A delightful town. I especially enjoyed the clambakes on the beach. Oh, those clams were delicious. We ate them right out of the shell, you know. And the girls—they would dance on the beach in beautiful dresses. The most beautiful dresses. But their feet would be bare! Imagine that. Such a provincial sight, and yet charming, too."

Professor Sprang paused, basking in that old lustrous memory. He was about Mother's age, I guessed, and maybe she'd been one of those girls on the beach. He'd have watched her from afar. The tallest girl. The swan. He'd have wanted to approach her, but would have known that there are all kinds of divides.

"Well now," he continued reflectively. "I feel more comfortable knowing you were raised in such a place. The right kind of place—with the right kind of people."

"Yes," I said, straightening my back. "Doesn't that make all the difference?"

Triangles and squares. Octagons and hexagons and circles. These were the shapes that my first test-takers, Mrs. DiRisio and her daughter, looked over in the pamphlets that I distributed. There were seven persons in the family, Mrs. DiRisio was quick to indicate. But only five lived at home. Last year her two eldest sons had left to look for work out West.

"California," Mrs. DiRisio murmured with such awe and disbelief that one would have thought California was adjacent to Antarctica. I had the impression that their departure had caused a rift in the family, or at least down the middle of their mother's heart.

At first, Mrs. DiRisio had been skeptical about my presence—the sight of a slight, thin-shouldered young man on her doorstep, even though I could have been a neighbor, maybe, with my dark hair and complexion. But I wore a suit and I could have been from Yale, too. She didn't fully trust boys from Yale, that institution that was near her neighborhood, Wooster Square, but separate, too. As if Wooster Square were a moat and Yale the castle it guarded.

Nervously, I'd outlined my purpose—exactly as Professor Spang had advised.

"Say the word 'Yale' as often as you can," he'd urged. "It's a magic word. Everyone wants to go to Yale even though they despise it. They despise it because they want to go. They walk by you and me and glance through our doors and windows. Some of the subjects even work here as maids, gardeners, janitors, plumbers. But they know they'll never be on the right side of this place, and that makes them bitter. This test—this is their chance to be a part of the real Yale. The right Yale."

I followed Professor Spang's advice. I told Mrs. DiRisio how the university had organized the study. How her family had been carefully selected for its sense of civic duty and its upstanding reputation in the community. How her family's participation would help scientists to study a little-understood region of the human brain.

But why *our* brains, Mrs. DiRisio wanted to know? Surely Yale had enough of its own.

I assured her that Yale wanted participants from different regions of New Haven—a true cross-section of the population. Of course, she and her family shouldn't have to give of their time for free. Yale was offering compensation: five dollars, to be paid in full at the conclusion of the study.

Eventually, Mrs. DiRisio had given in and all orneriness and skepticism drained from her brown eyes. She'd opened the door and let me inside. But I can't say if it was because of the word "Yale," or the money, or maybe my stiff, unpolished effort, for she was a mother and I was obviously green. Maybe I even looked a little like one of her sons, maybe like one of the two who had left.

"Can I offer you something?" she asked, wiping her hands on the stained apron she wore around her waist. It was dotted with tiny blue and pink flowers, and looked homemade. "Have you had supper?"

I was warmed by her generosity. I was warmed by her humble tenement inside this humble row house. Yet almost immediately I wanted to flee, or else tell her not to believe the speech I'd just given—people like she and I were merely puppets, manipulated by the hands of wealthy men in dark, stuffy rooms. I wanted to tell her that I was more like her than she knew. I recognized the smells of her cooking. She'd made sausage and peppers. It had been one of Pa's favorite meals and we'd eaten it often, although Mother always ate her share through pursed lips. "Peasant food," she'd called it.

"No thank you, ma'am. I've already eaten."

"How about a glass of milk?"

"Well, yes. All right," I conceded.

We walked to a low-ceilinged, shabby living room, then through a narrow corridor into the kitchen, a place that would have caused Professor Spang to cringe.

Ladies' stockings lay spread to drip-dry across a radiator. Dirty pots and pans and dishes sat in a tall, precarious pile in the sink. The kitchen floor hadn't been scrubbed in some time, and the wax was yellowed and peeling in places. Still, it was apparent to me that Mrs. DiRisio wasn't lazy. It was just that she had her priorities: the collars and blouses and handkerchiefs that lay stacked on the small kitchen table. She had embroidered these herself, I could see. Skeins of jewel-colored thread, silk ribbons, and a wooden tambour sat on the table, too.

I sipped at my glass of milk and debated whether I ought to talk more of the test or ask Mrs. DiRisio about her work. She did it to earn extra money for her family—I was sure of it. But I wondered what she thought about as she strained her eyes over those delicate stitches. Perhaps she got headaches from her work, as Mother did. Perhaps her customers were wealthy women who wanted their initials embroidered on all their clothes. I wanted to ask Mrs. DiRisio if she ever thought about those women and wondered how they spent their days.

Just then a little girl scampered into the room. She was a precocious thing, all bounce and stir, as if her body would stiffen if every limb wasn't used all of the time. A mass of cinnamon-colored curls encircled her head, and freckles dotted her face like an erratic constellation. I had the urge to pinch her cheeks, which were plump as ripe fruit.

Without the least reserve, she told me her name was Cecia.

Smiling, I asked, "How old are you, Cecia? You seem very grown-up."

"Eight," she asserted quickly, as if she were asked this often.

"Have you been helping your mother today?" Hearing this question pass through my lips unsettled me somehow, but I didn't know why.

The girl shifted uncomfortably, tugging at the bottom of her blouse until it came untucked. When Mrs. DiRisio frowned at her, she froze immediately, as if this were an old annoyance.

"Ceci helps me every day," Mrs. DiRisio said. "She helps me with the embroidery; we often get two or three orders in a single day. I stay awake late, but I can't keep up with it all." She shrugged, placing her hand affectionately on her daughter's head.

"She must have a good eye for the work," I replied.

"Oh yes, Ceci's very clever."

"But doesn't she go to school?"

Mrs. DiRisio's stare became a bit cool. "No, she has to work. We all work in this family. My boys and their father at the ammunitions factory down on George Street. Do you know the one?"

"I don't."

"I didn't suppose you would."

I wasn't oblivious to her needs, and I wished I could tell her about the work I used to do with Mother. In Stony Creek I knew of many children whose parents had taken them out of school. The truancy officers turned a blind eye to their nonattendance and to child labor laws. They knew that whatever sons brought in from working at the quarry, brickyard, or wharves might prevent a foreclosure or forestall a confiscation. And whatever daughters brought in from cleaning the hotels, selling pencils, or waiting hand and foot on the Cottagers, this made a difference, too. If not for Pa's insistence on my education, and Mother's high expectations of my brother, I had little doubt that my brother and I would have worked full-time, too.

Looking at Mrs. DiRisio, I brought the glass of milk to my lips again, but realized in my nervousness I'd guzzled it all.

"Here, let me get you more," Mrs. DiRisio insisted. She was trying to be amiable—moving quickly, as if nothing mattered quite so much as refilling my glass.

"Please don't."

But again those dark eyes were upon me, appraising, undecided. "Young man, we mightn't have much, but we still know how to treat a guest."

I hesitated. "Yes, ma'am."

"You can call me Marie."

"Marie," I repeated.

"And your name?"

"It's Charlie. Charlie Pietra."

"So you *are* Italian."

She'd opened the icebox and clenched the mostly empty milk bottle. Its glass had already started to sweat.

"You were wondering?"

"I was. I don't know of many Italian boys at Yale. There aren't many that make it, I imagine."

I smiled, turning my attention back to Cecia, who had climbed into the chair beside mine and was twisting a length of cherry-colored embroidery thread around her fingers.

"Marie, would you mind if I showed your daughter some pictures? For the study."

Mrs. DiRisio handed me the glass of milk and hovered close. She wanted to see the pictures first, no doubt wondering if the stranger she'd let into her house was up to no good after all.

But they were only shapes, this much was plain. There was nothing suspicious—or, God forbid, obscene—about them. She lodged no objection. But she did wonder about one thing.

"What of the five dollars?"

"It will be paid at the conclusion of the study," I repeated.

"Yes, but when is that?"

I'd posed this same question to Professor Spang. Yet he'd skirted it so many times I'd eventually given up asking. Realizing that Marie was too shrewd for ambiguity, I opened my satchel and took out a pencil and a sheet of paper.

"I'm sorry I don't know the exact date. But just so you know I'm honest, here's my address." I slid the paper across the table. "You'll know where to find me if there's any problem, which there shouldn't be. You have my word."

Mrs. DiRisio seemed satisfied then.

I opened the pamphlet for Cecia, showing her the shapes and asking her to name them. But my questions were too easy, even for a child, and the girl quickly looked for something else to occupy her attention. As I bent close, she extended her fingers, still tangled in embroidery thread, toward my face.

"You have very long eyelashes," she observed.

I blushed, drawing back.

"Pay attention," Mrs. DiRisio admonished.

But I couldn't blame the girl for losing interest. The naming of these shapes was a ruse, nothing but a sly entry into the actual test.

"It's meant to assure the subject that he is intelligent and that he will perform well," Professor Spang had said. "But the questions that follow are the ones that actually matter. They measure critical thinking skills, which is the true litmus of intelligence."

In the professor's gloomy office I'd hesitated, pondering a question for several moments before gathering the courage to utter it.

"But sir, how will the answers to the real questions prove anything? Even if the subjects score poorly, we won't know if they scored poorly because they are naturally incapable or because they never had the opportunity to learn."

How Professor Spang had laughed, an odd, chicken-like squawk that bore no resemblance to an honest chuckle. Again I'd noticed a change in him, a frenzied churning behind the eyes. Maybe the question had sounded banal to him. Or maybe he was tired of explaining himself to naïve new assistants.

"Charlie, I've already resolved that issue. And anyway, it's no concern of yours. I have over twenty years of experience in mental hygiene and psychometric test analysis. You'll just have to trust me."

I'd wanted to press him, but held back, unsure of myself, though sure that Professor Spang's intentions were dishonorable.

Here in the DiRisios' cluttered kitchen, I tried to squelch my worries. But I was tentative, hampered by guilt. My strong suspicion was that no matter what the test's integrity, and what its results, the professor would skew the data to support his own purpose. In the short time I'd known him, I'd not only come to abhor him, but to fear his extremism. If he were to know my true story, surely he would include me in the ranks of people he considered inferior. Already, I was surprised that my being Italian didn't distress him. Perhaps the tony ring of "Stony Creek" let him overlook my ancestry. My being a girl would have been a far worse insult. Yet I think he would have been most disgusted by my association with the quarry, with common labor and dirty immigrant hands. Race poisons, he called people like me.

Briefly, I'd flirted with finding a different work-study. But when I weighed this option, the first thing that sprang to mind was what Mother would say. She would consider my abandonment of the Department of Social Demography and Intelligence a failure. She would say, as she'd said so many times before, that education and wealth breed power. And that any person with power is entitled to do exactly as he pleases, Professor Spang included.

I told myself that even if I could switch work-studies, there was no guarantee that my next supervisor would be any less zealous or strange. Out of cowardice, I decided to make the best of what I'd been handed.

"Ceci," I said, easing away from my troubled thoughts. "Let's pretend you're older. You live in a house all your own with a long staircase that leads from one floor to the next. How will you sweep all those stairs? Will you start from the bottom or the top?"

"When I'm older, I'll make sure I don't have to sweep."

I bit back a smile. "So what will you do—in all the time you're not sweeping?"

"I'll be flying."

"Flying! Like a bird?"

"No, silly, like Amelia Earhart."

At that, Cecia took a little elfin leap from her seat and disappeared into another room, emerging seconds later with a clipping from the local paper, *The New Haven Register*. She thrust it into my hands. It was an article about Amelia, including a photograph of her standing debonairly in front of the propellers of a plane. She was wearing trousers and a cropped leather jacket. Her smile was girlish, frank, exhilarated.

"Oh, you want to be an aviator."

"An *aviatrix*," she corrected.

"I don't know where this fascination comes from," Mrs. DiRisio commented. She sighed, but there was a twinkle in her eye. "Ceci loves that Amelia. She wants to be just like her—tall and skinny, with that funny haircut. She wants to wear her ridiculous flying clothes, too—the cap and goggles, the whole kit and caboodle. I've told her, 'You're being silly.' But she says, 'Momma, you don't understand. *Every* girl wants to be like Amelia. Every girl wants to join the Ninety-Nines.' "

"The Ninety-Nines?"

"Don't you know it?" Ceci piped. "It's a club for female flyers. No boys allowed."

"Is that why you want to join? Because there won't be any boys?"

Ceci considered this question for several seconds before shaking her head. "It's because I want to fly—that's the only reason." She stood up on her chair and stretched out her arms. "I'm going to fly everywhere. Even places Amelia hasn't been."

Mrs. DiRisio grabbed Ceci's ankle so tightly the girl climbed down at once, her cheeks flushed with more excitement than embarrassment.

"To be an aviatrix—that's a dangerous job," I told her.

Ceci nodded gravely. "Yes, but I can do it. Why not?"

"There is a silver lining to this obsession of hers," Mrs. DiRisio revealed, having begun to embroider a handkerchief. Her hand was so practiced, she scarcely needed to see where the stitches landed. "I tell her that to fly her airplane, Amelia Earhart has to sit in a tiny seat for hours at a time—no food, no water, no nothing. And Ceci, she practices. She sits here in her chair embroidering for five hours in a row. She'll say, 'Momma, I can move my hands all I want because that's what Amelia has to do—keep her hands on the controls so that the plane stays up.' "

I couldn't envision Cecia keeping still for five minutes, let alone five hours. Yet I was fascinated that a girl so young could have dreams so grand. As a child in Stony Creek, I'd had my dreams, too. Mainly they had involved the seabirds: terns, gulls, and sandpipers looping and ripping swiftly through the sky. Any obstacle could be circumnavigated. Even a storm could be dodged with the right speed and loft. Yet even when I was no taller than a doorknob, I'd realized that wanting to be a seabird was a mere fancy, a naïve delight with all the heft of a light morning dew. Nevertheless, Ceci had taken the essence of my dream and made it viable. For if Amelia could fly—all the way across the Atlantic, just like Charles Lindbergh—why couldn't she?

Minutes went by and still I didn't resume the test. I was too busy imagining an older version of Ceci: tall and lean, but still freckled of face. She was standing beside her own gleaming silver plane. The engine whirred and she gazed down a landing strip, eyes veering into the sky. Eventually, Mrs. DiRisio asked me why I was so quiet. Was I getting hungry?

"Yes," I told her. "Maybe I am a little."

After that first visit, I met three dozen more families. I visited four colored families in Ward 19—the Dixwell district. I traveled to Fair Haven, a peninsula of New Haven that was home to hundreds of new immigrants: Russians, Germans, Poles, and the Irish. Here, the neighborhoods were cramped and rough. The men in these parts worked in factories, on the railroad, and even in a small trap rock quarry. Some worked as oystermen, shucking shells in briny work-rooms or repairing boats in wharf-side sheds. I spent most of my time with women and young children. Older, able-bodied men were already at work by the time I arrived. Either that, or they'd left Fair Haven for good.

The people I met told me stories about their pasts: families they'd left, adventures they'd embarked upon. They showed me prize possessions: an appliqué box, a jade rosary, a cameo made of shell, a hairbrush with a carved silver handle. They didn't apologize for their ramshackle homes, although I knew they were ill at ease around me. I could tell by the way they stared at my suit. They didn't know that I'd used pins to hem my trousers, or that I could wiggle my fingers through the holes in my pockets.

Of all the families Professor Spang had assigned, it was the first family—the DiRisios—that I visited most often. I'd taken a shine to them. Maybe it was because they were Italian and I saw a bit of Pa in the tarnished good looks of Angelo, Marie's husband. Maybe it was the shiny-brash Ceci, who had wheedled her way into my thoughts. Or maybe I liked the DiRisios simply because they were familiar. From the chipped dishes in the cupboard to the photograph of Marie's father on the mantel, I'd known this family even before we'd met.

Professor Spang later told me that five visits to each family would be sufficient. In that time I should be able to administer the test to everyone and write down my findings. But I'd called on the DiRisios five times in the first two weeks alone, and still I went back.

"I've been thinking about something," Mrs. DiRisio said to me one day over cups of black coffee. "Sometimes I talk to the Holy Virgin about it. Maybe it's blasphemous for me to say, but I consider Mary a friend. She was just a woman herself. She must understand."

"Understand what?"

"The things women want. What they hope for. I wanted to ask you, Charles. I know you're busy, but maybe you can use what you know to teach my boys? They were never in school very long."

She hesitated, peering into her steaming cup. "I just want them to know a little, so they can pick up a newspaper and not be ashamed." She fished in her pocket for something: a ten-dollar bill. "I don't know how much it would pay for—how many lessons, I mean."

She thrust the bill at me, but I shirked.

She sucked in her breath. "It's not enough."

"It's . . . it's plenty. But I don't want it."

Mrs. DiRisio's eyes, which shifted so effortlessly, went hard. I'd offended her sensibility again. "This family is not a charitable cause, Charles."

I bit at my lips, which were terribly chapped. Taking Mother's advice, I no longer smeared them in beeswax as I had in Stony Creek.

"Of course not. I don't want you to pay because, well, because we're friends now."

"It's because you pity me."

"No! You've given me so much. I want to return your kindness."

"And just what have I given you? Nothing—a few dinners."

"You've invited me into your home. You've made me feel welcome." Marie blushed. "It wouldn't be right."

"I do have one condition," I said slowly. "If I teach your sons to read, I'll want to teach Ceci, too."

"Ceci?"

It was my turn to stare into my cup of coffee. Neither of us had taken a single sip. "Marie, why shouldn't Ceci be able to read a newspaper, too?"

"Well, I never thought of it."

I tried a different tactic. "What if she becomes an aviatrix? She'll need to know how to read guides, maps, manuals . . ."

At that, Mrs. DiRisio let out a stifled little laugh. "She's a child! What do children know? When I was young I wanted to be a princess. Now I embroider handkerchiefs so that rich ladies can blow their noses into them."

"But it doesn't have to be like that for your daughter. You said it yourself—she's a clever girl."

"Ceci will continue to work, as I did. And when she's older, she'll marry."

"Of course."

"You say that like it's a crime."

"All I'm suggesting is that if we all followed tradition, nothing would ever change."

"And why should it?"

Swallowing my fear, I met her gaze. I wondered if she would understand things from Mother's perspective.

"Ceci could be the one whose photograph is in the newspapers, the one other girls want to emulate."

"Ah, but then she'd have to leave me."

At that moment I realized Marie and Mother had little in common. The eyes that shone at mine from across the table—they were hiding something soft and newly bruised, a wound that might yet heal clean. Mother's hid the most stubborn of scars.

"She wouldn't leave you, Marie. Not truly."

"Oh yes? And how do you know?"

I shrugged. I wished I could tell her about Pa, about how I'd found him again in a place I never would have anticipated. Instead I said nothing. I watched as Ceci blew into the room like a tempest. It was possible she'd heard everything, or nothing at all.

"Charles has decided that you ought to learn how to read," Marie said, her voice inscrutably monotone.

The little girl scowled. "Why should I?"

"Amelia knows how to read," I said.

"She does?"

"Of course. She's even written a book of her own. I saw it in the Yale library."

"What's its name?

"The Fun of It."

"The Fun of It," Ceci repeated, savoring the words. "Can I see it?"

"I'll get it for you and bring it here in a day or two. But you have to promise me you'll learn to read it."

Mrs. DiRisio had given up on her coffee. She stood and emptied the black liquid into the sink. With her back turned, she looked smaller and older, her back beginning to curve like a sickle. White tendrils streaked her hair, which was knotted back in a loose bun.

"Just don't forget my boys," I heard her mutter.

Harry and I had decided to eat more.

"Dense foods," Harry advised. "My dad says we should eat dense foods—like bananas. You can gain a pound a day if you eat enough bananas."

With this in mind, the two of us snatched fruit from the heaping baskets in Commons and stowed them in our pockets and satchels. We ate so many bananas that the smell of them started to make me nauseous.

"It's all right for freshmen to be small," Harry said. "But no one wants to be a small *sophomore.*"

We'd been in corrective exercise classes for weeks now, the both of us having been deemed physiologically underdeveloped. Harry's skinny legs had been cited. That, and the way he was always shaky and hunched. I heard the assistants wonder aloud, was it a problem of nerves?

I'd been harder to diagnose. Coach Roota liked my athleticism and dogged perseverance. But there was no getting around my size, how my shoulders and waist were woefully, rather effeminately, narrow. Then there was my voice—so high and weak, as if I hadn't even reached puberty.

Even so, I had potential, the coach had told me. Maybe I could even be a coxswain.

"What's a coxswain?" I asked Harry.

"It's the man on the crew team who shouts commands. The leader of the boat."

"Would I get to row?"

And though Harry was as rawboned as I, he looked at me tough-eyed and winced. "Heck no, Pietra."

By now Coach Roota had reviewed the letter from Doc Benson. One day he had taken me aside, his meaty hand like an anvil on my shoulder.

"I had a cousin that was burned, too," he'd whispered. His eyes conveyed tact, though his voice was still loud enough for anyone to hear. "It happened when we were kids. We'd gone camping. The canvas of our tent was waxed with paraffin to keep out the rain. We lit a candle inside, but we fell asleep and never blew it out."

He'd paused, reflecting. The memory still rattled him, and I'd wondered how he'd managed to escape as those licks of fire had grown higher.

"Where were you hurt worst?" he'd asked.

"I couldn't say. It's bad everywhere."

"Dr. Henrickson would like to have a look at you, even though your mother is against it. Maybe you don't feel right, but he's looked at a lot of unusual cases. There's nothing he hasn't seen."

By then some of the boys had started to glance in our direction, eyes alight with curiosity.

"I've been to more doctors than I can count," I'd told him. "And none of them could do a single thing. This thing I've got—this ailment—it's permanent."

"Don't be so hasty. Dr. Henrickson has more . . ."

"Sorry, Coach," I'd interrupted, but of course I hadn't been sorry at all.

Now that the orthopedic exams were over and Dr. Henrickson had skulked back to whatever cave he'd come from, I had less to worry about. Harry and I were placed in the same case group. Some of us were thin, others chubby and waddling, but we were all runts of the litter, and it was easy to see why we'd been lumped together.

We assembled in the gymnasium three days a week to improve our deficiencies. We were in the charge of Donald Allen, the same coaching assistant who had noticed me on the rooftop track. Donald put us on stationary bicycles and told us to ride in imaginary races. He made us do handstands against a wall as he counted to ten, playfully drawing out the nine as blood rushed in dizzying waves to our heads. He had us rolling medicine balls and huffing and puffing our way through calisthenics. Finally, he baited us with comments that were meant to be encouraging.

"Pull harder," he cried, his voice rising. "Faster. You can do it, chief! Let's get those legs good and strong. Are you a man or a mouse?"

"All he wants, deep down, is to put us on a stretching rack," Harry whispered.

Though I attended every exercise session, I didn't notice much improvement. I was fast—fast as before—but I hadn't put on much weight. Not even the bananas seemed to be helping. At night in my room I ran my hands along my torso, my arms, my legs, feeling the thin layer of muscle that lay over my bones.

Fortunately, despite a want of evidence, Donald was convinced I had made progress. "Your deficiencies aren't as obvious, especially in your lower body. See the improved muscle mass in your calves?" he asked one day. "I'd wager you're almost through with Corrective Exercises."

He'd uttered this in front of Harry and I could sense my friend's heart sinking, maybe all the way down to his rickety legs. A couple of weeks later, Donald invited me into one of Coach Roota's offices, a windowless room that smelled as acerbic as the rest of Payne Whitney.

"My hunch was right. Coach thinks you've come a long way and that your prognosis is good," he said. "Let's talk about what sport you'd like to join. Coach is optimistic, like I said, but still he has placed restrictions on what you can do."

"What kind of restrictions?"

"They have to do with, uh, your abnormalities." Donald nodded sympathetically to show me that he knew about the accident. Perhaps he'd watched me practice and wondered about my burns, all those scars knotty and raised, some still pink-painful. I wondered how many hands Doc Benson's letter had passed through.

"Mainly you need to stay covered up, right?" he asked. "There aren't many sports with head-to-toe uniforms. The most suitable for you, to my knowledge, is fencing."

But wasn't fencing an anachronism? When I heard the word, my mind conjured long-dead knights, maidens in castles. Thinking back to when Harry and I had first looked at the gymnasium directory, I remembered how the seventh-floor salon had caught my eye. One day I'd even made my way there. From atop a balcony, I'd peered into the large practice space. It had enormous mirrors on one wall and floor-to-ceiling windows on another. White masks with mesh fronts hung on wall pegs. In a corner, a battered jousting board looked as if it had endured years of torture.

I'd sat on a wooden folding chair next to a hill of jumbled athletic shoes. I'd watched fencers in identical white uniforms trickle into the room, playfully lunging and jousting, until the coach stilled them with a single word, foreign and indiscernible. He'd ordered them into pairs. And then—what magic—they had danced up and down the long strips adhered to the floor, swords raised in perfect synchronicity.

Donald leaned forward in his chair. "So what do you think?"

"Do fencers always wear so many clothes?"

"You betcha. Breeches, jackets, gloves, masks, plastrons, knee-length socks—the whole shebang. They're covered, all right."

"Sounds like something."

"But don't be fooled," Donald hastened. "With all that gear you'll still feel the blade."

"That doesn't matter to me."

"At least think it over. Consider your condition. Coach said the fire left you—delicate."

If Donald could see my body, "delicate" was probably not the first word that would jump to mind. But it didn't matter. Already I was fixated on those fencers, how there was no telling one from the other. Facing each other on the wide floor strips, the dark grills of their helmets as concealing as domino masks, they could have come off an assembly line—all the same make and model. There was no way to tell what they looked like underneath. And even if there was, swords barred the truth.

Back in the locker room, I hadn't counted on seeing Harry. But there he was—changed, but not showered. His hair was still damp with perspiration and he gave off a faintly fermented odor. I smiled at him guiltily, not knowing what to say. After some awkwardness, I muttered that I was going to my locker.

"I'll wait for you here," he called as I rounded a corner.

"No, I'll meet you back."

"It's no trouble."

"All right," I replied, wishing he would just go. "See you in a minute."

By then the locker room was mostly empty and I didn't hesitate before proceeding toward the closet. In the darkness I changed as fast as my hands would allow, my heart loud and heedless. This ritual—the fumbling, the clumsy fastening of buttons, the brilliant flash of fear—never got any easier.

When I returned to Harry I could see he had something to say; the passion of his thoughts seemed to beam straight through his translucent skin. Trying to avoid a scene, I spoke first.

"Listen, Harry, you'll escape Donald soon enough. He's an odd duck, but he has to come to his senses eventually. I swear it."

Harry shook his head. "You've got it all wrong. It's you I'm worried about, Pietra. Don't you understand? You're still vulnerable. It's obvious—at least to me."

At that pronouncement my heart just about gave out, a glutted and purple-swollen timepiece run out of ticks. I looked balefully at Harry, hoping to see what he knew without letting on that I had anything to hide.

"You're scared," he continued. "Scared to change out in the open because you don't want them to see you. I can sympathize."

He paused, pushing his spectacles up the bridge of his nose. He had taken a step forward, and I a step back, so that the small of my back pressed against the cold metal lockers.

"I know just how you feel."

"You do?"

"Yes. See, they caught me one day, too," he said, chin trembling, though his voice remained steady. "I was fourteen. It happened in school, in the locker room. They pulled me into a wet shower stall after practice. They came up from behind—taunting me, see?—four or five of them, and they were big guys, too. They took all my clothes and started tossing them around. I tried to get them back, but I've never been fast, like I told you, and I couldn't help it, Pietra, I started crying, like a baby, and the more I cried the more they jeered. Then one of them, this big ugly ape, he grabbed me by the shoulders and pinned me down. I cracked my head so hard on the floor I went out for a few seconds."

"Harry," I murmured, my body starting to rock against my will. Watching him struggle, I felt my lungs deflate.

"I thought that would be the end of it. But then another fellow— he spit on me. And the others, they thought it was really funny, the most hilarious thing they'd ever seen, morons; and they started, too. The bastard that had been holding me, he let go. But I couldn't move. It was as if . . . as if I was looking at myself from some faraway place. Only, the person I was seeing wasn't really me. He was just this pathetic, crippled creature and I wanted nothing to do with him. I didn't pity him, either, not even when they pulled down their pants and started pissing. Clean into my face, Pietra. Clean into my goddamn face."

Harry paused. He didn't look at me, but kept his eyes askance. I inhaled sharply, feeling like I hadn't breathed for hours. The air tasted toxic. I wanted to touch my friend, to reassure him somehow, but he looked like he wanted to be left alone.

"I missed a whole month of school after that. I fell behind in all my classes. My mother took me to a psychiatrist because I stopped eating. I don't know—I just wasn't hungry. I didn't have any interest in anything except getting out of that school, coming here, I suppose. But I never said who those guys were or what they did."

Harry's eyes, peppered with malice, turned to me then.

"I used to think it was because I'm Jewish, see, but now I think they just needed an excuse, any old excuse. Easier to pick on the shrimp, right? They called me 'runt,' 'ant,' silly childish names. And what does it matter really, because it's all over now. Right, Pietra? What's the use of trying to come up with an explanation? I'm a New Haven man now, and what the hell have those goons done to put themselves right? Nothing, I can bet you. Nothing at all."

I accompanied Harry back to his room in Durfee. We were quiet on the walk home. I thought I'd stay to keep him company, but he insisted on being alone. Maybe he was embarrassed that he'd told me so intimate a secret; maybe he now wondered if he'd made the right choice.

"I have to get through all of *Hamlet* tonight," he said, insinuating that I should go. When I lingered in the doorway, he added, "I'll be all right. I swear. Shoo already, will you? And stop giving me that pitying look."

"It's not pitying, stupid."

"Fine, compassionate, empathetic—whatever it is, I don't want to see it. No offense, Pietra."

"All right, you know where to find me."

"Yep."

So I left Harry's suite and walked toward my own. I had two classes that afternoon, yet I hoped to squeeze in a catnap. Harry's revelation had left me spent.

Approaching my room, I noticed that the door was ajar. How strange, for I always double-checked the lock. Inside, I found Wick and Phin.

"Hope you don't mind," Wick said with a wink. "The door was open."

Had it been? I wondered. The smile on my lips was tight as the fists I kept clenched at my sides.

"We were looking for a deck of cards," Wick continued. "Phin tossed his into the fireplace after I beat him at twenty-one the other night—the scamp. Have you got one, Charlie?"

I knew I didn't. But to appease my friend I grunted a "maybe," opened the door to my closet, and rummaged halfheartedly. With my back turned, I didn't notice Phin—how he silently opened the drawers of my desk, even the bottom drawer. It wasn't until I heard a playful whistle that I realized his discovery.

"Have mercy!" Phin exclaimed.

He was dangling something from his fingers: my girl's clothes—the ones I'd meant to stash somewhere else. I cursed myself for my stupidity. Mother had warned me a dozen times not to be careless.

"Give me those!" I blurted, managing to snatch only the skirt and blouse. My chemise and bloomers, crumpled from lying so long in the drawer, fell with a faint rustle to the floor. For an excruciatingly long moment, no one said a word. Then Wick smiled wide and patted me on the back.

"I always knew you were a Casanova, Charlie. Who was the girl? Has she got a friend? How on earth did you smuggle her in?"

"Yeah, Charlie? Who was she?" Phin urged. He watched me intently, without any of Wick's amiability.

"A gentleman never tells." I picked up the clothes from the ground, hoping they wouldn't notice how my hands had turned from fists into gelatin.

"Oh, you can tell us."

Though I looked pleadingly at Wick, he offered me no relief. "Sure you can, Charlie. We're your best chums, right? Who else in the world would you tell?"

At that, Wick flopped onto my bed, his legs so long that his feet dangled over the edge. He lit a cigarette and took a ruminative drag.

"Don't leave out the details, either," he added. "Like how she got out of here naked. That I really have to know. In fact, maybe I should take notes. This is definitely more important than my trigonometry test tomorrow."

"It was nothing. There's nothing to tell."

"Nothing! Girls' clothes in your drawer is not nothing. In fact, I'd say it's quite certainly and most decidedly *something*."

Pa had told me once that the best way to get out of a scrape is to let it heal. Right then I thought his suggestion was worth a try.

"Look, fellas, I've got to get some rest. I'm dog-tired."

"Sleepless night?" Wick teased.

"Not one wink, as you can imagine. So if you don't mind, you can take your card hunt elsewhere."

"But what about the story?" Phin asked. "We've got to hear it."

"I'll tell you later," I said, pushing aside Wick's legs so that I could sit on the bed. "Promise—some other time."

"When?" Phin pressed.

I picked at an invisible thread on my shirt. I even had the nerve to yawn. "Whenever you want. Just not now."

Wick stared at me a while longer, trying to coax me into saying more, anything, with those damn seductive eyes. But when I didn't give an inch, he rose. The cigarette was limp between his lips. He stretched his arms languorously and nodded toward Phin that they should leave.

"A man of mystery—I respect that," he said, plucking the cigarette from his mouth and gazing down at me like I was some star that had fallen from the sky and still smoldered with dazzling stubbornness on the ground.

WINTER

Chapter Seven

B LUSTERY WEATHER arrived, and with it a flurry of letters from
Mother. In my notes to her, I'd inquired about the Christmas
holiday and whether we would see each other. She wrote that she'd
love to have me home, but couldn't take the risk. She feared that by
now I would act as much like a boy as I resembled one. Miss Prowl
would notice. Lately, our landlady had been knocking on Mother's
door constantly. She came for a cup of sugar, a smidgen of butter, any
excuse for her to step inside the apartment and have a look around.

"She knows something's amiss, Adele," Mother conceded. "I fear
she's looking for clues. Fortunately, I always tear up your letters. I
hope you're remembering to do the same."

Mother revealed that Stony Creek had changed noticeably in my
absence. Work had slowed over at the quarry. Several snow showers
and hailstorms had halted the blasting and cutting. Discouraged, the
men went early to the saloons and left late. They complained about
money, spent what little they had on ale, and wondered how much
longer they'd be able to keep their jobs.

The quarrywomen, they were rationing. They counted the cans in
their pantries and larders. They diluted jars of honey with warm
water and hid the last of their preserves for truly dire days. Their children, Mother wrote, had learned not to complain when they were
served the same mealy stew five days in a row.

Mother said little about our own finances, and I didn't ask. Deep
down, maybe I didn't want to know.

Most of Mother's letters were similar, filled with questions about my classes and work-study—Had I decided what major I would be pursuing, she wanted to know, underlining the question. But one letter stood out. It was short, direct, and wrenching. At least, I thought, she hadn't tried to couch the news with trivialities.

Precious Adele,

A most unexpected thing has happened. You would never guess! Alfred and Joanna have written to me. Somehow they have learned of your father and brother's deaths. I don't know when or how they came upon the news. Nor do I know what their intention was in sending me a letter. Perhaps I oughtn't be so surprised, but somehow I thought even this most critical news would never reach them. After all this time I can scarcely make sense of my parents' intentions and I am wary of this attempt at contact. I have not yet decided if I will respond to their inquiry. Yet I have to admit I am a little touched.

Remain vigilant, dearest. I will do the same.

Always and ever,
Mother

I remembered how, years ago, Mother had craved Pa's attention above everything else. She was an only child, and as a girl had been doted on by her parents, and later by her many chums and admirers. She was used to the spotlight. Once her life began to revolve around her husband, she made every effort to beguile him: cooking his favorite foods from recipes handed down from his mother, insisting he take her on long twilight walks, grabbing his limp hand in her own whenever she could. Before Pa arrived home from the quarry, she would wash her underarms and change into a freshly ironed frock. She would perfume her skin and dust her long neck with lavender powder. I'd sit on her bed and watch her pinch her cheeks until they bloomed.

"I have to look beautiful," she'd say needlessly. I'd seen men stop dead in their tracks to stare, enchantment overpowering propriety. Mother would lift her chin, never looking crosswise.

As she waited for Pa, her face would gleam with hopefulness. Maybe this evening he wouldn't be so tired. He'd look at her anew— no, not anew, but the very way he'd looked at her long ago, back when they'd met. He'd notice how she'd styled her hair differently, how her legs were still lithe as a girl's, and he'd remember again just why he'd been so hungry to have her.

Yet invariably Pa would come home tired, settle in his slouched chair, and close his eyes. He didn't want to sleep, just to rest. But that would also mean he didn't want to be disturbed, at least not by Mother. Not even a waft of her powder or the aroma of his favorite dinner could rouse him. If he spoke at all, it was to talk to me—about what was happening in whichever book I was reading, or how my day at school had been.

Pa and I could communicate so effortlessly, sometimes I felt we had our own secret language, comprised as much by silence and gestures as by speech. I used to wonder if I reminded him of Mother when she was young, if I had inherited a shred of her charm and allure. I did not flatter myself that I did. More likely Pa bestowed attention on me because I reminded him of his own kin: solitary and obstinate, noticeably nonconformist in a town used to a careful social order. To Pa, I probably felt more like family than anyone else.

Still, our closeness came at the exclusion of Mother. She let her dissatisfaction be known by criticizing me for my laziness. When I was with Pa, more than anytime else, she berated me for forgetting to stir the pot of sauce, or for leaving so many crumbs on the table. She criticized the way I looked, how wild and snarled my hair had gotten, or how suntanned my face. My father would snap at her, "For the love of God, leave her be." But in so doing, he crossed that most objectionable of boundaries: siding with daughter instead of wife.

Guiltily, I acknowledged that Pa was worse than the men who spent their nights in the saloon. His vice was more destructive than bottle or mistress or cards. Mother might have succeeded in fighting a more commonplace foe, but she stood not a chance against her own child. The greater the magnetism between Pa and me, the equal the expulsion between he and Mother, and Mother and me. Consequences also came of the partnership between Charles and Mother. Every pull came with a push. From childhood I'd intuited this, yet I knew of no way to stop it.

Despite the tension between us, I admired Mother for her sense of duty. Hers was a constant, if embattled, devotion: caring for Pa as his lungs wore down, making sure Charles had every chance to escape the quarry, maintaining our fragile hold in Miss Prowl's house. With her looks and pedigree, there was always the chance that she could become a Cottager again. Once she put her mind to something, she almost always succeeded. Yet when she talked of a better future, her vision included all of us.

I couldn't deny that Mother was loyal. As to whether Pa was as committed, I didn't know. As to whether he would have chosen a different life if offered the chance, I feared to speculate.

Ceci and I had finished *The Fun of It* and were now on to Amelia's second book: *20 Hrs., 40 Min.,* the aviatrix's personal account of her flight over the Atlantic.

Ceci lapped up the pages hungrily. Wearing a leather flying helmet trimmed with rabbit fur, which her mother had no doubt sewn, she ran her finger along the lines as we read them, stopping me sometimes so she could sound out a word.

She was learning quickly, as quickly as her brothers Carlo and Freddie, whom I taught several nights a week. Together we convened around the DiRisios' crowded kitchen table, snacking on fried eggplant, minestrone, and chicken cutlets smothered in mozzarella cheese and marinara sauce. Now that I'd turned down Marie's payment, she had decided to barter with food. Even though the family made a paltry income, Marie was a shrewd shopper—able to coax vendors into selling her cheese and fresh fish for half the price, knowing which bakers gave out the last of their bread for pennies or even for free at the end of the day. She also knew the names of the local pawnshop keepers by heart. Sometimes her customers would pass on bits and baubles that they no longer wanted: a bent brass candle-holder, an earring that had lost its twin, a chipped figurine from a menagerie. Marie, being so affable, would accept these tokens with frothy gratitude, proclaiming how beautiful they were and how much she would cherish them. Then she would go directly to one of her preferred pawnshop keepers and shrewdly broker a deal for each. Almost all her profits went to foodstuffs. "Bad times or no, my people will eat well," she was fond of saying.

Sometimes, at our lessons, other eager pupils arrived: cousins, neighbors, friends, and not a few boys of questionable relation.

"I hope you don't mind," Mrs. DiRisio would say. "Word has got-ten out how good you are. People keep stopping by to ask if you'll teach their boys."

"The more the merrier," I assured her.

Angelo also took a seat around the table. A gentle-mannered man, Marie's husband was shy about participating, scratching his head and begging off whenever I asked him to read. Still, he seldom missed a lesson, listening raptly as I explained how to diagram a sentence.

Inspired by the curiosity of my pupils, I created lesson plans, sometimes weeks in advance. Once everyone around the table had mastered the alphabet, they memorized word lists and practiced penmanship and pronunciation. They learned to decipher a noun from a pronoun, a subject from a predicate. To keep the lessons lively, we read adventure stories from the library. We enacted plays from simple dialogues we wrote ourselves. We rummaged for newspapers and read them cover to cover. One day I assigned a one-page essay. The boys had to write about where they'd like to travel; Ceci, about the first place she'd fly.

The little girl told me she'd rather learn how to write a letter. "So I can answer my fans once they start sending me mail."

"Yes," I agreed, managing not to grin, "that makes sense."

It's true I hadn't anticipated how much time teaching would take. And it's also true I occasionally neglected my own studies as a result. I even skipped classes sometimes, Harry later chastising me with a waggle of the finger and a lash of the tongue.

"Did you sleep the day away, Pietra? Where on earth were you?"

The only class I never dared to miss was The Foundations of Biology, and only because there was a small part of me that still feared Phin.

Still, my grades didn't suffer. Midterm examinations came swiftly and passed with equal alacrity. I scored well enough to list the results in a letter to Mother. I told her, truthfully, that I appreciated every opportunity this experience afforded me. I continued to marvel at the number of books in Sterling, and I still pinched myself when I realized I had access to every one of them. Often, in the Stacks, I'd read aloud, softly, hoping that somewhere Pa could hear me. Whereas I'd chosen my reading randomly before, now I started to dig deeper into topics that I studied in my classes, often reading beyond the texts my professors assigned.

I realized that I enjoyed writing, too. When I took pen to paper to write an essay, thoughts that were once disparate and amorphous coalesced with stimulating rigor. Though the subjects I studied were wildly divergent, common themes emerged, and I had the sense that the world was both more intimately interconnected and spectacularly vast than I'd previously imagined. What freedom there was in having the time and the means to think without boundary. I hadn't known how high one could climb by piling ideas one on top of the next.

Despite these dizzying pleasures, though, I was much the same person I'd been in Stony Creek: flighty and prone to daydreaming. At night my thoughts still drifted, sometimes to Ceci or to Wick, sometimes all the way to the quarry path, or the beach, or the shallows where eels squiggled uneasily under Old Man Richter's watch. At times I even let myself sink under salty sprays and cold-rippled currents, all the way down to that retched skyhook, now barnacled and orange-rusted, just another old forgotten thing.

*   *   *

It was one of those rare winter days when the sun was so hot it could make the skin burn, when people left their overcoats and muffs and gloves inside even though the ground was coated in snow and icicles dripped impatiently from the rooftops, some crashing to the ground with heart-stopping aplomb, like daggers thrown from God's own hand.

I'd come to the DiRisios' tenement because Ceci had begged me. We were almost through with *20 Hrs., 40 Min.*, and the little girl couldn't wait until evening to read the last chapter.

Indoors she grew impatient and sulky as we leaned over the book. Her attention alternated between Amelia and the rays of sun beaming through the grimy windowpanes in the kitchen.

"Please, Charlie, let's go outside to read—our secret."

"I'm not going to be your coconspirator. You'll have to ask your mother first."

And surprisingly, perhaps because the bright sun was affecting us all, Mrs. DiRisio agreed.

Ceci put on her boots, her coat, and her omnipresent skullcap. She rushed through the rooms, grabbing my hand as she barreled past. "Come on! Before she changes her mind."

Outside, we walked several blocks simply because our antsy legs propelled us so. Eventually we realized we'd need a suitable place to read and returned to the stoop leading into Ceci's own house. Though the steps had been shoveled, we giggled about our cold backsides. I asked Ceci what we would do if the temperature suddenly plummeted. What if we froze right here, exactly as we were, for all of time? She stared at me solemnly before letting loose a wild, delighted squeal.

I don't know how long we read before the man appeared. From a distance he looked unassuming rather than alarming—just another fellow from the neighborhood making his way. It was Ceci who couldn't stop staring.

"Doesn't he look swish!" she declared, and her eyes must have been sharper than mine. It was only when he was very close that I saw how regal his clothing was: the gleam of a gold pin stuck through his lapel, the way his boots glistened shiny-clean despite the slush.

It was only when the man paused in front of the stoop to gaze at us that I realized he was President Angell.

I told myself I had nothing to fear. He probably wouldn't recognize me—wouldn't even know I was from Yale. And even if he did, I wasn't doing anything wrong. Why, at that moment I wasn't even playing hooky! I was antsy, then, when he insisted on staring at Ceci and me as if he'd never seen anything quite like us before. His bespectacled eyes affixed to our faces until I felt I had to say something, anything, to break the moment into smaller, more manageable pieces.

"How are you, sir? Strange weather we're having, isn't it?"

President Angell continued to stare, squinting through the sunlight at the book, and back at Ceci and me.

"It is," he said at last, looking as if he wanted to add something more.

My own mouth was slack and half-open, an idiot's mouth, ready to fill the air with empty words at the nearest opportunity. That opportunity wouldn't arise, though, for President Angell bowed suddenly and turned away, one glance back to make sure we weren't an illusion.

Ceci and I watched him as he continued in his elegant way down the street.

"Who was that?" she clamored.

"The president."

She seemed to weigh something in her mind, her rumination culminating in a doubtful expression. "But my father says Mr. Roosevelt uses a wheelchair."

"Ceci, that man was the president of *Yale.*"

"Oh. Is he as important as Mr. Roosevelt?"

"Not quite."

"But almost?" she insisted, hopeful that something tremendous had just happened. I didn't want to let her down.

"Maybe to some people," I replied.

On a frosty Thursday evening, Wick rapped on my door. With neither Harry nor Phin anywhere in sight, he asked me if I wanted to go out for a nightcap.

"I can't do another trigonometry problem or my brain will explode," he joked, clutching his head as if a detonation were imminent. Of course I said yes, grabbing my coat, looking briefly for my gloves but too distracted to see that they were right in front of me, lying on my bed, until Wick laughingly showed me. We hurried to the pub, a place called the Last Anchor. It wasn't a traditional Yale haunt, being a full mile from campus, but Wick said it was worth the trek.

"There are always characters there, Charlie. People you wouldn't *believe.*"

He walked close to me, the sleeves of our woolen coats brushing, but that was just his habit. I'd noticed that he walked this way with everyone, intimately, as if in collusion. The streetlights turned the banks of snow into lemon ice. The air was raw and sharp. When Wick asked me why I was shivering, I was glad to have an excuse.

The walk away from Yale and into hitherto unknown reaches of New Haven opened my eyes to something I hadn't seen before: a seedy, unsavory quality to the town. The places I visited for Professor Spang were not nearly as forsaken as what I saw now. The winds blew crosswise and I recognized sensations I'd felt only while observing the men around Stony Creek late at night: a shiver in the stomach, a ringing in the ears, a hot slick dart of energy all the way to my groin. We saw assorted watering holes and cheap-looking restaurants and stores that were either boarded up or chained down for the night. Women in cheap, tight dresses lounged against doorways or hung out open windows, swaths of skin exposed despite the cold. One or two of them stared at me encouragingly as I walked past, and I nearly forgot they saw me as something other than a wide-eyed girl.

Here and there we walked past signs advertising dance halls and cabarets and vaudeville, but Wick said in this part of town most of the shows offered a unique brand of entertainment. "If you get my meaning, Charlie."

Men entered these places with hats pulled low and coat sashes drawn tight. In the morning I imagined these men would shave their stubbly faces and rinse sour night tastes out of their mouths. But right now, nothing seemed regretful. Nothing seemed out of bounds.

Wick and I watched as one fellow contemplated a particularly run-down establishment. On his arm drooped a tired-looking blonde, the roots of her hair dingy-dark. She resisted his tug with playful vehemence until he whispered something in her ear. She laughed, acquiescing, and accompanied him inside.

"Have you ever been in such a place?" I asked.

"Sure. Haven't you?"

I shrugged, wanting to believe that he'd never expose himself to any sort of debauchery, that he wouldn't want to. But I knew otherwise. Sometimes after class he'd flourish a magazine he had curled up in his back pocket, and Phin and Harry would gather 'round. Those magazines were full of naked girls, their bodies curvy as violins. Every time I saw them, the pictures left me with a sting of inadequacy.

The Last Anchor turned out to be a dive. The layout was cramped and awkward, tables and unmatched chairs jumbled alongside a long bar overcrowded with bottles, the pressed tin ceiling only two feet from the top of Wick's head. The interior was warm thanks to a crackling fire, but the air was stuffy, as if the room hadn't been aired in years. The floorboards were warped, some raised a whole inch above the others, so that regular customers—even the worst drunkards—had learned to step gingerly. At the back were dark booths built right into the wall. Wick and I settled into one. I watched him run his fingertips over the tabletop, decoding the names whittled into the old wood.

Wick said he'd carve his, too, if we drank enough. "Just you wait, Charlie. The more soused I get, the more I'll babble on about how I want to make some mark on this world. But since I'm just a lazy lout, in the end I'll give up my dreams of becoming something, someone important, and settle for a scratch on this table."

I laughed at that, telling him I could believe he was a lout, but not that he was lazy.

"Please, Charlie, I'm bigheaded enough; you don't have to feed my ego. Everything's come too easily and too fast."

I paused. "Aren't you glad of that?"

"Glad? I should be. Instead, all I want is to be put in my place."

Wick ordered two bottles of ale from a barkeep, then continued, his voice dropping so that I knew he didn't want anyone else to hear. "What I'm trying to say is that I want to feel different, different from how I've felt for nineteen years, always getting what I want, never working for it. I know it sounds ridiculous, Charlie, but I can con just about anyone. It's time someone saw through me. You'd think someone would by now."

"You'd think so," I agreed.

"Girls especially. Girls are supposed to have female intuition. They're supposed to be able to sense if a fellow is sincere. But the birds I meet aren't very challenging, and that's a fact. They think I'm a swell guy from the start. I wish one of them would realize I'm a phony and would refuse to forgive me for it."

"But you're not a phony."

"Shucks, Charlie, I am! I'm much worse than you think. I seem ambitious but I'm not. I don't feel strongly about anything, really, except having fun. I just glide along the surface of things, smooth as you please. And my father hates me for it—you should see the letters he sends me."

Our drinks arrived and we chugged them. Wick still wanted to talk, his eyes unguarded as he stared at mine from across the table.

"Have you ever been in love, Charlie? Mercilessly in love? Maybe with that girl of yours from back home?"

I shook my head and downed the last of my drink.

"Me neither. And yet, I have a feeling that that's the only thing that can cure me of this—this apathy. Sometimes when I'm onstage I'll play a character in love and I'll taste it, just for a few seconds, what it would be like to be totally infatuated. But it fades—the ardor—because it never belonged to me in the first place. Do you know what I mean? Am I making any sense at all?"

"I—I think so."

And of course I knew all too well, not what it was like to glide along the surface of things, but what it was like to yearn. As Wick continued to ramble, we bent our heads closer across the table. We were drinking too much too quickly; another round of ales had come and gone. Though Wick's eyes brimmed with earnestness, I couldn't look at them for long. My gaze drifted to his lips, which were full, a little turned-down at the corners so that more than once I'd wondered if kissing might right them. But those eyes, they were to be avoided at any cost, for they were without filter. I feared certain emotions could pass as easily in as they could out. And then he would certainly see it: the ardor he pined for, scarlet and blistering in someone else.

"But what kind of girl will she be?" he asked. "I suppose I'll know when I see her."

He laughed suddenly, his somberness tapering. He made a toast—"To the road ahead, Charlie-boy, may it take us to places we haven't been before! To places we've always wanted to go!"—and we clanked our bottles so rapturously it's a wonder we didn't break them.

Minutes later, our privacy faded. People came by, one by one, each wanting to talk to Wick. They'd seen him here before, hadn't they? He was a Yale man, a local, maybe both? In any case, he reminded them of a nephew, a friend from back home, a fellow they'd met on their travels, a son who had grown up and moved away. Wick, he teased and bantered, flirting with an old crone about her cane, telling her that her legs looked good to *him*. And to the barkeep, who was sad-eyed, defeated-looking, Wick insisted on telling jokes until he coaxed a smile.

Watching quietly, I saw for the umpteenth time just what Wick had been talking about: how his charm was almost too potent. It superceded his real character. And I wondered, only briefly, my adoration soon squelching the question, what *was* his real character?

The more we drank, the more the Last Anchor started to soften, voices mellowing, edges crumbling, clinking bottles turning into fairy chimes. An hour later the place had reached its capacity, all the chairs and booths taken so that people were loitering around the bar, huddled together in rowdy groups, some dancing so close to the fire that their bodies glowed like embers.

As for what time Wick and I finally left, I couldn't say. In fact, the rest of that night remains a mystery. I remember only a rough outline, the details obscured by ale and by a peacock-colored concoction given to us by the barkeep just before we left. "Absinthe," he said. "It's on me. Don't mention it to management."

I remember we traveled home a different route.

"A shortcut," Wick had said, walking even closer than he had on the way there. Every now and then he'd clutch my arm and recite a bit of poetry—dirty, silly, nonsensical bits that made me laugh. His breath smelled malty, but there was something more to him, a fresh scent, on his clothes, on his skin, reminiscent somehow of the first snow of winter, piney and tingly and stinging.

"Will you be all right, Charlie?" he asked when we at last entered Phelps Gate. But I must have been tottering and so he followed me home. He asked me for the key to my suite and then to my room, and I remember smirking, thinking, why would he want such things? He had to fish for the keys in my pockets, and I giggled, no doubt effeminately, thinking he would find more than he'd bargained for if he kept it up.

Propping me up with one arm, he at last swung open the appropriate doors and hauled me inside. I remember we sat on my bed, close, too, close as chums in his eyes, probably, but I couldn't help but wonder if he felt even a fraction of what I felt. I was outrageously close to touching his face, to studying those fine bones, the irresistible crinkles around his eyes; close to whispering something in his ear, something I'd promised myself I wouldn't say; close to raking my fingers through his disheveled hair; outrageously close, even, to sucking on his fingers.

And now, in the sober-cold light of day, was I aghast? Ashamed? The truth is, if I could have done those things I would have.

I remember Wick taking off my coat and then my shoes, all with a practiced hand. Little doubt he'd done it before—on other inebriated friends, but more likely on a girl. A girl he'd undressed himself, starting with her feet. He pulled back the covers and gently tucked me inside, telling me, "It's okay, Charlie. You'll be fine in the morning. I know just how you feel. But you'll be swell—I'll check on you." I recall he caressed the side of my face briefly with those elegant sinewy fingers—a sign of love, if perhaps not the right sort of love.

I tried to sit up, anything to keep him there. But the room had started to spin. My eyes felt tight, as if someone were reining them in from my skull.

"Sweet dreams," he whispered as he rose, and I fell back. His sweet, wintry scent lingered in the air around my bed. When he closed the door behind him, I didn't hear it; I felt it, knowing that when I whispered back, it was only to myself.

To flaunt a sword—there was no more glorious a feeling.

Decked out in my fencing regalia, the long foil like an extension of my arm, I looked nothing like the girl Mother had known. I wore a stiff white jacket, tightly fitted and buttoned up the side. I sported white breeches to the knee, with long socks covering the rest of my legs. On my face rested a mask, its mesh front allowing me to see out, but no one to see in. A leather glove protected my right hand from my opponent's weapon. My left hand was the only part of my body exposed—the only piece of the original Adele. It was chafed and rough, still the hand of a laundress.

Though my sword wasn't sharp, still it could wound. Donald hadn't fibbed. Aimed at the right spot with the right amount of force, the tip left a bruise the size of a dime. A whip from the blade, too, branded and scored.

Within weeks I had dozens of marks all over my body. Yet I never felt them at the time of impact. Facing my opponent on the fencing strip—advancing, retreating, lunging forward with all my might—I felt nothing but my own volatility.

My coach, a Hungarian named Istvan Bodnár, said that fencing was passion tempered with forethought and precision. Watching me in practice, he said I still had to learn two of the three.

Though I was less skilled than almost all my teammates, I gained a reputation for being unpredictable, roaring down the strip with knees bent and sword raised. I lashed. I lammed. I planned intricate strategies only to abandon them at the last possible second. My physical improvement was slow, perhaps, but not so my mental improvement. Something lodged deep inside of me was loosening. That pearly shell was cracking. The more I fenced, the more I sensed it: the heavenly sweet rush of release.

I practiced with the team several times a week. Warm-ups consisted of runs up and down the stairs of Payne Whitney. There was footwork, stretching, and training with weights. In groups of two we perfected our blade-work, refining our parries until they were petite, forceful, and exact. We created sophisticated attacks and suitable defenses. We stood in front of padded targets mounted on the wall and tried for bull's eyes. We wore our battle scars proudly—slashes, lacerations, and, always, those coin-sized welts in various colorful stages of metamorphosis.

I was the smallest man on the team. I was the only one never to have fenced before. While my teammates wore guards in their pants, I slid a slim book over my bound breasts. And yet I had no doubt that I would become a potent force. My confidence was bolstered by Istvan

Bodnár. Like Coach Roota, he somehow sensed my potential, saying, "*Fiú*, I will tell you your greatest asset: there isn't enough of you to hit."

The Yale Freshmen Fencing Team played Columbia, Princeton, Harvard, and West Point. We sparred with local teams, too: the Milford School and the Hartford Fencer's Club. Being inexperienced, I seldom participated in official tournaments. But always I cheered from the sidelines—often louder than anyone else. I took comfort in the fact that my turn would come. It had to, for in fencing I had as much advantage as anyone else. It wasn't the strongest man who won, or the tallest, but the most cunning. A champion chose unforeseeable targets. He outfoxed, outwitted, outdanced, and outlasted. He was merciless, a saboteur, darting and weaving down the strip. A winner waited until the time was right. And when it was, finally, he closed his eyes and savored the moment, already knowing he'd struck true.

With final exams closing in, Wick, Phin, Harry, and I were holed up in the library for hours on end—although I spent much of that time reading in the Stacks. Occasionally we went stir-crazy, allowing Wick to lead us out of Sterling and into one of his harebrained adventures. In Commons, we seized dinner trays and with a great deal of effort, if not stealth, draped them with our coats and sneaked them out the door. From there, we tromped through the snow and slush to the highest reach of Hillhouse Avenue.

"Let's go!" Wick cried, running as fast as he could up that incline, the tray clenched in his hands. At the top of the hill he took a flying leap, landing belly-first on that makeshift sled, the momentum of his elastic legs having given him extraordinary propulsion. We watched him slip-slide down, gaining speed, too much speed, a small ridge in the snow sending him into the air, gravity sending him back down with a thud, and still he sailed, barely avoiding trees and shrubbery, a dozen possible collisions, until at last the arc of the hill gave way to level ground. He slowed enough to roll off his ride, yelling up at us that we'd better hang on. What a thrill. My God, what a feat of engineering.

The four of us sledded down the hill all afternoon, more or less successfully, exhausted and covered in snow.

Another day found us amid the droves of freshmen on Old Campus. It was dusk. Dozens of us were milling around, stretching our legs, talking and amusing ourselves in the waning minutes before dinner. I'm not sure how it started—who threw the first snowball or why—but pretty soon hundreds of snowballs were flying through the sky, hurtled from eager hands and landing indiscriminately. A few men yelled that we ought to make teams, that the residential colleges ought to play against one another. But through the tumult it was hard to see which face was under which hat, and it wasn't long before a frenzied free-for-all drowned out all reasonable pleas.

I reveled in the rabble. I couldn't bundle the snow fast enough, pitching half-formed balls with glee. I felt as I did while fencing: infallible, driven by instinct alone. And yet, how could I miss the voice from behind?

"Hey, you throw like a girl!"

Wheeling around I already knew I'd see Phin, his eyes indurate as always, so that I didn't know how serious he was or how seriously I should take him. I knelt down gently, almost deferentially, but only so I could form a pile of snowballs, packed hard as ice. One after the other I slung them, advancing a little more each time, until I was practically on top of him. And still I persisted, grinding dense gobs of snow into his face, cramming them into his mouth, so that maybe he'd stop hinting, so that maybe he'd just shut up.

I had both of my hands on him now. And Phin, he scarcely resisted, though he was a husky fellow, certainly stronger than I. I sensed that he wanted me to go on, that my miserable attack somehow gave him pleasure. Maybe what happened next was exactly what he'd hoped for.

"Hey, cool off, Charlie!" Wick yelled, grabbing me from behind and tearing me off my adversary. He threw me into a nearby snowbank, hard, too, so that my arm felt like it had broken off my shoulder. "What the devil's gotten into you?"

It didn't matter that I was out of breath: I had nothing to say. I'd been a fool to fall for such a petty jab.

"It's all right," Phin said, coughing harshly, clearing the wet snow from his mouth, his nostrils. He rose slowly, stiltedly. A martyr, I thought.

"Forget about it," he added with a wave of the hand.

And the surprising thing is—we did. Wick turned to lead Phin away from the commotion. He didn't say another word to me for the rest of the night. And even when he did start speaking to me, he didn't mention the incident, not even to ask why. Why had I blown my cork over something as petty as a snowball fight? Maybe he'd already heard Phin's account. Maybe he'd already figured out certain things. But of course, I didn't dare ask.

It was a relief when final exams got under way. With no time left for cramming, my classmates and I, armed with pencils and the same grim expression, marched to our fates.

All of the exams lasted two hours. Most of the time I finished with at least a half hour to spare. I knew I had time to reread what I'd written in my essays, to rethink the verbs I'd conjugated in Latin, or the identities and formulas I'd used in trigonometry. But the weight of my classmates' concentration bore me down. All of Harry's admonitions rattled through my head. I couldn't stop tapping my feet under my desk, so eager I was to be done, to put this first semester to rest. I knew I'd pass whether I checked my answers or not, so I'd rise from my chair early. I'd turn in my exam. Inevitably, the professor would smile at me kindly, if impersonally. He didn't remember my name, only that I was a good student. I was quiet, unremarkable, indistinguishable from the hundreds of boys he'd taught over the years. And that's exactly how Mother and I wanted it.

During the examination period I visited the post office daily. I both craved and feared Mother's letters. I wanted her to change her mind, to beg me to come home for the holidays. Or maybe she would offer to visit New Haven. Maybe just on Christmas day. We would wander the campus together, arm in arm. But no, there was laundry to do. The garments were taking longer to dry now that she had to hang them indoors. The fireplace was still out of service and the nights were frigid.

She was working harder, she wrote, but every little bit of money helped. She would like to see me, truly she would, but her absence would only fuel Miss Prowl's curiosity.

And there was something else—another mention of Mother's parents. She *had* written to them—a lengthy letter with details, but not too many, and certainly few about me, except the *fact* of me. Mother asked Mr. and Mrs. Mockleton if they had known that they had a granddaughter. She told them I was sweet and compliant and selfless. She confessed nothing strange. She told them I would be the apple of their eye, if ever we were to meet.

Mother assured me that a note to her parents would do no harm. Alfred and Joanna were kittens, she insisted, essentially clawless. She still didn't trust them, and had no desire to see them again, but they *were* her blood, and she was starting to realize that Pa may have been right all those years. By severing ties to her kin, she had also severed a part of herself.

And how different her tone! Gone was the bitterness and desire for revenge that had always peppered her talk. I'd never known Mother without vitriol, and I wondered what would happen if she were finally free of it. Maybe she would be like a girl again, the sylph-like Cottager who'd never had enough room on her dance card. Maybe visiting her parents meant a chance at revisiting the past.

These possibilities vexed me. To make matters worse, I was starting to feel lonely. Wick and Phin had left immediately after their last exams. Only Harry lingered, and even he would be departing soon, not to be back for three weeks—the duration of Yale's holiday break.

"When will you be off, Pietra?" he asked, stopping by my room hours before his departure. "Thought you would have left by now, seeing as you live so close."

"I'll be out of here soon."

"Is someone coming to get you?"

"I'm taking the train."

"Don't wait too long. The campus has gone into hibernation."

I agreed. The whole of New Haven seemed to slumber, even during the day, under so many layers of snow. Stores closed early, people stayed indoors. Gone were the boys trudging through Old Campus and Cross Campus, heads bent against the wind. Without the counterbalance of youth, the buildings of Yale seemed ancient and derelict, as if they'd been deserted for centuries rather than days. Most were locked and bolted and chained. Even Commons was shut, the cooks and waitresses and dishwashers probably as eager to flee as the students they served.

In all of Durfee, only three or four of us had stayed behind. But we stragglers seldom saw one another. I took my meals in my room, alone. I subsisted on bread, mainly, and sometimes cans of peas or beans or corn, whichever was cheapest. I missed the rich selection of Commons, even the darned bananas. Mrs. DiRisio had told me I could come to her home anytime—why, she'd feed me every day if she could. But I didn't want her knowing that I'd stayed at Yale through the break. I didn't want her pity. More than that, I didn't want her questions.

The days hobbled by. By myself so much of the time, I missed nearly everybody, but surprisingly, Ceci most of all. Until now I hadn't realized how much affection I felt for the girl. She'd become more a sibling than a pupil—a little sister whom I could advise using my own unlikely experience. The things I said to her were the same things I wished I could have told a younger version of myself.

Yet there would be no Ceci for nearly a month. No venturing to Wooster Square, either; I worried that Marie, or her husband or sons, would see me. Instead, I kept inside the perimeters of Yale—a barren, macabre, frozen Yale—until I grew so mopish I was eager to encounter anyone, even the old widow. Seeing her on the street in her shabby coat, the mink like a witchy charm around her neck, I no longer crossed to the other side. I nodded at her as we passed, looking into her eyes, one of them opaque, colorless. A glass eye, perhaps.

"Why aren't you wearing your kidskin gloves, Josefina? Mind you don't forget you're a lady."

But there was no way I could forget. When I returned home that day I saw a stark reminder: a spot on my knickers. Before Yale, I hadn't minded when the red tide crept in. I'd first started menstruating when I was thirteen. Since then my flow had followed a more or less predictable cycle: two days of cramps and mild nausea, followed by five of bleeding.

Mother used to buy Modess or Kotex at the store, but eventually she'd deemed the boxes an unnecessary expense.

"We're in the laundry business, after all." So we developed our own method, using a basket of rags in the larder. These we would soak overnight in a bucket to relax the stains, same as we did with the soiled items our customers brought in. We'd scrub the fabric with a brush until the worst of the marks were gone. But always the coppery imprints remained, and I'd feel bashful and exposed when the rags flapped on the line, though no one but Miss Prowl ever saw them.

Mother had given me those rags to take with me to Yale. "Consider them disposable now," she'd said, packing them into the carpetbag along with a dozen small paper sacks. I was to hide the bloody rags in the bags, to carry them far away from my room and from observant eyes. "Dispose of them anywhere," Mother had said, "so long as no one sees you."

One time I'd gone to Yale Station looking for a letter from Mother and found a box instead. I'd held it in my hands, shaken it, turned it at a dozen angles. It must be a gift, I decided, something lovely and sentimental. I'd felt giddy opening that package in my room, my legs curled underneath me on the bed like a little girl's. What a surprise, then, what a disappointment, to find a new batch of rags, a little note from Mother tucked inside.

"In case you run out, Adele. These are from an old flannel sheet. I thought we'd give it a new purpose."

She'd been sensible to send the parcel, I reasoned. She'd been thinking of me, of our complicity. And yet I couldn't help feeling dejected by the shabby, torn squares.

Since arriving in New Haven, I perceived menstruation differently. The dull petulant ache in my womb, the blood that oozed sticky-warm for days, the way my appetite spiked, then tapered— these were no longer minor annoyances Mother and I shared with a laugh. Even the smell seemed stronger now, more earthy and olid. Even repellent.

Each month I should have been prepared, but always the flow came as a surprise. When I saw it there, the first telltale stain—dark, clotted, incriminating—I scarcely believed it. How could it be that my own blood was alien now? As alien, even, as the name "Adele" written in Mother's careful script.

Another time on the street: not the widow, but someone just as familiar. She was window-shopping, like the others on Chapel Street, no one having much money these days. She was a large woman, rolls of fat around her midriff like automobile tires. She was standing in front of the W. L. Douglas Shoe Co., staring at a sign that read: "25,000 Pairs! All on Sale!" From the back she appeared youthful, in a coat that was fashionable but gaudy and poorly tailored. A size too small. It was her legs that gave her away. They were thick and buckled, especially at the ankles. Under her woolen stockings they were heavily veined—I was sure of it. Curious, I crept closer, until I was only an arm's length away. Where had I seen her before? She even smelled familiar, like a bottle of wine left open overnight.

Bold from loneliness, I resolved to tap her on the back. She'd turn around and then I'd know. But thank heavens I hesitated, snapping back my hand in the nick of time, shocked by my own stupidity. Had I been away from Stony Creek so long as to forget everybody? The woman looked like Miss Prowl. Probably *was* Miss Prowl—maybe in town to buy Christmas gifts. And if she saw me, why, every day I'd spent in New Haven would have been for naught.

I took a giant step back, then another. Scurrying away, I didn't glance back, not even to check if she'd turned around at the last moment, if she'd caught sight of a face that was incongruous with gentlemen's clothing. Faster now, I veered around elms, people, carts, bicycles. I tripped on a trolley line brimming with snowmelt, straightened myself, and kept going. I tried to put this latest brush with danger out of my mind. But inside I panicked, knowing that there were only so many brushes one could have before a collision.

Chapter Eight

CHRISTMAS arrived without company, or cheer, or the decorations that Mother had delighted in making: popcorn strung on string, cut-out snowflakes and angels, chains of colored paper links, candles propped in little tin cups. These were ways of escaping a plodding, unchanging life, I understood now. Little holiday excesses that ornamented Mother's otherwise dog-eared days.

I woke up late and kept to my room. Since the holiday break had begun, I'd had too little to do and too much time to think—a dangerous combination that left me almost as melancholy as I'd been following the accident. I cried often, always spontaneously. My thoughts would expectedly snag on the gnarled nail of death, and I couldn't pull away. In the turbulent weeks before Yale, I'd been able to concentrate on what Mother and I needed to do. I'd been able to push my grief far enough away to cope. But it had crept back, especially my sorrow over Pa. Some days I barely left my room. I nibbled at my food. Funny how sadness can obliterate pangs of hunger, how it can send you back to your bed long after the day has started.

I missed my busy schedule: classes, fencing practice, sojourns to the Stacks, my work-study trips, and, of course, my excursions to the DiRisios. Without constant distraction, the darkest of my thoughts flourished. They looped and twined around themselves, growing stronger as they united, like fibers in a rope. And I, hanging on for dear life at the end.

I got to wondering if I belonged at Yale at all, if I had the strength to be here, the courage, or the right. I wondered if I'd cheated Charles somehow, not consciously, but on a secret, rivalrous level.

Lying in my bed, bundled in blankets but comfortless, snow falling softly outside my window, I remembered Christmases past, how Mother had loved to create little projects for my brother and me. One holiday she'd spent the morning baking thin sheets of gingerbread. We were to build gingerbread houses, she'd explained, showing us how to join the hard pieces of baked dough with a thick white sugar paste. My house had been simple: a rudimentary box without the least hint of artistry. Charles's house, on the other hand, had been an opulent, teetering affair. He'd decorated all three stories with gumdrops, candy canes, and dyed frosting, cleverly using chocolate coins as shingles on the roof.

"Oh, Charles, how wonderful!" Mother had cried as he'd shown it off.

Knowing I couldn't compete, I hadn't bothered with decorations, settling for a plain roof. Only my house had been special, too, if one knew where to look. Inside, I'd inserted little people cut from the remainder of the gingerbread, their feet planted in place with gobs of paste. I'd used pieces of licorice as hinges on the door, so that it could open and shut. I'd swung that door over and over, pleased as punch, until Charles had snapped it off and popped it into his mouth.

Though I'd been young, I'd understood the sadism at the root of my brother's mischief, particularly when he said, "Tell Mother. Go on, I dare you. You know which one of us she'll believe."

Hours later and well into the night, my jaw clenched, I couldn't put his words out of my head. Finally, I'd climbed out of bed. When I was sure everyone was asleep, I'd tiptoed into the kitchen. There our houses still stood on the table, side by side. Carefully, I'd peeped through the gaping door frame of mine, noting that the people were missing now, too. For minutes I'd hovered there, statue-still. I'd wanted to pound Charles's house into crumbs. But in the end I just couldn't. It wasn't Mother's passionate condemnation or my brother's rage that worried me, but Pa's quiet disappointment.

In lieu of destruction, I'd picked off a lone gumdrop from Charles's house—one that would go unnoticed. I'd popped it into my mouth. I'd sucked and savored every last bit of its nubby sweetness. Then I'd returned to bed, only half-sated, and forced myself to sleep.

All Christmas day the snow didn't abate. When evening came it continued to fall. Only it became lighter, more airy, practically ethereal, so that suddenly I wanted to touch it. For the first time that day I got ready to face the world. Groggy from lack of movement, I walked to the lavatory. I showered leisurely, knowing that no one was there to see me. Slowly, I regained my energy. I dressed, combed my hair, and brushed my teeth. Then I went outside and lifted my face toward the sky, letting the flakes kiss my eyelids. They melted instantly on my skin. I resolved to go to a church, although religion didn't hold much of a place in my family's holiday traditions. Mother and Pa had never been able to agree on how Charles and I should be raised—Catholic or Protestant—and whilst they'd argued, opportunities for baptism and communion and Sunday mass had passed. Pa had insisted that we ought to have God in our lives in one form or another, but Mother had disagreed. After what she'd been through, she wasn't even sure God existed.

"And even if he did," she'd said, "he certainly doesn't understand *my* needs."

My family's lack of religious affiliation hadn't gone unnoticed by the people of Stony Creek, particularly by Miss Prowl. On Sundays, when other children had walked with their parents into town for service, Charles and I had read or played on the porch. Miss Prowl would see us and shake her head.

"Heathens," I'd heard her mutter.

Now I was older and supposedly knew better, but still I didn't choose a faith. Still I didn't know the ideological differences between an Episcopalian and a Baptist, a Russian Orthodox and a Presbyterian. Ignorant but intent, I resolved to enter the closest place, Battell Chapel. Although it was situated next to Durfee, I'd never been inside.

I'd never paid the chapel any attention, except perhaps as a timepiece. Along with Sterling Bell Tower's knell, Battell's bells rang every hour.

Upon entering Battell I was ashamed of my apathy. Its interior, though humble in size, was beautiful. The oak trimmings, charmingly stenciled walls, gold-paneled ceiling, and bold medieval symbols crowning the arch leading into the apse—all marked Battell as sublime: a place of worship, yes, but also a place *to* worship. The stained-glass windows, the colors of spring flowers, were the most striking element. Their inscriptions celebrated not only angels and saints, but also early professors of Yale.

One window in particular looked familiar: it depicted a man wrapped in pale robes standing between two columns as he gazed skyward. I realized the window might have been made by the Tiffany Company, whose style of jewelry and art Mother had loved to describe in detail. She'd told me stories about how Alfred had taken her to the Tiffany Company every year on her birthday until she was sixteen. He'd allowed her to pick a new trinket for her charm bracelet, one of the many indulgent items Mother had lost when she'd chosen Pa over her parents.

I had arrived in Battell in the middle of a service. Parishioners were squeezed tightly into the pews, bedecked in their Christmas best, inhaling incense and listening raptly as a minister read from a Bible on a lectern. I found a seat at the back and settled in as unobtrusively as I could. But still a woman turned to watch me. I didn't know if her stare was the result of my tardiness or if she simply didn't like the look of me. Whatever the case, she shook her head in annoyance.

I tried to listen to what the minister was saying, closing my eyes to concentrate. He was reading a story I was familiar with, how the angel of the Lord had announced Christ's arrival to the shepherds keeping watch over their flocks. I knew it because when weeks passed in between Miss Prowl's book donations, I'd turned to the Bible. Pa kept an old and tarnished one in the bedroom, not under a floorboard in secret, but beside the bed.

The minister described the baby swaddled in cloth and lying in a manger in Bethlehem. A baby born to a virgin, the holiest of miracles, he emphasized. But the unlikelihood of that notion—the sheer absurdity—made me uneasy. I was ignorant about Christianity, yes, but one thing was nevertheless clear to me: embracing it would require a leap of faith, a dilution of the literal and scientific, and a moratorium on questions. Without faith there was no way to believe the minister. But I must have had too little, for the longer I listened, the more illogical and sanctimonious he sounded. More and more, his tone resembled Professor Spang's.

"This is the word of the Lord," he said at last.

"Amen," said the lady who had watched me.

"Amen," I breathed, sliding out of the pew as stealthily as I could.

Outside again, I breathed in the cool air until I couldn't smell incense anymore. I thought briefly of trying another chapel, but odds were I'd be uncomfortable in every one. There was only one place that felt holy to me, while also welcoming and free of artifice, and so I walked to the steps of Sterling. I took off my gloves and rubbed the snow from a patch of granite. I sat down beside the cold pink rock, not caring that the temperature was certainly below freezing. I thought about home, and mainly about Pa, how he'd loved Christmas. He'd take Charles and me into his arms and tell us about how children in Italy left their shoes by the door so that an old woman who rode on a broom could fill them with candy and chocolate. He'd tell us about all the foods his mother had cooked, and how he and his brother, Francisco, had fought over the last of the sweet honey balls called *struffoli*.

Pa used to say that because Francisco was the youngest, the weight of family responsibility had never lain thick on his shoulders. He had never married and didn't have any children. Though his life as a musician meant irregular pay, always he seemed to have money in his pockets and a bounce to his step. And always, he seemed youthful.

"That's what happens when you move around so much," Pa had said. "Time can't catch up with you."

I'd wondered why Francisco didn't visit us. Why didn't we invite him to stay in our apartment? But Pa said his brother didn't accept invitations; he never knew where the days would take him. Why, at one point Francisco had even joined a circus: the Bringlebright Traveling Show. He'd played his trumpet in the circus band. He'd traveled in his own car on the circus train, which stopped in places like Tulsa, Boston, Tucson, Charleston, and Springfield. On the way he'd romanced a red-haired fire-eater who wore flimsy costumes.

"Cirella—that was her name," Pa had said. "She almost caught him, too. But not quite."

Pa said that Mother had met Francisco once, in the heady early days of their relationship. She hadn't liked him much, though. Whenever Pa mentioned his name, she'd clear her throat in irritation.

I'd asked Pa—did he miss his brother? Why didn't they insist on seeing one another? What if they forgot each other's faces? But Pa had laughed at that last question. "I have only to look in the mirror. Francisco looks like me, just more dashing."

Dashing. Romantic-eyed. Though I'd never admit it aloud, still I daydreamed about Francisco. In those dreams he'd visit Stony Creek and fall in love with me. Together, we'd sit on the granite bluffs, the sun silky on our faces, and he'd kiss me with lips that were like the summer sea: salty, warm, too tranquil to be trusted. Pa had a brother again; I, a beau. Yet whenever I tried to fit Mother into my thoughts, they withered. I told Pa once I wished we had a photograph of Francisco—something to make him real and lasting. But Pa had said his brother never posed for any. He couldn't keep still for long enough.

From far away I heard them—the bells of Battell tolling in sync with Sterling's peals. They rang boldly, marking the hour. But could it be so late? Two in the morning already. The snow had stopped, finally, and the sky was like slate against the blinking stars. I'd been thinking about Pa and Francisco for so long I might have been the last person in all of New Haven to be outdoors. I stood up and rubbed the numbness from my limbs. Returning to Durfee, I thought maybe I'd see the widow. But only my shadow, eerie-stretched under the streetlamps, kept me company on the way home.

Chapter Nine

WHEN SCHOOL resumed, there were fewer men in the Class of 1940. Harry noticed it first, how about thirty of our classmates hadn't made it back. Surprisingly, some of the wealthier boys—boys of Phin's stock and standing—were among the missing.

"Their families can't pay the tuition any longer," Harry told me. "The depression's affecting everyone, even the boys I used to be jealous of."

In a letter to Mother, I shared this news. She wrote back that misfortune's blade sometimes struck the privileged, too. She said that not as many Cottagers would be arriving this summer, either, and that according to Miss Prowl, some of their homes were being foreclosed.

Despite its diminishing numbers, my class did have something to celebrate: the coming of the Freshman Winter Ball. Almost immediately upon our return to Old Campus, the ball dominated discussion. The question asked most frequently was whether each man would bring a girl or take his chances among the dozens of coeds who would arrive from local women's colleges and Yale's sister schools. Harry told me he was determined to find a date before the ball—even if he had to resort to drastic measures.

"Up against men like Wick, I'll stand no chance," he said.

And so began Harry's crusade. Not to find any girl, but a girl who would be ogled and admired by every last hormone-driven yearling. Harry already had such a girl in mind. But as he told it, his chances of getting her were as slim as he was.

"I want to ask the Botticelli," he confided to me.

After seeing her that night in the diner, Harry had failed to take her up on her offer to meet again, blaming a bad case of the jitters. Ever since, he'd regretted it. Now that he'd made it through the first semester with excellent marks, he decided that he could officially begin his pursuit of women.

"After all, aren't they almost as important as schoolwork?" he asked me.

"Some would say they're more important."

"Would you say that?"

"Depends on the woman," I answered.

"We met the Botticelli at roughly ten-thirty on a Friday night," Harry said matter-of-factly. "If I'm at the diner at that time, there's a chance I'll see her again, right? Since there's so little time before the ball, I'll have to go every night. I'll keep going until I meet her again or I choke on those greasy cheeseburgers, whichever comes first."

I asked Harry, "If you do see her, how will you explain not coming when the napkin said?"

"You think she'll still be sore about that?"

"I don't know."

Harry took off his eyeglasses and wiped away the smudges with a handkerchief. "There's only one way—I'll have Wick write another poem, a poem of apology."

Wick, thrilled to take part in any scheme, duly complied. He asked Harry whether the poem could begin with "roses are red, violets are blue" and whether he minded dirty words. Both questions were met with horrified silence.

Once Harry's plan went into effect, I didn't see him much. True to his word, he went to the diner every night. Often, he would arrive after his last class and stay until closing. He brought his books and schoolwork with him. But the diner was not as hospitable as the library. He came into class looking exhausted, saying he'd been too nervous to study, having to look up from his reading every minute or two, every time another customer walked in. Still, he was determined to persevere, telling me, "Sometimes I think a tin can would have a better chance of wooing that girl. But other times I imagine how she'll look at me when she walks through the door—like she's been waiting for me."

A mere two days before the ball, Harry finally triumphed. He burst into my room late at night, clutching another napkin—heart-shaped, so I knew. Wordlessly, he plopped himself on my bed with jelly-legged elation.

"Let me see," I said, taking the napkin carefully from his hand.

"Don't rip it," he warned. "I'll be showing it to my grandchildren."

I unfolded the note gently. The curlicue writing was familiar. "You can join us, if you want," it read.

"That's it?" I asked.

"We talked mostly," Harry explained. "Face-to-face. I came over to her table."

"Did you ask her to the ball?"

"Of course. But there was a problem."

"What problem?"

Harry flipped onto his back. Churlishly, he stared at the ceiling. "Her friend was there—the same friend that was with her the first time."

"The plain one?"

"Yes."

"What of it?"

"Well, Ethel—Ethel's the Botticelli's real name—she said she wouldn't go to the ball with me unless her friend came, too. Her friend's name is Helen."

"What are you going to do? Take them both?"

"No! See, I sort of, I sort of said that *you* were sweet on Helen."

"What?"

"But Pietra, before you say anything, the girls—they remember you. They said there was something different about you. 'Special' was the word they used. And Helen, she looked so different tonight. Much better than when we first saw her. Some fellows might even find her pretty."

"Harry—"

"Please don't say no, Pietra! Ethel, she's the girl for me. You should have seen her in the skirt she was wearing. It was like she was trying to slay me."

Watching Harry practically convulse on my bed, his face as red as I'd ever seen it, his eyes glazed over with a combination of ecstasy and despair, I figured I had no choice.

"Fine, I'll go along with it, reluctantly—and only as a favor. But I'm warning you, Harry, don't even try—"

But by then Harry had sprung up, grinning like a Cheshire cat. He hugged me with such brute strength I swore he must have graduated from corrective exercises.

"Pietra," he told me, recovering enough of his composure to get the words out, "I swear, you'll be the first person we invite to the wedding."

An hour before the Freshman Ball, every last shower on Old Campus was running. I was sure that New Haven must experience a water shortage every year at this same time. Every local store had sold out of Burma Shave, hair pomade, and peppermints. Boys crowded in front of the mirrors in the lavatories, vying for space, smoothing their sideburns, relentlessly adjusting their ties, splashing cold water on their faces.

I ignored these rituals and went to Harry and Wick's room looking like I always did. The only special thing I'd done that day was visit a barber. Whenever my hair grew past my ears, the curls sprang out irrepressibly.

I found Harry in a muddle, unable to decide which of three ties to wear. He was worried about the smallest details, even how we ought to greet the girls.

"Should we play it safe or pretend we're smooth, Pietra? You understand we can't make any mistakes."

Wick was there, too. He looked debonair, in slim black slacks that had been tailored to emphasize his gangling legs. A top hat made him so tall he'd have to bend down to fit through doorways. Though he'd chosen not to bring a date, I had no doubt he'd find plenty of companionship.

"I'm gonna find a girlfriend tonight," he declared. "Or at least a girlfriend for the night."

Phin, our fourth musketeer, had decided not to attend the Ball.

"I tried to make him come, but he wouldn't," Wick told us. "He said if he's gonna neck with a girl, he'd rather do it in private than in front of us bozos. And speaking of necking—Harry, do you think Ethel kisses on the first date?"

"Of course not!"

"How do you know?"

"I talked to her, didn't I?"

"Yes, but how do you *know?* You can't until you try."

Harry looked at Wick testily, then turned his attention back to the ties.

"What do you think, Charlie?" Wick asked.

"If Harry can get through the night without fainting, that will be enough."

"And how!"

"Hey," Harry cried. "Are you know-it-alls going to help or not?"

Wick scrutinized the ties a moment before dubbing a paisley number the winner. Towering over Harry, he calmly tied the knot and smoothed out the creases.

"I think it's time," Wick said.

Harry took out his pocket watch. "No way—we have a half hour yet. If we're early, we'll look too eager."

"Time for a break," Wick corrected, reaching into his jacket and retrieving a box of Camels. Inside, there was only one cigarette. It was long, thin, and looked as if it had been rolled by hand. Wick examined it briefly before giving it to me.

"Smell it," he said. I complied, never having smelled a cigarette quite like it before. It was strange, cloying, exotic, oddly spicy.

"What is it?"

"I got it over break from an old chum at Choate. It's an herb. He said Mexicans smoke it to purify the soul. He said to save it for a special occasion. Tonight's as good a night as any, I reckon."

Harry took the cigarette from me, turning it over in his fingers. "It's marihuana, isn't it?" He pronounced the word *marihuana* as if it were an obscenity. "What do you have this for, Wick? If Angell ever found out, boy, he'd give us the boot faster than you can count to five."

"How would Angell find out? What do you think he does—sneak around Old Campus at night? He's probably home right now, feet on an ottoman, sipping a highball, making googly eyes at his wife."

"But the smell—it carries."

"So what? No one will know where it's coming from."

Harry walked about worriedly. "I don't think we should chance it, that's all. What if something goes wrong? I've heard it can make you hallucinate."

"Look at your hands, Harry." Harry did just that, and when he did, he was shocked to see that they weren't just trembling, but downright shaking.

"How is Ethel gonna feel when you hold her hand and yours is all twitchy?" Wick persisted. "This baby can make you relax, that's all I'm saying."

Harry had been fragile before, but now he was close to crumbling. The threat of Ethel's disappointment caused his whole body to quaver. I thought Wick's statement a little cruel and told Harry not to worry, the girls would have a first-class time—we'd see to that. But he didn't believe me. He said he'd try that queer-looking cigarette after all, if there was any chance it would ease his fright. Any chance at all that it would make him brave.

"Are you sure?" I asked.

"Sure I'm sure," he said briskly, taking a seat next to Wick on the floor. Watching them, I was reminded of our first day in New Haven. And in recalling that unexpected, music-filled prelude, I grew bold, deciding I, too, would try the cigarette. Out of the three of us, I had the most to lose, the most to fear. I'd tried not to think about Helen. I'd told myself I'd worry about her when the time came. That was the only way to cope: avoid possible calamities until the last possible moment. If I were to let myself fret about every last might-be and could-be, I might as well buy a ticket back to Stony Creek. And yet! I remembered Helen so vividly—how pale and tremulous she'd been. How quiet. She'd used her lank hair to shield her face, to shield herself, but from what? And in asking that question, I'd become interested in her—in who this mousy, bashful girl might really be. Maybe she'd reveal a bit of herself tonight, and maybe that bit would be as shiny as the glimmer of copper under patina.

Of course I was mortified at the thought of other things—like dancing with her, another girl, just my height. I could scarcely imagine what it would be like to hold her fingers, to touch her waist. How perverse these gestures seemed. How contrary to the natural order of things (not that I had any right to speak of the natural order).

Mother would need smelling salts if ever she were to find out. I hadn't mentioned the Freshman Ball in my letters. I didn't want to fill her head with disturbing possibilities, to make her think I'd taken our plan to unnecessary lengths. Watching Wick light the cigarette and take the first puff, I could admit only to myself that the thought of taking a girl to the dance was tantalizing. Like walking to the very brink of the quarry and wiggling my toes over the edge. Like thinking, maybe, of taking that final step, that plunge into thick rushing air, into nothing, a total abyss, not by accident but just because I could.

Wick said there was a special way to smoke the marihuana. But he didn't remember what that was, so we inhaled it like we would a normal cigarette. Still, I could tell something was different. When I exhaled, there was almost nothing to let out. And then Wick remembered, on the second pass, the cigarette now between Harry's agitated fingers, how his friend had said you have to hold the smoke in, way down in your gut. So Harry tried again, and to the surprise of all of us—and mostly Harry himself—he didn't start to cough or wheeze or hack, but held his breath almost like he'd been smoking those skinny cigarettes his whole life. Finally he exhaled, slowly, smoothly, a tear or two running down his face. A christening, I swear it. We expected something to happen; never had our friend been so expertly deviant. And something did. He began to giggle, without any nervousness at all, saying that he felt lifted, wide open. We pressed him for more details, but all he did was laugh.

It was Wick's turn again, but he gave the cigarette to me first, saying, "Do it like Harry did, Charlie-boy."

So I tried, conscious of the fact that the cigarette had grown stubby, that this would probably be my last turn. And maybe I'd absorbed the nervousness that Harry had shed. All I could think about was Wick sitting next to me, close as usual, so that our legs were touching, just a little but enough.

Wick watched me intently, coaching me to hold it in, hold it in, until I couldn't stand it anymore. And I did hold it in, thinking, whatever you say I'll do—surely you know that. Then, suddenly, I felt something, too. Not lifted or wide open, but tranquil and solitary, far away from my friends, from this smoky room, maybe even from myself.

Maybe I'd walked off that quarry ledge after all.

Wick put his hand on my shoulder. "You feel it, don't you?"

I nodded, holding out the cigarette, my arm moving so slowly the action didn't even seem real. Wick's hand grazed mine. The cigarette was between his lips now. What a picture-show moment: Wick big and theatrical in his glad rags, that face both chisel-sharp and vulnerable. I stared at it, trying to determine if it was mostly one way or the other. An eternal mystery, an infernal mystery. One that was never meant to be solved, for the pleasure was in the guessing. I watched Wick inhale deeply, his eyes closed, locked tight, like he was plunging into ecstasy, so that it was a shock when after a full minute he exhaled, flicked the burnt-down stub onto the floor, and declared, "Shit, fellas, I don't feel a thing."

*   *   *

We were late meeting the girls after all. A whole twenty-five minutes late, so they had gone from being casually concerned to downright fretful, tapping their kitten heels on the sidewalk.

Harry and I had decided to meet the girls in front of the diner. Ethel and Helen hadn't wanted us to come to their homes. Though I didn't know why, secretly I wondered if maybe they lived in the same poor neighborhoods I'd seen during my work-study trips. I wondered if one of the slanted shanties with thin clapboard walls and windowless holes belonged to Ethel's family and if she spent what little money she had on fancy fabrics and buttons and patterns so that she could look like a Cottager, or whatever it was a Cottager was called in New Haven.

Harry had said we couldn't possibly meet the girls in front of Commons, the location of the ball. "They'll be stolen by the first freshmen who lay eyes on 'em," he'd told me. So the diner it was. As Harry and I walked, I realized he was still acting strange—his speech fast and fearless and a little incomprehensible. But maybe I shouldn't have worried. As soon as we saw the girls, he didn't hesitate to drape his arm around Ethel's shoulders. And Ethel, maybe worried that she was going to be stood up, blushed with pleasure.

"Whatsa matter, Harry? You've been crying? Your eyes are all red," she said.

"Crying over you, baby," he responded, sounding so astonishingly un-Harry-like, I wished Wick could have heard him.

Meeting my date, I acted more reserved. I was feeling more like myself now, but some of the foggy feeling of the cigarette lingered. I was a little detached, a little withdrawn. I hesitated when I saw Helen, not altogether sure she was the same girl I'd met in the diner. She'd pulled back her curtainlike hair into a smooth knot at the nape of her neck. There was no missing her face now. It was shiny, pale white, and moonish. Harry'd been right that she looked different, better, maybe even pretty. Maybe if she weren't wilting with shyness.

Harry had hoped to spend as much time with Ethel as possible. Yet as we made our way to Commons, Ethel slipped from his side, and Helen from mine. The two girls huddled together, whispery and intimate, wreathed in a feminine, perfumy aura. Harry and I watched them as they walked ahead of us. They wore their coats draped about their shoulders. But still we could see a portion of their dresses—shiny and whisper-soft all the way to their ankles. Ethel wore canary-yellow, Helen a vivid maroon. And it was hard not to stare, with Ethel's short, turned-up curls bouncing jauntily and Helen's rhinestone comb winking coquettishly under the streetlamps.

We weren't the only ones to look. Inside a balloon- and streamer-festooned Commons, Harry and I took the girls' coats. When their dresses were revealed—silken silhouettes clinging softly to bosom, waist, and hips—I could feel dozens of eyes turn. A quick glance around told Harry and me that the man-to-woman ratio was as dismally disproportionate as the most desperate yearlings had feared. My friend's arm swiftly reappeared around Ethel, but I hadn't any nerve. The most I could do was walk a little closer to Helen—asking her if she was cold.

"Why don't I get you your coat again?"

"But how will anyone see my dress?" she asked.

Up close she smelled wonderful—of gardenias. I knew the scent because Mother had once owned some expensive French perfume that smelled the same way. She'd used it over a number of years, spraying it sparingly from an ornate cerulean bottle with a gold atomizer.

"I must conserve it," she'd told me. "I'll probably never be in Paris again. Oh, I shudder to think!"

I wondered how Helen had come by her perfume. Only, to ask this question would imply that she had the right to ask me one, too. I didn't want to open the gates, not when my mind was still murky-strange, and not when Wick caught my eye from across the room, sticking up his thumb ever so slightly so that I knew he approved of my date.

"Do you want something to drink? Some punch?" I asked Helen. Almost before she could answer, I told her I would be back in a flash and headed toward a table of refreshments, only I couldn't help detouring to Wick first. He was standing next to the stage, at the very back of Commons. Nearby, the band had started to warm up. He was watching everyone, but mostly the girls.

"Have you found one you like?" I asked.

"What? Oh, hey, I like them all. But that one stands out. See her over there? There's something about her."

"What is it?" I asked, too quickly and too seriously, not sure I wanted to know what made the girl in the blue dress different from the dozens of others roaming Commons.

"I've no idea." Wick tapped his top hat with an index finger. "That's why I keep looking."

The girl in the blue dress wasn't a classic beauty, but on this night she could have fooled most anyone. Cold, exertion, or rouge had rubied her cheeks, and her eyes were starry-bright with life, with that whirring hope and sense of exhilaration that some people call youthfulness. In later years she might become too round at the hips, even matronly. But for now she looked supple, a just-ripe fruit, with the kind of figure you see in advertisements for hosiery and skin cream. She knew her power—I could see that much in her pose, head thrown back, hand at cocked hip, her elbow creating a pointy-sharp triangle. Her large, slick teeth showed as her lips tweaked into a half smile. Her eyes flashed from behind a pair of spectacles that seemed, somehow, both unfashionable and terribly daring.

Knowing that Wick's eyes were on her, I went green. But I also felt admiration, for there was no denying that this girl was in her prime. Eventually she saw us staring, and smiled wider, a little devilishly, not hesitating to walk right over—I couldn't believe her nerve—and introduce herself. And wouldn't you just know it, her name sounded like mine: Ada. So almost at once my jealousy squeezed me tighter than ever, my own ribs a miserable corset. I choked out a half-hearted greeting, my voice snide to my own ears. She told us in a con-

fident, high-piping voice that she was in college over at Albertus
Magnus, only a stone's throw from Yale, did we know the school? She
revealed that she would have gone *here,* if only Yale had let her. She'd
even applied, to heck with the rules. But the letter had spelled it out.
"Despite your fine credentials and unquestionably distinguished academic record," she said, pretending to read from an imaginary letter,
"Yale does not presently permit women in its undergraduate program of studies."

Even so, this girl—Ada—had no intention of giving up, of pursuing her dream, that is. She was going to be a professor—not a teacher,
thank you very much—but a professor with a capital P. And the way
she said it, with saucy, no-nonsense conviction, we believed her. We
just had to.

Wick asked her how she liked the ball.

"It's not shabby—if you're partial to this sort of thing."

And what did she think of Yale men?

"You're all alike," she replied, laughing. "Too big for your
britches."

At this Wick grabbed his chest, feigning pain of the heart, only I
suspected he wasn't feigning at all.

As Ada spoke, she looked as much at me as she did at Wick. But to
me it was clear whom she favored. I knew from firsthand experience
that any girl in her right mind would take a shine to him.

Though I was jealous, I was also impressed. I'd never met a girl
like this. Of course I'd heard of girls going to college. Some of the
Cottagers' daughters did—to Smith and Wellesley and Mount
Holyoke and Barnard. But I'd supposed from the way they'd talked,
whimsically, dismissively, that they were just going as a diversion en
route to a homebound marriage and a half-dozen children. They
certainly didn't talk like Ada, who proclaimed she'd always known
she was going to be a historian.

"History's my only love," she said with her sly, twisty smile.

I knew I ought to go back to Helen, but I couldn't bear the
thought of leaving Wick in the company of this siren. So I stayed,

hoping that Helen had gone in search of Ethel, and that Harry was watching over the two of them.

Wick's eyes became wider with every word that came out of Ada's mouth. With any other girl, he would have moved closer, confident in himself, in his flirtations. But with Ada, who gave no sign of being besotted, he kept his distance.

"What's that in your pocket?" she asked him. "It's a flask, isn't it? Let's have a look, mister."

"What are you talking about?"

"Don't play dumb with me. I'd know that shape anywhere."

"It wouldn't be right," he dodged.

"Why are you carrying it if not to use it?"

"In case of emergencies."

"What do you think this is? We ran out of smart things to say five minutes ago."

"It wouldn't be right," he repeated.

"You mean it wouldn't be *ladylike.*"

"Well, yes, now that you get down to it."

"Wick, don't be so old-fashioned! I can have a drink if I want it. I've already poured a little of my own firewater into the punch bowl, if you want to know the truth. This party needs a kick in the seat."

"You didn't," Wick challenged.

"I most certainly did." At that, Ada opened her purse to reveal her own flask. Silver, like Wick's.

"Hot dog!" was all he could say.

A moment later the band started in earnest, and Ada began to tap her feet. "I'm wearing my dancing shoes," she said, adjusting the collar of her dress. "That's a hint. But in case you boys are dim, I'll ask outright. Would either of you care to dance?"

I couldn't believe it—a girl requesting a dance! How brazenly forward, how presumptuous! At the same time, I realized how absurd my disbelief was.

The music was translucent, bubbly, like the champagne the Cottagers sometimes drank outside the hotels in long-stemmed glasses.

Yet dancing was one skill Mother and I hadn't practiced. Although I knew basic steps, I didn't know how to lead a partner. I refused Ada as politely as I could, knowing that Wick wouldn't say no, and that my chaperoning was destined to cease.

All I could do was watch them as he offered his hand and she took it blithely. They were one of the first couples on the floor and certainly the best-looking, Ada's dress twirling a little at the hem, her ankles slim and shapely. And Wick—a fine dancer, his legs slippy-sure. Though it was he who led, it was Ada who seemed in charge, moving freely with a joyful abandon that belied her prim appearance. Dance after dance they continued, even when the floor became crowded. And dance after dance I stared, miserable.

Having volunteered to mind Ada's purse, I grew curious. Maybe more jealous than curious. Turning away from the dance floor, I twisted the star-shaped clasp. All I wanted was one clue into this girl's life. I rifled through the contents, carefully at first, then heedlessly, my sense of entitlement fueled by a burning resentment. Yet I found neither talisman nor pixie dust, just the flask and some ordinary items: coins tied into a lacy handkerchief, a tube of lipstick, a comb, a compact. Then I noticed it: at the bottom, a small book, maybe a diary. I looked up cautiously. The dance floor was thick now; I couldn't spot them. Perhaps that meant they couldn't spot me. Impetuously, I opened the book and scanned the pages, keen for any insight at all. But there were no dates and no entries, only lists of words, sketches of faces and buildings and trees, and quotes from women like Jane Austen, Belle Starr, and Victoria Woodhull. In the end I snapped shut the purse, feeling intrigued but little the wiser.

By now a few balloons, exhausted of their helium, wobbled drunkenly from the ceiling. I watched them as the band played louder, more furiously, egged on by the stamping of feet and the swinging of arms. Finally, Ada returned, moist-faced and ebullient.

"Did you have a sip?" she asked.

"What?"

"From the flask. You could have, you know."

"Oh. I—I didn't think to."

"Why not?"

Before I could answer, Wick returned too. From the look on his face, you'd think he'd been orphaned. He sidled up closer to Ada, but her posture stayed stiff and remote.

"I need to freshen up," she told us, not making eye contact with Wick, who stared at her desperately. She took the purse from my hands and gave me a wink. "Don't miss me too much."

"Hey, how's about one more dance?" Wick asked.

But already she'd slipped away, both Wick and I expecting her to turn around, at least to look back and wave. But she didn't; she kept going, the swell of the crowd rapidly closing in on her, that blue dress the color of a memory. So all Wick could do was stare, wistful-eyed. And all he could say was, "Wow, did you ever see anything like her?"

Now that I'd been gone so long, Helen would surely be in a mood. I went, finally, for that forgotten glass of punch. Then I remembered Ada's declaration and opted for a cup of strawberry soda pop instead. This I carried with me until I spotted my date. She was sitting at a table with Harry and Ethel, way off on the sidelines. Though she saw me looking at her, she refused to acknowledge me. When I sat beside her, she turned away and pushed the glass of pop aside.

"Harry already got me a drink," she scolded. "An hour ago."

Harry glanced at me a little scornfully. I couldn't tell if he was more angry with me for being ungentlemanly or for forcing him into a trio.

I hadn't a decent excuse for being tardy. And even if I had, I doubted it would hold water. Anger had straightened Helen's hunched back into something rigid and arrow-sharp. When she spoke, she addressed Harry and Ethel alone. I didn't try to make amends straight away. I waited for Harry and Ethel to make a hasty excuse, get up, and start dancing. And still I waited, hoping for a sign that Helen would forgive me, that we could start fresh somehow. When that moment didn't come, I knew I'd have to say something, anything, to save the night.

"I'm sorry, Helen, really I am. I shouldn't have left you alone like that. I lost track of things. Of time. What a lousy thing to do."

She turned toward me then, her moony face alight with pride and anger in equal measure. "Really, Charles, you're impossible."

"What?"

"All night you haven't shown a scrap of interest in me. You haven't talked to me. You haven't looked at me. You haven't said one nice thing about my dress. And now you have the gall—the nerve!—to spout ridiculous excuses. Have you any idea how to treat a girl?"

And perhaps—unlikely as it was—I hadn't. Nor had I any idea how to treat *this* girl, who wasn't timid after all. And yes, perhaps she was different, special, underappreciated, just as I'd suspected. Only there was a problem: I couldn't give her what she wanted. I'd escorted her to the ball out of caprice. Of course she'd expected more. She'd been hoping I would become her fella—she who was always overlooked for her more beautiful friend. There was no other way to explain the perfume, the dress, the satiny shoes, the careful taming of that listless hair. And now this: a rankling so sore it could only have sprung from hope.

"I have to tell you something, something important," I said, drawing my chair closer to hers, closing in on that gardenia nebula. Beneath the fierce flush of her skin, I saw the powdery delicacy of a young girl. "It's that—well. Here it is: I don't know what I'm doing. I haven't any idea, none at all. How do you like that?"

She said nothing for a moment, staring me in the eye, figuring something out. "What do you take me for, Charles?" she said finally. "A boob? I saw the way you were talking with that girl—the one wearing eyeglasses. You know what you're doing, all right. You certainly do. And you know something? I think you ought to take me home. Right this second. I know a Romeo when I see one."

"But we haven't even danced yet."

"That's because you haven't been here."

"Oh, let's forget all that, all right? I don't want to be anywhere else. I'm here with you now. You're the only one I'm looking at."

At that, Helen softened. I'd said what she'd needed to hear: a glimmer of a compliment, a hint of attraction. Maybe after the ball she'd turn my words over in her head. She'd discuss them with Ethel, examining them from all possible angles. She'd pick at this proclamation, searching for fresh meaning, the same way I sometimes excavated my conversations with Wick.

As we stood to dance, her face radiated an immaculate happiness. I felt sorry for her even as I fell into the blur of her perfume, like falling into a heap of flower petals. Mother said the gardenia was white, delicate, and exotic; it was a bloom that needed the spray of the Arabian Sea and a scorching sun. It was so intoxicating, she claimed, it could make you fall in love in minutes.

I slid one hand around Helen's waist, the fabric of her dress so silken I had to hold her firm. And in my other hand—her fingers— longer than mine, cool and supple. Our cheeks brushed. Hers felt as it looked—pliant, fragile, foreign. Her breasts, lofted high, pressed encouragingly against my chest, which was now so accustomed to bandaging it barely protested.

"I'm not a very good dancer," I warned.

"But Charles, dancing's the most natural thing in the world."

Yes, but what about leading, I wanted to ask? I stumbled a little at first, knocking her knees with mine, but finally realizing the trick: to exert more pressure on her back with my palm, cuing her to pivot, and turn, and spin. By the fourth song we had it right: gliding and swaying like we were an old pair. I felt suddenly content, coasting on the lingering effects of Wick's cigarette and on the toasty intimacy of the dense dance floor. The strains of music began to sound like romantic overtures. Above, the Commons' huge chandeliers had dimmed. The light fell dreamy-sheer through delicious dollops of crystal. And maybe we were in a dream, Helen and I, both half-believing in something that wasn't there. Until, out of the corner of my eye, I saw Wick. He had found Ada again, no doubt after a hunt. The two were dancing so slowly they were scarcely moving at all, just swaying. Though they were several yards away and intermittently blocked from view by other couples, still I could see he was smitten. He was gazing at her in a way he'd never gazed at me—*would* never gaze at me—rapture, tenderness, and amazement all tightly bound and bursting. I couldn't stop staring. Not even when Helen whispered to me that I was acting rude again and that she'd had quite enough. The girl in the eyeglasses wasn't *that* pretty.

"What do you see in her?"

I whispered back that it wasn't she who interested me.

"Prove it," Helen said.

So I did, pressing my mouth against hers, which was partly open in surprise, in accusation. When she didn't protest, I kissed her harder and deeper, like I meant it. And maybe I did, if only for that moment. Maybe the body can settle on misplaced desire, so long as the gardenias are blooming. So long as the heart stays bound.

Later that night Helen told me she didn't want me to walk her home. I agreed to walk her to the diner instead. It was long closed. A single bulb shone hesitantly from inside, scarcely granting outline to the tables, booths, and stools.

"I don't feel right leaving you here," I told her.

I felt strangely protective of this girl, who now preferred whispering to speaking, who leaned into my side as we walked, looking at me through eyes glazed with the sweet trust of newfound affection.

"It's only a short walk."

"So let me take you."

"Didn't I tell you about my father? He hates fellas your age. He'd treat you awful if he saw you, I just know it. He chased my last steady with a baseball bat down three blocks, no fooling."

I sensed she was lying, but I didn't let on. I tried to persuade her a second time: Why couldn't I walk her even part of the way? If her father saw me, I'd duck behind a tree, I joked. But she refused again and I relented.

It was midnight by the time I kissed her good night, this time chastely, for our luxe encounter had dimmed and I was eager to part her company. I thought she would walk away first. But when she stood still, the hem of her plummy dress swept to her knees by a breeze, I began my trek back to Durfee. As I rounded the corner she was still there, looking at me, maybe not wanting me to see which direction she needed to take.

Back in my dormitory room, I wasn't ready to turn in. All I could do was think about how Wick was probably still out with Ada. When the ball had ended, I'd caught a glimpse of them walking out of Commons arm in arm. Where were they now, and what were they doing? My mind conjured all sorts of possibilities, every one of which made my stomach cramp.

I shucked off my clothes and my bindings and threw them in a heap on my bed. I stood stark naked, running my hands through my bristly hair, along the knotty-lean contours of my body, not sure what to do. Just knowing I needed to do something, that lying motionless in my bed would feel awful, something like dying. I didn't want to sleep—and I didn't want to be alone. Maybe it was the last hurrah of that magical cigarette that made me restless, or maybe the moody shifts of the night. I didn't know. All I knew was that I had to get out.

I started to dress again, but the thought of putting on my bindings, of compressing myself into something neat and confined and false, was too much to bear. Squeezing my lumpish breasts with a combination of contempt and pride, I decided to wear my girl's clothes instead. After Phin had discovered them, I'd put them right back into the drawer. Now that the secret was out, it didn't matter where I put the evidence.

My skirt was in need of a good airing. It felt unfamiliar as it rustled around my bare legs. How strange the touch after my long sojourn as a young man! There was nothing to keep my legs from sliding together. The flow of fabric felt easy, unrestrictive, even indecent. The blouse, too, was weird to me now. I wanted to see if I looked as odd as I felt, but there was no mirror in the room, only in the lavatory. I had to content myself with looking down at the expanse of wrinkled cotton and remembering my spectral image in the mirror that hung over my dresser in Stony Creek.

And then, without warning, I had a plan. Or some semblance of a plan. I wasn't able to say that I knew what I was doing, only that I was determined to press on.

Pulling on my trousers, I tucked the length of my skirt awkwardly into the waistband. Although the extra fabric ballooned around my middle, I hid it well enough with my coat. This I buttoned to my chin so that the collar of my blouse didn't show. I pulled on long wool socks and my boy's shoes. I kept my hat low. All in all, I felt quite uncomfortable, though I was finally the person I'd been portraying: an amalgam of both sexes, passing by only the humblest margin as either.

Leaving Durfee, I greeted acquaintances hastily as I passed. With my coat on, I looked the same as I always did. I doubted anyone would notice the subtle buoyancy of my breasts, free beneath my winter layers, or the anxiousness threaded through my friendliness. I took the same path Wick and I had taken the day we'd walked to the Last Anchor. Without him, arm slung casually around my shoulders or sleeve brushing mine, I felt cagey. I walked with long, confident strides, trying my best to fool everyone.

Eventually, Yale gave way, university landmarks and buildings thinning until at last there was no sign of the school. I no longer recognized the faces I passed, and most appeared uneasy and aloof. Even the architecture seemed to caution my arrival. Factory buildings, hulking and windowless, dominated the area. Dark residues stained their sides, a sign of the potency of the now dormant smokestacks. Beneath my feet, the walkways had cracked wide in places, pushed out as if by angry subterranean creatures. Cobblestones were missing on the walks, the gaps cunningly covered with a thin snow, so that a single footstep could be treacherous.

The tenements were the most neglected of all. Many had the charred, blistered surface of a fire combated too late, or left to blaze on purpose. Fire escapes and balconies teetered. Shutters hung crookedly. Windows, particularly on the lower levels, had holes surrounded by intricate spiderwebs of crackled glass. In the alleys between the row houses, I saw the bright sparkle of shattered bottles.

Now and then a dog would appear, shivering and curious, its dirty flank rippled by jutting ribs. I wished I had some scrap of food to offer, but my pockets were empty. I whispered "sorry" as one mutt passed by skittishly, pausing to see if I was friend or foe. It was a pretty thing—or at least it would be if it were clean—with unusual brown and yellow markings and eyes darkly lined like an Egyptian pharaoh's. I put out my hand to pet it, but it continued onward, limping and distrustful. It was one of the many pets that had been pushed out of hungry homes and left to fend for themselves these last few years.

It seemed like a long time before I reached the unsavory places Wick and I had passed the night we'd gone to the Last Anchor. The streets here were exactly as I remembered them: dingy, ill-tended, bathed in as much shadow as light. The women were as I remembered them, too, loitering in a way that I knew, I just knew, what they were looking for.

I continued on, head down, zigzagging down several more blocks before choosing an alley, the darkest I could find. For a moment I worried someone might be watching.

"But who? Who do you expect, Adele?" I asked aloud. "The bogeyman?"

My eyes adjusted to the dark slowly. I saw outlines and halos at first, then the row of putrid-smelling trash cans. From behind one a puss let loose a savage yowl, then skittered away, choosing the shortest route, straight between my legs. I cried out too, alarmed, pinching myself into silence.

By now I was used to changing in the dark. Careful not to touch anything, even the walls of the tenements that flanked me, I pulled off my trousers. Then I removed my coat and put the trousers inside, balling up both items into a tidy, innocuous parcel and tucking it under my arm. I removed my hat, too, pausing uncertainly before leaving it there in the alley.

Same as when I left the custodian's closet in the Payne Whitney gymnasium: one deep breath before emerging anew. A girl this time, in summer clothes, and I would have shivered if I weren't so flushed with an anxious excitement. I already felt different, and I already walked differently, though my shoes and socks were all that remained of my boy's wardrobe. I cut back to where the late-night shows were playing, where the women beckoned with outstretched fingers, cooing "babyface," "honey," "sugar pie." But they no longer cooed at me, and I wasn't sure whether I felt better or worse for it.

As a boy I would have picked the show with care, reading the signs and taking my time. But as a girl I was hobbled by the weight of my decision and by the eyes that had begun to appraise me. I saw in them that I fit no easy category, being neither a good-time girl nor a steady on the arm of a masher. I was a curiosity: a girl alone and out-doors at this ungodly hour. Modestly, if unseasonably, dressed, a gamine with too-short hair and a tentative air, I was nothing if not the strangest of strangers.

I was relieved when I saw him. Tall and spindly, he looked a little like Wick, at least from behind. I caught only a glimpse of his profile, and I couldn't have said how old he was or if he was handsome or why I felt like I'd seen him before. But there was something familiar about him, about the ostentatious red plume in his hat, about his careless shuffling walk, and that was enough. At that moment, the possibility of him was enough; I can't explain it any better than that.

As he walked by I followed, trailing a good twenty yards behind. We continued on this way for a long time, until he finally chose a doorway, one of many he had paused before. I counted to one hun-dred, then followed him in. Inside was a foyer, dim and smelling of dust and ale and soiled things. The wallpaper had been expensive once, but it was now dingy and yellowed. On the floor, the butts of

cigars and cigarettes had been swept into little piles. Behind a counter
at the far side of the room a man stood. He was dressed like a bellhop
at one of the Stony Creek hotels: tasseled shoulders and a dozen shiny
buttons on his jacket. Next to the counter was a door with a brass
handle.

The man with the feathered hat lingered at the counter, his back
to me. He purchased a ticket and turned the brass handle, disappearing. I colored, feeling foolish when I drew the bellhop's attention. His
eyes started low, wandering from my shoes to my ankles, to the hem
of my rumpled skirt and beyond. The urge to flee came to me swiftly,
as it had so many times before.

"One for the late show?" he asked sarcastically. His voice was surprisingly high: it reminded me that I oughtn't speak. I couldn't even
remember how my regular voice sounded.

He held out his hand and continued, "It's a buck. It's always a
buck a show."

My wallet was stuck somewhere in the bundle of clothes. Flustered, I wiggled my hand into its middle and dug around for the
bulge of leather. The man tapped his fingers impatiently on the
countertop.

"Once the show's over, it's over," he warned, snatching the dollar I
finally handed to him. "No loitering around in here. I don't care what
the weather's like."

I nodded, eyes low as I reached for the handle. Abruptly, the man
stretched out his arm to block me. His whole demeanor had changed
in a flash, his expression faintly frightened.

"Say, you're not here for an audition, are you? I don't have any
girls on the list."

I smiled at him, thinking, let him wonder, then slipped through
the door.

I wasn't sure what I'd been expecting. Maybe girls like the ones in
Wick's dirty magazines: plump and frolicsome, eyes doll-numb. I
didn't count on this element of theater: a droopy curtain in front of a
small elevated stage. Before the stage sat rows of chairs, dozens of

rows for dozens of men. The only light in the room shone on the curtain. The seats in the back were safely dim. I didn't have to search long before I found him, in the very last row, the feather my beacon.

I sat exactly three seats away, not daring to turn in his direction but knowing he was aware of me, that he was trying not to show it. Maybe he had first noticed me before, when I'd trailed behind him like a dog. Like a runaway who needs someone to cling to.

I put the bundle of clothes on my lap and clenched it tight. Ahead of me I studied the silhouettes of scattered men slung back in their seats. From behind, these patrons seemed tattered and sad somehow. Just before the curtain rose, the man in the feathered hat stole a look at me. Just one. So quick I almost missed it.

The open stage revealed an upright piano on one side and two girls on the other. I wasn't sure what I was seeing at first. There was nothing raunchy about the girls, nothing in keeping with their after-midnight appearance in this seedy place. They wore flouncy skirts, fishnet stockings with lines in the back, and high-heeled shoes. They were made up to look like each other—the same coffee-colored waves parted on the same side, the same lipstick heavy on the curl of their lips. They were of similar height, too, one a little stouter than the other, broad at the bosom and waist where the other was svelte.

I tried to focus on one, but always my gaze reverted to both, pulled to the link of their hands, to the wiggle of two pairs of hips and the shuffle-slide of four feet across the boards. They danced in tandem to a tune being played on the piano by a man who looked like an older, more woebegone version of the bellhop. The slumped figures in the chairs had leaned forward. The man in the feathered hat had, too.

The pianist wasn't good. He played the same simple, whimsical ditty at various speeds, missing different notes at each turn. But the girls were used to his rough playing, anyone could see. They appeared eternally lighthearted, smiling, blowing kisses, and bending suggestively even when the song went sour. By the fourth repetition they had separated their hands just long enough to unbutton their blouses, slowly and with great flirtation, removing them finally, all eyes on their thick conical brassieres, the noise in the room escalating into a jumbled collection of hoots, bleats, and heavy exhalations.

When the man in the feathered hat changed seats, extinguishing the space between us, I wasn't surprised. The time of night, the duration of our proximity, the sight of so much skin—all must have given him courage. And anyway, this is what I'd been expecting when I'd set out: something uncertain, something a little risky. After a minute he leaned toward me and whispered into my ear. I was pretty—pretty enough to be onstage with the other girls. Had anyone ever told me that? His voice was unsteady, tinged with an accent I couldn't place. He wasn't used to this sort of thing, or else he was out of practice.

I glanced at him, trying to make out his face. It was strong-featured, maybe good-looking, maybe not. Suddenly, he seemed nothing like Wick.

He placed his hand on my knee awkwardly. I took the hat from his head and put it on my own. The feather felt silken and oily as I stroked it.

"Wouldn't have figured on seeing a girl here, in the audience," he went on. His words drifted into one another monotonously. "Wouldn't have figured on it, no. Must be my lucky night."

He moved his hand farther, to my thigh, but sensing a rigidity, he snatched it back. We kept our eyes glued to the girls onstage, now naked from the waist up. I wondered, struck by the randomness of the thought, if they had rouged their nipples.

It was just an impulse, to kiss him. Just an idea, so absurd that it somehow seemed logical. Everything must be logical at some time and in some place, I rationalized. I leaned in quickly, before I let myself reconsider. My lips mashed against his, inexpertly, obtrusively, and I shuddered. The kiss was nothing like the one I'd shared with Helen, which had been ardent, seeking, almost right. He had a potent, base taste.

Tobacco, I thought.

He paused, head tilting back. He was deciding on something. And maybe I would have fled, if he'd waited even one second longer, if he'd shown any more reserve, but he didn't. He leaned in, and this time when our lips met it wasn't so alarming. The feel of his mouth was warm, peculiar, not as pleasant as it was exciting. I let his hands twine around me, one about the waist, the other along the side of my breast. The sensation of novelty swept all reservations aside. There was nothing but the repetition of the sad piano and the stilted space of the seats, the hand rest between us a funny, blundering obstacle so that from time to time we would giggle humorlessly as we fumbled and tasted and stole whatever we wanted from the other.

He was greedier than I—this surprised me. I thought no one else could feel so lonely. Tentative at first, his touches became probes, powerfully insistent, leading my hand to his hardened penis, which poked out from his pants. I touched it awkwardly, then moved my fingers away. He was whispering about bringing me to his apartment; we'd have more privacy there. I wouldn't have to be so shy.

It was close, he said, nipping at the skin of my neck with his teeth. Right around the corner. When I didn't reply, he told me, his voice deepening, he didn't want to be alone, not tonight. He'd been alone too much lately. The last two years, if I wanted to know the truth. And he could see I didn't want to be alone, either.

Still, I didn't speak. I wouldn't compromise my last remaining shield.

We were still exploring each other when the saggy curtains closed, my hand finally molded around his long, thin penis, warm and sticky-moist in my palm. He put his hand around mine and showed me how to work it up and down. I obliged, fueled by a strange fusion of mischievousness, guilt, and shame. Still, I wasn't adrift in the moment, not like before. The craving to touch and be touched was passing quickly. When the piano stopped, I realized the show itself had been sustaining it. As if the girls and the little stage had provided a crude, temporary sanctuary. I drew away from the man at once, adjusting my messed blouse, pulling my skirt back over my knees.

Frantically, I searched for the bundle of clothes and found it on the floor. The man started to talk again, louder and more rapidly, his words almost indecipherable now. I noticed for the first time that he was older. He had lines and tiny nicks in his skin. His hair was receding from his forehead. His squinty eyes were alert, yes, but resentful, too. The light against the curtains seemed stronger now, but no less dull, like the stars in this part of town. It shone on something shifty and desperate between us. Something the man's touch had stoked and simultaneously enabled me to ignore.

I clutched the bundle and stood up, putting out my hand—the good-bye I'd learned at Yale, always applicable, surely. The man, still seated, stared at my outstretched fingers. Finally, he shook his head and laughed without humor.

"Fucking whore," he said.

I looked straight ahead as I fled, face red, but I wouldn't let him know he'd gotten to me. The bellhop watched me as I passed through the foyer. Outside in the cold, I saw that the streets were emptier. Only a few people now, bundled and shivery and grim. There was a chance that the man would follow me, that he would beg and taunt or else become aggressive. I'd seen all kinds of behavior standing outside the saloons of Stony Creek.

I was still wearing his hat, had known I was wearing it when I left him. But I hadn't wanted to return it—to give him anything else. Which isn't to say I wanted to keep it.

I hurried to the alley, looking over my shoulder every few yards. The smell in that narrow corridor seemed more foul now. I tried to breathe through my mouth as I untwisted my bundle and started to change. The little hairs on my arms and legs stood up. Something wasn't right, something under that sweet, lurid odor of rot. Something lurking as I pushed my feet through the legs of my pants. Buttons on my coat still undone, fingers shaking too much, I bumped against a trash can, slamming my hip. I cursed, loudly, too, though I'd sworn I'd keep quiet.

There was only one way into the alley and one way out. It would be easy to be cornered here, the walls too high for anyone to hear— and anyway, there was no one to come to my rescue. I pushed past the shifting shadows, half-expecting one to grab me, teetering, banging against those filthy cans again, strangely heavy on my feet. Until finally: open space, those anemic stars.

Halfway home, running hard, legs on fire, I realized I'd abandoned two perfectly good hats that night. But I wouldn't go back. I wouldn't chance seeing the man again, even if his face was already fading from memory. Even if by daybreak I'd hardly remember it at all.

Chapter Ten

M y two suits, being wool, couldn't be washed, and I'd wait until they were in truly wretched condition before plunking down money at the dry cleaner. As for my other clothes, these I laundered exactly once a week.

The other fellows around Durfee were less thrifty. They used the pricey Student Laundry Service, which meant they piled all their washables into big blue bins, which they left outside their dormitory rooms. The bins would disappear and miraculously reappear a day later, all the clothes newly washed and ironed. Alternatively, some students made private arrangements with local laundresses: women of all ages and matters of appearance who for a humble fee heaved burly sacks over their shoulders and stumble-plodded their way back to sinks, bathtubs, and washboards all over New Haven.

Had I mentioned the topic in a letter, Mother might have insisted that I have my laundry done like the rest of the boys. She might have reminded me how impressions count, more than anything else, and how lowbrow work like laundering was something to avoid. Even so, after all these years of washing clothes, I couldn't imagine paying someone else to do it.

I'd created my own routine, using the lavatory sink in the morning on Sundays, early enough that I'd been interrupted only once or twice by my confounded suitemates. I'd scrub out stains and odors and rinse and scrub some more, wringing fabric with red-knuckled hands, working with the facility and alacrity that come with practice, measuring by eye and instinct proportions of bleach to water. I'd bought some of the items I needed, thinking that over time these expenses would certainly be less than the cost of a service. Other items I stole from Commons or from the closet in the Payne Whiney Gymnasium where I changed. Under my bed I stowed white vinegar for grass stains, cornstarch for grease, ammonia for yellow smudges of sweat.

When I was through with the lavatory, I'd return with the sopping pile to my room. When I'd first moved in, I'd hammered hooks high on the walls at either end. On Sundays I'd take a coil of rope from atop my closet and hang it on the hooks: a makeshift clothesline. The clothes would drip-dry onto my floor, my bed, my desk, no matter how hard I'd squeezed. But when the radiator was running or my window was open on a sunny day, everything was ready by evening. I could take down the line and there was no proof. Nothing damning or strange.

I found comfort in my Sunday-morning ritual, the comfort of a familiar history. I didn't worry so much what my suitemates must think, what Phin or Wick would say if they happened to look under my bed. They could call me nothing worse than quirky or queer or penny-pinching. I wasn't washing my menstrual rags, after all.

But maybe I was a little too intrepid, not hesitating even an instant when Harry knocked on my door one Sunday afternoon; and me, at my desk, reading ahead in my biology text, cold beads of water intermittently falling on my head, on the pages of the book, calling, "Come on in, Harry. I had a feeling you'd try to drag me to Sterling."

How his jaw dropped when he saw the line. The clothes were carefully arranged with a bunch of clothespins I'd taken with me from Stony Creek—mementos, I'd thought at the time, stuffing them into the carpetbag with a rueful smile. Remembering the day we'd met, how our junky luggage had formed the basis of an alliance, I wouldn't have anticipated Harry's shock. But there it was, plain as punch. He stood atremble in the doorway.

"I didn't want to pay someone else," I said, shrugging. "What's the matter with that?"

"I didn't even say anything."

"You have a terrible poker face, Harry."

"I don't know how to wash clothes," he responded, his tone flat.

"Your mother never showed you?"

"My mother? Why would she?"

And then I realized what was bothering him: it wasn't that I'd done menial work, but that I'd done women's work. One was unsavory; the other, unfathomable.

"I'm saving money." I tried to sound blithe.

"Yeah, of course."

That's when my fury took hold, the fury of being misunderstood for so long, even if the basis of the misunderstanding was my own doing. I don't know why I got so angry, at that moment more than any other time at Yale. I hadn't realized how stifling it had become: this thin-walled house of intrigue and deception I'd closed myself into.

I slammed shut the book. My whole body jangled. My insides felt as molten-hot as the inside of the quarry coal house. Jabs of resentment blazed through my limbs. Every one of those jabs was directed—or misdirected—at Harry, who should have understood, who at the very least should have tried. Out of all the boys, he was the one who knew me best.

"Ah, forget about it. I don't care," I lied, clutching my books. "Let's just get out of here. I'm going nutty."

Harry buttoned his lip and followed me down the stairs. My gait was heavy and aggressive, his light and cautious. We walked a well-trod path. But we didn't walk side by side like we usually did. He was a step or two behind, bewildered, half-repentant, but not sure what for.

I had no desire to speak to him. Yet the next words out of his mouth changed everything. They made me see that he hadn't found the sagging clothesline pitiful or degrading or impotently feminine. My anger dwindled as quickly as it had swelled when he sighed heavily, reached out a hand to slow me down, and asked in a conspiratorial whisper, "Pietra, just tell me one thing: how much money do you save exactly?"

*   *   *

It was a slow Saturday afternoon at the DiRisios' tenement, no one much in the mood for studying, maybe because of all the food Marie was placing before us. Heaps of it, so that our engorged stomachs groaned for peace. Only boys encircled the table in the kitchen. Marie had sent Ceci to fetch a half-dozen rolls. But I knew the little girl would return soon. She'd never missed a lesson, never *wanted* to miss a lesson. Sure enough, ten minutes after she'd left, she reappeared, roaring into the tenement like a banshee, waving a flyer in one hand and a bag of bread in the other.

Out of breath, she thrust the crinkled paper at me—hollering something unintelligible, except for two words. The two words most often on her tongue: Amelia Earhart.

"She's coming," Ceci cried, gulping for air. "She's to speak at Woolsey Hall on Wednesday. This Wednesday!"

Though I feigned surprise, I'd already known about Amelia's scheduled appearance. The flyers were tacked up on every available surface on campus. *The Yale News* had been heralding her arrival for weeks. Yet I'd decided not to inform Ceci, believing that Marie would never give her permission to go. How surprising, then, when Marie, carrying a deep, steaming bowl of artichoke risotto, said, "Ceci, maybe Charlie will take you, if you ask him nicely. And if he doesn't already have an escort, of course."

Ceci came closer. She winked at me slyly. In her most polite voice, she asked if I'd take her and if we could go early—as early as possible—so that maybe, if we were very lucky, we could watch Amelia from the front row.

"I don't see why not," I replied.

She clapped her hands.

"But for now," I continued, "why don't you have a seat? Or else you'll fall behind. And I know you wouldn't want *that*."

Though Ceci was shivery with anticipation—she asked me if I thought her idol would be as spectacular in person as she was in her books—she nevertheless hunkered down with pencil in hand. She was poised to rewrite a passage I'd clipped from an old newspaper, even though it was of little interest at the moment, having nothing to do with sky, or wind, or wings.

Ceci and I did arrive early—two hours early, so early we'd brought our supper to eat under the domed rotunda of Memorial Hall. We were among the first in line.

"Numbers thirteen and fourteen," Ceci verified, counting the people ahead of us with a flutter of the finger. "We should have come an hour earlier."

"I had a class."

"You have those all the time."

I smiled, thinking that tonight Ceci looked like Amelia in miniature. As usual, the skullcap sat snugly on her head. I wouldn't have been surprised if she had taken to sleeping in it. Calf-length boots rode over the hems of her slacks. She wore a cream-colored blouse and a scarf tied around her neck. And then there was the pièce de résistance: a pinch-waist leather trench coat like the one Amelia was so often photographed wearing. It was rugged, oversized, a little tatty and oil-stained, but well made. When I'd come by the house for Ceci, I'd asked Marie where she'd found it. Sometimes Marie's rich patrons would donate clothing their own children had outgrown. I'd seen Ceci wearing things no person in Wooster Square could have afforded. But to my question about the coat, Marie had shrugged.

"When she put it on, it suited her," she'd replied, maybe wanting to forget a rare extravagance. "It just did."

Under the cap, even Ceci's hair looked like Amelia's—an untidy boyish crop. I asked her if she'd had it cut, but she put her finger to her lips. We wouldn't speak of her hair—at least until her mother noticed it.

We waited, nibbling on ham sandwiches and mouth-puckering dill pickles, until the line became so long it slithered out the door, all the way down College Street. Maybe it was Amelia's celebrity that drew so many boys. That and the fact that Yale's guest speakers were normally men. My classmates may have preferred Norma Shearer, Greta Garbo, Bette Davis, or Ginger Rogers, but Amelia, who was fetching in her own tomboyish sort of way, was nothing to scoff at.

At last the doors to Woolsey Hall were unlocked and pushed open. Ceci made a mad dash for the front row, urging me to hurry in a way that reminded me of Harry. I walked slowly, however, wanting to set a good example. But if the truth be known, I was nearly as excited as she. After reading so much about Amelia, I, too, wondered what she'd be like in person, if she'd disappoint or somehow rise to our dizzying expectations.

Fifteen minutes later, Woolsey was filled to capacity. Ceci gushed and bounced in her seat, ignoring my halfhearted admonitions to sit still. The boys around us chatted and laughed lustfully. We were all eager to catch sight of Amelia. The newspapers had branded myriad images of her onto our brains: Amelia leaning roguishly against her plane, Amelia waving good-naturedly at the crowds, Amelia looking venturesome in her flight goggles as her admirers waved banners: AMELIA, WE LOVE YOU. THREE CHEERS FOR LADY LINDY.

At precisely 7:30 Dean Walden strode onto the stage. Though the dean possessed neither President Angell's popularity nor his charisma, still the audience cheered. Forgetting myself, I stamped my feet and clamored with the rest.

The dean began a diligent speech about Amelia, but it did little to appease us. Not when it was Amelia herself we longed for. Ten minutes passed and our clamor, now rising to a shrill cry, drowned out the microphone Dean Walden stood behind. Droplets of sweat dotted his forehead. The whole room felt giddy and charged, as if a thunderstorm had slipped inside and was brewing atop the vaults and recesses of Woolsey's celestial ceiling.

Somewhere in the middle of that volatility she emerged. We noticed her confidence at once, how her eyes were mirthful, dancing with pleasure. Beside me, Ceci lurched forward, gripping my hand, no doubt wishing she could climb right onto the stage.

Amelia walked straight to the podium. The dean was still pondering his speech, eyes painstakingly scanning the notes before him. When he did notice her beside him, he stopped mid-sentence, disconcerted until she placed her hand on his forearm. A light and charming touch—and wasn't that what she was known for? Ceci and I had read about it in the papers, how she could win over anyone with her clever, off-kilter ways.

For a moment the dean seemed annoyed, but then he gave in, as the rest of us already had.

Our cheers grew louder, braver. From atop the stage she took them in with a gracious wave. Her eyes were widely set, and the space between them gave her a frank, childlike quality. But where was her devil-may-care expression—that ferocity that allowed her to fly above clouds, almost into outer space? I saw no sign of it as Dean Walden nudged her to take his place. She was taller than I'd imagined, her frame elongated by her monochromatic clothes: camel-colored trousers and jacket, a white flower pinned to the lapel. She looked younger than her age, which Ceci had reminded me in the rotunda was thirty-nine. Nearly the same age as Marie.

"Isn't she splendid?" Ceci whispered.

And indeed she was. But it was difficult to say why. It might have been because a creature adored and mythologized by the press now appeared before us in the flesh. Or maybe it was the way she hesitated as the applause died down. Her downcast eyes gave away her nervousness. They made her within our reach.

It was a relief when she finally took control, warning us with a coquettish smile, "Quiet down. Hush now." We settled into a silent reverie, all eyes on that slim frame. Her tone was calm, almost lulling, as she began a prepared speech about air transportation. At first it was enough simply to gaze at her, to take her in. But quite soon we longed for a sudden laugh, a random interjection, something capricious, anything that would give us a glimpse of the person beneath the careful string of words, rehearsed a hundred times if once.

The minutes ticked solemnly. She talked about aviation's beginnings: the Wright brothers and their adventures at Kitty Hawk, the bravery of the Great War's fighter pilots, Harriet Quimby's flight across the English Channel. She noted how far the world had come, America in particular. The last thirty years had brought about a whirlwind of advancement in aviation, wonders hitherto inconceivable. Beside me I could feel Ceci stir. Perhaps the girl had anticipated what Amelia would say next.

Leaning into the microphone, at last ignoring her notes, the aviatrix's voice went low and husky. She made each of us feel like we were her one and only confidant.

"Romance and beauty," she murmured. "No other phase of modern progress maintains such a measure of romance and beauty as aviation. But more than that, no other phase exemplifies the relationship between science and women. Air travel is as available to women as it is to men. I'm living proof of that. Perhaps I'm speaking to the wrong audience on this matter, but I believe women must take full advantage of opportunities in flight. It's—what can I call it?—our destiny."

She paused, sizing up her audience, continuing, "Sometimes girls, especially those whose tastes aren't routine, don't get a fair break. Too many of us have been bred to timidity. That is why those who escape must run, not stroll, toward what they desire. They mustn't look back. They mustn't question their own instincts. And they mustn't listen to the naysayers. If they can only follow their own true course, well then, they will be as renowned for their bravery as the greatest men are."

At that, I knew for certain that Amelia's splendor had nothing to do with how she wore her clothes or how many reporters were getting the scoop on her. It had only to do with what she thought and what she was willing to say, not only in her books, but here in the epicenter of Yale, surrounded by hundreds of young men, one little girl, and me.

From that point on, she talked about the new directions of air travel: how someday airplanes would be like sky-bound trains, transporting hundreds of people on a daily basis; how the average American would think of the sky as his own personal road map— and the airplane as his automobile. We lived for a while in her head, seeing clouds and bursts of blue throttle past. We let ourselves pretend that we, too, had helmed a plane through parts uncharted, through a universe in flux. In that we shared a moment with her, intimate in its controlled fervor, so, too, did we share some of her spirit. Each of us fell in love with her, or deeper in love. But there was a haunting quality to her speech, too, for we knew she would leave us. For her, time on land was not as precious as time in the sky.

We realized she had finished when she finally stepped out of her own fever. She let our stares penetrate, her cheeks blooming with color. Quiet she stood, so quiet that if we listened carefully we could hear the tapping of her shoes behind the podium. It took the reappearance of Dean Walden, the mortal to her goddess, to snap us out of our trance. The dean stood on the side of the stage as Amelia invited questions. Hands flew into the air eagerly. She pointed to one.

"Despite what you imply, flying is not impervious to peril," said a voice from the back of Woolsey. A lad with a shock of dark hair stood up. "What safety precautions do you take?"

"Well, I never meant to imply that flying is completely safe," she said carefully. "Even with precautions there is always some danger. The unknown is part and parcel of flying. My plane is meticulously inspected between flights for mechanical problems. I fly with a radio transmitter, of course, and often with a trailing wire. I sometimes carry a parachute and a life raft, although I've never actually used either. But mostly I don't think about those things. I think about the flight ahead—I try to enjoy myself."

"Do you think your sex makes you more vulnerable to fatigue or to the other stresses of flying?" the dark-haired boy continued.

"I don't think so, no, though many would like to say otherwise."

Her tone was humorous enough to blunt any sharpness. The lad asked another question, this one about her competence with Morse code. But Amelia ignored him and pointed to another person. He asked what sort of motor was on her plane.

"A Wasp motor, stupid," I heard Ceci say under her breath.

"I myself still fly a Wasp," Amelia replied. "Those of you who have followed my career know that it has carried me over the North Atlantic, over half the Pacific, and many times across this continent."

"Do you fly because you're bored with your husband?" someone else wanted to know.

Among the snickers, Amelia let out a hearty laugh. "I fly because I want to, that's why. Women must try to do things as men have tried. When we fail, our failure must be a challenge to others."

"Is it true that you are to begin your solo flight around the world this year?"

"Yes. I will begin the first leg next month from Hawaii. After this stop and one other, I will devote myself exclusively to training and preparing."

"But isn't it too dangerous? For anyone, I mean, regardless of sex?"

She hesitated then, feeling for a glass of water that sat on the edge of the podium. She sipped for several seconds, and in that small ambiguous span I felt a queer ache in my heart. When she spoke again, she looked at us dreamily, as if she were seeing us anew.

"I have a feeling that there is just about one more good flight left in my system. Anyway, when I have finished this job, I mean to give up long-distance stunt flying for good. I've had a very fruitful career, and of course it will continue, but perhaps not at the same velocity."

"Do you mean to start a family?"

"My, you Yale men waste no time getting personal!" She laughed some more, this time more shrilly, and sipped again from the glass. "Normally I don't touch this subject, but I'll say this: my husband and I have thought about having children, of course we have. But so far I haven't been on the ground long enough to consider changing diapers and preparing bottles. After this next flight, perhaps we'll have the kind of time we'll need—and that's all I'll say about the matter."

"And who shall be your heir to the throne of female aviation?"

Amelia seemed relieved to be on to another topic. She set down the glass and scanned the audience as if pretending to pick a contest winner. Then she pointed at none other than Ceci.

"Young girls like this one here. Young girls will go on to fly to the most distant reaches known to man. They'll exceed expectations because they must. That is what modern progress is in any field: breaking records, sometimes breaking laws." She looked over her shoulder slyly. "Just don't tell the dean I said that."

At that, the audience let out a collective whoop.

She answered a few more questions, seeming to regain her composure, before thanking us for coming to see her. "I must go and rest," she told us. "I'll be flying again before I know it."

As Amelia bid everyone good night, boys filtered out, loping and in no rush, for maybe she would linger and descend from the stage to shake their hands, maybe even to plant kisses on their cheeks. Ceci was still aglow from the attention Amelia had paid her. She refused to budge from her seat. I reminded her that her mother had set a strict curfew, but she wasn't persuaded.

"I can't leave yet. How can I?"

Ceci grabbed the underside of her chair to show me she meant business. Amelia was still on the stage, speaking privately with Dean Walden. She gave no indication that she would further interact with the audience. Still, I saw that I had as much chance of removing Ceci from Woolsey Hall as I did of removing the skullcap from her head. Instead of arguing, I tried to think of what excuse I would tell Marie.

Eventually, Dean Walden left the stage, followed by Amelia. Ceci clung to the hope that her beloved would pass by again, but I told her that Woolsey must have a back door, that Amelia may have left already.

"Listen, you'll see her again," I reasoned. "She gives speeches all the time, and in so many places. She might visit Connecticut again. Or, if not, surely you'll see her somewhere else."

"But what if I don't, Charlie?"

And I realized I oughtn't dangle any promises. I didn't know what would be—if Ceci would see Amelia a dozen more times or never again. I hadn't forgotten about the cracks in the granite.

Waning prospects weighted the passing minutes. The two of us were alone now, no boys' chatter or footsteps for company, nothing but the silent sheen of Woolsey's gilt adornments, their beauty chill and aloof at this hour. I had decided to let Ceci choose when we ought to leave. I wouldn't be the one to dash her hopes.

The longer we waited, the more obvious it became that we wouldn't get any closer to Amelia that night. But as Ceci told it, she'd been sure this would be her chance not only to see Amelia, but maybe even to become her friend.

"Maybe when you're an aviatrix, you and she will be friends," I said.

Ceci didn't look at me, but she did unhook her hands from the underside of her seat. She placed them carefully in her lap.

Eventually the lights shut off. In the dim Ceci stood up, her chin quivering gently. I'd never seen her cry before, and I wondered if this was the prelude.

"Maybe," she said. "Maybe when I'm a member of the Ninety-Nines, Amelia and I will be dear chums. Like you and me."

"You and I."

"Right, you and I."

I nodded vigorously. Through dead light Ceci peered into my eyes. "She looked tired at the end, didn't she?" she asked.

"Yes."

"I didn't think she got tired."

"Everyone does at some point, right?"

"But I never thought of her like that."

"Like what?"

"Like someone who has to worry about—about ordinary things."

I took Ceci's hand in my own for the second time that night. Gingerly, so as not to bump against the chairs in the dark, we moved in dispirited procession out the door. The air outside was damp and hard, rubbing raw against our faces. As I stooped down to pull the sash tighter on Ceci's coat and to wrap her scarf around her neck, I thought beyond her comfort or my own. I thought about Amelia. I couldn't help but hope that she was already tucked into bed, safe and warm.

It was written in the snow. Emblazoned was more like it: I LOVE ADA.

Simple, childish, though not without a shiver of romance. Something I would have expected to see carved into the bark of an elm or into the old tables of the Last Anchor. The letters—bold and upper-case—were huge, fifteen feet tall and equally wide, each one. They were written with diluted red dye. Wick had explained that he'd bought gallons of it, in big sealed drums, at a nearby hardware store where the owner's wife had taken a shine to him.

"The old dame even gave me a discount," Wick told us.

Getting the dye had been the easy part, apparently.

"It was getting the barrel that almost killed me," Wick continued.

Phin, Harry, and I were sitting on a wood fence on Old Campus, lined up like a flock of perched birds. From our vantage point, the letters were as striking as giant exclamation points. Our bemused classmates strolled past, pausing, admiring, wondering. Watching them react was like discovering Wick's handiwork over and over again. Yet the more people tromped by, the more injured the letters became. Already, the first "A" in "ADA" had gone bent and smeared.

"Looks more like 'IDA' now," Harry remarked.

"No matter," Wick replied. "I'm sure there's a perfectly decent-looking Ida somewhere in this town."

Wick was telling us the story of how he'd done it, how he'd rolled an empty fifty-gallon barrel all the way from one of the ammunitions factories, maybe even from the one where Marie's husband and sons worked.

"It was a heavy sucker," he said, "filled with gunpowder before they emptied it. That's appropriate, given what I know about Ada, right? Anyhow, I gave some guy—there for security, I suppose—five dollars for the thing. It's worthless, but he was a big guy, and as soon as he saw me, he knew he could get something outta me. And as soon as I saw him I knew he would get it too. The man was a colossus.

"I gave him the money and rolled this baby home. Mind you, I decided to do this at three in the morning, right after the snowfall ended. The ground was totally white—like a blank canvas. Not that I'm an artist, but what can I say? I was inspired.

"I bought hose, too, a few days back—yards and yards of it. While you were sleeping, Harry, I connected it to the faucet of the sink and snaked it out the window. I filled the barrel with water, added some of the dye, and mixed it all up with a stick. I'd thought through the whole scheme, but when it came time to write the letters, I couldn't lift the barrel. I couldn't even tip it! Thank god Roota wasn't there or I would have been back in corrective exercises for sure."

"How'd you do it, then?" Phin asked. He was smoking a cigarette, arms and legs elevated, splayed out in front of him. He was balancing on the narrow beam of the fence with an athleticism the rest of us could only aspire to.

"That's the beauty of it, really. At three in the morning who the hell could I ask? All you bastards were sleeping. That's when the wizard appeared."

"Oh, come off it," Harry muttered.

"Harry, you're much too practical for your own good. I swear, you remind me of my father. Any second now you'll be lecturing me about ethics and responsibility."

"You honestly want us to believe you saw a wizard?"

"All right, he didn't look like a wizard. Wasn't dressed like one, anyway."

"What was he dressed like, then?"

"A tramp, a hobo, your typical vagabond. But I knew straight away it was a disguise. You know how I knew? When I saw him there next to me, there were no tracks in the snow. Not a single print. It was like he'd descended from the sky or flew or something. I said to him,

'I'm here at the mercy of love. I'm nothing but a bowed and humble servant at the feet of a princess.' He nodded like he knew my whole story."

"Or like he was in a drunken stupor," Phin added.

"Where was his magic wand?" Harry wanted to know.

"He did have a walking stick, now that I think about it. And a beard, grizzled and gray, not white like you'd think. But the point is, fellas, he had the strength of five men. Ten. He picked up that barrel like it was nothing and poured exactly where I told him to. All I had to do was fill the barrel with the hose water and mix in the dye a few times. It was the easiest test of love I've ever had."

"How many *have* you had?" I asked.

Wick ignored my question, leaned over, and grabbed the cigarette out of Phin's mouth. He smoked with a broody air. "I tried to give him some dough when we were through. His hands were all red from the dye, bloody-looking almost, and I felt bad. I wanted to repay him. But he said he couldn't take my money—not for something like this."

"How honorable," Harry sniffed.

"But he did take your coat," Phin observed.

I, too, had wondered why Wick was wearing two sweaters, one layered thickly over the other. Only Wick could succeed in looking debonair given such bulkiness.

"It was the least I could do." Wick shrugged. "Anyway, his had all these stains. The dye—along with crud and grime."

"Was your wallet in the pocket?"

"Heck no."

"Who cares about your magical assistant," Harry said. "What we want to know is—how did Ada react?"

Wick dropped the cigarette into the snow. It slipped through the white fluff as it burned out. A smile crept across his lips. He looked down, and if I didn't know him better, I'd swear he was being coy.

"To quote Charlie, a gentleman never tells."

"Oh no, you're not getting off that easy," Harry prodded. "Not after you made us listen to that wizard babble."

"All right, all right. She liked it, okay? Of course she did. I brought her here at sunrise. The sky was perfect: hazy, pink, beautiful. There was no one around. Even the wizard was long gone. She saw the message and just stared and stared."

"And?" Harry asked.

"And—she started laughing. She said I was a fool. But a romantic fool."

"And?"

Wick sighed, embarrassed, a willing victim. "She came upstairs. She was in our room while you were sleeping, Harry. Holy Joe, you could sleep through a freight train."

Harry shook his head.

"But it wasn't what you think. Well, heck, maybe it was halfway to what you think."

"Fine, we get the picture," I muttered.

"Speak for yourself, Pietra," Harry piped. "I could use some details."

"Like I said, we got halfway."

"The top half or the bottom?"

"Harry, for god's sake, I thought that the Botticelli would have cured your hormones by now."

"She hasn't been returning my telephone calls. Her crotchety old mother answers, but she won't tell me where Ethel is and why she doesn't want to talk to me. I think I've ruined it—*chort!* And I don't even know why."

Harry sounded so suddenly defeated, so despairing, that in gentlemanly solidarity we at once terminated discussion of Wick's coup and turned our attention, instead, to why females are so careless with men's hearts and so unpredictable with everything else. I could have offered some ideas of my own. I still hadn't determined why I'd gone to the show that night, for instance, and why I'd done what I had with the man in the feathered hat. It was as if I'd been carried there by some deep-seated primal impulse, and though I didn't particularly regret what had happened, it did make me wonder if girls, by design, needed to immerse themselves in trouble every once in a while.

So I had theories, yes, not that I could have voiced them. Instead, I listened to Harry and Wick, mostly, because Phin cared little for dissecting the female mind. Women were the great unanswerable question, he'd once said. Why waste time on philosophies that don't go anywhere, just 'round and 'round, an endlessly spinning wheel? When you get right down to it, women were more mysterious than they had any right to be.

Phin fished out another cigarette and stared at the students staring at Wick's message. And I stared, too, just at the very last letter, letting myself imagine it wiped out clean, the name finished off the right way.

SPRING

Chapter Eleven

ALTHOUGH I still visited the post office daily, Mother's letters arrived less frequently. Sometimes weeks would pass before I'd see the familiar stationery in my box. I attributed the lapse to spring. The coming of warm weather also meant the coming of Cottagers. They brought with them mountains of clothing needing to be aired, laundered, and set to dry in the sun. Spring had always been our busiest time of year. Linen and cotton tablecloths, draperies, bedsheets, dresses, shirts, trousers, pinafores, and smocks constantly flapped on the clothesline. I would use so much bleach that the insides of my hands would turn white while the backs would brown.

When finally a letter from Mother did arrive, I didn't wait to return to my dormitory, tearing it open then and there and skimming it as I walked. I was eager for a taste of home.

My Adele,

The crocuses have sprung up in cheerful yellow and purple abundance, some beside lingering patches of ice. They grow, I think, in defiance of winter rather than in celebration of spring. I remember how you used to love to spot the first crocus, and the first snowdrop and johnny-jump-up too. I often wish you were here to point them out.

I appreciate the latest news on your work-study program and classes. But you still haven't told me if this second semester is much different from the first. I imagine that you are finally at ease and that the trials and foibles of those first months seem as inconsequen-

tial now as they did trying then. Nevertheless, I hope you are still minding yourself and not pursuing unnecessary kinships. It is when one relaxes that one is most vulnerable, I have always believed.

Many people have brought their laundry these past weeks. I scarcely begin one load when another arrives on the doorstep. I have been working past sunset, just as you and I used to do. Right now I write you by moonlight.

I see that I've already written three paragraphs and yet I haven't told you my most important news. So let me announce it. I have corresponded several more times with my mother and father. I never believed that a full reconciliation might be possible, but now I realize that it is, in fact, already under way. My parents are ever so eager to meet you, Adele. I have told them that due to financial constraints, I was forced to send you to your father's cousins, who live in New Haven. Alfred and Joanna were so appalled that they promptly sent me a check for a considerable sum. They believe you ought to come back to live with me. They say families ought to stick together. Isn't that something your father used to say?

They also suggested that you and I visit Philadelphia (the sooner the better). Could you spare the time away from your studies? You could spend as much time as you pleased in their library, Adele. And if any books caught your fancy, why, I'm certain you could take them with you. This is a strange proposition, I realize. My parents and I have been at odds for as long you've been alive. Nevertheless, I hope you will recognize the benefits that could be gained if all of us were to forgive one another.

I eagerly await your thoughts on this matter. Write soon, my daughter.

All my love,
Mother

P.S. I am enclosing a portion of the money sent by my parents. Enjoy, but spend wisely.

After finishing the letter, I was so flummoxed I didn't know what to do. Screwing shut my eyes, I tried to imagine what a visit to the home of Mr. and Mrs. Mockleton would be like. But try as I might, all I could see was their photograph next to the fireplace. I could not remove them from the frame and insert them into a real house with real people. I could not place them among everyday things: wildflowers tipping out of a jar, potatoes boiling in a pot, bits of dirt on the floor trekked in from outside. The Mockletons, in my mind, were motionless, plastic. Shop-window mannequins forever wearing the same indifferent expression.

Maybe my portrayal wasn't fair. But then, my grandparents had given me every reason to judge them harshly. Pa and Charles had lived and worked and died without the Mockletons' interest or concern, never mind support. My grandparents did not deserve my forgiveness. Maybe they did not even deserve my tolerance.

Mother wanted a prompt response, but I didn't have one for her. Instead, I had questions. These I wrote out carefully on a piece of paper, wondering as I wrote whether I would mail them to Mother. I wanted to know so much. How much time would a visit entail— three days, a week, two weeks? It was possible I could miss my classes without falling behind, but I couldn't leave my work-study. Professor Spang would never have it. Nor could I drop my tutoring for long. Ceci and the rest of the DiRisio gang were making too much progress for sudden abandonment. More than anything, though, I wanted to know the purpose of the visit. Was our aim to gain the Mockletons' affection? Acceptance? To see if they could stomach our company? To grovel our way into their hearts so that we would have access to their coffers?

I was sure Joanna and Alfred would be pleased by how beautiful Mother still was. But they would look me up and down like a rare specimen plucked from an exotic land. A specimen not to be touched, but poked at with a stick at safe distance. I wondered specifically what they would think of my haircut. Surely they would lose their smug smiles when they saw it. They'd hoped I might be pretty, sophisticated, refined. They'd hoped I'd taken after Mother's side—*their* side. They'd never figured me for a Bowery Boy, that much I was sure of.

The more I thought about the visit, the more squeamish I became. Mother's letter might be only the beginning. A full reconciliation could also mean a transition back to her former life. A life in Philadelphia. I'm sure that's what she'd pined for all these years—to wear silk drawers, sip wine from crystal flutes, travel whenever she pleased, and deposit her dirty clothing into the arms of a maid. Mother's wounded pride had prohibited her from resolving her differences with Alfred and Joanna. Yet if they admitted error, surely Mother would accept their apology. Surely she would find a way.

The DiRisios' tenement looked brand-new, from the recently cleaned floors to the ceiling, which was vined with colorful streamers. Marie had draped a bright tablecloth across the table in the kitchen, and it was on this night, as on many nights, packed with food: great bowls of pasta in red, pink, and white sauces, mushrooms marinating in olive oil, flounder floating in puddles of butter and garlic, sautéed escarole, spinach pie, lamb rubbed with thyme and rosemary. And then the desserts, so many Marie had moved them from the crowded table to the almost-as-crowded counter. Macaroons, almond biscotti, ricotta pie, cookies dotted with pine nuts, fat cannoli with cream oozing out their ends.

When I entered the tenement, the aroma of those foods shook my senses awake. So did the racket of excited voices. Everywhere people were laughing and talking, sitting on all available surfaces, standing where there weren't any more. I meandered a few minutes, tentative, surveying the scene. Marie found me in this way, staring shyly at some random fixed point. She grabbed me, kissed me on the cheek, and thrust a stack of plates into my hands.

"Would you mind, Charlie? I've got a hundred things to do."

I didn't mind at all. Sometime during these months of visits, Marie had eased up on formality. She'd begun to treat me less like a guest, more like a member of the family. This newfound intimacy wasn't necessarily accompanied by disclosure; she didn't try to pry out information on Stony Creek or my family, in any case. But somehow I think she suspected not that I was pretending, but that I fit more comfortably into her world than in most others.

"Don't give my sister a chipped one," she added.

"Which one . . ."

"The one with the hooked nose. She got that from my father. I was spared, thank heavens." Marie laughed, and I caught a fruity whiff of wine on her breath. I'd spotted several open bottles in the kitchen, and now that I looked more carefully, I saw that half the guests were clasping mugs, and jars, and ill-matching glasses.

Marie had told me weeks ago about the party: Angelo's fiftieth birthday. Originally she had planned it as a surprise, but she'd changed her mind when the guest list topped forty. Marie realized her husband would catch on when he saw how much food she would have to prepare, how she'd have to rearrange the furniture to make room. While the full number of guests hadn't arrived yet, there were enough people to cause considerable congestion in the small rooms and narrow corridors. I carried the plates gingerly.

Marie owned many dishes, many more than Mother owned, but few of them coordinated, and even fewer were free of defect. The most beautiful of her mismatched ensemble were of delicate, nearly transparent china. Some were accented with jewel-colored enamel, or rimmed with gold or silver. Others were an immaculate white. All of these finer pieces were hand-me-downs, Marie had told me. They'd come from one of the ladies she embroidered for. The woman would give Marie a few dishes every time one from her latest collection broke. She would give the rest to the Salvation Army, or else throw them away.

"Sometimes I swear she breaks them on purpose, just to give herself something to do," Marie had said. "Just so she can spend more of her husband's money! Not that it was hard-earned. Imagine, when the rest of the country is skimping and scraping and counting every last nickel, when the breadlines stretch on for blocks, *she* walks into Malley's like she owns the place."

I had to flip through all the plates before finding a perfect one: the ivory glaze crackled just so, rosebuds around the rim. This I safely delivered to the woman I presumed to be Marie's sister. She was sitting on a cozy love seat. Smiling up at me, she took the plate with one hand and motioned for me to sit beside her with the other.

"Marie's told me how well you teach her children," she said. "I think it's marvelous what you do."

My hands bracing the plate pile in my lap, I gazed at her shyly. She was a compact, fattish woman with a waddled chin and exactly the sort of nose one wouldn't want to inherit. I had to look hard to find her resemblance to Marie, but noticed it finally in the heart shape of her upper lip, in the appraising angle of her stare.

"Thank you, ma'am."

"My name is Edna. You can call me 'Aunt Edna.'"

"I'm Charlie."

"Of course. Marie tells me everything. She says you're a Yale man. Is that true? You look so remarkably—young."

One of Marie's sons, Carlo, came by at that moment. He held out a platter of stuffed olives and gave me a little wink. Get away while you still can, it read. He turned the platter so that Edna could plop several olives onto her plate and one into her mouth. As she chewed, she nodded vigorously, encouraging me to fill the silence.

"I do go to Yale, yes. I'm lucky to be there."

I wondered at my feeble answer, then decided it must have something to do with being caught off guard in the DiRisios' home, the one place in New Haven aside from the steps of Sterling in which I normally felt entirely comfortable.

Marie's sister swallowed, and I watched the lump travel down the short course of her throat. "If you don't mind my asking, why do you do it? Teach, I mean. You must be so busy with classes and that sort of thing. Do you consider teaching your calling?"

"I enjoy it is all. Being around Marie, Angelo, the kids—they're a very nice family."

"Yes, certainly. But tell me, what are you looking to do after you finish? Teaching, it's a rewarding profession. But there are so many other kinds of work that would better fulfill, well, other needs."

"I don't know what I'll do yet, ma'am."

"Maybe medicine. Have you thought about becoming a physician? Marie tells me you're very intelligent. 'Sharp as a whip,' she says."

"No, I don't think medicine would suit me."

"Why not?"

Mother had asked me the very same question in one of her letters. She'd also inquired whether I'd developed a greater interest in law, mentioning not for the first time that Yale had an excellent graduate program.

I'd treated these questions the same way I'd treated the topic of Silvio: briefly, noncommittally. However much Mother feared I wasn't thinking about my future, *our* future, I was—just in my own way. I habitually listened to what other fellows said they were planning to do after graduation and wondered if banking, architecture, engineering, or chemistry might be right for me, too. Then there was my course work, which I used as a rough gauge of my potential. I wondered if my facility with Latin conjugations meant that I was well suited to languages, or if my grades in biology foretold a career as a veterinarian or a botanist. All I knew for certain was that even those classes I most enjoyed paled in comparison to my favorite pastimes: reading in the Stacks alone or, better yet, teaching and preparing lessons for Ceci and the gang. My pupils had made so much progress these past few months that they could hardly be called beginners anymore. The boys were learning to distinguish between various styles of writing. Angelo was fixed on writing a perfect paragraph, "no mistakes." And Ceci, Ceci was filling whole pages, whole notebooks, with stories and poems and daily accounts.

I relished our lessons more than ever, though they weren't without difficulty. Freddie and Carlo would kick each other under the table, or Angelo would insist that he understood a concept, only to admit later that he did not grasp it at all. Still, week to week, I noted progress, an undeniable upward tilt. How thrilled I was to be part of that escalation.

Could Mother have spied on our lessons, she wouldn't have understood my zeal. She who had been schooled by a team of tutors—"not only for traditional academics, Adele, but for posture, diction, dance, even tennis"—wouldn't have understood the little spark that shot down my spine when I heard Ceci correctly pronounce a word she'd never seen before or when Angelo's face suddenly lit up with beamy, long-suffering comprehension. She wouldn't have approved of my interest in teaching as a profession, certainly not, not when she'd slipped jewelry off her skin to get me here.

Our financial future was still foremost on Mother's mind. That was surely why she was so eager to reunite with her parents. I worried about money, too, but lately I agonized more over my identity. Still, Mother hadn't come out and said it: that to succeed I'd need to continue as a young man indefinitely. Maybe that was because she had decided on an alternative. Maybe making amends with the Mockletons also meant an end to my illegitimate journey to New Haven.

"Really, I thought that's what most college men did. Study medicine." The cheerful, tinny voice of Edna reminded me suddenly that Mother wasn't the only person concerned about my future.

"I don't know, ma'am, maybe they do."

"Well, shouldn't you know?"

I shrugged.

"But you're young—still considering things?"

"I haven't ruled anything out."

She seemed halfway satisfied with that answer, satisfied enough to pop another olive into her mouth. I took that moment as my chance, nodding at the plates, telling Edna I had to distribute them, joking that Marie would have my head if I didn't.

"It was very nice to meet you," I added as I stood up, fumbling to keep the plates balanced.

"But I wanted you to meet someone. My daughter. She's here— over there, well, somewhere. Find me later, will you, and I'll introduce you?"

"Sure," I said, knowing I would make no such effort.

For several minutes I approached strangers, trying to unload my wares. I had little luck. Most of the guests were content to eat their food off napkins or their bare hands. I made sure neither Marie nor her sister was watching, then put the rest of the pile onto a newly vacated chair. Ceci found me soon after, seeming to sense my guilt.

"Want to escape?" she asked me.

"Do I ever."

"Let's go to my room," she said, head bobbing through the crowd as she tugged me along. Being the only girl in a family of boys, Ceci had never had to share her room, which was fortunate given that it was literally an oversized closet. Marie had said that it had been used as a pantry twenty years ago, before the one-family house had been converted into its current state: four choppy, graceless units.

Ceci's room contained nothing but a tiny mattress and several wood crates, painted in vivid colors, one stacked on top of the next to create makeshift shelves. With so little space, she made good use of her walls. These were plastered with pictures of Amelia, her Lockheed Vega plane, and an enormous map of the world. Little thumbtacks marked all the countries Amelia had ever traveled to or over. Ceci used Marie's embroidery thread to create lines connecting the tacks: the actual routes Amelia had taken, a different color for every trip. Along the margin of the map, Ceci had written notes about the particulars of each flight: dates of travel, altitude, base speed, number of fuel and rest stops, equipment on board, weather conditions, if Amelia had flown by herself or with the help of a navigator. These notes I'd helped her with at first. But I was pleased to see a slew of more recent scrawlings. These she'd made without my consultation. I was even more pleased to see a new thread color: violet. This route,

Ceci explained to me now, was not one Amelia had flown, but one that Ceci herself wanted to try.

"I won't be able to take flight lessons till I'm eighteen. And even then, I'll have to start off slow. Amelia didn't fly 'cross the Atlantic the day she got her pilot's license, you know. It might take me two years to learn how to fly, and then another two to fly this route."

Ceci stared at the map, eyes fixed on the winding journey of the purple thread. "I just hope no one else flies it first."

"Let's keep our fingers crossed."

"No sirree, that's bad luck."

"Bad luck?"

"Freddie told me the wish gets caught between your fingers."

"Oh, he must be right. No crossed fingers, then."

"Crossed toes are okay."

"Can you cross your toes?"

"I've been practicing."

"Can you do it?"

"Not yet."

I leaned against the wall, my arm crooked to support my head, glad that I no longer had a pile of plates to contend with.

"How do you like the party?" I asked her.

"It's not bad."

"Why are we hiding here, then?"

"I thought you wanted to get away."

"I thought *you* wanted to get away."

Fidgety, Ceci looped a stray thread around its rightful tack. "There are so many people out there; I don't know half of them. All day I've been waiting for my brothers from California to come. They'd want to celebrate my father's birthday, wouldn't they? They didn't come last year, either."

"How could they?" I leaned over to draw a line with my finger from Connecticut to California. "How many miles is that, anyway?"

"About three thousand," Ceci said.

"It would take them weeks to get here by car or rail."

"I know. I was just hoping." She paused, adding, "I've been writing to them. Long letters. Mother thinks I'm doing my lessons. She doesn't know I've been doing some of Carlo's chores in exchange for stamp money."

"How many letters have you sent?"

"Twelve. But gosh, what's the use? My brothers don't know how to read."

"Maybe they've asked someone to read your letters aloud."

"I hope so."

Watching Ceci's glum face, I realized how much I wanted to convince her that her letters were worthwhile no matter what happened after she mailed them. Only months ago she'd been able to read all of ten words, and now she swallowed whole books, memorized entire speeches Amelia had made, penned stories about planes she would like to fly. Ceci had recently written a list of topics she wanted to learn about, including celestial navigation, dead reckoning, relative bearing, and gravitational acceleration. I'd agreed to supply books from Sterling Library on one topic each week. These she pored over day and night; Marie complained that Ceci had taken to sleeping on a book rather than her pillow.

I enjoyed feeding the little girl's appetite, but lately I felt guilty about it, too. Although Ceci looked to me for guidance, I was too deceitful to be called a true teacher. One of the reasons I related to Ceci was because she was a girl, a girl who didn't fit a conventional mold. Through her I remembered some of my own girlhood rebellion: reading the afternoon away in my stone cubby when I should have been helping Mother; outsprinting Charles on the quarry path, my skirt tied between my legs so I wouldn't trip; telling Pa how one day I'd go with him to find Francisco, even if our search took us over the Sahara and across the mighty Amazon. I related to Ceci because both of us were females living on the brink of acceptability. Whether she knew it or not, this commonality served as the backbone of our friendship. To continue letting Ceci believe that I was anything but a young woman would only deepen the betrayal. I was a hypocrite to tell her that girls could aspire to be anything when my own life was full of cowardly compromise. It occurred to me then, more urgently than before, that I had three options: to go on infinitely this way, in a clandestine life that didn't belong to me; to do an about-face and confront the very same realities as my young friend; or to continue to balance uneasily—and quite gracelessly—between the two.

There was a letter in my mailbox, but it wasn't scented with rosewater. I'd been expecting it for some time. Mother had never been one for patience.

> *My darling,*
>
> *Why have you not responded? Did you receive my last letter? If you did, then you know I must reply to the request of my parents. They want us to visit them in Philadelphia as soon as possible. After all I have told them about you, they're anxious to make your acquaintance.*
>
> *You'll love Philadelphia, Adele. That much I can promise you. You will finally have the chance to do all the things a young woman should: attend the theater and the opera, visit a proper dressmaker and hatter, mingle with like-minded company. I am afraid I must press you for an answer. I myself am eager to see Philadelphia again and have my heart set on you as my companion.*
>
> *Put your life at Yale aside for a moment, Adele. I expect a most immediate reply.*
>
> *Eagerly and ever yours,*
> *Mother*

Chapter Twelve

HARRY AND I were finishing our third round of egg salad sand-wiches in Commons, trying to eat more despite our already full stomachs, when Wick came dashing out of nowhere. Phin came striding behind him, spinning his finger by the side of his head: a warning that Wick was planning something cockamamie.

This time Wick wanted to explore Yale's labyrinthine under-belly—the tunnels that ran beneath the university and reached like tentacles to Sterling Library, the Payne Whitney Gymnasium, all of the university's most vital organs, maybe even the tombs of the secret societies. As he talked, I could feel myself surrendering, despite my reservations, despite my better judgment. I was left to wonder—was it even possible to say no to Wick?

We knew of the tunnels. Everyone in New Haven did. You could almost feel them beneath you as you walked the campus, the hollow thump of empty space below. But there were rumors, like how grue-some pagan rituals took place there, or how they were kept boiling-hot to deter prowlers, indeed, to scald them outright. The plumes of steam that occasionally screamed up from the grates lent credence to such talk.

Still, Wick couldn't be dissuaded, no matter how many times Harry shook his head. He unfolded a well-marked map of the cam-pus. Here was where he thought the tunnels went, he told us, using a pencil as a pointer, circling and marking as he went along. "And here's where we'll burrow in."

We tried to convince him that this plan was different from sledding down a hill on stolen trays or stealing the pickled brain from Professor Thatcher's shelf or from our most recent antics: dressing up Nathan Hale as Little Bo-Peep, climbing up the Sterling Bell Tower and resetting the clock, and sticking a TYPHOID FEVER HERE—KEEP OUT! sign into Dean Walden's front lawn. It was a misdeed on par with smoking marihuana—something that could get us kicked out of school, or at least suspended. If we got caught, our parents would be notified. We asked Wick if he really wanted to get a first-class whooping from his father. We told him we had the right to know—in the interest of bodily security—where he had gotten his information.

"Like I told you, I did a little research."

"You can't expect us to follow you blindly," Harry argued. "Give us *something*, at least."

"All right, all right. Gee whiz, you fellows are such sissies. A senior told me about the tunnels—that's how I know. He went down there himself his freshman year. Satisfied?"

"Maybe he was pulling your leg."

"He wasn't," Wick protested, and here was where his enthusiasm could so easily convert into irritation. He couldn't understand, he said, why some people forsook grand opportunities. He demanded to know why there was no sense of adventure left in this world. "The man I talked to tunneled into all sorts of weird buildings and rooms. He said you can't believe what's underneath this university. He said, even, that there's a way into the Payne Whitney pools. He took a girl there for a three A.M. dip."

That was just the piece of information Harry needed. Maybe he wasn't thinking of just any girl, but of Ethel, sprung dewy-wet from the pool like Venus from the sea. Phin and I capitulated once Harry did, and then Wick immediately started to tally the things we'd need: drinking water, flashlights, a compass, tools, and bread crumbs—like in that fairy tale—to mark our way back.

"What if the rats eat them?" Harry wanted to know.

And we agreed—there could be rats or snakes, roaches or dragons. Just about anything could live down there.

"We can use my poker chips," Phin volunteered, solving the quandary.

Wick had already decided where we'd enter, and the hour—2:00 A.M., a time when the campus was virtually dead. Even the patrolmen started to snooze on their beats, their billy clubs hanging flaccid. And in talking about the logistics, we became more worked up, giddy as schoolgirls. Harry was as inspired as the rest of us, until he looked down suddenly, his cheeks paling as he asked, "But what if we get trapped in the tunnels? How will anyone know to find us?"

Wick quickly returned fire. "So why don't you write a note, Harry? We'll leave it in our room—in case we go missing. Then they'll know where to find our remains."

We went on the night Wick chose, an inauspicious Wednesday—the four of us, in head-to-toe black. Only, Harry and I didn't own any black clothes and had to borrow ours from Wick and Phin. We entered through a manhole on Cross Campus. Though Cross Campus was an open area, and a little too conspicuous for comfort, it also marked a main artery of the tunnel system. Wick tried in vain to pry open the manhole cover himself, then Phin lent him a hand. Harry, the last one down, managed with great effort to slide the cover back most of the way. Since we planned to come out at the same place, we didn't want to seal the hole entirely.

We descended a rickety, rusted steel ladder. It hung down a good fifteen feet; then there were several more feet of air we needed to drop through to hit the ground. When we'd all jumped, we plunged our flashlights into the catacombic still. The light sliced open just enough space to reveal passages in four directions. Staring at the map, Wick chose one and signaled us to follow. The tunnels were almost as hot as we'd feared—a humid, dribbly hot, the kind that drenches you in sweat. As we followed Wick through the corridors,

Phin tossed a poker chip every few yards. The little red circles looked disarmingly festive against the grimy concrete floor.

Our flashlights illuminated only a few feet of darkness at a time. And things got worse when Harry's flamed out. The shadows and the narrowness of the corridors made us jumpy, restless, a little miffed. When we talked at all, it was in brusque whispers. Wick was our leader, as always, and we followed behind him single file. He stopped often to check the map. As the minutes waned, I began to question his ability to shepherd.

"We're under High Street now, I think," he said. "Let's go another fifty paces. Fellas, we're bound for the tomb of Skull and Bones."

Only, when we turned the next corner, the passage stopped abruptly. Tipping our flashlights, we saw there was nowhere to go except back—or up. Another steel ladder jutted up to a small circular door in the ceiling.

"It must lead inside some building or else there would be a manhole," Wick said, eyeing the door, and so we agreed to follow him. Even if we didn't know where we were going, at least we could escape our claustrophobia.

Phin wove his hands together, an impromptu stirrup, and gave Wick a boost to the ladder's base. He climbed hastily. For several long minutes he fumbled with the handle of the door, a corroded steel wheel. But when he couldn't force it, Phin got a boost up from me and took Wick's place. In one swift motion he cranked it clockwise. The door sprung open on thick deteriorated hinges, releasing a dense cloud of rust particles. We didn't dare breathe until the air had cleared. Then, one by one, we helped each other reach the ladder. To get the last man up, Wick hung by his knees from the lowest rung and pulled Harry up with his hands.

We couldn't see anything at first. It was even darker here than in the tunnels. Our flashlights shone weak as stars in a storm. But gradually we realized we were standing in a huge, high-ceilinged place dominated by dozens of eerie, odd-shaped objects. They appeared to us like frozen animals, herded together in hunched clusters and covered in woolly fur. We were terrified, none of us admitting it, until finally Wick dared to walk up to one and touch it, yanking back his hand as if in pain, chuckling at our yelps.

"Relax," he said. "It's a blanket, not a pelt."

He pulled it off slowly, painstakingly, and what was underneath took our breath away: a golden harp, bright as a sunburst, even in this lightless place. Harry caressed her shining strings. She sounded like a siren's song.

Inspired, we made our way around the room, which seemed endless; Harry piped up that he'd found only one wall so far, walked right into it, actually. We peeled away blanket after blanket, believing we'd happened across a treasure trove. Here were pieces of furniture fit for a palace, ancient and finely wrought pieces, their surfaces lacquered-gleaming and decorated with platinum, gold, and enamel. The Cottagers have furniture like this, I thought. Tables, chairs, wardrobes, and dressers, their ornate cabriole legs ending in hooves and claws and talons, some clutching crystal balls. Here were paintings, too: portraits of rich women wearing lace, satin, and gem chokers. There were biblical scenes, landscapes, still lifes of fruit bowls and artfully arranged fowl, Madonnas embracing fat children. Wick suspected one self-portrait a Rembrandt, but he couldn't accept the idea.

"It couldn't be—why the hell would something like that be *here*?"

We set about opening sealed boxes—smaller treasures now—wrapped in yards of velvet and brocade: jewelry, statuettes, coins, vases, an ebony chess set, a scroll with a scene of crisscrossing bamboo shoots. Phin, Wick, and I had become a team, moving from cluster to cluster, pile to pile. Harry, alone, still rummaged about the larger pieces. He yanked off more blankets with the dash and fanfare of a matador. We could hear his heavy, avid exhalations.

Wick joked, "Geez, Harry, sounds like Ethel's necking you."

Harry ignored him for the time being, but his breathing got even louder when he found the trunk. It was a mammoth thing, larger than any trunk I'd ever seen before. Certainly not something one person—or even two people—could heft. Harry fooled around with the lock, then surprised us when he caught sight of a fire iron and used it to smash the latch.

Wick couldn't resist. "You've got all this pent-up passion. Where's your girl when you need her?"

"Oh, drop dead. You're one to talk. I haven't seen Ada around much, either. Maybe they've both found new beaus."

"It's possible."

"Those dames are conspiring to ruin us."

"Can't argue with that."

"How long do you think it'll take?"

"I can't speak for you, but I'll be nothing but a bleeding heart and some dry bones by the weekend."

"Need help with that?" Phin broke in, observing that Harry could barely get this hands around the trunk cover, never mind lift it. Harry moved to the side, and together he and Phin hoisted it up. It groaned with every inch. Commanding the space inside was a book, a whopper of a book—but certainly nothing as delectably exciting as we'd been anticipating.

Wick shrugged and walked away. Phin and I stayed a little longer, watching Harry's face transform from curious to intrigued. He ran Phin's flashlight over the ancient-looking tome, then began to wipe off the dust with a blanket. Harry enlisted Phin to help him haul the book out of the trunk entirely. Together, they placed it on the ground, Phin with a thump so loud Harry cried out, "No, you twit! Careful! We don't know what we're dealing with."

"It's just an old book. We've got enough of those in Sterling," Wick uttered, his back turned. "So far the harp and the fake Rembrandt are the duckiest things we've found."

But Harry wouldn't give up so easily. He was on his knees now, carefully turning the pages, which were the size of elephant ears.

"Incredible," he whispered.

"What is it?" Phin asked.

"My best guess? The Gutenberg Bible."

And I'll admit I didn't know a thing about the Gutenberg Bible, had never heard of it, in fact. Yet it must have been something. Even Wick abandoned his foraging to look.

"It's got to be phony," Wick said, shaking his head. "This place is full of fakes. It's a pawnbroker's dream!"

"It's real. I think it's real."

"Nope."

"Really, look," Harry said, caressing a page. "Vellum. It's vellum."

"What the fiddle is vellum?" Phin asked, taking the words right out of my mouth.

"Calfskin, usually. People used to use it as paper."

"Why does that matter?"

"Because the vellum could date this book. The Gutenberg Bibles were printed—on vellum—in the fifteenth century."

"Can you read it?"

"Of course, it's Latin. But that doesn't matter."

"Why not?" I chimed.

Harry sighed the sigh he reserved for our most blatant displays of ignorance. "Because it's not what it says that's important. The Gutenberg is famous for three things." He ticked them off on his fingers. "First, it's beautifully wrought. Second, it's the first book printed with moveable type—as opposed to someone copying a book by hand. And third, it's rare. Only a few copies have lasted until now."

Wick waved off Harry's speech. "As I said before, if any stuff in this wonderland were real, it would have been ransacked ages ago."

"It sure looks real," Harry insisted, pushing up his glasses. "And this place doesn't have the easiest access."

My thrill diminished a little at that moment, the wonder and awe of learning about the Bible cut by resentment. If the Bible was indeed authentic, it would be ignoble for Yale to keep it here. Even at the risk of theft, it ought to be available to many. Yale had no right to hoard it, or these other fine things. Maybe, though, Yale wasn't hoarding anything. Maybe, so spoiled by its own prosperity and affluence, the university had simply forgotten part of its own bounty.

I got to thinking about some of the places I'd been for my work-study—places in New Haven that no one ever saw except for the people who lived there. In these isolated, stagnant regions, even the youngest children worked. They journeyed to lumberyards, building lots, construction sites, and the precincts of factories. They searched for anything saleable: lumps of coal, chips of wood, screws, bolts, and cogs. Amid the garbage in alleys and along street gutters, they found chair legs, shoehorns, cracked canisters, wicker baskets, and pot handles. I'd seen a child as young as four hauling a gunnysack over his shoulder. Maybe he'd been making his way to a back-street seller. Maybe he could trade in the day's find for a few pennies.

There was no question that in parts of New Haven, like in certain parts of Stony Creek, a few pennies could make all the difference. A few pennies and Marie wouldn't have to convince her husband that her old shoes suited her just fine, that they could live with drafty windows for another few years. Until their sons out West struck it rich and came home full-pocketed.

I would have loved to touch the Gutenberg, to feel the same sense of wonder that Harry was experiencing, to marvel at the wealth at our fingertips. But I hadn't the chance. Everything happened so fast, Wick turning at a noise, a startling rumpus, something fallen—off in the distance, or was it a door being swung? We were looking at Wick's face through our three flashlights, his beauty magnified by the trinity. His expression turned somber, then scared. We were running even before he told us to. Charging blindly, manically, headlong into pieces of furniture, stumbling over the blankets we had minutes ago torn off, scraping our knees, tearing up the palms of our hands. The flashlights like flickers from a nightmare, the flashes and winks of terror that remain in consciousness. Fear rising in our throats, the taste of it rancid, sour, like something decomposing in our mouths. Any second now I expected a yell, someone caught from behind, someone being pummeled or hauled off.

We weren't a pack anymore. One flashlight had been thrown. Its yellow trail fell dead on the dirty floorboards. I heard Harry's breathing. He was behind me, somewhere. But I couldn't locate Wick or Phin, and I didn't dare yell; I didn't want to give myself away.

It was Wick who found the round hatchway door. He called, "Here, hey, over here. Hurry!" until we finally found ourselves crowded together, bumbling, vulnerable, blind as a nest of squirming baby animals. Wick pushed Phin through the hole in the floor, to catch the rest of us when he got down. Harry was next, and then Wick and I had an absurdly chivalrous jostling match, wasting precious seconds. I won and Wick scampered down the shaky ladder, calling, "Let's go, Pietra! Don't be a daredevil."

I shuddered at his lapse: the one part of my name that was true. Traceable.

I just about leapt onto the ladder, yanking the heavy metal door with both hands. It fell with a fierce thud. Halfway down the rungs, still surging with adrenaline, I jumped; I don't know why. Perhaps I miscalculated how far down I still had to go. Tumbling, limbs contorted, I twisted my ankle as I landed, falling into a crouch, but Phin pulled me up and set me right. We were off, following that trail of poker chips, the four of us sprinting on the trust of two meager flashlights, me with a nasty limp.

Somehow we made it all the way back to our entrance under Cross Campus. I was still dizzy from the fall. My ankle throbbed, the pain so bad I thought I might keel over. The humiliation that image provoked made me bite through the ache.

Catching his breath, Wick noticed how my pants were torn at the knee, blood staining the shredded fabric in an ever-expanding blob. I tried to shrug off his concern. But Wick was suddenly worried, even doting.

"Hey champ, why didn't you tell us?" He knelt down to inspect the damage, rolling up my pants' leg with care. "You ripped yourself pretty good," he continued, dabbing at the open wound with the cuff of his shirt, using his spit, even, to clean the blood along the gash. "The landing could have been better, but I'll give you three stars for the dive."

I started to laugh, trying hard not to sound giggly-girlish. But no one noticed because they were laughing too, nervous, still unsettled by the uncertainty of that noise and by our hasty exit. We were feeling guilty, most of all. Like we'd escaped a certain fate. Like we'd snuck a peak at the goods under Mother Yale's skirt. And maybe we had.

Clearly, it was time to go home. Except Wick was arguing with us, saying that the four of us were a cowardly lot—weak in spirit, not the stuff of Yale men—if we ran like girls all the way back just because of a little scare. We had to march on, he declared. But we were tired and hot, and my knee and ankle were quitting on me. We didn't even know what time it was. The hazy, peach-hued light from the partially uncovered manhole shone like a crescent moon. It was a tempting sight, to be sure. Yet Wick was adamant.

"That room might only be the tip of the iceberg, boys. Who knows what else is down here? At the very least we ought to try for Skull and Bones. It would be criminal not to."

"It would be criminal to stay," Harry sniffed.

"Do you wish you hadn't come, Harry? Do you wish you hadn't seen the Gutenberg?"

And Harry had to admit he was glad for the chance to see it, even if his roommate thought it was a counterfeit.

"Who am I to judge?" Wick retorted, backpedaling. "It's a damn fairy tale, this place, a fairy tale and nightmare combined. But I have to admit, it's bewitched me."

He strode off, and like a bunch of hapless idiots we followed. He chose a different direction this time. The corridors were increasingly confining, the ceilings so low Wick and Phin had to bend their heads. Even then the boys managed to knock against the odd beam or pipe, cursing and laughing and hopped up. Harry and I had lost our enthusiasm, the both of us waiting for some imminent disaster. We walked briskly in that blistering maze, taking sips of water from the jugs in our satchels, Phin still dropping chips, saying he was running low, almost out of bets. Harry was fiddling with the compass and occasionally telling us that we were proceeding northwest or southeast. But it didn't matter, because we couldn't translate this information to the map. Wick stuffed it into his pocket with a shrug.

We were reaching the end of our patience, at least Harry and I, when the four of us met with the unmistakable odor of chlorine. It wafted harshly through the corridor, burning the insides of our noses. We didn't make the connection at first. Maybe we were lightheaded from the heat, but then Wick's face lit up. That irresistible spark of joy alighted in his eyes, and we realized where we were. We quickened our pace; even I ignored my limp and trotted on. The wound had started to bleed again, but I didn't care. We followed the stinging chemical trail until it became so overpowering we knew we must be close.

"Where the deuce is the way in?" Phin demanded.

"There," Harry said after a few minutes, pointing a flashlight at an overhead grate that was within striking distance. We worried that the grate would be welded shut, but it wasn't. Wick turned the few screws that held it in place. Then he popped it up and slid it aside. The opening was just wide enough to slip through. Grabbing the edges, Wick hauled himself up halfway, his long legs seemingly disembodied. Then he disappeared into the room above, which was pitch-black, and we weren't absolutely certain that he'd made it until he cried, "Eureka!"

"Shut your mouth!" I whispered through a smile.

The rest of us jacked ourselves through the opening. We searched for a light, but even when we found a switch, nothing happened.

"They must turn it off from a central source," Phin said.

And then Wick couldn't wait any longer. He turned off one flashlight and threw it aside recklessly. Whooping and hollering, he peeled off his shirt and pants, banging his chest with his fists like a cracker-barrel caveman, running crazily until he found the edge of the pool. He jumped high, tucking himself tightly into a cannonball. The splash was whiplash loud, then we heard only a sloshing sound. I wondered if he'd gone in at the shallow end and cracked his head open. The beam of the one remaining flashlight skimmed the surface of the water.

"Wick?" Harry called. But still we heard nothing, nothing at all, until Harry gasped. There was another splash. Harry had plunged into the water too, flashlight, clothes, and all. Wick was laughing, even when Harry spat out a mouthful of water and composed himself enough to knock his roommate upside the head.

"Bastard!" he cried. "You owe me a pair of shoes."

"That, my friend, was worth ten pairs of shoes."

Sullenly, Harry pulled the soaking, double-tied laces of his drenched oxfords and set the pair alongside the pool. He laid out his socks, too. Stripping off all his clothes, he wrung out each article carefully and placed it flat. Then, with stealthy deliberation, he hurled himself onto Wick and dunked his roommate's head under the water for as long as he could hold it there. Wick twisted free and wrestled raucously with Harry, who started to giggle irately, saying his glasses had fallen off. Crikey! Good God! Wick had better find them or there'd be hell to pay.

A moment later the floating flashlight went dead and there was no light left to speak of.

Wick began to dive, disappearing to the bottom of the pool for two minutes at a time, gulping for air when he popped up, saying he might owe his roommate new eyeglasses, too. Harry, meanwhile, relaxed a little. He even said, "Who needs glasses in the dark, anyway?" The pool felt darn good. "I could stay here all night."

I could almost make him out, back adrift on black water, white feet paddling, head listing.

A sudden fierce splatter meant Phin had gone in too. To make sure, I felt alongside the edge of the pool until I found another pile of clothes. My three friends were naked, or near naked, and I was the lone man out. But I couldn't deny that I craved the water, craved entrance into this ridiculous, harebrained spectacle. I knew if I thought too much I wouldn't do it, so I took quick, deep breaths and shed my clothes, even my bindings, off in a corner. I touched my body, the outthrust hip bones, the fringe at my groin, the smooth run of skin. Then I felt tentatively along the moist, slick tiled walls. My bare feet skimmed the rough floor. My senses were on high alert. I made sure that there were still three voices, and that they were all coming from the water. My toes curled over the edge of the pool.

I jumped in on the side opposite the boys. The deep end, I realized, when my feet didn't touch the bottom. Exhaling a bubbly breath, I let my body fall slowly, the water chill, shivery, and embracive. It penetrated my ears, sealing them off. I opened my eyes to see nothing but a blue-black abyss. I had the discombobulating sensation that I was in the sea, somehow. I felt so far down that I didn't know where the surface was. Maybe I was close to that moldering skyhook. Or maybe I was somewhere else, in an enormous womb, flipping and tumbling weightless in thick amniotic juices, growing and changing, readying myself for a final exit.

Counting all the times I'd swum in the Long Island Sound, I'd never been underwater for so long. I didn't need to breathe; I didn't want to breathe. My mouth opened like a shored fish's. My eyes peered into oblivion. What a relief, I thought, to finally let go.

From behind, someone grabbed me about the waist. Scissor-kicking, he hoisted me to the surface and my head emerged. The feel of air was startling, foreign. I didn't breathe, not until my rescuer had walloped me on the back, hard. I choked, a stream of water erupting out of my mouth. When I finally caught my breath, he asked me how I was. The voice belonged to Wick.

I couldn't reply at first; my throat felt as if I'd swallowed gasoline. My body hurt, too. I was sure my knee was still bleeding, that it was turning the water around it pink. But I muttered as best I could, "Fine, I think." As soon as he heard that, he hooked his hands under my arms and sent me flying. I don't know if he felt the sides of my breasts. I don't know if he realized my skin was softer than his, my rib cage too small. He laughed half-angrily, half-affectionately, in the way only Wick could, as I landed with a great jarring spray. But I didn't know what he was thinking—or even if he was thinking at all.

"Shucks. You scared the living daylights out of me, Pietra," came his voice through the darkness. "Thought you were a goner."

"It's not that easy to get rid of me," I told him as I floundered.

"Good, 'cause I wouldn't want you gone."

He disappeared again, his agile body sluicing through liquid. After a few moments I felt a hand stroke my side. It rested briefly on my hip, then on my waist. I grabbed it and held it, thinking that yes, these were Wick's fingers, no other touch would make me quiver. Plunging under again, I let my hand creep up his arm. I explored its length, its viny-sleek strength, the muscles clean and taut, not an ounce of unnecessary flesh. The arm wound around me, holding me firm. Wick's body pressed into mine, and I savored the twine of limbs, the cling of wet skin. Our mouths met, our tongues exploring gently at first, then urgently, even fiercely, the stubble of his chin rough—not a boy's face, but a man's, I realized. I thought one of us would break away, but neither did. We clung to each other, our bodies submerged in coiled suspension, mouths brushing, hands seeking. My sex grew swollen, slippy-hot, and needful.

I took his hand in mine and drew it to my lips, thinking everything is dreamy in this lulling, undulating place; everything is possible—even the junction of bodies.

But the hand slinked from my grasp, slowly, almost apologetically it seemed, and I couldn't find it again. The dark water heaved and pitched as he disentangled himself and floated away, rolling soundlessly under the surface. My lungs retched. I came up to breathe, finding no tangible divider between water and air, one world and another. Everything was blending now. Colliding. My heart, once whizzing, skidded to a halt. I wanted to call out his name, but I feared my voice would betray me, that Harry and Phin would hear the yearning.

I treaded water for several long minutes, hoping he would change his mind and come back to me. But when he didn't, my body chilled. Taking care not to make any noise, I climbed out of the pool and stood shivering, hugging myself tightly, the wedge of flesh between my thighs the only warm place left. I listened to the boys in the pool, as if nothing had happened, three voices hollering and goofing, and I'd never felt so separate, bitter droplets dribbling down my shins, tipping over my nipples, which were hard as copper rivets. Then I fumbled my way back, back to where I'd left my clothes.

I found my way without difficulty. I hadn't consulted a map, but I knew approximately where Ada must live—surely the same tired, straggly part of town where Helen and Ethel resided. It was an area of New Haven few Yale students ventured to. Not as terrifically run-down as Fair Haven, but still, a far cry from the university's marble pillars and chandeliers.

I may have found Ada's street, Cantor Boulevard, by chance, but I knew which house was hers: number 165. I'd seen it on the library card she kept in her wallet, when I'd rummaged about her purse the night of the Freshman Ball. Perhaps I'd anticipated that I would eventually seek her out. Ada, more than any young woman I'd ever met, seemed to know how to get what she wanted.

Ada's house appeared to me exactly the opposite of Ada herself. It was shabby, in a run-of-the-mill kind of way. Narrow and small, without window boxes, a door knocker, planters, or any other pretense of adornment, it attracted no attention, save pity. Its brick hide was dingy and crumbly. The chimney tipped gloomily to one side. I knew there must be activity there—the windows weren't shuttered, a light shone from a window on the second floor. But it *looked* dead.

Not knowing exactly what I was doing there—what exactly I hoped to achieve—I loitered. I loitered first in front of her house, and then, because I felt exposed, on the other side of the street. I couldn't have frittered away more than fifteen minutes when I saw a man exiting the front door.

He was drunk—this I sensed immediately. Even from a distance, I could see how he stumbled, like the men who leave pubs only at closing time. He paced about errantly; then, seeming to think better of it, he sat in a clumsy heap on the front steps. The last light of day illuminated another fact about the man: he was filthy. His clothes were yellowed and threadbare. His too-long hair seemed as if it hadn't seen a comb in weeks. I could scarcely tell how his face looked under a bristly, unkempt beard.

The door creaked open again. This time Ada appeared. Somehow, I wasn't surprised by her association with the drunkard. Her life couldn't possibly have been as idyllic and enviable as I'd imagined it to be.

I hunched behind a shrub (it was a low, sparse shrub, and small as I was, I had no doubt that I looked both conspicuous and ridiculous). Ada sat next to the man. She bent her face close to his ear and whispered something. Whatever she said achieved no result. She took his arm and tugged it. Again, he didn't respond. When Ada yanked a second time, he moaned and stamped his feet like a child throwing a tantrum. He was a large man, much larger a person than Ada, and his physicality frightened me. Ada didn't flinch, however. She ordered the man to stand up, which he did, finally. He leaned into her so that he wouldn't tip, and she took his weight capably, obligingly, as if this situation were unexceptional. She was still speaking to him when she caught sight of me. Her gaze lingered, then she murmured gently to the man and led him inside. The door fell shut behind them, and I tried to imagine the rest: maybe Ada would lead the inebriate to his bed, or maybe he would pass out cold on the floor before she got him there.

I rose from my hiding place and returned to the front of Ada's house. She didn't keep me waiting long. Her eyeglasses were propped high on her nose when she next emerged. The blue ribbons she wore in her hair seemed to accentuate her indignation. (Ada, always and ever, would remind me of the color blue.)

"Did Wick put you up to this?" she asked. "*Did* Wick put you up to this?" she repeated. "Why are you here, Charles?"

Her tough act was persuasive. Even so, I knew she must be exhausted. Having a sick father drains a person.

"I told Wick I wasn't comfortable with his being around my house," she continued. "It would be very disrespectful if he ignored my wishes and sent . . . a scout."

Outside of the Freshman Ball, I hadn't ever been this near to her. Even then, the lights had been dim and my racing heart had kept me from noticing subtle things, like how her skin looked fresh-scrubbed and radiant. I wondered how it was possible that she and the man shared the same run-down dwelling. It was remarkable that his taint hadn't had a visible effect on her.

"I'm not here because of Wick," I said finally. "And—I'm sorry I saw your father like that."

As soon as the words came out, I couldn't believe I'd spoken them. I hadn't intended to sound so harsh. She put one hand over her face and looked as if she might start to cry. Guiltily, I wrapped my arm about her shoulders and held her, letting her body tremble against mine. I rubbed her back and said, "Shh, shh, it's okay—everything's going to be all right," because I didn't know what else to say, and because I would have wanted to hear the same thing. She had wilted, her head bent, her shoulders bowed; I appeared taller as a result. I leaned my nose into the zigzag part of her hair. No doubt Wick had buried his nose in the exact same place.

After several minutes she composed herself, wiping smudges off her eyeglasses and taking deep breaths. Her posture straightened, and a flush of color returned to her face.

"Do you want to go for a walk?" I asked.

"I think so," she answered, sniffing. I took a handkerchief out of the pocket of my jacket and handed it to her.

"Is there somewhere we can go?" She knew what I meant—somewhere secluded.

"Sure, there's a place not far from here, a little park—well, not really a park, more of a garden." She sighed. "It used to be nice."

"That sounds perfect," I said, and the two of us walked in silence until her house was well out of sight.

"How did you know he was my father?" she asked.

"I'm not sure exactly. I had a sense of it."

"I don't suppose your father drinks?"

"My father—his problems were different."

"Sorry."

"No, don't be sorry." I didn't want her to be ashamed or embarrassed. I wanted her to feel perfectly at ease with me, for only then could I ask her what I wanted to.

Ada nodded faintly. "Here it is," she said, when we came upon an overgrown field. Bushes and trees flanked three of its four sides. There were a few scattered houses nearby, but the air was still. We seemed quite alone. "I don't think it's a park—not officially. It's probably private property. But no one's ever used it, not that I've seen."

It looked like a lost garden. Striped grass commingled with crab grass, clover, onion grass, and dandelions. It was impossible to determine, as I scrutinized the violets and fanned ferns, which plants grew wild and which had been cultivated. Moss crept over flat stones and brambles ran rampant over several low benches. Vines wrapped the private parts of naked, limbless statues, as if planned by a prudish overseer. The whole place was at once lovely, sad, and ethereal. It was easy to envision it, in a different time, as lively, a place for picnics, croquet, and leisurely strolls, but now the only creatures who rejoiced here were the bumblebees that flitted flower to flower.

"My brother and I used to come here," Ada explained. "We'd play cowboys and Indians."

"I didn't know you had a brother."

She smiled. "Why would you?

"How old is he?"

"Fourteen. Still a baby."

"Are you close?"

"Well, sure. Aren't all brothers and sisters? We still come here once in a blue moon."

"To play cowboys and Indians?"

She cast me a gamesome look. "I come to study now. No one can bother me if they don't know where to find me." She paused, seeming to decide on something. "I know it looked bad, Charles—what you saw back there."

"It didn't look bad."

"It did."

"I've seen worse, believe me."

"Really?" She asked this with genuine curiosity. "Because sometimes, when Wick tells me about you boys, your lives sound blissful."

"Smoke and mirrors," I assured her. She looked like she didn't believe me. I bent down to decapitate a flossy-headed dandelion wand, wondering how much I would tell her. "My family's got its troubles, too."

"What sort of troubles?"

"Well, my father was a dreamer, but not the healthy sort. His dreams just made him restless." I'd seldom said a negative word about Pa, and it didn't feel good, this admission.

"Not everyone can act on their dreams. He has you to take care of."

"That's true," I said flatly. "Anyhow, it doesn't matter—my father passed away."

"When?"

"Ages ago, it seems like."

We went silent, settling down on a little mossy patch. At this level, the grasses appeared very tall. The whole garden seemed to encircle us protectively.

"Does Wick know your father's gone?"

"I keep it to myself mostly."

"Yes, I think I would do the same."

"My pa's got this brother," I heard myself blurt. "His name is Francisco. He's been around the world and back—to all seven continents, my father used to say. He's had more adventures than you could fit in a book. I think Francisco got the life my father wanted."

Ada shrugged.

"Yes, that's the way life goes, isn't it?" I continued. "But still, I wish he would have tried a little harder to be like Francisco. For his own sake. Maybe he would have been happier."

"He wasn't happy with your mother?"

I stared at her. "How did you know that?"

"I didn't. It was only a guess."

I stared at her half-admiringly, half-crossly. She seemed suddenly less disciplined than I'd had her figured, and more discomfited. I wondered, audaciously, if she thought I was sweet on her.

"Did Wick send you here or not?" she asked.

"I told you he didn't."

"Why is it you came to see me, then?"

"There's something—see, something I've been wanting to ask you." I swallowed hard. "You don't happen to have your flask, do you?"

"Of course not, Charles—don't be ridiculous."

What I said next came out in a blundering, breathless spurt. "I want you to tell me about your life, Ada. I want to know about your school, what your history program is like, what you'll do when you graduate. When you become a professor, where you'll teach. Will you make enough money to live on your own—without ever getting married?"

"I don't understand. Why are you asking me all this?"

I chewed at my lower lip. "If I tell you something—something that might sound crazy—will you promise not to tell anyone?"

"I—I suppose so."

"No, Ada, you have to swear."

"Okay, I swear. Now what's all this about?"

I didn't want to, but I didn't see another way. I started to unbutton my shirt. My fingertips tingled with fear, and the taste of bile rose up in my throat.

"This—this doesn't feel right, Charles," she whispered.

"Here," I said. Three buttons down, I exposed a few inches of the elasticized band, the silvery flash of a pin.

"What are you doing? What's going on?" She didn't sound scared or upset, just confused. She averted her eyes until I grabbed her hand and squeezed it. I told her to look at me. I begged her to.

"This is what I wanted you to see."

At last she relented, her jaw hardening as she comprehended what I'd kept hidden. "You've been . . . all this time?"

"No one knows. I'm only showing you because—well, I don't know why, except that I thought, maybe, you could help me."

"*Help* you?"

"Yes, see, I want to know how you do it. I'm going to teach—I realize that now—but I don't know how much longer I can stay and fake my way through. I'm betraying everyone, Wick and Harry, every single person I've met in New Haven. I want to continue my studies—more than anything—but I don't want to keep pretending."

Still her jaw appeared rigid, tight. Still her hand was clenched in mine. I released it self-consciously.

"There are no two ways about it," she said finally. "You must stay at Yale."

"Stay?"

"Stay," she said emphatically. "I told you how Yale admitted that I was qualified, but still wouldn't let me enroll. You've found a way in. You've found a way around their absurd, archaic rules, Charles Pietra. I'm downright jealous."

"They would kick me out if they knew."

"Of course they would. You're upsetting the balance of their system. Yet you're hardly the first to do such a thing. Haven't you heard of Deborah Sampson or Renée Bordereau or George Sand? Sampson battled in the Revolutionary War, and Bordereau in the French Revolution. Sand was a female novelist whom everyone assumed was male. I'm sure there are a dozen more examples of women pretending to be male to achieve what was otherwise forbidden. My point being," she continued, "that it doesn't matter what you look like under your clothes. That's no one's business but your own. What counts is that you're the first female undergraduate at Yale."

"Would you do it if you were me?"

Her expression grew increasingly impetuous. "What do *you* think?"

"And what about after?" She must have caught the weariness in my voice. I had only so much endurance.

"You'll find a way to be yourself again—I'm sure of it." She hesitated, seeming to weigh her thoughts. "It's a sacrifice," she said finally. "A temporary sacrifice. That's how you must regard it."

"A temporary sacrifice," I repeated. Framing it this way made the shame and guilt fade. It even made me feel proud, like I had a righteous mission to accomplish and not a fool's errand.

Ada leaned over, much the way I'd seen her bend close to her father. Carefully, quite deliberately, she began to button my shirt. I watched her moisten her lips with the tip of her tongue. I could see my own reflection in the lenses of her eyeglasses. I tried, for once, to see neither one sex nor the other.

"There you are," she said, guiding the last button through its hole. She smoothed the shirt over the elastic band. "Good as new."

We looked at each other again, not guardedly this time but as confidantes, and I understood completely why Wick desired her as his muse.

"You can come to me, you know, if you need someone to talk to," she said. "I'd be hurt if you didn't."

"All right. I will." I leaned back onto a mossy bank, savoring a calm I hadn't felt since reading in my granite nook, deep in the quarry. The best thing about Ada, I determined, was not just what she said, but what she didn't have to say. I didn't need to ask her to keep things quiet. In the still of her secret garden, her discretion could not have felt more sure.

Chapter Thirteen

I'D FINISHED administering the tests to Professor Spang's subjects
and compiling the data onto large gridded ledgers long ago. Now
that I was no longer scouting about New Haven, my work schedule
revolved around the professor's office. In that drab, weakly lighted
place I sat patiently, pencil poised, writing letters, articles, booklets,
and monographs as the professor dictated them. He liked to pace as he
talked, clopping about the room in his elevator shoes, occasionally
exclaiming, "Strike that! Now listen: here's how I want it." He was loud,
too, as if we were in a bustling newsroom rather than a private office.

Afterward, I would sit at a little wood desk, small enough for a
child, and use his bulky black Remington Rand typewriter to tran-
scribe my notes. I was grateful for the clatter of that machine. The
noise served as an aural divider between Spang and myself.

When I was finished typing, he would review each page, revising
and correcting. He would dab his index finger on his little pink
tongue as he turned the sheets. Then I would retype the document,
making the necessary adjustments. At first Spang would check the
second version, too. But as the weeks passed, and my presence
seemed a little more natural to him, he trusted me more. He trusted
me, even, to organize his files, to mail letters and parcels, to take
charge of certain communications.

"As long as you're here, I might as well make good use of you," he
told me.

And he did. Much of my office work pertained to the data gathered from my work-study, but some of it was personal: I typed

263

Spang's correspondence with colleagues in other states, even in other countries, and with his friends at the American Eugenics Society, the Race Betterment Foundation, the American Breeders Association, and the National Education Association's Committee on Racial Well-Being. I typed for two or three hours at a clip, using only my index fingers. Always I was slow and flustered. Maybe it was that I had trouble seeing; the office was as sepulchral as on my first rainy day. But I never inquired about drawing the curtains or turning on an extra lamp. Something about the professor's waxy skin and jumpy rabbit eyes warned against light.

Sometimes Spang would offer me a cashew, or further reminisce about his summers in Stony Creek, or read aloud something that amused him—something in a newspaper column or a letter. He would chortle, entertained by his own strange brand of humor. He never seemed to notice that I found his jocularity ridiculous.

But for these interludes and the rat-tat-tat of the Remington, we existed in silence. I tried to ward off his chilly presence, to forget I was breathing in his wet, earthy odor. But, of course, I couldn't forget what it was that I was typing.

As my disgust mounted, I would attempt to rationalize Spang's influence and my relationship to it. Spang floats in the bubble of academia, I would tell myself. His ideas on human worth exist more in theory than in reality. But when I carried his mail to the post office every day, buying stamps out of the pocket change he gave me, I could almost see those letters traveling across fields and valleys, mountains and seas. The ideas in those envelopes not only fed the faithful eugenicists, they drew new devotees. They nourished a movement—a movement I was supporting.

Trapped as he was in his foul office, Spang nevertheless knew a lot of people. He wrote to affiliates in western Europe, complaining of the "inferior stock" coming from eastern and southern Europe. He disseminated articles on how Gypsies, homosexuals, Jews, Negroes, Chinese, and Japanese were polluting the gene pool here in America. He drew parallels between economically and socially forsaken people and physical defectiveness. Using terms like "Darwinian," "Mendelian," and "dysgenic," he purported that a devastating trend was taking place right under our noses. The less fit were outreproducing the more fit. The solution, he clamored—and which I typed time and again—was to implement the four s's: segregation, sterilization, selected breeding, and stricter immigration policy. Only then might the racial hygiene of this nation be restored. Only then might we be vindicated.

The "we," of course, being a precious few.

Sometimes I would arrive to his office and discover photographs tacked to the wall: shaved human heads, their cranial proportions charted, harsh and ragged stitches zigzagging across the scalps; or hands and feet side by side, analyzed and diagrammed and stuck with pins. Bold block print exclaimed "Feeble-minded," "Epileptic," "Imbecilic," and below these captions, pictures of sickly-looking babies, their faces x-ed out.

There were phrenology heads, and posters of dark-skinned, dark-haired children. THIS IS THE FACE OF HUMAN JUNK, one admonished. Others cautioned, SOME AMERICANS ARE BORN TO BE A BURDEN and NONE IS ENOUGH FOR THE POLISH AND HUNGARI-ANS. These posters changed over time, as Spang received new mementos from his colleagues. But one quote was always tacked up, its curled corners giving away its owner's unwavering belief in its dogma: THE CROSS BETWEEN A WHITE MAN AND AN INDIAN IS AN INDIAN; THE CROSS BETWEEN A WHITE MAN AND A NEGRO IS A NEGRO.

One day Spang decided that we would both take the afternoon off. We would watch a movie, he teased, the sides of his face wet, sweat seeping into the furrows of his forehead. I couldn't believe we would be leaving his office, and sure enough, as we walked, Spang glanced back uneasily. His face was pallid and queasy-looking. His stacked shoes clicked rapidly against the flagstones. He wondered aloud if his enemies were watching him. We were in the midst of a war, make no mistake about that. And there would be casualties. Did I realize that?

I grunted noncommittally. It didn't matter; Spang wasn't really listening.

We walked in tandem, but a certain distance apart—a respectable distance. I feared passersby would assume we were associated, although I had to admit, shamefully, that we were. I wondered if Spang had given much thought to my last name, to my being half Italian. Sometimes I suspected he was just waiting for me to make a significant mistake so he could exchange me for someone else. Other times I thought he trusted me implicitly.

On the way to the tiny cinema, Spang joked about the five-dollar compensation we'd promised the test-takers. He'd been surprised at how many of them had actually demanded the money.

"Thought they'd forget about it. Alcoholism, sloth, and truancy tend to fray the memory."

I didn't respond. Prying the money out of him had been like prying out stubborn teeth. Even now, I'd compensated only half the test-takers. The DiRisios I'd guiltily paid out of my own pocket months earlier, after Marie's worried face had gotten the better of me.

Once in the cinema, we were two of twenty or so viewers. Some were professors I recognized from around campus; some were students. The film was called the *The Black Stork*. Once the lights went low, I closed my eyes. Working with Spang, I'd seen too much of this type of thing already; now I had to hear it, too. On-screen, a doctor tried to convince a worried mother that her newborn son was too diseased to be kept alive. The doctor wanted to terminate nourishment and medical care.

You'll see, it will be better this way, he insisted, and the mother, after cinematic exposure to all the dark turns her child could take on its way to adulthood, had to agree. Better that another child not grow up defective and prone to criminal tendencies.

"This film was released years ago," Spang said as the movie ended and the lights were turned on. I blinked. My head felt strangely tipsy atop my neck. "But Charles, you see that it's as relevant as ever."

Week after week I returned to Spang's den, that despicable hole, dreading it a little more each time. At the start of my work-study, I had thought about asking Mother's advice. I wondered what she would have said about Spang. In all likelihood she would suppress her criticism and advise me to do the same. She would tell me yet again that the rules were different for the privileged. "Have you forgotten how much money you're being paid to write the opinions of this little man? Just hunker down and do what you're told."

I'd thought about opening up to Harry, too, but in the end I'd kept the predicament to myself. The second semester was coming to a close, anyway. Quite soon I would be done with the whole of my freshman year. There was no point in stirring the pot now. Next year I would request a new work-study, one having nothing to do with Yale's Department of Social Demography and Intelligence. Next year I would pretend I hadn't set foot in the office of Joshua Cecil Spang, Ph.D., and that I hadn't walked with him, side by side.

I would have made it, too, straight through to the end, except that I'd grown used to deceit. By now it was a habit.

It started very slowly, my mutiny, with small things here and there. I'd change a sentence or two on a second draft, the one Spang usually didn't check. Or I'd misaddress an envelope and cross out the return address so that the post office had no way of delivering the mail or sending it back. Some of the envelopes ended up in the garbage, too; they just clear fell out of my hands and into a trash can.

When the old coot didn't catch me I grew bolder, hacking away at that typewriter, glancing over my shoulder to make sure he was still at his desk. I deleted and added whole paragraphs as I saw fit, manipulating his theories, reworking his conclusions. I pointed out inconsistencies in the data, how not all of it could be forced into basic Mendelian templates. Posing as Spang himself, I questioned how complex traits could be defined so laxly and simplistically, how characteristics as multifaceted and intangible as humor or loyalty could spring from a single cause. I concluded many of his papers by imploring eugenicists to reevaluate findings in light of procedural flaws, everything from the failure to account for environmental influences to false quantification.

Late at night, in my room, I wrote Spang's signature hundreds of times. I liked to practice naked at my desk. Sometimes I ran a free hand along my dark skin, feeling my body's bumps and angles. Sometimes I felt my head, too—the shape of it under my hair. I imagined myself dismantled, my every part charted and labeled in a medical text. When I'd learned Spang's signature by heart, I sent an entire counterfeit letter to one of his colleagues, a professor at the University of Munich. I asked him please not to write back.

"Please consider the issues herewith carefully and pass them on if you find them of value," I typed. "I look forward to the eventual day when I will have the pleasure of meeting you in person and discussing this subject matter in detail. But in the meantime, I'm afraid I won't have adequate opportunity to correspond with you. It is my work that keeps me captive. You see, there is so much to do, and so many others to reach."

I comforted myself by thinking of how infrequently Spang left his office. There was little chance he'd ever meet any of his overseas cohorts face-to-face.

Then came the day when Spang brought up the article.

"This isn't a small-time affair," he pointed out. The prestigious *Journal of Human Heredity* would be printing it. Every single one of his colleagues and competitors would see it, even the big cheese at Yale.

"This is my chance," he told me. "I knew it would come."

He wanted to know if I could stay late at the office from here on in. He might need me on the weekends, too. Putting out an article of this kind in an efficient manner would require extra manpower.

And though I'd promised extra study sessions to the DiRisios, I said, "Of course. Oh, yes. I'm always at your disposal, Professor Spang."

We worked until late at night. Spang added black coffee, dried figs, and chocolate caramels to his sparse diet. He would become overexcited and his eyes would bulge. His shirts would sag under increasingly large sweat stains. I was surprised he had procrastinated this long on a project he must have had some prior knowledge of. Truly, there were nights that seemed endless—nights I stayed at his office until even the stars nodded off. I listened, transcribed, and typed, an endless, draining cycle. I saw Spang's face more than Harry's or Wick's or Ceci's.

The more time wore on, the more frantic Spang became. Feigning concern, I reassured him that everything would be fine. His article would be in the mail on time, and it would be a plum. There was no doubt about it: he would do Yale proud. But I worked with deliberate sloth, allowing the hours to flit by with just enough to show for them, allowing Spang to bite his nails down to the stubs.

Those last two weeks, careworn and visibly agitated, he detoured from usual procedure. He still hadn't produced the last third of the article, and he complained of writer's block. Panicked, he checked my typewritten sheets more hastily, and never got around to glancing at the second drafts. His files became miserably and inexplicably disorganized. Did I mind going through them again? he'd ask me. He swore he'd put the "Grant" file next to the "Glick," but here it was in the "Closed Case" drawer. And he'd been looking for the survey on the Wysocki family for days. He must have misplaced it.

"How stupid of me," he exclaimed.

Mere days before his deadline, he began to stutter. He complained of myriad ailments: a backache one day, a sour stomach the next. He paced in circles until he grew dizzy. He had to lie down, he told me. Take a catnap. Just this one time.

"When you get as old as I am, the parts start to rust. You'll understand, Charles. Eventually."

Whenever he fell asleep, I would make the most of the opportunity by mucking up the files or moving all the posters and photographs on the wall a couple inches in one direction. I'd switch the positions of his desk items: a paperweight, a stack of folders, a carton of paper clips. I'd rub dull every pencil in his canister. Sometimes I swiped cashews and tucked them into the sheets of his roll-away bed.

It was clear from Spang's dubious hygiene that he wasn't spending his nights at home.

If he was snoring hard, I'd get up the confidence to steal important documents. He had all kinds of things that didn't belong to him: birth certificates, marriage licenses, vaccination notices. I feared to know where these items had come from and what had become of their owners. Most likely the documents belonged to those who had been sacrificed in the name of scientific research.

Eventually, Spang would ask me if I'd seen it—whatever it was I'd filched. He'd swear he'd left it there—on a chair, in the drawer, in the "Liu" or "Grubman" file. He'd complain of too much work, even for a man with his drive and stamina. I'd help him with his search, my countenance properly distraught, a tacit sign that I was as committed to this article as he was.

He didn't catch on to my monkeying. I was careful, purposely inconsistent. Some days I meddled mercilessly. Other days I was almost—but not quite—a model assistant.

His office had become a demolition site of hastily scribbled notes, unopened letters, and scattered documentation. Had Spang not been so worn out, he would have sensed it in the air: the threat to his dominion. It was imminent now.

Most of his naps lasted between fifteen and twenty minutes. The longest one I'd timed at twenty-four. I waited until I understood his habits completely before making my move, the one that truly mattered.

He took a single nap that evening. I had to wait four hours before he finally nodded off. Watching his eyelids carefully, I coaxed the ledgers from underneath his sedated arms. These were the same ledgers I'd given him after my work-study rounds. Usually he kept them well guarded, locked in the middle drawer of his desk. But today he'd spread them on his desk and scrutinized them, an unsharpened pencil tucked behind his ear.

Numbers filled the columns and rows. They marked the presence, absence, and degree of certain traits among family members, often across multiple generations. Spang referred to the numbers as "pedigree scores." I saw that he'd used the scores to create graphs that resembled family trees. These eugenical graphs differed from genealogies, however. In addition to names, dates, and family connections, Spang's trees contained notes on what he perceived to be each person's physical, mental, and temperamental qualities.

On Spang's trees I recognized many names: the families I'd visited, people who had invited me into their homes, shared with me the last tea in their cupboards. But my written observations had changed. Negative traits now replaced both neutral and positive findings. I scanned the list with my finger and found the DiRisio family. All the names were there: Marie, Angelo, Carlo, Freddie, and Ceci. According to the new figures, every one of them qualified as feeble-minded. Descriptions like "slow-learning," "suspected imbecility," "developmentally impaired," and "permanent cognitive dysfunction" followed each name. I forgot to breathe. A sickening tide of repulsion rose in me. And then I saw it: my name cited at the bottom of the ledger. My name listed as one of the study's contributing researchers. Spang must have thought I'd be thrilled.

I stood over his slumped body. In his sleep, his mouth made strange sucking sounds. Little gray gobs had gathered at the corners of his lips. I was closer than I'd ever been to him, to his tallowy hair and odd, slightly nauseating funk. And then it struck me just what it was that he smelled like. The same odor that had spilled out of the medical station on the day of the accident: the fleeting state between death and rot.

Spang entrusted me with the final parcel. I conceded that his faith in me probably had less to do with my competency than with his reluctance to leave his office, his sanctuary.

The professor handed me the final article after he reviewed it. He watched me wrap it into a tidy parcel and address it properly. But he couldn't see how I swapped it on my way to the post office with the other parcel in my satchel. This one was thinner than it ought to have been. Pages were missing, and those that remained were nothing like Spang's dictations. I was especially proud of the conclusion, how I'd conceded that all of the professor's prior findings had been a wash. Slowly but surely the eugenics movement was revealing itself to be a pseudoscience, as improbable as spontaneous generation or the flat earth theory. I quoted the geneticist Thomas Hunt Morgan, explaining that the problem with eugenics was one of definition. The diagnosis of human elements was a highly subjective and idiosyncratic matter. The personal bias of the data collector, the partial nature of the tests themselves, and the social and cultural differences between collector and subject invariably obstructed credible, reliable dialogue. The attempt to define "native intelligence" thus resulted, more often than not, in faulty findings and deeply flawed research.

All in all, I made an effort to debunk everything Spang held dear. And then, on the last page, I signed his name with a flourish.

Spang, having said that the strongest always prevail, saluted me as I left. I walked decisively to the post office, a spring to my step. I tried to imagine his reaction once the article came out. I couldn't decide whether he would respond with quiet outrage or a ranting tirade. It all depended on which would be harder for him: reluctantly affirming his new stance, or swallowing his pride and admitting that he'd let himself be duped by a swarthy amateur. My money, what little I had of it, was on his ego.

Of course, for me, there would be consequences. Spang might turn to Yale's executive committee. The school might put me on academic probation or throw me out altogether. Mother might be unable to forgive my trespass. Maybe other lies would be exposed. But no matter what happened, the DiRisios wouldn't abandon me. This I was sure of. In a new era of ambiguity, I clung to this one conviction.

He'd slipped me a note, of all things, he who had no trouble barging into rooms, shimmying through windows, and climbing over locked gates. He didn't knock, either; I knew this because I was there when he did it, when he passed the note through the crevice under my door. I was in my room, thinking about him in fact, thinking of how he'd been avoiding me since the tunnels. Several times I'd happened by—not quite by chance—the room he shared with Harry, but he was never there. Nor could I find him at the usual haunts. I kept thinking I'd catch him lollygagging around the smoke shop, sweet-talking female passersby, or standing in the middle of a courtyard delivering some half-baked, delirious tale. But as usual, Wick defied every expectation.

As luck would have it, I caught up with him, finally, smack in the middle of Old Campus. It was one of the few moments when my mind wasn't on him, which was probably why we crossed paths. It seemed to me that fate delighted in working this way: withholding what one wants until one is, for only the briefest of moments, safe in the relative tranquility of distraction. I was rifling through my satchel, searching for a misplaced essay that was due in a matter of minutes. Wick was walking with Phin, who was listening as raptly as he always did. It was Phin who saw me. I stopped dead on the stone walkway, the lost essay at last in hand, crowing, "Hello! Where have you chaps been?" Instantly I wondered if I sounded desperate.

"Hardly anywhere—it's a damned shame," Phin replied. "Got any bright ideas? We're bored as all hell."

"Ideas?" I tried to find Wick's eyes. They slanted eastward.

Suddenly, Phin's face lit like a lantern. "Holy mike, I forgot there's a soccer game on. Davenport's playing Saybrook for the title. I said I'd give the D-boys a hand. Anyone else want to jump in? We're going to Mory's to celebrate afterward—winners and losers."

"I've got to study," I hastened, glancing again at Wick, although I had no better plans than to deliver my essay and continue moping about. I prayed Wick would hear what lay beneath my offhanded-ness. I wanted so much to talk to him, alone, but he didn't notice, or more likely, he didn't want to. He managed, somehow, to acknowl-edge me without really seeing me at all: a quick smile, a sidelong glance. Then he told Phin, sure, he was up for it, maybe he'd play too—play on the Saybrook side, if they'd have him. It was traitorous, what they were doing, but he'd take part anyway, just to rattle the traditionalists.

My heart fractured as soon as he left. Days later it still felt broken. And now this: a folded note, not even in an envelope. It seemed too casual—careless, even. Already the paper was sullied from its crawl over the floorboards.

I tiptoed across the room to fetch it, not wanting Wick to know I was here waiting for him, waiting for something exactly like this. I sat on the floor, feeling brittle as tinder. I realized the creative impress Wick was capable of: his every action toward Ada had revealed it. I knew his tender side, too. A love letter would have been spangled with poetry, glazed in gold, written in blood. It would have been something smoldering, anguished, grand, and full of impossible fantasy. A note under the door, I knew, was not one.

Already I swiped at the tears, madly, nearly scratching my face with my close-clipped nails.

"Criminy," I muttered, before I'd read anything. For a moment I wondered where I'd picked up the word; I'd never heard or used it in Stony Creek. And further, I wondered if Mother had ever said it, back when she'd been young, sassy, a little blasé, cinching a cigarette between two fingers, trying out rough words just to startle the boys and to impress her friends.

"Criminy," I said again, biting until my teeth hurt, the physical pain more bearable than the mental.

Dear Charlie,

How can I put your mind at ease? This is my foremost concern, the only reason I've been able to kick my muddled self into motion and finally give you this letter. I tried before, but I turned lily-livered. Anyhow, here it is, better late than never, I suppose.

The first thing I want to tell you is that your secret is safe. I'll never tell anyone, not even Phin or Harry. I'll carry it through the rest of Yale, through all my life, if you want me to. I swear it. I swear it on the Gutenberg.

And now, what else can I tell you? Here is where my thoughts run dry. I'm not sure how long I've known the truth about you, Charlie. Looking back, maybe you gave off a hint or two, and maybe I responded with a hint or two of my own. But I must question the accuracy of my memory. In light of what happened that night in the tunnels, all the conversations and adventures we've shared have taken on new meaning.

In the pool we made a leap of faith. I don't dwell on the right or wrong of it, or if what we did was natural. All of that seems pointless and stupid. Instead, I think of how you came to be here. I wonder what you used to look like, if your hair was long, if you had other lovers. I won't ask you for any answers, not that I have the right. I don't know anything about you anymore, Charlie. What the deuce, I don't even know your real name!

I've tried to get this off my chest for many days. There isn't a delicate way to say it. See, I don't think we should ever speak of what happened. I don't have the courage for what it would take. I told you before I'm a fraud. Always have been, always will be. You didn't believe me, but it's true. Don't hate me for it—please. If I lost your friendship as well as your affections, I don't know what I'd do.

I'm sorry, Charlie, really I am.

Wick

The disappointment wasn't what got me. I'd expected as much. There was nothing shocking about what Wick had to say. I followed the same protocol as with Mother's letters, tearing the sheet carefully, until the sentences were halved, then quartered, and finally transformed into meaninglessness.

I didn't feel anguished, either. Somehow I'd suspected it would end this way, quite unlike how it should: no clamoring or passionate embrace, nothing very dramatic, nothing that mirrored the intensity of what I felt, of what I'd hoped Wick felt, too. It was the impassiveness that bothered me most.

I pulled out a drawer in my desk and poked around for a stone—the only pebble left from Stony Creek that I hadn't discarded. I set the memento into a tin drinking cup, then heated the bottom with a series of short-lived matches. The air reeked of phosphorous. When the stone was piping-hot, I tipped it into a rag and picked a place on my arm, high, just below the slope of my shoulder. Biting my lower lip, I pressed the stone into my flesh until it sizzled, the same smell as gristle steaming in a pot. The sting was startling enough that I dropped the cloth, pebble and all. Drawing a deep breath, I took a gander at the perfect black circle, the flesh already transforming into a pus-filled boil. It would scar, I hoped. It would become a permanent reminder, not of the pact I'd made with Mother, but of the pact I'd just made with myself.

In the time between the mailing of Spang's article and its publication, I lived in a daze. There were things I should have done, precautions I ought to have taken. I should have visited the bursar's office and asked what my financial options were—if I could work full-time and still be a student. I should have worked on a good defense. I should have written to Mother regarding the Mockletons. I'd never responded to her about them. In fact I hadn't written her at all, not for weeks.

Maybe, subconsciously, I'd understood that the ground beneath us was shaky. The rocks were starting to tumble, cracking open as they smashed to the ground. New chinks were splintering wide. Old fractures were healing through the unstoppable intensity of heat, pressure, and time. Maybe I'd known, somehow, that when Mother and I next communicated, our landscape would be completely different.

I counted what little money I had left and set a stricter budget for myself. For the first time in my life, I silently thanked Joanna and Alfred. Without the money from their check, I wouldn't have been able to stay at Yale through the end of the semester. I wondered how

Mother was faring with the laundry business. Surely by now she'd run out of jewelry to sell. We'd never discussed it: how we'd make it for three more years. I supposed we'd always hoped for the best. Too bad we didn't have any way to prepare for the worst.

When Wick, Phin, and Harry headed for the diner, Commons, or Sterling, I stayed in my room. Being around Wick was too painful. I felt like the new skin underneath my burn: vernal, tender, not yet ready for the fierceness of life. To his credit, Wick seemed to be making an effort at restoring our friendship. When we happened across each other, he looked me in the eye. Sometimes he joked and teased like he used to. Only, something had changed. He didn't touch me, didn't drape his arm over my shoulders or ruffle my hair with his hand. When I went to bed, I would strain to remember those moments in the pool. But as the days passed, the memories started to fade. Like autumn leaves pressed into a book, they lost their brilliance over time, more brown than gold, more rust than red.

The boys invited me to join them like they always did, but I found new excuses. It got to the point where Harry slinked into my room one day, hunched and worried, asking me outright what the heck was wrong. Was it my pop? Lots of families had been worn down by the bust. Lots of people—decent, hardworking people—had lost their jobs. Why, unemployment was almost to be expected—and it was certainly nothing to be ashamed of, no reason to be depressed.

"No, it's not that," I replied.

But Harry, ever suspicious, forged ahead. "Is there anything I can do? I don't have much money—that's no secret. But I can give you what I can, Pietra. We can share. We're like brothers, you and I. I wouldn't be able to stand this place without you."

I'll admit Harry's confession almost moved me to tears, so I had to play it tough, turning away, pretending to be absorbed in whatever book I'd arbitrarily opened. I had to keep myself from spilling the truth, everything from how I'd sabotaged my work-study to how I couldn't quit pining for Wick. More than anything, I needed a confidant. But it couldn't be Harry. Maybe it couldn't be anyone.

I scrunched my eyes to keep in the wet. "Get out of here, will you?
I have work to do."

"Since when did you start studying?"

"Since now."

"Like hell," he said, but still he left, stiffly and hesitantly, not
knowing how much of our exchange was a joke, how much I was still
hiding.

When I grew too antsy to stay in my room, I went to the Stacks. It
still had the ability to ease my mind. And still I sought its quietest,
most remote corners. Thus, when I heard the sound one night, my
first reaction was to doubt it had even happened. I resumed my reading, only slightly distracted. Then I heard it again. It was louder this
time, a low groan, nearly an animal's cry. I pushed back my chair
slowly—to avoid squeaking, not wanting to be heard—and I'll admit
I was scared when I heard it a third time. I realized where it was coming from, several shelves beyond, maybe in a place I'd been myself—
a secluded corner, too dark for reading once the sun goes down and
the windowpanes darken.

I crept closer, hearing other things, too: sighs, fabric rubbing
against itself. And I wasn't a fool; I knew what these sounds might
mean. I remembered what the quarrymen had talked about. I'd seen
them outside the saloons at night, leading woozy, wobbly, disheveled
girls into shadowy alleys. Sometimes the girls laughed, sometimes
they protested. But always they went. I'd even heard Pa and Mother,
ages ago, their ardor muted by the walls and by my own desire not to
listen, not to know. But I wanted to know now. So much so that I crept
as close as I dared. The sounds were on the other side of a shelf. I
could hear everything: hoarse murmurs, the friction of skin. But I
couldn't see a thing.

Slowly, I pulled two books from an overstuffed row, creating a
slim vertical window, a peephole. But still, all I could see was darkness. I knew I oughtn't, but already I'd come too close, close enough
to tiptoe to the very end of the row and to lean around, neck craned,
eyes wide as dinner plates.

I expected to see plump feminine thighs, a skirt bunched around the waist, curly swaths of hair. Instead I spied two sets of trousers pushed down to the ankles, two boys, one bent over and pressed against a wall, the side of his face pressed, too. And the boy behind him, shirtless, compact and muscular, with the kind of build Coach Roota always extols. He had his hands firmly planted on the other boy's shoulders, rocking against his backside forcefully, but not without a certain rhythm and grace. I was so shocked I forgot I was still holding the books. They slipped out of my slack-scatty fingers, falling with a thud that made all of us jump. The boys' hands raced to cover, to protect, to pull up and tuck and belt, and I knew I couldn't undo what I'd done, but how I wished I could have when the shirtless boy turned.

We locked eyes. His were gray and hard like ball bearings. And in our gaze so much was explained and so much was decided, like how I'd learned his secret, and how he'd always known mine. When, where, and how he'd found out I didn't know. Maybe he'd suspected from the beginning, from that very first day, when he'd had to vie with me for Wick's attention. By now Phin must have been an expert at keeping secrets, he who hid his under expensive wool blazers, cashmere sweaters, and argyle socks, under a sneer and a carefully tended tough-guy act.

We stared at each other a long time, neither of us wanting to be the first to look away, to show cowardice, shame, or vulnerability. Somehow in that face-off the scorn drained. Phin's partner darted off, face hidden in his hands, and still Phin and I peered at one another, not even blinking, until we both wore down.

"Swear I won't say anything if you won't," he gave in and whispered.

"I swear, too," I replied, and there it was, how simple: a tincture of trust. An awareness that we'd achieved balance, finally, by the symmetry of our scandals.

Chapter Fourteen

L IKE SO MUCH ELSE in life, the rain poured all at once, a torrential splashy sheet of it. Near the end of April, I received two important letters in my mailbox on the same day. One was from Spang. The other was from none other than the office of President Angell. I shoved my hand to the very back of the box, half-expecting one from Mother, too, but I didn't find it.

I was trying my best to be optimistic, but I couldn't help but wonder if Angell intended to expel me for what I'd done in my work-study. These might very well be my last days in New Haven.

I was due to see Spang later in the week. His letter didn't give away much, just the perfunctory information. We'd be meeting in his office, of course. I noted that the letter was handwritten, not typed on the black Remington. I wondered if Spang even knew how to work the machine, or if he'd always had someone else to do it.

There was no telling what had become of him since I'd left him at his desk, content in the knowledge that he'd finished the article he'd set out to write. I tried not to anticipate, but still I did. Remembering Spang's fondness for violent, militaristic talk, I considered taking a knife with me. But the idea of pinching one from Commons seemed ridiculous, even melodramatic. Instead, I tucked a sharpened pencil into my pocket. This and my fading courage were all that I took with me.

On the day of our meeting, as was our custom, I knocked twice before Spang invited me in.

"Shut the door behind you," he commanded, as if I would have forgotten.

His office was different than before. Neater. There were newspapers fanned out on his desk, but the room was otherwise tidy and uncluttered. Books sat on shelves rather than on the floor. Letters had been carefully opened and placed into stacks. I didn't spy a single crumb or cashew. Spang sat behind his desk, his fingers spread out over a copy of *The Boston Globe*.

"Charles, how interesting to be in your company again. I've been thinking about you. And I'll bet you've been thinking about me." His voice was noxiously sweet, like we were long-lost lovers. "Have a seat. Don't be shy," he said.

And so I wasn't. I sat down, mindful of where the pencil was in my jacket pocket. Wondering how long it would take me, if need be, to grab it and position it right.

"Let's get started, shall we?" he asked. His lips spread into a tight smile. "I've spent many hours analyzing this ordeal—this ordeal that you, Charles, are responsible for. And I've concluded it can be framed in two ways. Either impudence and a dangerous susceptibility to propaganda led you to decide to sabotage me. Or—you were coerced by someone else: most likely a strong coalition of my enemies. Given your limitations, I've concluded that the latter theory is more probable. Believing it helps me to despise you less. It almost makes me feel sorry for you."

He sighed deeply, pausing for a long moment. "I must admit, Charles, I had misgivings about you from the first. As soon as you walked through my door I sensed something very queer about you. I've never had another pupil act like you have—so confidently, so willing to give his all. Now I see I should have trusted my instincts. But in life, as in science, the truth is always more apparent in retrospect."

He was staring at me, at my face, but I had the sensation that he was scrutinizing something very particular: maybe the pores on my skin, or the absence of any sign of hair. When his gaze broke, I was surprised by the expression that took hold: disappointment.

"My boy," he said, a little sadly, "a more astute and worldly apprentice would have realized that his role was to bolster an existing hypothesis, not to challenge it."

I cleared my throat and kept my voice low. There was no telling what this meeting could degenerate into.

"But sir, surely we don't mean to ignore the truth."

"The truth?"

"I've seen the DiRisios for myself. I've been to their home many times. And I'm sorry, but they're not as you identified them. They're nothing like it."

The professor straightened himself in his chair. His face, glossy with fresh sweat, grew more grim. His pale hair seemed wispier than usual.

"Do you have any sense of what you've done, Charles? Any sense at all? You've sacrificed my entire career. And for what? To protect this miserable family—what are they called? The *DiRisios*?" He spat each syllable with disgust. "How did they do it, boy? That's what I want to know. How did they indoctrinate you?"

When I didn't reply, he added, "What irks me most is that I've gotten only praise for your barrel of bullshit."

He waved at the newspapers before him. "They're all raves, if you can believe it."

I had no idea what the consensus on the article was, having seen only a single review in *The Yale News*. HEAR, HEAR!, the headline had blared. PROFESSOR JOSHUA CECIL SPANG KEEPS YALE AHEAD OF THE INTELLECTUAL CURVE.

"Teachers, plumbers, nurses, clerics, even judges—they're writing me in droves," Spang went on. "Some are sending telegrams. They congratulate me for being one of the few leaders in my field to see through the haze, to have the courage to denounce the persecution of immigrant groups. One even had the nerve to say that eugenics was falling out of fashion!"

He laughed mirthlessly. "I've never received so many lauds, not ever. Even Angell sent me a fruit basket. The whole situation is spectacularly cruel. I'm simultaneously at the zenith of my career and the lowest depth of my academic integrity."

"Professor Spang, I—" I didn't know what I was going to say, exactly. But whatever it was, Spang wouldn't be interrupted.

"Shut up!" he snapped, fingertips pressing into the newspapers until his chewed-up nails went white. "You've said enough already. Now I will speak." His voice was insistent. "I've thought this through very carefully—what our stations will be from this point forward. It goes without saying that tact and discretion will be crucial. I'll go about my business and you'll go about yours, and we'll cease all contact from this time on. You will not come to this office. You will not mention my name. You will not allude to the incident—not even subtly—not verbally nor in writing. I cannot stress this enough. You will not discuss it with your friends, family, or even with strangers. If even one person finds out that this article is a counterfeit, by God, I'll have you expelled faster than you can nod that idiotic head of yours. Have I made myself clear?"

"Crystal, sir."

"Good. Obviously your work-study under my tutelage will cease. I will personally oversee the transfer of your apprenticeship to another party for your sophomore year. And there's one last thing."

I looked at him expectantly.

"I never want to see your face again. I mean it. If I do, if we ever cross paths again and you somehow get in my way, I'll make damn sure you go down this time. You'll fall so hard you'll be begging for mercy. You'll be clinging for your worthless life, you thankless little prick. You sanctimonious son-of-a-bitch."

I rose and started for the door before things got any hotter, but still Spang seethed. He rose, too, taunting, "And to think you came from Stony Creek. What a waste. What would your father say? Have you asked yourself *that*?"

I straightened my posture as I reached for the doorknob. No cowering, not anymore. But even the upright know when it's time to disappear.

*   *   *

For the first time since the pool, Wick and I were alone together. He'd invited me on an adventure, and so we'd found ourselves, on a blowy bright spring afternoon, armed with a skein of string and a kite he'd fashioned himself. Proudly, he showed it to me: cellophane pulled tightly over crossed wooden sticks, hand-glued, and the tail long, trimmed with bows.

We were standing in the middle of Old Campus, the wind teasing our hair and pulling at our clothes. Harry had appeared briefly, but he was on a studying binge and duly scuttled off. Now it was just the two of us, and a faint, sullen discomfort. The elephant in the room had morphed into a considerably smaller creature, but still it was there.

All around us boys were scurrying. The end of the year was approaching faster than any of us could fathom. Some yearlings coped by cramming harder, dashing to the library at all hours. Others, like Wick and I, couldn't be rushed. We had a kite, and what else did we need when the sun was spilling through the clouds and the grass looked so tempting we kicked off our shoes and socks and let the blades massage our feet.

"We have to name this contraption," he announced. "How about Victoria?"

"Too stuffy."

"Constance?"

"Too prudish."

"Eula?"

I smiled. "Eula reminds me of ukulele. Why does it have to be a girl's name?"

"I don't know—it just seems like a girl. Say," he leaned in close, smiled teasingly, "what did you say your name was? Your *other* name?"

With Wick there was no time to think, no sense in trying to be rational or judicious. "Adele."

"Adele," he repeated, releasing the kite into a sudden gale. The string unspooled faster than he could manage, so there were ungainly knots along her trajectory. But still she soared, she sailed, she dove only to rise again. The skein of string grew slender. I wondered if the end would slip away before Wick could catch it. Harder she pulled, now only a speck among the clouds, her tail wiggly and slight.

"She wants her freedom," Wick said with a laugh. "Why am I not surprised?"

He reined her in, little by little, until it seemed he had her under control. Except—she made one last wobbly, desperate bid for liberty, plunging into a dangerous territory of trees Wick had so far avoided, navigating past one elm only to snag at the top of another.

Wick yanked, lightly at first, then insistently, but she wouldn't dislodge. And then we heard it from the ground: a sharp tearing. When next Wick pulled, there was no resistance. But still the kite didn't give.

"Fine, I'll fetch her myself," he said, putting on his shoes and shimmying up the wide trunk, past the strong base limbs, up ten feet, then twenty, thirty, and more, up to where the branches were unreliably slender. Maybe they could hold a man's weight and maybe they couldn't, but one thing was certain: the kite rested on twigs that could scarcely support a sparrow.

With a resigned yelp, he finally scampered down, swinging from the lowest branch like Tarzan.

"Just my luck," he clowned, jumping to the ground, his knees bending on impact. "Another woman out of reach."

Flustered, I sat down on the ground. He threw himself beside me and picked a blade, twirling it between his fingers. After receiving his letter, I thought I knew what he wanted, but now I wasn't so sure—and, truth be told, I was grateful for the ambiguity. We were quiet for a time. In that quiescence something stirred inside of me: an overwhelming urge to tell him everything. I wanted to purge myself of my whole history, back to the beginning, even before the accident, and more: I wanted to tell him how my heart still ached when I thought of him, sometimes so painfully I lost my breath. I wanted to ask him—did he not feel even a little of what I felt? And if not, why not?

Wick flipped onto his back and looked at me—intently, I thought—but then he shut his eyes. His turned-down lips were full, pillowy, the most lovely sight I'd ever seen. And his closed eyelids, threaded with filigree-fine capillaries, burgundy-rich, they were lovelier still.

If ever there was a time to speak, this was it—before our first year ended, before a part of our history was sealed. Only I wouldn't let myself. I looked around at the buildings, the purposeful faces of my classmates, the books that they carried, which surely had sentences underlined, notes streaming down the margins: the precious flow of free thought. Seconds wound into minutes. Wick's eyes reopened, turning with dozy affection toward me. His gaze was dreamy, sensual, entirely distressing.

I didn't want the moment to change into something disappointing, and I was quite sure it would. Thus I found the resilience to stand up, with effort, to brush off my trousers and grumble about an assignment I'd forgotten about, what trouble I'd be in. Wick protested in his jokey, good-natured way. There was an anxious edge to his tone—an edge that made me realize I might not be the only one who was unsatisfied. It wasn't easy to leave, but I did, casting thin excuses in my wake. He said my name once more: "Adele." I swear I heard it. But much as I wanted to turn around, I wouldn't let myself. It wasn't that I'd grown brave or that I cared any less. On the contrary. I just wanted to hold on to the ambiguity a bit longer, for as long as he'd let me.

Chapter Fifteen

S HE SAT AS STILL as a woman posing before an artist: legs crossed
neatly at the knee, long fingers folded in her lap. Her hair, secured
with a jade comb, was more golden than I remembered, no doubt
lightened by the spring sun. It was golden like the gleaming jewelry
she'd worn, like the finely spun metallic thread Marie embroidered
with.

In the time since I'd been away, I'd forgotten certain details of her
face: the sleek ridge of her nose, the cool glisten of her forehead. I'd
forgotten, too, how harrowing her beauty could be. How, in her presence, I always felt small, dark, somehow impure.

Whenever I pictured Mother she was in Stony Creek, tirelessly
washing laundry, or adjusting her hat in a hand glass, or staring out a
window, her gaze fixed on the ever-lapping Sound. How surreal,
then, to see her here, sitting rigid-backed on my bed.

Her absence made her seem even more regal. The new and subtle
lines about her eyes harmonized with the firmness of her jaw. Her
lips, wizened-tight with worry after the passing of Charles and Pa,
now budded red and fulsome. She was thinner than I remembered,
but more striking for the lack of flesh: her cheekbones sharp enough
to draw blood, her neck as ivory-hard as an elephant's tusk. This was
how she'd looked when Pa had met her, I thought. This was why he
hadn't been able to resist.

She didn't move as I watched her.

"I thought it better not to wait any longer," she said. "Better to
come in person."

"But how—how did you get in?"

"Really, Adele, is that all you can say?"

Embarrassed and flustered, I dropped my things and started toward her. I'm not sure what I expected when I wrapped my arms around her shoulders, but not this: stiffness, resistance, even distaste. I went to kiss her cheek and she turned away. My lips brushed a stray wisp of perfumed hair.

Be patient, I told myself, quailing. It's been such a long time, we don't really know each other anymore.

"Did you come by train?" I asked lightly.

She responded by peeling the white gloves from her hands. She did it delicately, finger by finger. Beneath the fabric her hands were still soft, lovely.

"I'm sorry I haven't written you, Mother. You must be so disappointed, and you have every right to be. You see, I've—"

Her gaze silenced me; those narrowing feline eyes had always had a discouraging effect. I'd forgotten how powerful she was, how much power she wielded over me. Her letters could not compare with the potency of her presence.

"No excuses, please. Spare me that, at least. Barring death or illness—neither of which appears to have afflicted you—there isn't a single reason why you couldn't have sent a response. I made it clear that we're at a crossroads, Adele. But more than that, I *am* your mother."

She watched me expectantly. When I didn't reply—not out of pettishness, but because I didn't know which answer would satisfy her—she set the gloves on her lap and sighed.

"My God, Adele, you seem more boyish than ever."

"Isn't that the point?" I wanted to demand. Instead, I took several steps back and shut the door. My suitemates might be home, and wouldn't this be an earful! I wondered if I ought to stay here, on the other side of the room, and keep my distance. Always, with Mother, it was impossible to know.

"I wasn't as candid in my recent letters as I wanted to be," she continued. "I didn't tell you how much my parents regret the way they treated me. They regret never meeting you or Charles." She hesitated, affected, perhaps, by the sound of my brother's name in this place.

"I want you to know that I took that trip to Philadelphia without you, Adele. And it was superb, sublime, everything I imagined it could be. There were champagne toasts, tea parties, midnight carriage rides, trips to the theater. My parents have expanded their manse. Now there are so many rooms they've named them to keep track. Believe me, I could have stayed forever. But I came back for you."

I stared at her blankly. No wonder she'd always assumed I was lazy; I was a spellbound dolt in her company.

"Oh, Adele, seeing you here, the way you live—well, we have our work cut out for us. Obviously we'll have to focus on your demeanor and conversational skills, to start. Maybe we'll travel before we leave for Philadelphia. That will give us time, at least. Where shall we go? Rome? No, Vienna, perhaps. Oh, you'd love Vienna. The air there is so sweet and fortifying. The whole town is like a sanatorium. It's the perfect place to retrain the mind."

"Mother, I can't come with you," I blurted.

Unperturbed, she smiled.

"It's not easy for me to explain," I hastened.

And how. I had no idea how to tell her the truth without shattering her trust. I needed to show her that, for all my misadventures, for all my trepidation, I couldn't stand the thought of leaving.

"I have to finish my studies," I said clumsily.

"And what about after you graduate, sweetheart? What will happen to you then? You can't go on being your brother forever."

"I'm not *being* Charles."

Mother uncrossed, then recrossed her legs. She was still perfectly composed. "Oh no? Who are you, then? Certainly not the Adele I know."

"But that's what we agreed on!"

She sighed moodily, signs of impatience appearing now.

"Adele, in the absence of other opportunities, our plan made sense. But now something better has come along—something altogether splendid—and you want to ignore it. Don't be a fool. You can have anything you want in Philadelphia, served on a platter with garnish! You'll never have a chance like this again."

"But I'll never have the chance to be here again."

"What can you possibly gain by staying?"

"Mother, everything, simply everything. My studies, my books, my friends, my fencing, my—"

"No. For heaven's sake, it's ridiculous that we're even having this discussion."

"And what if I refuse to come?"

"You can't."

"Why?"

"For one thing, you haven't the money. And for another, I'm not asking for your permission. I have every intention of leaving this room with you in tow. I would never have believed it if I hadn't seen it for myself. Who would have thought that my meek, impressionable daughter would turn out bigheaded?"

That set me back. It made me wonder if maybe I was as hopelessly juvenile as she thought. Perhaps I had overestimated myself all this time. Even now, like a child, I wanted to please her, to see her face light up the way it had around my brother. I couldn't pretend otherwise.

I thought back to a time when Charles, Mother, Pa, and I had traveled to the quarry. One of the drillers had sworn he'd seen the face of Jesus Christ in the rock, and though everyone assumed he'd probably been drinking, or else inhaled too much granite powder, still we went. Out of curiosity, I suppose. Or boredom. It was a Sunday, and the rest of the town was in church. We had the quarry to ourselves. I remembered feeling both excited and guilty, not sure if we were on our way to honoring or disrespecting the sacred.

On a steep bluff we found it. It protruded right out of the stone: a lumpy, contorted face. An agonized face. Pa said the driller must have chipped it that way on purpose. Maybe he'd done it at night, by lamplight.

"It's obviously a ludicrous ploy for attention," Mother said.

"Maybe he didn't do it on purpose," Pa countered. "You can't stare at this damn stone too long. It can make you see things. It can make you do things you don't want to do."

To me, the face looked like it could have been natural, maybe because it was so crude. I had to squint to determine the features: two crooks for eyes, a jag of a mouth, a jutting chin. All in all, the face didn't look like Jesus Christ's—or however Jesus Christ's face was supposed to look. I'd always assumed that the son of God would be pale, august, aristocratic, rather like Mother and Charles. But this primitive, rough-hewn mug seemed more ominous than hallowed.

Mother had examined the face for only a moment before rolling her eyes and sauntering off. She'd set down the picnic blanket nearby, a spread of fruits and cheeses. I'd sat next to her, rubbing apples and pears with my apron. The last thing she pulled from the basket was a bunch of grapes—a rare summer treat. I'd laughed with delight, never having seen its equal. How succulent those fat purple beads looked, how perfectly decadent, their skins glistening wetly under the heat of the sun.

"Where'd you find them?" Surely something this exotic couldn't have grown on the local arbors, and I'd never seen their like at the market.

She'd smiled coyly, handling the ambrosial cluster gingerly. "You know, Adele, my mother used to say that the way to test a young woman's gentility was through grapes."

Pa, who had just turned from the face, overheard our conversation and loped over. I remember how tall and handsome he looked. Surely at that time he'd been the handsomest man in Stony Creek.

"Gertie, don't you start with that nonsense. Not again."

"Nonsense? These are basic manners I'm teaching. I didn't realize there was something wrong with our children having manners."

"They have manners."

"One of them, anyway."

Pa, as always, had taken my side, warning her to leave me alone. I didn't need to be raised as Joanna and Alfred had raised her.

"What's that supposed to mean?" she demanded.

"It means that she's fine the way she is. Better than fine. She doesn't need to be made into a Cottager."

"Why? Are you afraid she'll end up like me?"

"Come to think of it, yes, that's exactly what I'm afraid of."

With that he'd stalked off, stride jerky, hands thrust into his pockets. Needing only a few seconds to recover, Mother kept her voice singsong sweet and perfectly even.

"This is what my mother would ask, Adele: 'What is the proper way to pass grapes at the dinner table?'"

I'd been anxious, still caught up in my parents' exchange. I wondered how Mother hid the strain so well.

"To pass them one by one?"

"No," she snipped. "A lady breaks off a small cluster at the stem." With a twist of the wrist she demonstrated. "Then she passes the cluster. See? It's vulgar to pick them off individually. It's something your father's people would do."

I'd failed another of Mother's tests, and as usual, I'd be punished. She called Charles over to her so that he could have the first taste. He shoved the grapes into his mouth as if they were in infinite supply. I was disgusted, thinking how I would have savored each and every one. Soon Mother was sampling them too, the both of them comparing their sticky fingers, laughing at the ejaculatory burst in each bite. Sprawled out on the blanket, one hand cradling his head, Charles had watched me, gloating as he chewed, his tongue and the insides of his lips violet-stained from the skins. I'd bit into a pockmarked apple, looking away, wondering where Pa had gone to, when we could leave from here. I was sore with him for abandoning me in such a predicament.

In the still of my dormitory room, the alliance Mother and I shared seemed suddenly flimsy. Much less substantial than stone, and yet just as hard, just as heavy.

"I know you'll be disappointed," I told her. "But I won't go to the Mockletons with you." My somberness caused her to wince. She had the same unstable, overwrought look she'd had when I'd cut off my hair.

"Haven't you heard anything I've said, Adele? This isn't for you to choose. If you don't come with me, I'll be forced to tell Yale who you are. I don't want that, believe me I don't. But you're toeing the line now."

The resentment would linger, I knew; it would taint the blood for years to come, probably for whole generations. But I didn't see another way.

"And I'll tell your parents I've been studying at Yale all this time— at your encouragement. Do you think Alfred and Joanna will approve? Do you think they'll still take you back?"

The hurt in Mother's eyes caused me to swipe at my own welling tears. We couldn't both win, but still I hated myself for volleying with her.

"I don't understand why you refuse to give them a chance," she lashed. "They're sorry, deeply sorry. I've told you that."

"But are they sorry for how they treated Pa? Do you think they ever gave *him* a chance? Have you even considered that maybe the only reason they've decided to see you is because he's dead?"

She touched her brow: a sign that one of her headaches was coming on. Now I'd reached her—truly and deeply. Even so, I didn't underestimate her.

"Despite what you think, your father wasn't a saint. He never loved anyone—even you—half as much as himself."

"How can you say that? What about the way he loved Francisco? You can't deny that."

"Adele, please." She let out a sharp shrill laugh. "Let me make one thing perfectly clear: there is no Francisco. Your father was an only child."

Vehemently, I argued that she was crazy, nothing but a bitter liar. But in her stoicism I saw the coarsest kind of truth. And somehow it all fit: how Pa had prized imagination above all else, how he'd longed for more and yet never really seen past the clouds.

"As time passes, I realize something else," she continued. "Your father could have been Francisco. He *wanted* to be Francisco, more than anything. But he was too much of a coward."

Even if what she was saying were true, even if she managed to contaminate my memories, I wouldn't let her denigrate Pa any further. I understood where my loyalties lay, and where hers lay, too.

"I want you to leave. Please, Mother."

With that, the pith of her beauty snapped. She faded a little before my eyes. I approached her hesitantly, hoping for some sort of truce, something that transcended all the sad, despicable things we'd said and probably would never be able to forgive. But she rebuffed me again. And I couldn't blame her, not even when she stood up and slapped me across the face. Squarely, with the cold ball of her palm.

"You truly want to leave it like this? The way my parents and I did? I'll play the game again if you want me to. I've got loads of practice. And I'll win, Adele. You can count on that."

"Mother, please, I've been trying to explain to you—I need to stay. I've learned so much. I've read dozens and dozens of books about concepts and places I didn't even know existed. My classes, they make me think and question things that I never thought to question before. I've made friends—Harry, and Wick, and Phin—and they care about me, Mother. We have such fun together. You know I never had friends before, not in Stony Creek. And then there's Ceci. I didn't tell you about her because I thought you might get angry. She's a little girl I teach—the smartest sprite you'd ever meet. She didn't know how to read, but I showed her how, Mother, and I have a knack for it—teaching. All my pupils say so. I've never felt quite so good about myself as I have since being in New Haven. Our plan makes more sense to me now because it's not just about me. I see the benefits that—"

"It's not just about *you*? That's the most ridiculous thing I ever heard. Of course it's not about you. You're not the one scraping money together to pay the bills Yale keeps sending. You're not the one worried to death about the problems that lie ahead. You're not the one who's left behind in that ridiculous town with its ignorant, spiteful people itching to see us wither away. You've forgotten all about your benefactor."

"Mother, that's not true."

"That's what I'm hearing," she insisted. "You've been misled by this silly Ceci and your friends. They wouldn't care a whit about you if they knew the truth. Don't delude yourself. You've got one other person in this world to fend for you, and that's me. I'm the one who's come back for you, after all. Can't you see I didn't have to?"

"Maybe you shouldn't have."

"Adele, I wish you could hear how foolish you sound. I should never have given you so much responsibility—it's my fault. Now come along. Stop these antics."

"I told you, Mother, I'm not coming."

"I have two tickets to Philadelphia, and I can afford to throw one away. I'm willing to take you, Adele. See, I don't bury my head in the sand after I've made mistakes—not like your father. But I won't pay for you to stay here and embarrass yourself or me any longer."

"Then maybe it's time we parted," I said, facing her.

My hand moved from my sore face to the burn under the sleeve of my shirt. Its steady ache was improbably comforting. Warily, Mother put the gloves back on her hands. She didn't appear angry or unhappy; whatever she was thinking was so deeply and inscrutably embedded that I had no sense of its nature, only that it was final.

"What will you tell the Mockletons?" I asked her. Something would have to be sacrificed in return for my ingratitude and selfishness. I'd placed my future ahead of Mother's and I would accept my comeuppance now. It was only fair; it was only just. One strike wasn't enough.

"The truth, my love. That you're dead."

In that way it happened—Mother left a wale so enormous I couldn't possibly hide it. It grew so large it swallowed my eye, turning it into a sightless slit.

Harry came around later that day, startled and concerned at first, then amused. I was resting on my bed, intermittently applying ice to the injury. He wouldn't stop firing questions. I wouldn't tell him what had happened, and the longer I withheld information, the more freely his imagination roamed. Although I hadn't seen Helen since the ball, he got it into his head that she was the perpetrator.

"Because you acted like such a cad! You kissed her—in front of everybody, Pietra. Then you never went out with her again."

"And you think she slugged me for it now?"

"Well, the proof's right there!"

Despite the pain, that made me smile. Maybe Helen had crossed his mind, Harry explained, because he was getting back with Ethel. At least he hoped he was.

"I thought she wasn't speaking to you," I said.

"Now she is. Now that I sent her flowers."

"Flowers? How chivalrous."

He smirked.

"She asked you to come over?" I continued.

"No. She sent me a letter. A love letter. Can you believe it?"

"What's so hard to believe about the Botticelli sending you a love letter?"

"If you have to ask, you're ready for the loony bin."

I turned the bag of ice and a dribble of condensation rolled down my cheek. "So what are you going to do?"

Normally, Harry would have sensed that I was hiding something, but he was too busy basking, and I couldn't blame him.

"What the heck do you think I'm gonna do, genius? First things first. More flowers. Then I gotta get Wick's advice."

"Maybe you should ask him for his manual."

"His what?

"His manual."

"Oh, it's a joke."

"Not a very good one, I gather."

"No," he agreed. "You'd better take it easy. She must've knocked the wits right out of you."

I didn't sleep most of the night before my appointment with President Angell. I tossed about in my bed, periodically breaking into a sweat, then shaking in the damp. I wasn't thinking about Angell, but about Mother. After our confrontation, she'd slammed the door, her expression an amalgam of rage, exhaustion, but also finality. My returning to Stony Creek for the summer certainly wasn't an option anymore. I didn't even know if Mother would still be in Miss Prowl's house. Maybe she'd already hung a sign on the door: SORRY—OUT OF BUSINESS. Maybe she'd already packed her things, discarding the most tattered and unflattering, and taken a train to Philadelphia. I doubted Charles's grave was enough to keep her home. And I knew Pa's wasn't.

Now that my choices were limited, I wondered if I ought to stay put. Harry had mentioned he wanted to try to find work in New Haven—delivering newspapers, shucking oysters, painting houses, shoveling coal, anything he could get.

"New York will be there after graduation," he'd told me.

"Yeah, and Ethel's here now."

For that quip, he'd slugged me in the arm.

"Maybe I'll stay, too," I said.

"I thought you were going to work for your father—up at the quarry."

"The quarry's not hiring. Not anymore."

"It's just as well. You better get used to a different line of work. You won't be hauling stone after you get your diploma."

I'd thought about that—how strange, and strangely wonderful, it sounded.

"What about Wick?" I asked, trying to sound nonchalant. "Where's he off to this summer?"

"He hasn't told you?" Harry asked. "He and Phin are going to work at the same place—Phin's father's rag. Lucky bastards. They'll probably get paid a bundle, too."

This made me think more of what work Harry and I could hope to find. The forecast didn't look rosy. The end of the year had seen dozens more students leave for failure to pay tuition. Even classmates whose great-grandfathers lived on in busts and portraits had been forced to flee campus. Classmates whose surnames graced buildings, streets, benches, and statues, whose families used to own plantations, hotels, companies, whole cities. They'd packed quietly. They'd scarcely said their good-byes, maybe thinking they'd be back. Maybe next year. Two years at the most. It couldn't end this way.

The harsh truth was that Harry and I would be lucky to find *any* work in New Haven. Maybe I could start my own laundry business. But that would pay little, not enough for room and board, and certainly not enough for savings for the coming school year. I couldn't even depend on another work-study. For all I knew, Spang had already dragged my name through the mud.

Toward dawn, I finally fell into a restless sleep, worries woven coarsely through my dreams like flax fibers through silk. Every so often I awoke, startled and discombobulated, only vaguely aware that early morning had given way to late, and that noon had come with the chiming of Battell Chapel's bells. At last there was no avoiding the new day. Groggily I rose and dressed, then went to the lavatory, disturbed to see that my face had changed overnight. It was pinched and blanched, its color sucked out as if by a midnight demon. The only spot of brightness was the bruise.

I dressed carefully, smoothing my hair and the creases on my trousers. Even so, I looked like a hooligan.

Leaving the dormitory, I stopped in Commons. Though I had no appetite, I knew I would need to gather my strength for Angell. I'd need to be quick on my feet, to refute his accusations with some semblance of conviction.

I didn't want to linger. I was in no mood to chat with anybody, or to field questions about my eye. But I couldn't avoid the hoots and hollers coming from a table off in the corner. Wick, Harry, and Phin gleefully waved their napkins in the air, calling me a cowboy, a hoodlum, their hero. Embarrassed, I made a gesture as if to slit my neck.

"Quiet!" I mouthed.

But that only inspired them to root louder. Wick was standing on the table now, as if he needed to be any taller. He saluted me smartly. As usual, I couldn't resist his teasing. Putting a sandwich on my tray, I made my way toward that rowdy table.

"What the hell did you do to yourself, kiddo?" Wick asked. "I told you to stay away from the mob."

I shrugged.

"Taking a vow of silence, eh? Harry thinks it has something to do with your old sweetheart."

"Nah, Helen's not capable of this."

"I don't know. 'Hell hath no fury' and all that."

There was the old glimmer of playfulness in Wick's eye. Phin chuckled and shook his head. I wrapped the sandwich in a napkin, put it in my jacket, and turned to leave, but Wick wasn't finished with me.

"Another rendezvous? Gee whiz, your calendar is full. Think you can pencil us in for later? We're going to play another prank on Thatcher. He's replaced the class mascot. Now that the pickled brain has been gone for so long, he's brought in—you won't believe it—a full-size stuffed antelope." The proverbial villain, he cackled and rubbed his hands together.

"I don't know." I found I didn't have the strength to banter any longer.

"What do you mean, you don't know? This is going to be the crowning prank of our year. A stuffed antelope," Wick repeated. "You must comprehend the possibilities."

"I comprehend them, all right."

"Then come with us."

"I'll try."

I didn't know what other answer to give. Everything from here on in would depend upon Angell.

Wick sat down. He brooded as I waved hastily and walked out of Commons, those high ceilings and colossal columns observing me in silence. I tried to stop myself from asking certain questions, but it was useless; they clanged about my head anyhow. I wondered if I'd ever eat another meal at Yale with my friends. I wondered if that would be the last expression I'd ever see on Wick's face.

I had a little time before the appointment, so I set out for the steps of Sterling. Only, as I sat down and ran my fingers along the granite stipples, splotches, and whorls, I didn't feel comforted. It wasn't the stone that felt alien, but the memories it evoked: all the sojourns I'd shared with my father, all the nostalgic musings. I didn't know which of them were real anymore.

"Pa, why did you lie to me?" I asked aloud. The air, the still of stone, stole my words as soon as I spoke them. I'd never felt so alone.

When I reached President Angell's office, I was immediately ushered inside by a prim-looking young woman in a smart suit and matching gloves. Though I smiled at her, she didn't smile back, maintaining a reserved and slightly dour air.

She knows why I'm here, I thought.

"President Angell will be along in a moment," the woman told me tartly, pointing to a chair. I sat meekly, examining my bruise with a finger. Looking around with my one good eye, I noted that the interior of the president's office mirrored the rest of Yale. Its decor suggested tradition, splendor, and conservatism. Yet there were flares of the unexpected, too: a jar of feathers on the desk, a picture of a delighted Angell shaking hands with Clark Gable, and in the corner, a fat tabby that was either too contented or too sleepy to pay me any mind. The cat distracted me—this touch of the normal and domestic in such an extraordinary situation.

I'm not sure how long I sat there—long enough to wallow in worry, certainly. Long enough to get up and stroke the cat's head just to occupy my mind.

"Ah, you're here," I heard a voice say from behind. With a start, I flew back to my seat.

"How are you, sir?" I asked, my voice too high.

He looked well indeed, in a suit as impeccably white as the one he'd worn to the Freshman Rally, as white as the snow on the day he'd passed Ceci and me on the stoop. He positively sparkled, from the diamond stud in his tie tack to the shine of his spectacles.

"I'm fine, Charles."

He took a seat beside me, rather than behind his desk. I drew back my legs, anxious over the lack of boundary between us.

"And you? If I might ask, where did you get that bruise? Not from a fight, I hope."

"Oh no, sir."

I glanced away self-consciously, still in awe that he'd known my name.

"Good. Now then, are you aware that I'm retiring?" He said this without reserve, as if it were the most natural of introductions.

"I wasn't. No, sir."

"Yes, Yale has been a remarkable home to me for nearly sixteen years, but it's time for a change, I think. I've accepted an offer to be the educational counselor of the National Broadcasting Company. It's too good an opportunity to pass up. Plus, I'll admit that my wife is always nagging me to spend more time with her. She says Yale is a demanding mistress. She's right, you know."

I nodded, though I couldn't imagine where this talk was leading. I stared at the cat, unable to hold eye contact with Angell for long.

"Before leaving Yale, however, I want to recognize a few individuals. Individuals who have changed the course of this university in ways large and small. It's been brought to my attention, Charles, that you might be one of those people."

My toes tapped nervously on the floor when he pulled a paper from his breast pocket. This, I knew, would be my undoing. It was either a damning letter from Mother, or else Spang had changed his mind about how we ought to leave things.

"This is from a young girl. I first saw her when she was with you, I believe. You were sitting on the steps in front of her house. She wrote to inform me what a splendid teacher you are. She said that without you she wouldn't have been able to pen this letter, or any letter at all. You're the one who taught her how to read and write. You're the one who made a difference. Maybe *the* difference, Charles. The critical one."

"The letter's from Ceci?"

He chuckled at my incredulousness.

"Yes, Cecia DiRisio. I was so impressed by her note, I decided to visit her myself. Well, Cecia and her mother—who is quite a chef, by the way—informed me that the girl is not your only pupil. You also teach her father, brothers, and many of the neighborhood children. Throughout the year you came to their house several times a week. And still you had time to participate on the fencing team, assist in a highly impactful work-study, earn high marks, and have a little fun." He winked at me as my eyes grew wide. "It is within my jurisdiction to check these things.

"In only your first year," he continued, "you've shown purposeful-ness, creative vision, and civic responsibility. You've lived precisely in the spirit in which Yale was intended. I must say, Charles, I'm proud of you. And I'm sure your parents are proud, too."

"I . . ."

"You what? You thought I was going to punish you for the black eye?"

I laughed awkwardly.

"Boys will be boys," he said. "I've had a few shiners in my life, too."

Struggling to recover from this bombshell, I told him that I didn't think of the DiRisios like that—like an obligation. "They're more like family," I argued.

"All the better." He continued, "Charles, there are a few scholarships I want to talk to you about. They were designed to reward students like yourself, students who perform valuable services to the community. There are not as many as in earlier years, as you can imagine, but still, I think you are worthy of one of the handful that are left.

"The scholarship I want to grant you will cover tuition as well as room and board for your remaining three years at Yale, contingent—of course—upon the continuation of your literacy efforts. And if I might speak more on that topic—I'd like to see an expansion of this type of work: more beneficial relationships between Yale students and townsfolk, more conscientious engagement. I have in mind such a program. It would have students regularly teaching reading and writing skills to people in the community. I would like your help in structuring it. Such a program would surely enrich all parties, just as it has in your case. The DiRisios speak so fondly of you.

"What we'll need first is a detailed proposal. It should include information on how students will find appropriate families to work with, the exact nature and duration of the program, and a standardized approach to how it will be taught. Will the Yale students need to be trained before they're sent off? Where shall the parties meet? The proposal I want you to write must address all of these questions. Incidentally, I've already spoken with my successor about the program. He understands that a push for greater literacy in New Haven is a worthy cause. We both agree that your scholarship ought to commence immediately, Charles, which would mean that you would start work on the project this summer."

I was thrilled, staggered. But something this splendid had to have a catch.

"Sir, if I might inquire—" I said cautiously. "Have you spoken with Professor Spang recently?"

"Professor Spang? Well, now that I think of it, yes. After the publication of his recent article, I had a word with him."

He paused, and I waited breathlessly.

"I don't recall his mentioning anything about you, however."

"No, I don't suppose. I played a very small role in the production of the article."

"Well," President Angell chuckled, "you are only a freshman. Everything in good time, son. Everything in good time."

"Sir," I said, "I wonder—did Professor Spang happen to mention my work-study? What will become of it, I mean?"

Behind his spectacles, President Angell's eyes brightened.

"Charles, I suppose I haven't made myself entirely clear. Organizing the literacy program will *be* your new work-study."

There's a hazy lull between wakefulness and sleep when there's no clear demarcation between reality and dreams. I wasn't sure how Wick knew to come to me during that moment, but he did. I didn't hear my window squeak open, although it must have; I didn't hear the scuffle of his shoes as he scaled Durfee's brick walls with a hand-rigged rope-and-pulley system, although surely he'd made some noise. I drowsed, if not soundly, then at least fitfully, through his entrance.

I awoke only when he touched my hair. I opened my eyes and saw him sitting on the edge of my bed, his eyes dancing a little in the darkness. He was smiling, but he put his fingers to his lips, which made me realize, even in my groggy state, that he was worried about getting caught. His fingers continued to slide through my hair, to caress the back of my neck, and I responded in kind, pulling him to me, kissing him deeply on the mouth. He disentangled himself from my arms and wrestled off his clothes. In his underwear he slipped into my bed and lay beside me, against me, his hands rubbing my back, my side, my thighs. Still I was caught somewhere between wakefulness and slumber, neither wholly aware nor wholly unaware, and maybe that's why I settled into a kind of trance, my eyes closing when his did, my mind conscious of the lazy tracing of his fingers on my body, his breath slow and deep, the piney scent of him, which had become synonymous with sensations both consuming and crushing.

I know we must have fallen asleep together because when I awoke again, the sky outside my window showed signs of daylight. He wasn't beside me any longer, but on his feet, pulling on his trousers and stretching his arms.

"Where are you going?" I asked.

"Back to my room," he said softly.

"Wait," I said, forcing myself to sit up.

He sighed, looking nervous, one hand ripping through the morning mayhem of his hair. "If I don't leave now, I'll be found out. I wouldn't be surprised if Harry were up already."

"Oh, don't worry about Harry. Come back to bed—just for a minute." Suddenly and uncomfortably aware of my nakedness, I pulled the sheet taut to my underarms.

"I can't," Wick insisted.

"I thought, after your note and all, that this sort of thing wouldn't happen again."

"I thought so, too."

"So why did it?" I felt my chin lift.

Wick gave up on dressing himself and sat again upon the bed. Without his armor of confidence, he seemed younger.

"Because I can't stop thinking about what happened, Adele, that's why. Holding back and doing nothing doesn't seem right—but neither does sneaking into your room in the middle of the night." He let out a cheerless chuckle. "Where does that leave us? Stuck in limbo, I suppose."

"This isn't the sort of thing that can be decided overnight. It's complicated."

"So what do you propose?"

"That we don't try to sort this out just now."

"When, then?"

"Why do we need a timeline?"

"Geez, Adele, it's like this doesn't bother you at all."

"Of course it does. But I'm tired of trying to make things neat and tidy when they can't be that way."

"So you're suggesting that we do exactly as we please, to hell with logic."

"*No,* I'm suggesting that you come back to bed. That would be logical, you know. When was the last time you got up at the crack of dawn? This will disrupt your whole schedule."

Finally I coaxed a smile. This was the best I would get from him, I thought, as he turned into something like the old Wick, raucously throwing himself down upon the bed, wrapping me so tightly in his arms that I couldn't stop giggling. His decision to stay didn't bring me comfort or ease my doubts or make me feel even remotely safe in his affections, but it was something, something definite, and after so much uncertainty, I was determined not to take it for granted.

Chapter Sixteen

D IDN'T YOU hear me, Pietra?" Harry asked. "I told you I signed a lease on a place—a place for the summer. And I need a roommate. It's on the sixth floor of an old building in Fair Haven. I hope you don't mind the walk. The water's a little rusty. And there are probably a few cockroaches. Maybe some mice, too. But everything else is shipshape, or at least manageable. We'll split the rent fifty-fifty. If you don't have anything lined up. You don't, do you? You haven't said anything."

"Sounds good. I'm in," I muttered absently.

"But if you're in, where are you going?"

He was in my room watching me pack some things: handkerchiefs, my toothbrush, clean socks. Most of the boys in Durfee had already folded their clothes into suitcases, unfastened posters from their walls, and removed all evidence of their previous habitation. I wondered if Wick had thought about me as he'd snapped shut his bags.

I told Harry I was going to Stony Creek.

At once he offered to accompany me. He wanted to see the stone that I was so mesmerized by—those perilous bluffs that I swore were more astonishing than anything we'd seen at Yale, more astonishing, even, than the treasure in the tunnels. But I told him I needed to go alone.

"Don't give me that look, Harry. I'll be back before you know it."

"So mysterious. Always so god-awful mysterious."

I hadn't yet told him about President Angell's offer. I would when I returned, every juicy detail. But first a pilgrimage home, just for a day or two, in time for the arrival of the last Cottagers in their shiny automobiles and hand-sewn gloves and crisp new walking suits. In time to watch them unlock their homes with big brass keys, domestics scurrying about to clear the dust, to air the rooms, to prepare old-fashioneds, watercress sandwiches, and ladyfingers.

Thus another languid summer would commence. Maybe Alfred and Joanna would come, too. They'd rent that old Victorian they'd used so long ago, the one with the sky-high turret and the road of broken oyster shells. They'd invite Mother to stay with them. Together, they'd sit under enormous umbrellas on the beach, reminiscing about the old times, the best times, flipping casually through books and turning a blind eye to the occasional dark-skinned man who dared to cool his feet in the water. They'd pretend that their own numbers weren't dwindling, that most of the mansions didn't need a new coat of paint.

And maybe it was possible to go back, to bend history's direction. But not for me. I was returning for something else, something personal. I wanted to smell the changing tides and to stare at tiny fish darting through tidal pools; to run up the quarry path, my old skirts aflutter; to sit beside Pa's grave and try to understand him, try to understand my brother, too, how it all went wrong.

At night I'd sleep on the beach, let the spongy-wet sand mold around my body. If I got up the nerve, I'd walk up the old porch steps and curl up in Miss Prowl's rocker, the sound of night insects in my ears. Then, in the morning, I'd lay in the pink calm of my quarry hideaway, Pa's restless clouds on the loose above. When the sun started to sink and the rock beneath me began to cool, I'd realize it was time to leave Stony Creek for good. But still I'd tarry, just for a few minutes. Above, exuberant gulls would swerve and coast and spin. My resentment would disappear, now that I knew, finally, what it was they saw. How the world looks on high.

Acknowledgments

I EXTEND DEEPEST GRATITUDE to my agent, Rosalie Siegel, and to comrades Trina Beck, Erin Mary Greene, Nina Wolarsky, and Mayumi Repp. Grateful acknowledgments to Deborah Deford and those who contributed to the fascinating text *Flesh and Stone: Stony Creek and the Age of Granite;* the librarians at Yale University's Manuscripts and Archives; and Richard Hegel, municipal historian for the city of New Haven. For providing an inspiring amount of encouragement throughout the writing and editing process, loving thanks to my husband, Basil Petrov, and my parents, Radha and Sue Prasad. Last, but certainly not least, I applaud Greer Hendricks, Judith Curr, Hannah Morrill, Sarah Walsh, and the rest of the talented staff at Atria Books for their dedication and insight.

On Borrowed Wings

Chandra Prasad

A Readers Club Guide

Summary

On Borrowed Wings is the impeccably researched and imaginatively written story of Adele Pietra, a bright and restless girl raised by an unhappy couple in the granite town of Stony Creek, Connecticut. Determined not to follow in her mother's footsteps and marry a quarryman, Adele spends the summer of 1936 dreaming of escape and adventure. When her brother, Charles, is killed in a mining accident, she sees her chance and, assuming Charles's identity and gender, enrolls as a freshman at Yale. Adele befriends a lively crew of undergraduate boys, including charismatic troublemaker Wick Foster. Despite her admirable navigation of Yale's rigorous social and academic pressures, great obstacles spring up along the way. Her work with a mentally unsound eugenics professor, her inconvenient crush on Wick, and her mother's unexpected meddling threaten to put an end to Adele's masquerade and her chance for a better life.

1. *On Borrowed Wings* contains rich and historically accurate detail about a place few people have experienced firsthand. What did you learn about the collegiate experience in the first half of the twentieth century, and about Yale in particular? What interested you most? What aspects of Yale's history would you have liked to have seen explored more?

2. When Amelia Earhart gives her speech at Yale, the students ask her pointedly personal questions about her home life and whether she plans to have children. What does this scene reveal about the expectations of women in the 1930s? Does this change your attitude toward the risks Adele takes by impersonating a man? Discuss the issue of gender roles in the book.

3. Discuss the various meanings of the book's title. Consider recurring motifs such as birds, flight, and the ways in which several characters borrow other identities.

4. Early in the novel Adele speculates on her mother's reasons for trying to force her to marry a stonecutter: "I'd think that maybe she couldn't envision my life as different from hers because she was confined by her own example. . . . I didn't know at that moment, and even later, to be honest, I'd never know for sure" (p. 15). What do you think of her mother's motives?

5. Adele's mother is an extremely complicated character—she's haughty, intimidating, and ambitious—but she displays unexpected moments of kindness. She ultimately has a stormy rela-

tionship with her daughter. What is your opinion of her by the book's end? Do you find her a sympathetic character?

6. Discuss the role of deception in the book. Do you think the author believes deception is acceptable when directed toward the right cause? Consider the evidence Adele alters in Professor Spang's study, Adele's work with the DiRisios, and her falsified identity at Yale.

7. Why does Adele follow the stranger to the burlesque show? Why does she feel compelled to have contact with him?

8. Wick thinks that falling in love will cure him of his phoniness. Do you think that it will? Can love help people correct their shortcomings?

9. When Adele discovers Phin in the library, she learns that he has a secret that might be nearly as damning as her own. How do these secrets create a bond between the two? What are the similarities in their situations? How would the consequences of their exposure differ?

10. What is the significance of the story behind her father's "brother," Francisco? Given her parents' relationship, why do you think her mother withholds the secret about Francisco until the end of the book? How does this change Adele's feelings about her family? How does this revelation affect Adele's understanding of her own situation and her own character? What does it seem to say about societal limitations versus the limitations of our own character?

11. Harry is Jewish, Phin is gay, Adele is in disguise, and Wick feels his whole personality is fraudulent. Discuss how these friends are all outsiders. What is the significance of their status? How are other characters outsiders in their own ways?

12. When her mother tells Adele the truth about her "uncle" Francisco and calls Adele's father a coward, Adele makes a decision: "Even if what she was saying were true, even if she managed to contaminate my memories, I wouldn't let her denigrate Pa any further. I understood where my loyalties lay, and where hers lay, too" (p. 296). How does the book explore the issue of loyalty? Consider the various alliances between Adele's family members and friends.

13. Were you satisfied with the book's ending, and the way things were left with Wick? Do you agree with Adele's decision to cut ties with her mother and return to Yale? Given the many questions left unanswered at the book's end, what do you think will happen? Will Adele be able to reenter society as a female, or will she be caught before completing her studies? What might the consequences of her deception be? Aside from going to Philadelphia, what might Adele's other options have been?

ENHANCE YOUR READING GROUP

1. Read other coming-of-age "Ivy lit," such as F. Scott Fitzgerald's *This Side of Paradise* (Princeton) or Thomas Wolfe's *Of Time and the River* (Harvard).

2. Read up on the real-life Amelia Earhart: http://en.wikipedia.org/wiki/Amelia_earhart and www.ameliaearhart.com.

3. Prepare a delicious Italian potluck like the DiRisio family's, including such favorites as artichoke risotto, pasta, lamb, and ricotta pie. Find great recipes in *Every Night Italian,* by Giuliano Hazan, or on www.foodnetwork.com/food/recipes.

4. Learn more about Chandra Prasad at www.chandraprasad.com.

A Conversation with Chandra Prasad

1. How did you develop the idea for this novel? Your characters are extremely complex; are they based on anyone in particular?

One seed for this novel was planted during my junior year of college. In an American history class focusing on women in the South, my professor talked briefly about females who had co-opted the male identity in order to assume roles that would have been barred to them otherwise. I became interested in the idea of altering one's gender in order to thrive, if not simply to survive. Since I knew that Yale had opened its doors to undergraduate women only in 1969, *On Borrowed Wings* seemed to take shape in my head with an ease all its own. Both the women throughout history who have dared to impersonate men and the first undergraduate females at Yale inspired the main character, Adele.

2. How did you conduct your research? As a Yale graduate, did you learn anything surprising about your alma mater? What do you think are the most significant changes Yale has undergone during the last century (aside from its decision to admit women!).

In terms of research, I had the privilege of speaking with a couple of older gentlemen who had attended Yale in the 1940s. Though the book is set earlier, their recollections were very helpful as I tried to reconstruct the university of that era. I read books about the history of Yale, New Haven, and Stony Creek, and I spent time in area historical societies. I also pored over yearbooks, journals, newspapers, and photographs in the Yale University archive. The photographs, in particular, intrigued me because they spoke of a university that I am familiar with now but which was so strikingly different in the 1930s. Then, the boys at Yale were mostly from a certain echelon, of course. But what struck me as I was doing research was that this echelon was undergoing a drastic change. Even among the very wealthy, the Depression took a toxic toll. Many boys who had come from moneyed families were hard hit and floundering. Also, once World War II began, a significant number of Yalies joined the military, leaving New Haven behind. Immigration, industrial and technological change, and swiftly shifting sociopolitical tides altered the basic rubric of family units and whole communities. The world was changing at a brutal pace, and the university had to keep up.

3. **What drew you to the real historical characters in the novel, particularly Amelia Earhart and President Angell, and how did you go about writing their characters?**

Of course Amelia is one of those legends, like Marilyn Monroe or James Dean, who never quite leaves the imagination. With all of our sophisticated advances in science, especially in the areas of deep-sea exploration and forensics, we still don't know what happened to her, and where her final resting place is. When Amelia appears in the novel, it is a bittersweet moment because the reader knows that she will soon disappear forever. There is something so poignant about that. As for Angell, he's a different sort of historical figure, because not a whole lot has been written about him. His professional accomplishments are well documented, but not so his personal life. Creatively, I could be a little bit more flexible with him.

4. **In your research, did you come across documented cases of women attending all-male universities under assumed identities?**

No, I did not find any—at least not in the twentieth century. I'm sure there are cases, though. I'd be surprised if there weren't!

5. You've written both fiction and nonfiction on a variety of subjects including the job market, the multiracial experience, and the circus. *On Borrowed Wings* is a complicated examination of gender. Do you make a conscious decision to explore certain issues in your work, or do you just start writing and see where your thoughts take you?

As a multiracial female, I'm naturally attracted to the topics of gender and ethnicity, and tend to gravitate toward an exploration of personal identity in much of my work. However, in fiction I don't try to drive home any particular points. When fiction does that, it tends to be preachy. I'd rather tell the story clearly, draw the characters as the multifaceted people I think they would be, and let the reader draw his own conclusions.

6. Women have long posed as men in order to gain access to restricted opportunities. Are there any particular stories, fictional or otherwise, that inspired you in the writing of this book? What has your own experience taught you about such social boundaries as race, class, and gender, and what did you hope to explore in this book with regard to these issues?

Since childhood I've been intrigued by women who utterly defy rules and expectations. The more drastic the story, the more fascinated I am. Anne Bonny and Mary Read are two women who successfully posed as male pirates in the 1700s. Both were known to be fiery, fierce, and quite terrifying. In 1916 Adeline and Augusta Van Buren became the first women to motorcycle their way across America. Several times along their journey, they were arrested for wearing men's clothing, which seems absurd now. Then there was Katie Sandwina, a spectacularly powerful circus strongwoman who was born in 1884. She could carry her husband above her head using only one arm. These are just a handful of examples. There are so many extraordinary women who have tread radically into male territory. They make me realize that once certain boundaries are crossed, they fade, even disappear. Again, I don't really want to impose this notion on the reader. But I do hope that Adele's experience offers food for thought on how far women have come.

7. Who are your favorite writers and biggest influences? What are you currently reading?

I adore Joyce Carol Oates and Louise Erdrich. Both are absolutely inspiring to me—Oates because of the powerful, unique, nearly hypnotic rhythm of her prose, Erdrich because of the searing beauty of her stories. I've read Erdrich's *Love Medicine* about a million times. Somehow it always manages to enchant me and rip my heart out at the same time. My general "favorite authors" list changes year to year, even month to month. I suppose a lot of people have that experience. Right now—in no particular order—the list includes Jane Austen, E. L. Doctorow, John Irving, John Knowles, Willa Cather, Jeanette Winterson, Lucy Maud Montgomery, Stephen King, O. Henry, Harper Lee, Toni Morrison, and Mark Twain. As far as current reading goes, I just reread Oates's *Black Water*, which was such a gutsy book not only because of its content, but also because of its highly unusual narrative structure. I'm now starting *Middlesex*, by Jeffrey Eugenides. After that I'm going to dive into this year's *Best American Short Stories*.

8. In certain scenes, such as the one at the Winter Ball, it's almost easy to forget that Adele is actually a woman and to believe she is just one of the guys. It's fascinating how gender lines can become blurred so easily. Did you consciously make any kind of switch in the way you wrote her point of view when she was in costume?

In trying to be one of the boys, Adele doesn't always know what she is doing, especially when she first arrives at the university. She is steeped in the male identity only three quarters of the way. There is always that last quarter sticking up jaggedly above the surface, a perceptible reminder that she can't control everything about herself. I felt the exposure along with Adele. I consciously made a switch to a male perspective; still, some of the best passages turned out to be the ones I was a little apprehensive about—because Adele would have been a little apprehensive too.

9. Do you feel that Adele's mother is a sympathetic character, or do you consider her one of the novel's villains? She isn't as harmful as someone like Professor Spang, but she causes her fair share of damage.

To a large extent Mother is in control and cognizant of her ability to manipulate. This much is undeniable when she parts ways with her daughter, and even before, when she shows such favoritism toward her son. But there is a layer of softness to her too. She is not purely villainous, in my opinion (then again, the worst villains are seldom thoroughly evil). When writing about Mother I tried to keep in mind that she was estranged from her parents, and that she experienced a lot of anguish because of that deep familial wound. She is not exempt from her behavior because of the pain, of course. But the grief, the profound resentment—these are things she has carried around for a long time. At some point they poisoned her.

10. The end of the novel opens a new chapter in Adele's life just as we are saying good-bye to her. Do you have an idea of what might happen to her after her first year at Yale or do you prefer to think of her future as open-ended?

I'm so fond of Adele, I like to think she makes it through the rest of Yale. I like to think she influences many more people through her literacy campaign, and that the bond she shares with Ceci grows. Of course I wonder if Adele goes back to living as a female. But when I consider her future, that is not my largest concern. I'd rather she be focused on the external world.